A CHRISTMAS GIFT

As the daughter of the local cinema manager, Sally Brewer has always dreamed of stardom. When she gets offered a theatre job in London, any fancy notions she has are quickly dashed when faced with the reality of long hours with no prospect of a speaking part. But all this goes out of Sally's mind once the nightly hail of German bombs start to rain down on London. She joins the newly-formed ENSA and is soon raising morale all over the bombed-out city – there is little time for love.

Eileen Ramsay

writing

A CHRISTMAS GIFT

as. Ruby Jackson

A CHRISTMAS GIFT

by

Ruby Jackson

Magna Large Print Books
Long Preston, North Yorkshire,
BD23 4ND, England.

British Library Cataloguing in Publication Data.

Jackson, Ruby
    A Christmas gift.

    A catalogue record of this book is
    available from the British Library

    ISBN   978-0-7505-3901-2

First published in Great Britain by Harper
An imprint of HarperCollins*Publishers* 2014

Copyright © HarperCollins*Publishers* 2014

Cover illustration by arrangement with HarperCollins Publishers

Ruby Jackson asserts the moral right to be identified as the author of this work

Published in Large Print 2015 by arrangement with
HarperCollins Publishers

Magna Large Print is an imprint of Library Magna Books Ltd.

Printed and bound in Great Britain by
T.J. (International) Ltd., Cornwall, PL28 8RW

ACKNOWLEDGEMENTS

Writing this story really brought home to me that this writer, at least, does not write alone.

My thanks are due once again to Dr Mike Still, Dartford, Dr Andrea Turner, Fortnum and Mason, and helpful staff at The Savoy and The Ritz, London.

Special thanks to Sylvie and Pascal Iovanovitch for introducing me to Corsica, its history, its beauty, its food and, not to forget, The French Foreign Legion!

Two members of ENSA definitely inspired me to write as true and as interesting a story as I could. The first was the beautiful Vivienne Hole, the only member of ENSA to be killed during the war – she was only nineteen years old. The second a war widow, Josephine, whose courageous and poignant story inspired the creation of my character Millie.

The fact-filled story of ENSA, *Greasepaint and Cordite*, written by Andy Merriman, was a tremendous source of information and inspiration and I enjoyed singing along with the CDs – ENSA Complete Shows.

The articles and books I have read on Basil Dean and Lesley Henson are too numerous to mention, but thank you all.

I am also very grateful for the information available on the internet about London theatres and the story of London during WWII, and I depended very much on the 'London A to Z' given to me for Christmas by my eldest grandchild because he liked the colour! Me too, B!

As always, thanks to my agent, Teresa Chris, my editor, Kate Bradley, and all the other talented people who make the wheels go round. And to my husband and family, I simply could not function without you.

This book is for my American sisters,
Susan A, Trisha S, and Holly McG

ONE

January 1945. Somewhere in Egypt

Not for the first time Sally wondered how she would cope. They were so young, younger even than the boys who had been at school with her – children some of them, not even the slightest shadow of down on their soft, young faces.

'Pull yourself together, Sally Brewer. You've seen injured servicemen before.'

I know, she argued with herself, but they were all nicely bandaged and in clean hospital beds. She shuddered as she relived climbing out of the lorry to find herself turning to face three field ambulances. From each ambulance, injured men in bloodied, torn uniforms were carried gently, but as rapidly as possible, into the field hospital.

What use here was a pretty girl in a pretty dress? It was capable hands they needed.

Sebastian, as always, was just behind her, and, as always, seemed to read her thoughts. 'Come along, Sally, there are medicines that don't come from a pill bottle. A smile from your beautiful eyes does wonders. I know. I've seen it. Wear the silver frock tonight. They'll think you're the Christmas fairy.'

Two days later.

'Come on, Sally darling, let's go over that num-

13

ber again.'

Sally pulled off her uncomfortable but very flattering long blond wig and threw it across the room at Prince Charming who did not, at that moment, look at all attractive. His blond peruke was bouncing on the top of his own thick brown hair and likely to fall off at any moment.

He caught Sally's wig, stuck it on top of his slipping peruke and ogled her. 'Arr, but you're a dainty wench, and I don't doubt these soldier lads'll be slobbering at your door in a minute.' Just as quickly he changed back to serious. 'I can hear the clumping of the great clods already, Sal, and we have to get the number right.'

'The only thing that can be heard approaching over sand, Sebastian, is an armoured vehicle. These men are not clods, and I have the dratted number right.'

'Darling,' he held out his arms in supplication, 'it's not my fault we're doing panto in the desert in January. I think the CO sounds like a really decent chap. Imagine some of the permanently constipated officers we've met over the years suggesting a pantomime. And Father Christmas. Wait till you see me as Santa Claus.'

'They'll never believe that you're Santa, Sebastian, you're too tall and too thin.'

'Picky. Let me tell you, Cinderella, that when the engineers and two of the nurses from the hospital have finished with me, Father Christmas himself will have doubts about his authenticity. Think, Sal. Some of these boys have been away from home for two, even three, Christmases. Realistically, odds are that more than one of the youngsters who follow you around like puppies will never see another Christmas. Lovely idea to have a late one and it is only January. Pretty please, I'd rather not dance by myself. One does look rather a fool.'

The ENSA company was stationed in an abandoned settlement somewhere, they believed, in the Egyptian desert. Apart from a half-finished aircraft hangar, their accommodation consisted of a ruined, deconsecrated church, its dilapidated hall and several barely standing wooden huts. There was one rather tired-looking date palm growing, or perhaps not – they could not be sure.

One of the young soldiers from the army base had told Sally that the presence of the tree showed that there was, or at least had been, water there. 'All you need to survive in the desert,' he had assured her almost gleefully. 'Perfect food, the date; it's got everything one needs to sustain life.'

Fervently Sally prayed that his theory would never have to be put to the test.

Now, as even the usually sunny Sebastian began to growl, she uncoiled herself from the rather elderly armchair and stretched. 'All this agony and it's not as if there'll be even one child in the audience.'

'*Au contraire, mon ange,* some of those boys aren't twenty yet. The hangar will be packed with children in uniforms, and all of them needing a good laugh or to ogle a gorgeous girl. Come along, let's give it a twirl – and show a bit more leg this time.'

'Show yours; they're better than mine, and besides, it's a waltz. Millie's instructions were decorum, decorum and ... and decorum.'

15

'Come on, Cinders, wrap that shawl round your waist as if it's your ball gown. Then – with decorum – use your thumb and middle finger to lift your skirt oh so frightfully genteelly. That's it. Gadzooks, I saw some calf there. Scrumptious.'

'You are an idiot.'

'But lovable. You, Cinderella, were lifting the wrong side; left hand for skirts while dancing, right hand for while climbing stairs. Good rule.'

'Whose rule?'

Sebastian smiled rakishly. 'Grandmamma's. A truly terrifying woman, as you know, darling, so please don't force me to send for her.'

Sally said nothing. She had heard of her co-star's formidable grandmother many times before but whether the lady actually existed she still, after almost four years, had no knowledge.

They left the hut styled 'Stars' Dressing Room' and moved to the war-scarred hangar, which was serving as a theatre.

'The engineers, bless them, have made this place almost presentable,' Sally said, looking round admiringly.

'The boys will be pleased. We should cut down the date palm and decorate it.'

'Don't even think about it, Sebastian. The lads I was talking to yesterday swear they'll get dates from it soon.'

In the surrounding area, several companies of Allied troops were stationed and too many of them were in the makeshift wards. Most waited for orders and trained for who knew what day after day. Some would be repatriated, possibly in the plane that would take the ENSA company home. Some were still too ill to move and would be forced to remain until the overstretched medical team got them well enough to travel.

It was the wounded whom Sally thought of most often and for whom she worked. As leading lady of this small troupe, she would star as Cinderella but she would also be expected to sing and dance in choreographed short pieces and, since both she and Sebastian had acted on stage and had appeared in film – he was a former child star – and were quite well known, they would take part in several selections from popular plays or films.

Sally loved every minute of her work with ENSA. She knew just how much a favourite song, a smile, a touch of the hand, a blown kiss meant to so many of these men and she worked just as hard on a hastily knocked-up stage – thanks to the Corps of Engineers – as she did on the London stage. She knew Sebastian well, having worked with him in several productions and shared his London flat. At another time, he could have been an Academy Award contender. Perhaps he would be some day. And so to the waltz of the handsome prince in his satin suit and his mysterious princess in her glorious gown and dazzling glass slippers.

'Let's try to work it out with my hand on your shoulder,' Sally suggested. 'Once we're in sync I'll try hitching up poor old Cinders' magic frock. You hum something.'

His right hand immediately found its way to the top of her hip. Once that touch would have set her on fire but that was long ago now. Sally smiled, not at all sad to acknowledge it now meant only

17

that her partner was ready to dance.

For once he did not begin.

'Hum, Sebastian.'

'I hate being asked to hum. All I can think of is "Rum and Coca-Cola" and I'm sure that's not three-four time.' He hummed the calypso.

'Where's the dratted pianist when you want him?' Sally muttered in exasperation.

'Do you know, my angel, that your frown has just reminded me that one of the Russians, Tchaikovsky perhaps, wrote a ballet, *Cinderella?*'

'Bound to be a waltz in it and that would be rather terrif, wouldn't it? Hum it.'

Sebastian saluted. 'I would, *mein Führer*, but the old brain must be slipping a gear because nothing is coming.' He looked at her face and saw signs of an impending storm. 'I'll just count. Right, one two, three, one two three...' He stopped counting and dancing and incidentally stood on Sally's foot at the same time.

'Good Lord,' he yelped.

'You called, m'lord?' came a voice from behind the stage, and a burly man in an elderly overall walked across to the piano.

'Gus, my angel, just when we needed you. Cinderella can't waltz, comes of doing nothing all day but sitting by the fireside poking the cinders. Can you produce a waltz, perhaps from Tchai-kovsky's ballet?'

Gus pulled up the ramshackle stool that stood near the piano. He and Sally looked at it rather doubtfully. 'How's this theatre's insurance cover, Seb? These little beauties are worth a fortune.' He wiggled ten short, stubby fingers before them.

'What's left of my entire Christmas and blessed New Year's Day alcohol allowance,' said Seb by way of answer. 'Even in sunny downtown Egyptian desert there appeared the odd bottle of something to go with the turkey. Rather an odd bouquet, like pressed dates.'

'I put my faith in the army,' said Gus, tentatively approaching the stool. He pressed down on it. There was a crack like the sound of a pistol shot. 'Solid as a rock,' he lied, and sat down. He played a few notes and stood up. 'This hasn't been tuned since it was built and the bloody thing's a Bechstein. Should be shot, whoever owned it.'

'It's a piano, Gus.'

'It's a helluva lot more than that; it's a casualty of war, Seb. This here is one of the greats. You should know that. How the hell did it ever get here? Unforgivable.'

'Can you do something to help it, Gus?' Sally asked gently. She was surprised by just how upset this burly man was, and, although he was new to this company, she knew that he had managed to survive some gruelling years in the conflict.

Gus smiled. 'I sure as hell am not going to plonk out a waltz or anything else on it for you till I've had a good look inside. If you can hum a few bars I'll whistle Cinderella's waltz from the ballet, Prince Lanky Legs.'

He did not wait for Sebastian to answer but began to whistle a lovely tune. Gus's whistle was in a class of its own, a musical instrument.

Cinderella and her prince waltzed effortlessly round the stage. Sally was quiet when they stopped. She had danced, eyes closed, safe in

19

Sebastian's familiar arms to music she thought she knew. For a few minutes she had been a world away from war and disaster, dirt and pain.

'Thank you, Gus. That was perfect. Was it the Cinderella waltz?'

'Naw, haven't heard that. That was vintage Irving Berlin.' He took Sally into a hold and began to dance with her, singing as they moved.

A familiar cold splinter pierced Sally's heart. She tried to ignore it and smile. '"What'll I Do" ... lovely old melody, Gus. I do hope you can heal the piano.'

'I'll do my best – and then I'll see who I can blackmail into sending it back to Blighty with other equipment.'

'They'll say it's not equipment, Gus; hardly the same as a three-ton lorry.'

'It's Equipment – vital to mental health, His Majesty's Forces of. Watch me. I can out-argue any barrister.'

Two weeks later, the company climbed into the cab of a large army lorry to be driven, together with a few lucky soldiers who were being re-patriated, to the nearest safe aerodrome. Sally had driven over every type of surface in every kind of weather – over hills, across riverbeds, through swollen rivers – but the trip across the desert was one of the most unpleasant. First, there was no actual road; secondly, it was so hot that it was difficult to breathe, and just touching a metal part of the lorry could cause quite a painful burn. Sally's preconceptions of Egyptian scenery had suffered several blows on this trip. She had expected miles and miles of sand dunes, with here and there a small oasis, exactly what she seen night after night in the films she loved watching from the projectionist's booth at the Dartford cinema where her father had worked since his return from the battlefields of the Great War. Yes, there were miles of sand dunes, but to her surprise there were hills – not tall dunes but actual hills – most multi-striped by coloured bands of what one of the soldiers told her were minerals. Once she saw a camel, his robed rider seemingly oblivious of their presence as he made his measured, stately way across the sands.

He has to be able to see us, she thought, but he chooses to ignore us. Whose side is he on?

The almost biblical figures disappeared from view just as a wind sprang up. In a moment the air was full of stinging grains of sand that invaded everywhere: eyes, hair, mouth, the tiniest un-covered area of skin. It was as if they were being stung by a million malevolent bees. Sally covered her face and her hands were attacked. She was grateful that sensibly she had decided to wear trousers for the journey but how she wished she had worn a long-sleeved blouse.

'Here, miss, take my shirt.' A young soldier had removed his long-sleeved khaki shirt and was offering it to her.

'Oh, how kind,' she said, 'but I can't take your shirt.'

'I'm used to the sand, miss, and me mum'll be right pleased with me helping Miss Sally Brewer. She were a cleaner at the Adelphi years ago; always said you was one of the nicest lasses as came through the doors.'

'Write your address on this paper,' said Sebastian. 'When we get home, Miss Brewer will send you a signed picture and one for your mum.'

Sally had been wondering what on earth she could do in return for the soldier's help, but once again Sebastian had stepped in, knowing exactly how to handle the situation. She had been to see a play at the Adelphi, but had never worked there and so was quite sure that the young soldier's mother did not know her at all.

'I'll wear your shirt till we're aboard,' she told the young soldier, 'but then you must take it back. Can't have you found short of uniform.' Then she told him stories of her friends Daisy and Rose Petrie, who were both in the women's services. Neither Daisy nor Rose would have recognised themselves but they would have applauded Sally's ability to tell believable tall tales.

Much later than expected, the lorry reached the aerodrome where an Albemarle transport plane was waiting.

In the notoriously uncomfortable aeroplane, Sally sat huddled in blankets. It was too noisy for her to attempt to sleep, but lulled by the drone of the engines, she allowed her thoughts to wander and memories flooded her mind.

Monday, 4 September 1939

Sally was awake long before the bell of her alarm clock shattered the silence. Yesterday had come the terrible news that Britain was at war and she, like thousands of others, had lain awake for hours worrying about the future. But her future, she decided now with rising excitement, was secure. She hurried along the little passageway to the bathroom where she spent some time – and most of the hot water – getting ready for this most important day. She had a new costume to wear, bought for her by her three best friends. The last word in fashion and perfectly suited to her tall slim figure, it was bound to make her stand out, to show the director that she was destined for success. Today Dartford, tomorrow London and ... Sally laughed at her own ambition ... some day – Hollywood.

She took out her lipstick and then replaced it in her little purse. Her parents would not approve of bright red lips before breakfast. She could apply it, as she had done time without number, on the way to her appointment. But she could at least apply mascara to enhance the blue of her eyes, and ensure her long blue-black hair was perfectly in place.

'Oh, Sally pet, how grown-up you are,' her mother, who looked as if she had not slept at all, greeted her as she walked into the little kitchen. 'Ever so sophisticated,' she added, shaking her head in happy disbelief.

'I need to impress the director of the school, Mum. I want to come home tonight to you and Dad and tell you about all the opportunities I'll have.' Spontaneously she hugged her mother. 'I want to show you that I was right not to accept a place at a university. You'll see, Mum, the stage is where I belong.'

'Then eat your breakfast before you head off, our Sally, or you'll be too weak to make any impression.' Her father who, like her mother, was still in his comfy old dressing gown, had come in and was sitting in his usual place. 'You look right nice, but I never heard Margaret Lockwood's stomach rumble.'

Sally laughed as she sat down beside him. 'You're right, Dad, it would take the bloom off a bit, wouldn't it? But please, Mum, just toast and a cuppa; I'm too excited to eat.'

Exactly forty-three minutes later, she was standing before the closed door of Oliver Dantry's Theatrical Training School, sure that her life-long dream was shattered. On the door was a notice.

DUE TO UNFORESEEN
CIRCUMSTANCES CLOSED
FOR THE DURATION.

Below the huge black letters was a small hand-written sentence: 'I'm sorry and will be contacting all students.'

It was signed simply 'Oliver'.

Sally was so gripped by shock she was scarcely able to breathe. As she collapsed against the forbidding notice, careless of the costume of which she had been so proud, her thoughts were racing one another round and round in her feverishly working brain.

It could not be true. There had to be some ghastly mistake. What were 'unforeseen circumstances'? The actual outbreak of war? But what had war to do with a college closing down, the college she had worked so hard to be permitted to enter? All those dreams of working in a jolly theatre company, earning the respect of the other actors, of getting a big break, playing a glamorous leading role to universal acclaim ... and then, very soon after, the movies – it was all supposed to start here, today, at Oliver Dantry's Theatrical Training School.

She pictured her parents. Her mother would be making quite sure that her spotless home was indeed spotless. Her father would be in his beloved projection booth, handling the magical reels of film with experienced, caring hands; those films that had been her inspiration since she was old enough to sit still in front of them, starring actors whose faces were as familiar to her as her own. Her parents would be thinking of her, imagining her excitement as she sat in a college classroom – if there was a classroom in a theatre school – trying to persuade themselves that they were pleased that their only child had abandoned the prospect of a university degree for a dubious future in the theatre.

What could she do? Hammering on the door would solve nothing. It was obvious that the building was empty. 'The duration'? How long was 'the duration'? 'Over by Christmas.' That was the pathetic little phrase that appeared in all her school history books. The Great War had gone on for years after that first Christmas.

'No, no, no...' Sally sobbed loudly. Eventually her weeping abated and then, embarrassed in case she might be seen, she blew her nose in a most unladylike fashion, took a deep breath, straightened her spine, and walked away smartly.

Sitting in the Albemarle, she moved slightly, in an attempt both to banish the memory and to make herself a little more comfortable. She was not proud of how she had behaved that day and preferred instead to remember when a letter had finally arrived from Oliver Dantry.

It hadn't started out as a red-letter day. She had expected to begin working full time as an usherette in the cinema now her theatrical training had fallen through. Selling ice cream and bars of chocolate was no substitute but she knew she had to do something useful. But that hadn't come about either. Her parents said nothing but they must have been thinking that had she accepted a university place she would now be preparing herself for a prestigious future. They had made no secret of their dreams that their bright, talented, only child should have a good education, and go on to be the first member of either family to graduate from a university.

'I've ruined all their plans,' Sally scolded herself. 'I'll never be able to make them proud of me. Because of my wilful pride I have neither university place nor theatrical training. Look at me, cosseted, spoiled Sally. If the Government hadn't closed all theatres and cinemas I'd be a cinema usherette; that's a long way from top of the bill. Instead of studying literature at university I'm taking a first-aid class – and I know I'd be useless in an emergency.'

She closed the leaflet 'How to Prepare Your Home for an Air Raid' as her mother called from the bathroom, 'Sally, be a love and turn on the gas under the milk pan while I fix my curlers; your dad should be passing on his fire-watching round and maybe he'll pop in for some cocoa.'

Sally hurried to the kitchen. This, at least, she could do.

'Sorry I forgot, love, there's a letter for you, typed address, in the dresser drawer; didn't want it to get covered in flour when I was baking.'

Sally, who had just taken the box of matches down from the shelf, dropped it, turned and pulled open the drawer. Her mother, still in the bathroom, smiled as she heard her rip open the letter.

The door opened and Ernie Brewer came in just as Elsie gave her head a final pat and walked into the kitchen where the milk was still cold on the stove. She lit the gas and waited while Sally finished the letter. While her parents stood watching Sally smiled broadly and read the letter again.

She finished, clutched the letter to her breast, threw her arms round her uniformed father, who was closest, and shouted, 'I've got a job.'

Her doting parents were not surprised when their daughter burst into loud but happy tears. Elsie made cocoa while she waited for the ever-emotional Sally to be calm and at last all three were able to sit down and talk.

'It's from Oliver, Mr Dantry. He says he talked to a friend of his in the Dartford Rep and, even though the theatre is dark–' she looked at her parents to see if they understood the term – 'they're willing to take me on as an apprentice. Learning from the ground up, he calls it. I'll have to do

27

everything: look after props, keep scripts in order, help with costumes, scenery too, if they think I'm any good, even make tea for the professional cast. I can start immediately, tomorrow if I want.'

'Very kind of Mr Dantry to think of you, Sally, but actually I've just heard some good news too.'

Eyes wide, Ernie's wife and daughter looked at him.

Elsie spoke first. 'Oh, Ernie, it's not...?'

He was too full of emotion to speak but nodded. Then, once again in control of himself, said, 'To-morrow, love, all cinemas and places of enter-tainment are to reopen. I know it's been only a few days but some big wigs 'as managed to show the Government what a stupid thing closing us down was in the first place.'

'Oh, Dad, that is fantastic news. You've got a job again.'

'And so do thousands of other people all over the country, even you, love, if you ever need it.'

Sally looked at him pityingly. 'Daddy, I've got a chance to become an actress, but if you need me on my days off I'll come in and give you a hand.'

'And get to watch the film in return, little minx. Bet in a thousand years you'll never guess what film we've been promised soon as it's available.'

Sally stood up. 'Let me get you more cocoa.'

'Sorry, love, duty calls. You two, don't wait up.'

'What film?' called Sally, but the only reply was a laugh and the sound of a closing door.

Next morning Sally went to the little theatre to find the few surviving members of the company sharing a bottle of sparkling wine. Elliott Staines, the director and – usually – leading man, intro-

28

duced Sally and even gave her a small glass of wine. Everyone was in a state almost of euphoria. Three young actors had joined up as soon as war was declared, two box office staff had been evacuated; the cleaning staff had been dismissed when the order to close had been received and so the company was sadly depleted.

'It'll get worse,' Paul Ridley, the second director complained. 'No offence, Sally, but that's why we were so glad to get you. I doubt we'll keep you long – Churchill will want you in the services – but while you're here, we'll work you to death. Believe me, a rep is the best place to learn your craft.'

Sally believed him and, for some time, had never been happier. She loved the smell of the theatre. Without the cleaning staff, dust and dirt were everywhere. Their smells mingled with the lingering perfumes of stage make-up, stale sweat, coffee, cigarette smoke, even beer, and Sally, newest member not of the cast but of the workforce, spent hours cleaning. It was not as she had pictured her first position but she reminded herself that at least she was actually working in the theatre.

She could smile now when she remembered her first theatrical experiences, those early days of endless hours of ironing frilled shirts or lace jabots, hours of cranking out pages of scripts on the ancient stencil duplicator, and of finding, to her stunned surprise, that she had a talent for designing and painting scenery. Less productive hours were spent making and serving endless cups of tea that in time grew weaker and weaker as rationing marched across the land.

29

It wasn't too ghastly, she mused now. I read every script and memorised almost all the words. I learned to judge what was good and what was so-so and what was just plain bad acting. I must have been the best-read skivvy in the history of English theatre. And I met Sebastian, and I fell in love.

Early December 1939

'The Theatre Royal?' she repeated.

Elliott Staines smiled at her. 'Of course, darling. *The* Theatre Royal, Drury Lane. Actually, my chum Connie Marshall has a teeny part – vitally important, naturally.' He held up an envelope. 'And she's sent me two tickets. Do come; vitally important for you to see and be seen.'

'Vitally important' – Elliott's favourite words.

'Elliott, you are kind. I'd love to but ... my parents tend to worry, especially if I'm out late. We'd be really late getting back, wouldn't we?'

He looked at her sadly. 'Dahling, was I mis-informed? They assured me that we were hiring an adult, a woman of the world. Come on, London's not very far away. We'll take my car; up and back in three shakes.'

Sally felt deeply embarrassed: a child who needed Daddy's permission to do anything. Her parents had heard of Elliott. When she had told them excitedly that a real actor, who had been in a film and had acted in theatres in London, was both the senior actor and co-owner of the theatre, her father's tone told her nothing of his opinion of the actor.

'Well, what d'you think of that, Elsie? Elliott Staines, of all people? Goodness, he used to be famous; come down in the world a bit, hasn't he?'

Elliott's sarcasm had made her blush but she promised to ask her parents' permission. Knowing perfectly well that she would get it, she decided to run around in her lunch break looking for a dress suitable for a visit to the Theatre Royal, on Drury Lane, a theatre whose name she saw in huge capitals in her mind. Elliott hadn't exactly said, but surely his friend would say hello. There were one or two experienced actors in Dartford Rep but Constance Marshall, Elliott's chum, was known worldwide. As a young actress, Constance had been famous for her portrayal of Shakespearean heroines; in later years she had played queens but now she tended to appear in small character parts. To meet her would be so exciting and Sally was sure that there was absolutely nothing in her very well-stocked wardrobe elegant enough to be worn in a London theatre.

She was passing the second-hand clothes shop on the High Street that had recently been opened by the WVS when, in the large picture window she saw, not a dress but a cloak. A cloak designed for magical evenings, for nights at the opera, for moonlit strolls, and certainly it was perfect for wearing by an aspiring actress who wanted – needed – to be noticed.

'Mum'll have a fit,' said Sally to herself as she walked in. She had never been in the second-hand

31

shop where her friend Grace's sister worked but she knew immediately that this was a very different place. The single room was large, airy and spotlessly clean. The clothes were hanging on racks that were not too crowded, the better to show off each item. Even the two women who stood one behind the counter, the other primping a rather dashing hat on a stand near the window, were different. It was obvious that neither would ever need to buy from a second-hand shop.

'May I help you?' asked the one behind the counter and her voice reinforced what Sally had just been thinking. She wondered now if she could learn to speak like the lady. That accent would be perfect for some parts.

'I'd like to see the blue cloak in the window, please.'

'Exquisite, isn't it? Maude, you're closer. Be an angel and bring the young lady the evening cloak.'

'In a jiff, Fedora.' Maude's voice was pleasant but not in the same league as that of the elegant Fedora.

Sally tried to memorise the sounds – as well as the strange name.

And then, somehow she was before a mirror and the cloak was on her shoulders. The blue of the velvet made her eyes appear bluer, deeper and brighter than ever. Whatever it cost, she had to own this wonderful cloak.

'What a picture,' said Fedora. 'Honestly, Maude, doesn't it look as if it was made for her?'

Maude looked at Sally, seeing her neat skirt, well-ironed blouse and hand-knitted cardigan. 'Not frightfully practical, but yes, very lovely. For something special, may I ask?'

Sally had been bursting to tell someone, anyone. 'I'm going to London, to the Theatre Royal, actually; it's more or less on Drury Lane. I'm a guest of Miss Constance Marshall.'

'Good heavens, surely all theatres closed a few days after war was declared?' said Maude. 'And as for Connie Marshall, I thought she retired years ago.'

'Obviously not.' Fedora turned to Sally. 'Forgive Maude, she's decided not to read the newspapers until the end of this ghastly war.' In a louder voice she added, 'The theatres have been reopened, Maude.' She turned back to Sally. 'That does sound like a perfectly lovely evening, my dear. I'm afraid the cloak is rather expensive. It's by a top designer, and the money is going to war charities.' She looked as if she was at war with herself.

'We've had it three weeks and no one has even looked at it,' Maude reminded her.

'Two pounds ten shillings,' said Fedora at last. 'I know that's a lot but I can't let it go for less.'

Sally had winced but she had to have the cloak. It was as if the designer had had her in mind when he had created it. 'I have five shillings in my bag but I have the rest in my Post Office account.' She fished her purse out of her bag and emptied the coins it contained onto the counter. 'Could I put this as a down payment, please? I have to go back to work now but I'll take the money out tomorrow. Honestly, I will come back.'

'I can't let you take it with you, dear, not without payment.'

'I understand, but please take my five shillings

33

– a deposit, as it were. I swear I'll come back to-morrow with the rest.'

'Of course we'll take it. The cloak was made for you, wasn't it?' said Maude.

A few minutes later, Sally, feeling as light as a soap bubble, left the shop and hurried back to the theatre. Her father would be unhappy about the amount of money she had spent on a cloak for one evening but he would also say that it was her own hard-earned money and, if she chose to waste it, that was entirely up to her.

Neither parent had been particularly happy about her going to a London theatre with an actor older than her own father.

'Of course, seeing and hearing Ivor Novello is quite wonderful, pet,' said Elsie, 'but we just don't like the idea of our young daughter being alone with this man, with any man.'

'Mum, he's my boss and he was famous once – even you and Dad know that. And I'll only be alone with him while he's driving us to London and back again right after the performance. Don't spoil this, please. What if I actually meet Miss Marshall?' She dreamed of meeting Novello, the star, but surely that was much too wonderful even to mention.

'Very nice, I'm sure,' said Bert. 'I think we should let her go, love,' he turned to his daughter, 'but he picks you up here, Sally, and he'll shake my hand and tell me exactly what time you'll get home – and it had better be not long after the play ends.'

Just over two weeks later, Sally sat, a mere five

rows from the stage of the Tamise Theatre, admiring the classic profile of the world-famous Ivor Novello as he starred in his own musical *The Dancing Years*. Only now, towards the close of the performance, was she able to breathe properly, for Fedora had been perfectly correct and the production had been forced to change theatres early in September. Elliott had been so sure of himself that he had never examined the tickets and had driven to Drury Lane to find the theatre completely deserted. There he lost his temper and shouted some words that Sally was glad she did not understand, but recovered in time to drive to the Tamise Theatre where he again embarrassed Sally by pushing his way through the waiting crowds.

At last she was relaxed after twice resorting to pinching her arm to assure herself that she was indeed in a London theatre, that she was enveloped in a strikingly lovely blue velvet cloak, and that the great man himself had actually spoken to her.

She'd been so excited to meet Connie Marshall, who was rather grand and gracious. It was just before curtain up, and visitors shouldn't have been backstage, but Connie found time to ask Sally very kindly about her theatrical career and Sally was saved from revealing the disappointing truth when her mouth literally dried up at the sight of the great – and very handsome – star of musical theatre approaching behind the elderly actress.

'Enjoy, poppet, sorry, got to fly,' was all he had said as Connie quickly introduced Sally, but he had spoken to her and she would never forget it.

She wished she could forget Elliott's closeness.

His right hand strayed several times to her knee and when she had joked that she needed to pinch herself, she had not liked the tone of his voice when he said that he would be delighted to do the pinching. As the evening wore on she became more and more sure that she had made a dreadful mistake in accepting the older actor's invitation. She almost wept as she realised that had she not accepted, one of the most famous men in the entire world of musical theatre would never have smiled at her or spoken to her.

The curtain went down. The theatre exploded with cheers and clapping and stamping feet as the audience stood up. Back came the cast, bowing modestly, kissing flowers that were thrown and often sending them back to the original thrower. It was wonderful, but at the back of Sally's mind was a band of cold fear.

He'll take me straight home, she told herself. He promised. Everything will be all right.

'Come along, darling. We're going backstage for drinkies.'

'But it's late, Elliott, and you said we'd leave after the performance.'

'And we will, sweet child, but first we have to do the polite, you know. Must get rid of the black mark I earned. We'll pop in on old Connie again – she is a darling, isn't she? Can't think of anyone else who would risk Ivor's wrath just before a performance but then, she is so terribly fond of me. If he's not too besieged, we'll see darling Ivor and have some champers. Ever had champers, Sally B?'

Champagne was not something ever served in

the Brewer house. How exciting. It was a dream ... except for that niggle of worry. But, of course there would be no problem; they worked together. Elliott was merely being theatrical and silly.

'I can't stay long, Elliott. My parents will worry.'

'You're not a child, Sally. Silly girl. Here we are.'

Seeing that the great man's dressing room was already packed full, Sally turned to leave but Elliott held her hand painfully and pulled her along behind him through the crowd.

The air rang with cries of 'Dahling', 'Wonderful', even 'Mahvellous!!' The practical Petrie twins would be amazed to learn that 'Mahvellous' and 'Dahling' were actual words, Sally thought.

'Wherever did you find this perfect little peach, Staines?'

Sally heard the question and at the same time felt an arm going around her waist. 'Stop that,' she began, but she felt herself being pulled even closer to a large man in a scarlet evening jacket.

'What a beauty,' the voice continued as the man's other hand began to rove over Sally's back and down her hips. 'Yum, yum, you can't keep her to yourself.'

'Let go of me,' Sally, heedless of the fact that she was surrounded by many of the nation's theatrical stars, hissed out the words, accompanying them with a sharp kick.

The hands dropped immediately but a well-known and heretofore much-admired face pressed itself closer to Sally's. 'Oh, I do like a little ingénue with a sparkle.' One hand grasped Sally's arm. 'Go

37

halves, Elliott darling, and I might just be able to...'

Sally looked up into the face of Conrad Blessington and, although she was frightened, angry and disappointed, she noted that the once so-handsome face had developed heavy jowls. There were dark shadows, not of illness, she thought, but of dissipation. Had the actor she had so admired always been as vulgar as the man holding her now?

Sally wrenched herself free and praying, first, that no one had paid any attention, and secondly, that she would not burst into tears, pushed her way past the two men and headed for the door. She gave thought to nothing but the need to get as far away from men like Elliott Staines and his friend as possible.

'Why, there you are,' said a voice. 'I waited an age and had quite given up hope of seeing you this evening.'

A young man – and Sally was not so upset that she did not see that he was extremely handsome – was standing beside her and smiling at her as if they were old friends.

'Bit of a crush, isn't it, but super evening? Didn't you think the last number was absolutely divine?'

Whoever he was, he gave her no chance to reply, not that she was capable of saying anything, but bundled her through the crowd – which parted for him – and out of the star's dressing room.

'Sebastian Brady,' he introduced himself. 'I take it that I'm correct and you didn't want to stay with those two old lechers?'

Sally looked up at him, into the perfect face

38

that she and her friends had fallen in love with when he had made his film debut as a prefect in the film *Goodbye, Mr Chips*.

Sebastian Brady. What must he think of her? Wildly Sally groped for a handkerchief. The young actor pressed his own into her hand.

'Where do you live?'

'Dartford.'

'Bloody hell. Oh, I do apologise. Has to be better than Portsmouth. Is there a late train?'

Sally blew her nose again. 'I have no idea. Elliott drove us.'

'So, no train ticket either?'

Tears started in Sally's eyes. How foolish she felt.

'You'll have to trust me then. Straight off, I think you're a lovely girl but my grandmother brought me up, she trusts, to be a gentleman. Come along. I've never been to Dartford. It'll be good for me.'

'You do know where it is?'

'Not the slightest idea.' He laughed at her worried expression. 'But I do have a fabulous invention, Miss Expressive Face. It's called a road map.'

'Very funny.'

They laughed together. He drove her home and as he negotiated the route he chatted of this, that and everything in between. It was as if they had known each other for ever. She was embarrassed to see the slightest chink of light through the blackout curtains in her parents' bedroom.

'Parents still awake, Sally? Don't be embarrassed. Be grateful. If I still lived at home, Grandmamma would be sitting up in the library waiting.'

She would have liked to ask about his parents but was still too aware that he was an actual film star. Instead she thanked him sincerely for his kindness. Then they said goodbye. He watched her until she had disappeared into the house. Sally waved and assumed that she would never see him again.

TWO

As always the house was in darkness when Sally let herself in and locked the front door. She smiled. Did they really think she did not know they were lying awake? She longed to tell them about Sebastian. How would her father react when he heard that a real film star, who had appeared in a film actually shown by his projector, had driven his daughter home from London?

Next morning she woke up to the sorrowful realisation that she had grown up overnight. She knew that she was about to lie to her parents. Never before had it occurred to her to lie; it had never been necessary. Sally brushed her hair until her head ached but she felt no better about her deception. At the breakfast table Ernie was unimpressed by her tale, glad that his daughter had been delivered home safely, but only the arrival on his doorstep of the King or perhaps, Mr Churchill, the Prime Minister, would have impressed him.

'And what about Mr Staines, love? Why didn't he bring you home as he promised?'

No matter how hard she tried, Sally knew she was blushing. She prepared to lie, hoping that most of what she was about to say was the truth. 'Mr Staines knows Ivor Novello, Dad, actually *knows* him. I was introduced to him.' She held out her right hand. 'Look at that hand. Ivor Novello shook it.'

Her father did not seem enthused by either the story or the hand and so Sally rattled on. 'There was a party, and I was invited too but I knew you and Mum would worry. Sebastian was there, one of the cast, and he offered to drive me home.'

'Very nice, I'm sure.'

'It was kind, Ernie, wasn't it?' Elsie put a plate in front of Sally. 'Eat up, pet. We didn't expect you up for breakfast – thought you'd take advantage and have a nice, long lie-in. You can tell Dad and me all about the evening when we get back from church.' She walked over to the stove and picked up the fat brown teapot. 'I noticed you caught your evening cloak on a nail or tack; I'll mend it and give it a good brush today.'

Sally had no remembrance of having snagged her beautiful cloak but she readily gave her mother permission to mend it. Elsie Brewer, like Daisy and Rose's mother Flora Petrie, was an expert with a needle and thread.

'I'll have to hurry, Mum. I want to meet Daisy and Rose before church; they'll want to hear everything.'

Sally was anxious not only to tell her friends everything that had happened the previous evening but also to ask for advice as to what to do. The thought of returning to the theatre and

41

Elliott Staines made her feel physically ill.

'You cannot let him spoil your career, Sally. Tell him hands off or your father will be there to see him.'

'I haven't told Dad, Daisy; that really would be the end of my career.'

The twins looked at her and then at each other. 'Sam,' they said together.

Sally was aghast. 'I can't tell Sam. Besides, where is he?'

'No idea, but you could put a picture of him on your worktable or whatever you have in a theatre. He'd make two of your Elliott. Accept no more invitations – if he's got the courage to ask you out – and mention Sebastian every so often. You know, a few words like, "You'll never believe what Sebastian said about..." and mention any big name you can think of. He'll stay clear, honest he will. He doesn't want to offend the big boys.'

Deep inside, Sally hoped that she would see Sebastian again, but he had said nothing about keeping in touch. Meeting a gorgeous actor and being driven home by him was a fairy tale. Once upon a time she had believed in fairy tales but she was now quite grown up.

Sally kept her friends hints in mind when she returned to the theatre. Elliott, suffering from a headache, brought on, he insisted, by winter sun glinting at him through leaves, had remained at home.

'He's a martyr to it, poor lamb. I'm afraid it makes for more work for you, Sally dear. Will you read Elliott's lines to Archie?' the director asked.

Sally picked up the script. Reading lines was

certainly a step up from typing out a new copy. The character being played by Elliott was – surprise, surprise – an ageing roué and Sally wondered if she dared try to change her voice. She could sound a little like a young man; an aged man was harder and her efforts might not be appreciated. Last time she had tried characterisation she had been told firmly, 'Just read the bloody lines, love.'

It was the nearest Sally got to real acting that week and was not a bad way to spend an afternoon. Archie Everest, better known to theatregoers as Giles Wentworth, was what was termed 'a reliable actor' and he was certainly better than Elliott and a great deal quieter.

'Dad's at the cinema, pet. Did you have a good day?' When Sally arrived home she found her mother in the kitchen doing the family ironing.

Without Elliott's presence, Sally's day had been much better than she had expected. 'Super, Mum, I had to read one of the parts. It was really interesting and Archie Everest is such a good actor. He gave me–' She stopped in mid-sentence. 'Oh, you've got my cloak. Where was the snag? I certainly don't remember catching it but the theatre was so crowded.'

Elsie put down her iron. 'Never mind the snag. Just guess what I found in the lining?' She reached up to a shelf above the cooker where several commemorative cups sat and took down one she had bought when the family visited the Empire Exhibition in Glasgow the previous year.

'Look.' She held out her hand.

'You're joking, Mum. That must have come from a Christmas cracker.'

'When did you ever see something like that in a cracker, love? I almost ironed over the top of it. There's a hole in the right pocket of your cloak. I think it slipped through and one of the stones must have caught on the lining. Otherwise it could have ended anywhere, in a gutter, down a drain.'

Sally was still staring in awe at what appeared to be a gold ring set with three large red stones, each surrounded by tiny white sparkling stones.

'Rubies and diamonds in real gold, Sally.'

Sally shook her head. 'They can't be real, Mum.'

'The lady who gave that cloak to charity could afford rubies and diamonds. We'll have to find her and give it back, love.'

Sally sat down at the table. 'Rubies and diamonds. Gosh. If they're real it must be worth a fortune.'

Elsie looked at the tiny diamond in her engagement ring. 'Daddy saved up for four years for this, Sally. Forty pounds it cost. The insurance man said we'd need to insure it for...' Elsie stopped as if the enormity of the amount was too shocking. 'Near two hundred, love,' she whispered, 'and that's for one diamond and there's twelve in this ring. Put it on. You've got ever such lovely hands and I'd like to see it on before we go to the police station.'

Sally slipped the ring on to her right hand and admired both the ring and her carefully manicured nails. 'Sets it off nicely, but, Mum, we'll be

44

quicker going tomorrow to the second-hand shop. I'll go on my lunch break. They'll know who brought in the cloak.'

Ernie would have liked to get rid of the ring straight away. 'That's worth a fortune, Sally, and I don't want it in my house. What kind of woman doesn't know she's lost a valuable ring?'

Neither his wife nor his daughter had the slightest idea how to answer that question.

'I'll put it in the safe at the cinema. Be better there.'

'But I won't be able to get it from you and take it to the shop, Dad. No one knows it's here. It'll be safe for one night.'

As usual Sally had her way and next day, carrying her packed lunch, she took the ring back to the shop. Neither Maude nor Fedora was on duty. Sally deliberated about speaking to the sole person there today. She had a relationship of sorts with the other two women; she trusted them. Her mind went back and forth. Of course, this woman was bound to be honest or Fedora would not have hired her. Therefore she should tell her the story of the ring. But she could not help thinking that this situation was almost like something one would see in a film. She would hand over the ring and the woman and the ring would disappear.

Sally smiled at her own foolishness.

'I bought the most beautiful evening cloak here,' she started.

'We don't take back sold items.'

The words were uttered so forcibly that Sally's original plan changed immediately. 'I'm thrilled with the cape. I wanted, if possible, to thank the lady who donated it.'

'We don't discuss our sponsors but you can be assured that our quality items come from only the finest homes. We have actually dealt with a titled gentleman recently.' She stopped abruptly as if she realised she was being too talkative.

'Of course, but do thank him and his wife,' said Sally with a beaming smile as she turned and hurried from the shop. She knew exactly who would know where any local aristocrat lived.

Petrie's Groceries and Fine Teas had been dealing with every stratum of Dartford society for as long as Sally had known them. She waited only until her family and, she hoped, the Petrie family had eaten their evening meal before hurrying over to the familiar flat above the shop to speak to her friend Daisy, who worked full time in the grocery.

Ron, the Petries' youngest son, opened the door. 'Well, if it isn't Margaret Lockwood herself. How's the world of bright lights, Maggie?'

Sally laughed. 'The girls in, Ron?'

'And where else would they be on a weeknight? Go on up. Rose is washing her hair but everyone else is in the front room listening to the wireless.'

A few minutes later, Daisy and Sally were in the kitchen, the door firmly shut against intruders.

'Well, what do you think of that?'

Daisy gazed at the ring. She tentatively stretched out a hand towards it.

'Try it on; it'll be too big but watch how it sparkles.'

Daisy slipped it on and gazed in awe. It was much too big for her petite hand, but when she

46

held it up the stones contrasted prettily with her green eyes and short dark hair. 'Is it real? It can't be real. It looks like something the Queen would have.'

'Dad thinks it's real and of course I have to return it. The owner must be frantic, poor woman. I would be, wouldn't you?'

They were silent for a moment as they stood silently, just watching the stones sparkle as light hit them.

'I want you to help me find the owner, Daisy, because she must be a customer.'

'Sorry, Sally, our customers can't afford diamonds and rubies. We sell cheese and porridge oats and tinned peas. Rich people don't eat porridge.'

'Perhaps they don't, but they drink fine teas.'

The friends sank back in their chairs as this truth hit them.

'You do some of the deliveries, Daisy.'

'I can't tell you customers' names, Sally, and certainly not their addresses.'

Sally sighed and Daisy recognised it, for once, as a genuine note of unhappiness. Sally was capable of showing a whole host of feelings, one after the other,

'I wish I could help but the business is built on trust.'

'Golly, I'm not going to steal something. I want to give this back.'

'Take it back to—' began Daisy.

'I did. That was the first idea but it didn't feel right and I just have this strange feeling that it's really important for me to return it in person.'

As with the sighs, Daisy was familiar with the feelings. 'There's the bathwater going. Rose is coming. Put the kettle on while I tell Mum we'll bring the cocoa in to them.'

Sally did as she was bid. They had enacted this scenario countless times over the years: the twins with Sally and sometimes their friend Grace, drinking cocoa in the kitchen, discussing great secret matters while their parents and brothers remained out of the way. Rose, Daisy's non-identical twin, wearing a well-worn pink fluffy dressing gown, which was a bit short with her height, and a very damp towel round her long, wet corn-coloured hair, joined them.

'Hello, I thought I heard the door. You don't mind if I dry my hair in here?' She carried on as Sally agreed. 'How was the first day back? Did you skewer the old toad?'

'He's ill.'

'I bet. No doubt the gorgeous Sebastian warned him off. Are you seeing him again?'

'Get in front of the fire, Rose. Mum'll explode if she sees your hair dripping all over the floor.' Daisy plonked down a chair for her sister. 'Show her the ring while I make her some cocoa, Sally.'

The next few minutes were taken up with much trying on and oohing and aahing over the ring.

'It has to belong to–'

'Ouch, Daisy. That hurt. And what's the harm in telling Sally? She's hardly likely to burgle the place; she wants to take the ring back.'

'Yes, and the way to do it is to return to the shop, speak to the Fedora lady and get her to contact them. Keep your dad happy by letting him put it in the safe, Sally. Fedora whoever will telephone them – they're bound to have a telephone – and one careless owner will tell her to instruct you to bring it out. Who knows, maybe she loves theatre and you'll become friends and she'll help you in your career.'

'You are silly, Daisy, but maybe that is the best way. I'll handle it tomorrow.'

'Phil and Ron will walk you home.'

'What on earth for? They've never done it before.'

'Because, Lady Griselda, thou art wearing the family jewels.'

'Who's the actress here, Daisy Petrie? But you're right. I'm off and I'll tell you what happens.'

Nothing 'happened' for several days and then one lunch hour, Maude was standing outside the shop waving frantically.

'Has Fedora managed to talk to them?'

'At last. Come in and we'll tell you. You're a very lucky girl. Proves that doing the right thing is … the right thing.'

Sally looked at her watch and decided she had just enough time to speak to the ladies and still be at the theatre ready for rehearsal. 'Very well, but I mustn't be late.'

Maude ushered her into the shop.

'Dear Sally,' Fedora walked over from the counter where she had been making a display of donated hats and gloves. 'I have some wonderful news for you.'

'You've spoken to the owner?'

'Two days ago and Sally, you are such a lucky young woman. The ring is yours.' She stopped talking but her beaming smile told Sally how pleased she was.

'Sorry, but this doesn't make sense. I bought the cape...'

'As far as the owner ... the *former* owner is concerned, you also bought everything that was in the cloak, too. It's yours, Sally, legally.'

'What about his wife?'

Fedora reached a supplicating hand towards Maude. 'Maudie, you tell her.'

'It's an age-old story. A young man buys a ring for his wife whom he loves. A year later she decides that she no longer loves him or anything he gave her. She walked out leaving almost everything behind, clothes, jewellery etcetera.'

'But she probably didn't know that the ring was in the lining.'

'Trust me, Sally, she doesn't care. As far as he is concerned the ring means nothing to him either. He values it at less than you paid for the cloak. He was surprisingly rude about that.'

'That makes no sense. It's obviously valuable.'

'Don't look a gift horse in the mouth, young woman,' Fedora said sternly. 'As far as the shop is concerned, the subject is closed. Now you'd best hurry.'

Sally stood speechless. Even the words 'thank you' refused to come. She turned and almost ran from the shop. The ring was hers but did she want it? It meant heartache, at least for the husband. Would she think of his broken dream if she were to wear the ring?

Work, she decided. She would get to the theatre and forget the ring and her beautiful cloak; she

50

would never wear it again.

Some of Fedora's words ran around in her head as she hurried.

'I should have gone through the pockets, I'll admit that, but I couldn't somehow. My dear Maude is known to his family and it would have seemed somehow intrusive. I should have reminded her that I hadn't done it. We usually go through everything, of course, just in case something's been forgotten, but I've only ever found used bus tickets or soiled handkerchiefs – so unpleasant. I can't tell you how sorry I am to have put you in an embarrassing position. I do wish I'd been in when you came back first, Sally.' She stopped, obviously extremely perplexed. 'I've never worked a day in my life until this damned war. Oh, do excuse my language but I made a silly mistake, which then involved you, and I do abhor feeling inadequate to a situation.' She took a deep breath. 'Still, it's turned out fortunate for you. The jewels in the ring are real and the owner was adamant that an honest girl like you should have it. You're a very lucky young lady and must be sure to insure it.'

Thinking about this as she returned to the theatre that afternoon, Sally sighed. Her parents would never allow her to keep the ring no matter what the owner had said.

'Heat of the moment, Sally,' her father said that evening. 'People say things they don't mean when they're angry or upset. She'll want it back. Give it to me and I'll lock it away.'

London – and Dartford itself – were being

51

blitzed by the German air force before Sally heard of the ring again, and by then she had been so busy that she had almost forgotten about it.

The country was experiencing the reality of war and the entire population of Britain was expected to pull together. Both younger Petrie brothers had joined the Forces. Rose and Daisy continued with their work but complained loudly that they were not doing enough. Grace and Sally took a first-aid class, and then one day, early in 1940, Grace, who had started a small vegetable garden in what passed for a garden behind her sister's squalid little house, disappeared. Her friends were anxious about her, but they could only think that she had gone to join the war effort.

In the months that followed, appalling things happened in Europe and night after night that first summer of the war, Dartford residents, like Londoners, sought safety from the fighting that raged above and around them.

The little theatre decided to put on a revue in an attempt to brighten the lives of the community. Sally was given a starring role, both singing and dancing. Her only claim to being a dancer was that, before she was old enough to go to school, she had attended a Tiny Tots dancing class in the church hall. Her part in the dance class's production was as 'Special Fairy Guard', and she had stood to attention for the entire performance. It was years before she discovered that the teachers had told her distressed parents that their lovely daughter did not know her right foot from her left. Luckily Elliott – who was minding his P's and Q's – and a middle-aged actress, Marguerite du

Bois (real name, Maggie Wood), who had, at one time, been quite well known, had years of experience of being what they called 'hoofers'. They had coached Sally when the small troupe had put on entertainments over the Christmas period.

'You'll be fine, Sally. I'll go over the routines with you,' offered Maggie. 'Heck, I choreographed most of them and, in that dim and distant past, Elliott was a beautiful mover. I know, hard to believe, but it's true. Come on, show me what you did at Tiny Tots.'

As yet, apart from standing well, Sally did not have much of a repertoire but she was graceful and elegant and worked hard. She began to enjoy herself as Maggie encouraged her and congratulated her on definite improvement.

'Listen to the music, Sally. It will tell you what to do.'

Sally listened and she learned.

She was not too happy with one of the outfits she was expected to wear. The shorts were definitely the shortest ones she had ever worn. She tried to picture her father's face.

'My father will have a fit, Maggie, and while I'm talking about costume, the dress for the waltz is cut much too low.'

'Take it up with Wardrobe, lovey.'

'I am Wardrobe.'

'Then fix it but don't blame me when Elliott sees – or rather doesn't see.'

Sally took the offending gown home and after uttering a few choice words, Elsie agreed to rework the top. 'And don't let your father see it till I'm finished or you'll be out of that theatre before you can say…' She could not think of what to say but Sally understood her perfectly.

So did Elliott, and as opening night drew closer, Sally blossomed.

Sebastian Brady sent her a 'Break a Leg' card, perhaps not the best choice to send someone dancing on stage for the first time, but Sally was thrilled and wondered how he had known. He enlightened her when he came backstage to see her after the last performance of the revue.

'The world of the theatre is surprisingly small, Sally. We keep an eye on one another. I didn't manage to see you in your first show – was involved in a war film – but I do read the reviews, as, of course, do others more important than I. You're gathering good press. The frock in the last number was a tad virginal but I must say that the skirt was perfect for movement. How are you enjoying the work?'

'Even appearing in a Shakespeare play seems such a long way off.' Sally looked at him through the dressing-table mirror. He was real, though as tall, dark and handsome as any fairy-tale prince. His presence was not a figment of her imagination. She hadn't seen him since he'd brought her home from that ghastly after-show party, but she'd thought of him often. But had he come especially to see her or was he merely on his way somewhere else? She leaned forward to study her face closely as she wiped off the greasepaint, and suddenly he was standing behind her, cotton wool in his hand.

'You're not stripping down the old door in the hall, darling. Gently. Rubbing on the delicate skin under the eyes like that will lift the make-up, yes, but it will stretch the skin.' He smiled into her mirrored eyes naughtily. 'You don't really want to look like old Maggie years before your time, do you?'

She said nothing, every atom of her being signalling furiously that it was aware of his presence. And he knew how she felt; somehow she could tell. What was he going to do? Was he another Elliott? Somehow, for one crazy moment, she did not care.

Sebastian finished the gentle cleaning and stood back. 'There, that's better. And now, is there a hostelry in this town that will give us a pot of tea and a sandwich? I want to discuss a new project with you and then I really must tootle back up to town. Haven't quite used all my petrol coupons, thank God. No idea how I'll exist when they run out. I shall have to emulate the hobos during the American Depression.' He looked at her, sadly shaking his head. 'You have no idea what I'm talking about, do you? Didn't you do any American history or lit?'

'Of course: the Civil War, the War of Independence, and I've just finished reading *Gone with the Wind*.'

He laughed. 'Read backstage, Sally, not just plays, but novels by writers from all over the world, and read history. Now, if you're coming for a cup of char, change your frock, although you'd be a sensation walking into the Copper Kettle or whatever in that.'

He went off and Sally changed into a white silk cowl-necked sweater and black trousers, thrust her feet into high-heeled black sandals, grabbed her jacket and her handbag, and turned off the lights.

THREE

October 1940, London

The Theatre Royal. Soon the wonderful old theatre would be as familiar to her as the little house attached to the cinema in Dartford. Each day as she tried to find the safest way to the theatre from the hostel in Camden, where she was now living, Sally cheered herself by remembering that. She assured her concerned parents that her area of London was relatively peaceful, preferring that they not know how many nights she and her fellow residents spent crowding into only marginally safe shelters. She never told her parents how afraid she was of the underground, having decided that travelling under ground was definitely safer and quicker than catching a bus or a tram, even if any were running.

Sally, like thousands of others before her, had fallen completely in love with the magnificence that had been London, and cried inside every time she was forced to see the devastation that months of bombing was causing. These days, she closed her eyes as she travelled and tried not to wince when she found that the gracious church, museum, private house that she had seen only yesterday was today a ruin.

But the Theatre Royal was still there and Sally was now doing what she had always wanted to do.

She was being taught how to perform, as she was now a probationary member of the Entertainments National Service Association or ENSA, as it had become known. It was a real acting job, and, better still, it was war work, with the vital role of entertaining His Majesty's Armed Forces and so keeping up morale. The delicious icing on the lovely cake was that the magnificent world-famous theatre was now her 'university'. Once she had wept because she could not see a play there and now, a few months later, she walked into and out of that hallowed place five or six days a week. In the first weeks she did not know that several of the offices had once been dressing rooms, or that ENSA would not have constant use of the stage as it was being shared by other groups, and was still needed for auditions. She learned that what had been the Stalls Bar was now a recording studio where at times she herself would participate in ENSA broadcasts to troops abroad and, of course, the first thing she learned was that the theatre had its own air-raid shelter in what had once been the Staff Bar.

'Wherever you are, you hear the warning, you drop everything and come here. Everyone get that?' Max Hunter, the director looked, as it seemed, into the eyes of every new recruit and waited until they nodded affirmatively.

Sebastian Brady was only one of thousands of professional actors, singers, dancers, musicians, comedians – many of them world famous – who were prepared to give up their time to entertaining servicemen wherever they were in the fields of war, although a long, tough battle had had to be

57

fought and won before ENSA came into being.

'Basil Dean and Lesley Henson were the creative brains behind the idea of ENSA, Sally,' he told her. 'They both served in the Great War, and had done some entertaining in the field. After the war, they went back to acting and filming and, of course, since they started the film careers of stars like Gracie Fields and George Formby, they had great contacts. But they had to fight to get ENSA off the ground as so much money was needed for actual warfare. Eventually the NAAFI helped out financially and now, I think everyone in Government believes in our work.'

Sebastian had worked with both men and he had recommended Sally.

'She has natural talent,' he had told them, 'and, thankfully, hasn't had time to develop bad habits by working too long for the wrong people. Some of your training will make a duckling into a little swan and, while we're talking about ducklings, there's no ugly one here – she's a stunner.'

Sally had been called in for an audition.

When, over breakfast at home, she opened the letter requesting she attend, for a minute or two she was excited. Bubbles of joy burst inside her and she pictured them sending out tiny sparkling lights. Then realisation cancelled her euphoria. An audition? What on earth was she to do; how could she impress? Professional, experienced performers would be auditioning – what chance did she stand?

She wondered if she dared contact Sebastian for advice but decided against it. 'I can't compete against a professional, Mum; they'll laugh me off the stage.'

'Don't be silly, love. You were really good in the school plays, Shakespeare and Shaw and ... writers like that. Besides, you have a nice singing voice. They'll want to see all your talents so sing a song; one of the ones we hear soldiers asking for on the wireless. "The Nearness of You" is a big favourite, or "I Get Along Without You Very Well". Your dad loves to hear you singing that around the house. I'd go for that one. Or you could recite a speech. You were so good as Juliet, and you can't do better than Shakespeare, can you now? Wish I had time to make you a new frock. I thought your white Juliet dress was beautiful, and with your lovely hair hanging down on your shoulders ... you'll be perfect, Sally, you will.'

'What if they ask me to dance?'

'They won't; they know you're studying to be an actress. Actresses don't dance; they speak.'

Sally hoped her mother was right; even with Maggie's tuition she knew she would never be dancing at Sadler's Wells.

She scarcely ate and hardly slept in the days before her audition but she did practise a few songs and went over and over Juliet's 'Wherefore art thou Romeo?' speech until she and her parents were all heartily tired of it.

The day of the audition dawned and Sally was appalled to see the length of the waiting line of candidates. Not only was she terrified but she decided that every female in the queue was not only prettier and more sophisticated, but also more intelligent than she. She barely managed to control her terror when she found herself standing on the actual stage where England's theatrical greats had stood – it was some time before she knew that 'her' Theatre Royal was the third to stand on that hallowed spot, the previous ones having burned to the ground – and eventually went home so stricken with nerves that she couldn't eat for a whole day.

Thankfully they had not asked her to dance, they had asked her to walk across the stage, had listened to a few lines of her well-rehearsed Shakespeare and a verse of the poignant love song, then thanked her and called the next candidate. She had been quite sure that she had failed in every department. And then the letter came. She had been accepted. Somehow, miraculously, Sally Brewer was now a probationary member of ENSA.

There could, however, be no celebration in the Brewer household that night as Ernie was due at the cinema.

He hugged his daughter to him. 'I never felt more like – what's it they say – painting the town red, Sally, but the show must go on, as we showbiz folks say. Can hardly believe my little girl'll be saying it soon, too. Course we'll miss you, love, and you know your old dad, I'll always worry about you, every moment, but you're a clever, sensible girl and you won't do anything stupid.'

'Of course not.'

'And remember, you can come home at any time if anything worries you. Just get on a train. Right?'

'Right, Dad.'

She returned his hug. 'I'll come with you and Mum; I'll sell the potato crisps and the ice cream.

Probably be the last time I'll ever work with you.'

'Oh, don't say that, love; that's sad,' said Elsie.

'You'd rather I stayed here selling Smith's crisps, Mum?' Sally teased her mother.

Elsie pulled on her coat. 'Don't be daft, but I don't like saying "the last time".'

'Get a move on,' teased Ernie, 'or it'll be the last time either of you will work for me.'

Sally enjoyed her last evening as a cinema usherette and next morning went to the theatre to resign.

'Dahling, absolutely the wrong decision,' Elliott said bluntly. 'You'll hate it, and I know they hold up names like Olivier and Richardson before your ambitious little eyes, but they'll never join that motley crew. Would you take ten quid a week for the tours they'll offer when you could be earning hundreds on the legitimate stage? You can't believe a world-famous actor like Ralph Richardson will go traipsing all over the country to act in draughty church halls and old barns, and as for following the troops... He's a star. Good heavens, someone even told me they had snaffled Gracie Fields. I ask you, *the* Gracie Fields. You've more chance of meeting her here, Sally, and besides, only last night we decided to stage a Noël Coward. Bit of a chestnut, *Private Lives*, but the punters do love it. Believe me, darling Sally, "resting" actors are queuing up like housewives outside the butcher's, hoping that they'll be taken on, and face it, sweetie, all with more training and experience than you.'

He walked round the desk to lay his hand on her shoulder. Automatically Sally tensed and he

61

moved away, smiling at her jovially.

'Sally dahling, we have decided that you will make a lovely Sybil. Now can you abandon that opportunity for something that probably won't get off the ground?'

'Yes,' Sally had answered emphatically.

It was a decision she never regretted.

The day before she left to live in London, Sally returned to the clothes shop where she had bought her cloak to see if there was anything suitable to wear in her new life, and in the hope of being able to say goodbye to Maude and Fedora. She was delighted to see that both the ladies were in the shop. They were talking to a man in naval uniform.

'Good heavens, here she is,' called Fedora, and all three turned to look at Sally. 'Sally, this is...' she hesitated and then continued, 'the ... original owner of the ring.'

'Former owner,' said the young man, holding out his hand to Sally. 'Jonathon Galbraith, or just Jon is perfectly fine.'

'Sally Brewer, Just Jon.' Sally, surprised by her nonchalance, blushed furiously.

He smiled and, for the first time in her life, Sally was aware of how much a smile can change appearance. At first sight, Just Jon had been austere, controlled. She would have guessed that he was twice her age but now ten years melted away as quickly as light snow melts under a winter sun. 'Miss Brewer, I'm just about to rejoin my ship so it's a happy chance that we should meet here.' He looked around and obviously came to a decision. 'Would you have time to have coffee or tea with me? It would only take a few minutes and I really would like to thank you for trying to return the ring.'

'I'm on my way...' began Sally, but he already had his hand under her elbow. 'I won't keep Miss Brewer too long, ladies,' he said with another charming smile as he propelled Sally out of the shop.

A few minutes later they were seated at a table in a nearby café, and had ordered tea, which was just as well, for apart from cocoa, tea was almost all the café served.

'The ring is in the safe at the cinema, Mr Galbraith, and my father will give it to you as soon as you ask him.'

'No, I don't want it, Miss Brewer. Sell it, if you don't like it.'

The waitress put the cups on the table so forcibly that tea spilled over into the saucers. She did not apologise.

'Everything in the world's going to pot right now,' Jon said as he dried Sally's saucer with a clean handkerchief. 'I believe Fedora's told you that I bought the ring for my wife because she liked it. Now my wife no longer wants me or anything to do with me and has sailed for America, I think – she always wanted me to take her there – or possibly she has returned to Malta where her family live. She has not done me the courtesy of telling me. I will not tell you what she said I might do with the belongings she chose to leave but I assure you that the ring is yours.'

Without warning he changed the subject. 'Maudie tells me you are to study acting.' He stopped and, for the first time, really looked at her. 'I know you find this entire scenario distasteful, Miss Brewer, but I do thank you for trying to return the ring.'

'But of course I needed to return it. It was the proper thing to do.'

Sally had not really paid attention to what he was saying. Instead she was looking at him, this man she had only just met but who had featured in her thoughts. She could not remember what she had thought he might look like, but she knew, somehow, that he looked just right.

She liked fair hair, like that of her friend Daisy's brothers, but now knew that brown hair was perfect especially when matched by brown eyes that revealed sadness. She knew little about uniforms but enough to know that this was a naval uniform. The markings told her that Just Jon was an officer, probably of fairly high rank. She felt sad as reality struck her. She had just met him. How unlikely it was that she would ever see him again.

He clasped his hands and put them lightly on the table. 'It is yours,' he said again, 'and I'm happy to sign a letter confirming that. If you've fallen in love with it, then enjoy wearing it. But my advice would be to sell it; it might make years of study more comfortable.' He sipped his tea while he watched Sally think about what he had just said and then he stood up. He held out his hand and Sally stood and put her hand in his. She felt a tremor. Was it her hand or his? 'Again please accept my apologies for my inexcusable rudeness. I should have been congratulating you on your honesty – God knows I've seen so little of it lately.' Still he held her hand as he looked into her eyes. 'May I wish you all success in your endeavours. I look forward to seeing your name in lights, Miss Brewer.'

'Thank you, Mr Galbraith.'

He smiled and again his face changed. 'Do you know, I rather like being Just Jon.'

Sally blushed. 'I was rude,' she began.

'No,' he drew out the syllable. 'You were enchanting. On this exercise I shall remember a beautiful girl calling me Just Jon.'

Then, as his gaze continued to hold her own and she saw admiration in his eyes, she suddenly felt shy and had to look away.

At the door he turned and raised his hand in farewell. 'Don't change, Sally Brewer.'

And he was gone, leaving payment for their tea discreetly beside his saucer.

Sally sat down for a moment, her mind and body in turmoil. *Maudie, not Maude; they must know each other very well. An aunt, perhaps. No, she's not ... not like Fedora.* A strange and unrecognised thrill of excitement made her shiver. *Just Jon, what have you done to me?* She stood up, hoping that her legs would continue to hold her upright. Fortunately, they seemed to have recovered from the shakiness they had exhibited under the small table and she walked quite easily from the café.

Just Jon.

Jon. Somehow that small word seemed to Sally the most perfect possible name for a man. The images of the delightful Sebastian that always seemed to be at the very front of her brain had somehow been replaced – and so suddenly – by

65

the image of a man she had seen once. Again, she felt a pang of real pain. No, that could not be. What on earth had happened to her? Was this what so many of those wonderful films she had watched repeatedly as an impressionable teenager had led her to believe lay in store? One day she would meet a man and fall headlong into everlasting love. This man? He was not as tall as Sebastian but somehow he looked stronger. The width of the shoulders perhaps? Sebastian was beautiful. Jon was not. There was too much strength there for beauty, plus power, and an easy air of command. The film magazines would have called him handsome. Sebastian too, had a lovely voice but it did not set her pulses racing as a few minutes' conversation with Jon had done. Somehow she knew that his voice would echo in her sleep.

Sally shook her head and hurried back towards the shop but then she decided that she was incapable of having a sensible conversation with the two ladies and so she changed direction and walked towards the park.

From the days when they had first been allowed to play without adult supervision this had been a favourite place for Sally and her close friends. They had loved strolling around the vibrant flowerbeds, or lying on the meticulously mown lawns talking of everything and nothing. Many plans had been hatched here and some of them had even come to fruition. Now Sally walked but the park no longer gave her the solace it had once so easily dispensed. How could she have forgotten the changes war had caused? Where there had been beds of glorious roses, there were now trenches. Sally looked up at the sky and her heart, which had been beating happily only a few seconds before, almost stopped in terror. Any second a German aircraft – Dartford residents knew the names and could recognise most of them – a Heinkel or a Messerschmitt, could come screaming out of nowhere, and if she was not killed immediately she might just have time to jump into one of the trenches.

'Stupid, stupid Sally,' she said aloud and turning, ran as quickly as she could out of the park and home.

Life was not always the film with the happy ending but today, her last day at home for some time, had brought something very special and she would allow nothing, not even fear of an air raid, to spoil it.

She acted, quite perfectly, the part of 'happy girl who has had one of her dreams come blissfully true'.

She found her mother rehanging the blackout curtains in the front room.

'Mum, they're black. Washing them so often is just making work for yourself, but you'll never guess what happened!' She waited for a response and none came. 'Mum?'

'Yes, I won't guess so tell me.'

'I'm in...' Sally could scarcely believe what she had been about to say and quickly recovered herself. 'I'm in a bit of a pickle. I went to the shop to say goodbye to the ladies but didn't get a chance. The nicest man was there, a naval officer, handsome, lovely voice, proper gentleman, but, Mum – he bought the ring.'

67

'From you? How?'

'No, of course not. It's just like Fedora said. He bought it for his wife but she's left him. He says she doesn't want it and that I can keep it.'

'Never.' Elsie's facial expression said clearly that she had heard tales of rich men who bought valuable jewels for young girls. 'And where is he now, Sally?'

Sally looked at her mother and could see all the doubts and worries running across her pleasant face. 'I'm surprised at you. Right now he's rejoining his ship; I told you he was in the navy. I'll never see him again,' and she burst into tears and ran to her room.

Elsie looked after her, shaking her head. 'Sarah Bernhardt,' she said, and sighed. 'Didn't I say the university would be calmer?'

Since Sally had not mentioned the ring in some time, her parents had also let it slip from their minds. Ernie saw the box he had put it in each time he opened the cinema safe, but it was as if the family simply hoped that the problem would just go away.

Sally lay on her lemon and green quilt and looked up at the white ceiling but no answers to her questions were written there. 'Why?' she groaned, 'why did he have to come today? Why did I decide to speak to *Maudie?* And why didn't she tell me she knew... Jon, Just Jon, so well?'

Sally turned over in anguish and buried her face in the quilt and was still there when her mother came in to remind her that she still had packing to do.

The next morning her parents travelled up to

London with her to see her settled in the boarding house where she was to live while she was taking classes at the theatre. Apart from Ernie saying that the ring would remain in the safe until Mr Galbraith was next on leave, the question of whether or not Sally would keep it was not mentioned.

Sally enjoyed every moment of her training as the year seemed to rush towards its end. Like the other residents, she handed in her ration card, and even though meat, butter, sugar and tea had been rationed for some time, the meals were adequate. In no way were they like her mother's tasty meals, but they were more than acceptable.

The other residents were older and had known one another for some time. Although they were polite, even friendly, Sally doubted that she would make any close friends from among them. The ENSA groups training or rehearsing at the theatre became a substitute for her family; she grew closer to Sebastian, whom she had known longest. They held hands as they walked around town; occasionally he would throw his arm round her shoulders. 'Are you the teeniest bit in love with me yet?' was a fairly regular question that Sally did not take seriously.

Her personal life suffered some blows as her friends in Dartford dealt with one tragedy after another. How, she wondered, could dear Mrs Petrie cope with the death of Ron, her youngest son, and the always nagging possibility that her eldest child, Sam, was also dead? She looked forward to at least one day at home, possibly as

69

far away as the Christmas period; a letter was nice, yes, but a warm hug would be much better. Maybe she could get away some Sunday. If trains were running she should have time to get home, see the families and get back before Mrs Shuttlecock, her landlady, locked up.

Having made this decision, it was with lighter steps that Sally made her way back to her digs one autumn evening after a strenuous dance workout. She, like her Dartford friends, had always been fit and active, but dancing had uncovered muscles she had never known she had – and every single one ached.

Supper was a deep bowl of delicious vegetable soup – every vegetable grown in Mrs Shuttlecock's garden – followed by a thick slice of toast and cheese and a cup of tea.

'My Henry laid out all the beds and planted vegetables and strawberries too before he joined up. Didn't need to as he had a job what was on the special list that could easy have kept him out of the Forces – reserved occupations, that's it, reserved – but "It's my duty to King and country," he said, and they'll give him his job back when he comes home.' Mrs Shuttlecock related this story to each new arrival.

Sally had just begun to undress for her weekly bath when the air-raid warning sounded. No time to dress again and so she pulled her pyjamas on over her underwear, grabbed a cardigan and a coat, shoved her feet into her short, lined boots and headed for the door.

'Remember your gas mask and papers, Sally,' yelled one of the other residents as Sally passed the pile of bags at the back door without picking up her bag. She smiled her thanks and retrieved her bag of important documents, her birth certificate, the letter from Oliver Dantry, the acceptance letter from ENSA, a few pictures of her childhood friends, and her gas mask, and ran out into the neatly ordered garden. (Mrs Shuttlecock, of course, had all the ration books in her very large bag.)

There was no time to admire the chrysanthemums or the fine crop of cabbages camouflaging the roof of the Anderson shelter. Inside, Mrs Shuttlecock had made it as comfortable as possible with cushions and blankets, and Thermos flasks full of tea or cocoa, which sometimes returned unopened to the kitchen but which more often lately had been a late supper in the shelter as the bombers roared overhead. There was an elderly wireless, which seemed to sound better when it was set on the specially painted orange box that the local greengrocer had traded for some home-grown potatoes and a jar of Mrs Shuttlecock's strawberry jam. Nothing seemed to be able to mask the damp smell of earth that permeated the papers, blankets, cushions, and even their clothes if they stayed there any length of time as, unfortunately, they often did.

They tried to keep themselves amused by reading, listening to the wireless, playing cards and even listening to the tales – most of them probably with little truth in them – that were told them by Liz Sweep, who worked in a very expensive West End department store. She always started in the same way: 'Wait till you hear this, girls, and sparing your blushes, Mrs S,' and then she would carry on, using, naturally, her everyday voice instead of the highly affected one she adopted when dealing with surprised or amused customers.

'Me and Doreen was having a chat; worked off our feet all morning, we were. Would you believe the Christmas goodies is coming in and we make such a lot of money in the weeks before but everything's got to be just so. Anyways, we were taking a breather and this funny little foreign woman grabs my arm and says, "Stop with trivial chatter" – cheeky cow – "and be so kind as to tell me where English Christmas crackers are being."

'Neither of us had the slightest – in the Christmas department they was setting up, I suppose, but I says – trying to be helpful – "I'm sure you'll find them over there, Modome," and I stretched out my arm to point her in the right direction.' Liz stopped to make sure that her audience was spellbound. Pleased with what she saw, she carried on. 'And would you believe I knocked over our entire arrangement of Christmas "suggestions for the lady in your life" work what we'd spent the entire morning making look fabulous. Ever so artistic, Doreen is. The blo– sorry, Mrs S, things went everywhere, behind us, beneath us; they rolled under counters, one really lovely Limoges compact fell out of its box and rolled off, heading for the front door. If no one stopped it, it'll be in Richmond by now. The foreign woman shrieked and ran and the floor manager comes over and gives us a ticking off. Doreen's crying and her mascara's run so far down it's on her chin and he says to her, "Clean yourself up. And get back here immediately.""

'Did you tell him what really happened, Liz?' asked one of the older women. 'Or did you blame it on the customer?'

Liz had the grace to look a little shamefaced. 'Thought about it for a second – can't afford to lose my job, can I, and it were an accident but you have to watch out for the dead posh ones or the foreign ones – they're usually duchesses or ambassadors' wives and they can tell you round is square and Management tells you to agree with them. Doreen and me's got to pay for the breakages but I'll do it since she never really done anything.'

With mixed feelings about the story, the women were delighted to hear the all clear soon after. Gratefully they made their way along the garden path to the house. Less than fifteen minutes later everyone was sound asleep.

Mrs Shuttlecock woke them up early and they staggered downstairs, still half asleep but appreciating the smells coming from the pretty dining room.

'You'd think we'd get used to interrupted sleep,' groaned a girl who worked in Camden market.

'We will,' said Liz, immaculately dressed and perfectly made up as usual. 'My sister says she thought she'd never get a full night's sleep again after being up half the night nursing her kids, but she says, soon as they're weaned, everything goes back to normal.'

'Nice to know, Liz, thanks,' mumbled the others, eating their breakfasts of scrambled eggs with fried bacon bits in them.

'Fantastic breakfast, Mrs B.'

'No more real eggs till next month, probably. Anyone know a nice farmer?'

Of course Sally knew Alf Humble, tenant of the farm near Dartford where she and her three special friends had played or picked strawberries. Strange to think that Grace had chosen to join the Women's Land Army. *And what connection to farming could a girl like Grace have had? Did enjoy growing her sprouts, mind you.*

Sally's thoughts went everywhere as she tried to get to the theatre. Here and there was evidence of the previous night's raid and, like every other pedestrian, she had to watch where she put her feet. Smoke drifted across the city and it was impossible to judge where most damage had been done. Eventually she turned into Catherine Street and stopped dead in horror. Several Auxiliary Fire Service taxis with their trailer pumps stood outside the theatre. A group of rather tired-looking teenage boys, none older than seventeen or thereabouts, straddled their bicycles, feet firmly on the ground but each ready at a moment's notice to cycle off with a message or a plea for more help from other AFS units. A WVS van was near the grey taxis, and exhausted firemen and some men – three clerics among them – who had obviously been helping, were being offered hot tea. The hard-working members of the WVS seemed to turn up with their tea wagon wherever succour was needed. One reminded Sally of Fedora, every hair still in place. For the first time that morning, she smiled.

Dirty water was everywhere but from where she

74

stood, Sally could not see exactly what had happened to the theatre.

And then a mug of tea was pushed into her hand and there was Sebastian. He looked tired and his brown hair was liberally sprinkled with ash.

'You've been here all night? How bad is it?'

'Max has been here since around one. He rang me just before he left his apartment – took me half an hour or so to get here. There he is leaning against the wall. And no, his hair didn't turn grey overnight, it's ash; I don't think he's noticed it. It's even on his moustache – shows what a handsome devil he'll be in his sixties. The men with him are the all-powerful gods of this theatre, Sir Seymour Hicks, and, of course you'll remember Basil and Lesley from your audition. We plebs rarely see them but Seymour has that office at the end of the main foyer and Basil's is in what was the boardroom. Don't remember where Lesley is but at least one of them is here every day. As to damage, a bomb, high-explosive probably, crashed through into the rear circle just before midnight. It caused a fire, which has done extensive damage, but they tell me the fire brigade is sure it's under control. Debris landed everywhere and so we can't do a thing until we've had a massive clean-up. But the good news is that no great or lasting damage has been done to the building.'

'Will we have to wait till the repairs are completed?'

'What repairs, my little innocent? Every builder, slater, joiner, carpenter in Britain is working all out. We'll fix what we can ourselves. Actors are only one part of a theatre, remember. We have a brilliant back-stage crew who'll get to work as soon as they're allowed into the building. Restoration? I'd imagine that is low down on London's priority list. A year or two at the best, I think.'

He yawned, and Sally, seeing that the tea in his mug was obviously cold, exchanged it for hers, which he drank gratefully.

'Any ... oh Sebastian, was anyone inside?'

He nodded. 'Night staff. No fatalities, a few minor injuries. What a wake-up call. Sally darling, those boys have been cycling all over London begging for water and carrying it back here. Could you give the WVS a hand getting tea to them and something to eat – if humanly possible?'

Sally was more than happy to help out and the Voluntary Service ladies were delighted to have an extra pair of hands. 'Splendid lads,' said one, 'absolutely splendid, and look at them, my dear, they're scarcely more than children, aren't they?'

Sally smiled and carried on with her tea serving until all the cyclists, whose tired eyes had brightened immediately an extremely pretty young woman had spoken to them, had been fed. As she returned to Sebastian she saw that the men with Max had shaken hands with him and were walking off in another direction. Max himself came to join them.

'They've gone for breakfast and will be back later when they're told it's safe to enter the theatre. In the meantime I'm going to bed; I suggest you do the same, Seb. Come back tomorrow, Sally; we'll be working, even if it's only sweeping floors.'

He walked off and they watched him. Usually

76

straight as a guardsman and light of foot, his bent figure seemed to shuffle to the end of the road before disappearing round the corner.

'What about the others?'

'Anyone turns up, they'll see they have a day off. Max and the general manager will contact as many of us by phone as possible. You're welcome to come home with me, Sally, but I won't be great company. I want a bath and my bed.'

'Thanks, but I'll see you tomorrow. I have letters to write.'

Sally did try to keep up with her friends, who had all promised to be in touch regularly, but she never seemed to have time. If she had a break, she needed to rest, or there was something for her to learn.

'A letter a day for a week,' she told herself, and as soon as she reached her digs she sat down at her dressing table and began the first.

Dear Mum and Dad,

You'll probably hear that the theatre was hit by a bomb last night. Don't worry, I was sound asleep in my digs and didn't know a thing about it till I got to the theatre. I went up to town as soon as I'd had breakfast; Mrs Shuttlecock serves a good breakfast and you'd like her, Mum, as she tells us every morning that breakfast is the most important meal of the day.

The director says the damage is minimal and we'll be up and running as soon as the mess is cleared up. Seems the bomb caused a fire and its nose shot off and went straight through the backs of several rows of seats but, thankfully, the safety curtain saved the stage. Would you believe some theatre workers were

*actually asleep in their offices, and some of the typists,
who were working late, put on their tin helmets and
went back to work? Incredible people, don't you
think? I hope I'd be half as brave.*

*Now I have to write to Daisy as I haven't heard
from her in ages. 'Course, since I never seem to have
time to write letters, I can hardly expect to get any.*

Love to you both,
Sally

FOUR

Late 1940

On the first day that the whole company assembled after the bombing, Max reinforced
Sebastian's comments that it would probably be
years before the building was ready to reopen as
a fully working theatre.

There were gasps from all corners.

'Now what? Have the powers that be found us
a new venue or are most of us back on the
breadline?'

'Neither,' said Max with a cheery grin. 'Believe it
or not, ENSA is staying put. We don't use the rear
circle; we'll manage without the pit, and so all we
need do is make some adjustments as to avail-
ability of dressing rooms and rehearsal space.'

Everyone heard the collective gasp of relief.

Max seemed to look directly at each and every
one of them. 'Right, so look for notices on doors

because what was a storeroom last week may well be a VIP's office now. At last count there were twelve companies in ENSA but there may well be more as the need grows, and the managerial staff from each one will have to come here for general meetings. So, be thoughtful. I know you'll give it your best and in a few days we'll be completely at home again.'

Sally, who had managed to get home for a few hours to put her mother's mind at rest, was aware that it was a while since she had spent any time with her oldest friends and she missed their closeness. Rose Petrie was still hard at work in the Vickers munitions factory and Grace, according to Mrs Petrie, was working on a farm somewhere in the wilds of Scotland. But the most amazing and exciting news of all was that Daisy – little Daisy, who was always thought to be delicate – had been learning to fly an aeroplane and had actually joined the WAAF. Would any or all be home for Christmas? Would she, or was Christmas without family a very small sacrifice that she would be asked to make?

How strange. A picture of a sailor had come unbidden into her mind. Thousands of sailors, soldiers, airmen, nurses – indeed, everyone involved in this blasted war – would probably not be going home for Christmas.

They're all in great danger every minute of the day and night and they get on with the job. Grow up, Sally, you're in no danger, not every day, anyway. I'll think of them wherever they are: the Petrie brothers, Daisy, the chap who's teaching her to fly – and … Jon, Just Jon.

79

Sally did mean to be brave, but during a morning break she found herself asking Sebastian if they might be given a day off during what she had used to call the Christmas holidays.

'A day off? Sally, you're not serious. *"You're in the army now",*' he sang.

Sally, her heart still somewhere in the pit of her stomach, looked up at him and, for once, did not find herself thinking how very beautiful he was, perhaps too beautiful. 'Does that mean we don't celebrate Christmas?'

'Have one of these biscuits; Grandmamma sent them and I swear there's an egg and a teaspoon of sugar in them somewhere.'

Sally took one of the drab-looking biscuits and dunked it in her tea. 'Are you ever serious?'

'Of course. When I tell you you're practically perfect, I'm serious.'

Sally pretended to believe him. 'And what do I need to be absolutely perfect?'

He smiled but Sally thought that it was not his usual smile but one with a tinge of sadness. Why should joking with a chum make him sad?

'I wouldn't expect you to love me as I love you, Sally Brewer, champion fairy guard of the Tiny Tots dance troupe, but if you could love me a little...?'

'But I...' Sally had been about to say, 'But I do love you, Sebastian,' when some instinct stopped her. She did love him, of course she did. When close to him or even when apart, she felt somehow different; something in her had changed. How could she not love someone who was kind and gentle, unfailingly patient and polite and

80

amazingly handsome? Again, the image of the man in naval uniform flashed across her mind but melted away as quickly as it had appeared, leaving her somehow frustrated. *What is this? He stays in my head like a tune that keeps repeating.*

She forced herself to ignore Just Jon. 'You're being silly, Sebastian, and haven't answered my question.'

'Very well, *mon ange,* we will acknowledge the advent of Christmas this year but leave is, I believe, totally out of the question. I hear – and should not be telling you so "Mum's the word" – that we are taking Christmas joy to some casualties of this blasted war. Now, control yourself when I tell you that you are going to be the Christmas fairy dispensing little gifts to children – yes, I know, someone should tell the War Office that children do get hurt when bombs are dropped on their homes – and after what passes for cake and fruit juice, I will, in my Prince Charming satin suit and buckled shoes, waltz you out of Children's to Maternity – don't groan, darling, it's Christmas – and after that we're doing a slightly naughty little play in Men's Casualty; *Spiced Shakespeare,* I think they're calling it.'

'Just the two of us?'

'Of course.'

He saw her expression of abject dismay and took pity on her. 'No, silly, everyone in our group will be there and, with luck, a few more seasoned performers will join us. It's for our war wounded and I know they'd prefer George Formby, but quite a few of them will feel much better after a discreet glimpse of your lovely legs.'

81

Her heart beating with excitement, Sally smiled. At last she had a starring role – as a fairy – but at least she was the only fairy. She decided that it would be quite fun to dance with Prince Sebastian along the hospital corridors. What she would be required to say in a spiced-up version of something from the huge canon of the Swan of Avon, she shuddered to think, but it was in a good cause.

'I'm actually going to be billed as a member of an ENSA troupe, Sebastian?'

'You are indeed. Eventually we will all have uniforms, just like the other Services.'

'Uniforms? For actors and singers, comedians and hoofers?'

'For ENSA and, unlike the other services, we automatically become officers.'

'Officers? I rather like the sound of that.'

'It simply means you can use NAAFI canteens. Now to work.'

Sally was no Vera Lynn but she created what the director termed 'a pleasant sound' and as a result of concentrated professional teaching she was improving in every way. Besides, she was pretty, taking her loveliness for granted so that few of her female colleagues resented her. She knew that she had a great deal to learn and was determined to improve, and the more established performers basked in her admiration.

Having little knowledge of children, her ability to play the 'good' fairy worried her, but the young patients recognised her genuine kindness and they loved her appearance.

'You're a perfect Christmas fairy, Sally,' Sebastian congratulated her as they left the children's ward. 'All the little girls want to look just like you when they grow up, and, *Deo volente*, they will grow up. Now glide with me down the corridor on fairy gossamer wings and we'll enchant all the new mothers.'

Sally climbed into bed that night with her hot-water bottle and her writing case, put her cold feet on the not-quite-hot-enough bottle and wrote first to Daisy, both to congratulate her on her exciting life and also to ask her all about the mystery flying teacher, and then to her parents.

She had been told that she would be allowed to go to Dartford for at least a few hours over the holidays, but she wanted her parents to know about her first ENSA performance as quickly as possible.

My frock was every little girl's dream, and I had a 'diamond' crown made of silver paper we'd been collecting for weeks. Don't worry, every piece has been straightened out and will be delivered to the collection points after Christmas. Sebastian and I danced – he did look perfect as Prince Charming – and all the new mothers in Maternity loved him. He is a dear, walked round the ward and kissed every patient and at least two of the nurses. Then we did a bit from The Taming of the Shrew. *Max spiced it up a bit although I remember it quite well from school and I didn't think it needed spicing; don't worry, Mum, I was the sister and really all I had to do was look pretty. But I have a credit in a Shakespeare play to put on my CV. Yippee.*

Sebastian took me to an actors' club for lunch and

I had a glass of champagne – very sophisticated.

See you soon, I hope, but ENSA is part of the Forces and we have to obey orders. Give my love to everyone.

Sally

On Christmas Day, the company visited a convalescent home in what had been, just a few months before, a stately home. She was to remember the luxury of the house with grateful nostalgia many times in the years ahead. The wards in this hospital were like no ward she had seen before. The ceilings had carved cornices, and holly with vibrant red berries nestling among the leaves covered the mantelpieces; candles, red, silver, gold stood among the holly leaves and in the hall an enormous Christmas tree proclaimed the glories of Christmas past. In the late afternoon, after their prepared performance and their spontaneous carol singing, the troupe joined ambulatory patients, medical staff and even a few family members in a panelled dining room where they enjoyed a Christmas tea.

They returned to London on Boxing Day and Sally found herself working harder than ever.

Max, having received more requests for performances than they could possibly handle, was not in the best of moods, and after the barest of civilities brought them up to date with his immediate plans.

'I've sketched out a few new ideas. Everyone's thoughts are welcome – if you have an idea, share it. It seems musicals are the things to cheer the troops, comedians, of course, and divinely lovely girls – that's you, Sally. What do you think you'd look like in a blond wig?'

'An idiot in a blond wig.'

'Keep your comedy for the war-wounded.'

'Sorry.'

'Take a tea-break everyone; we can't use the stage today since another group has first dibs and so let's meet in twenty minutes in the storeroom.' He saw the disgruntled looks and attempted to mollify his tired troupe. 'I know it's full of scenery from *The Dancing Years*, filing cabinets, costumes from everything under the sun, but at least for this afternoon they have promised not to bring in anything else and so we will have some space.'

'You grab two mugs of tea, Sally, and I'll beetle off and snaffle two chairs. It's every man for himself today,' said Sebastian.

His clever if somewhat selfish plan did get them two comfortable chairs – for once all four legs of each were the same length.

Sally, who had been about to tell him that she'd just heard of the tragic death of Grace's sister, Megan, in an air raid over Dartford, decided not to spread any misery but concentrate on the morning's work. 'I've blotted my copybook with Max, Sebastian. What did you think of what I said?'

'You expressed my exact thoughts, but you are – for the moment – only a tiny spoke in a great wheel. The powers that be say they need you to be two different girls. Can you do a Scottish or perhaps an Irish accent?'

'Not so I'd fool a native.'

'Trust me, you'll be able to fool anyone when

85

Lalita has finished with you.'

'Who on earth is Lalita?'

'Lalita Cruz; she's Mexican. Isn't that incredibly exotic? She's fluent in only the Lord knows how many languages and each spoken with the correct accent; frightening woman. She used to do miracles with tenors in the opera, but came to us saying actors were more biddable, and besides, it's for the war effort.'

'Is she nice?'

'Brewer, Sally, Miss, you do ask the most irrelevant questions. "Is she nice?" Who cares, little one? All that is important is whether or not she can teach and, believe you me, she can. But I'll warn you that she doesn't take prisoners. So work hard today, get yourself off to bed as early as poss, have a good night's sleep and you'll be brilliant at nine tomorrow morning.'

'Well, look who's grabbed the best chairs.' The others arrived *en masse*. 'Sally in the alley; the boss's favourite.'

'That's enough–' began Sebastian but he was stopped by a forceful hand.

'Shove over, Seb,' said Ken Whyte, one of the actors, 'and make room for your elders and betters.'

Obligingly Sebastian removed himself from the chair and went to sit down on the floor with his back against the wall, where he attempted to make Sally laugh by pulling funny faces. Max ignored him, merely stepping over the long legs stretched out, and announced, 'I've agreed to put on shows at two military bases in the south of England, and later in the year, possibly March, a third base in the north-east. Unfortunately none of these bases has one of the fantastic new purpose-built garrison theatres, but never mind. We'll take what we're given. Our programme for the next few months will be more or less the same each time, and so by the time we hit Northumberland – if that's where we're going – you should be word-, note- and step-perfect. By the end of this bloody war, I'll have you all on Broadway, the West End, luxury liners sailing to tropical climes; you name it, we'll do it.'

'Any real chance of a trip to Europe, Max?' asked Millicent Burgess, a former member of a professional ballet company, who had joined their ranks just before Christmas.

'So far only those prepared to lay down their lives for their friends and enemies are being offered European holidays, love, but with some of the greats prepared to chance it, who knows what'll happen? Any particular holiday resort in mind?'

There was no reply to Max's sarcasm but Sally saw that the slim young woman looked absolutely devastated. She had turned so pale that the blusher she had put on her cheeks stood out almost like the make-up of a circus clown. Surely Max's words hadn't upset her to that extent. Sally waited until they were dismissed and moved in beside Millicent as they returned to the dressing rooms.

'Max isn't usually so unpleasant, Millicent...' she began.

'Millie's fine. And Max is a rank amateur where pain-in-the-arse directors are concerned.'

They walked on in silence and Sally was at a loss. She tried again. 'I'm so looking forward to seeing you dance. I'm ashamed to admit that I've never been to an actual ballet performance.'

'Take yourself off to Sadler's Wells. You won't get "an actual ballet performance" from me. I think I was hired as a hoofer, not a ballerina. Now, if you'll excuse me, Miss Goody Two-Shoes, I'm starving.'

She opened a dressing-room door and shut it behind her with an almighty crash. Stunned, Sally stood for a moment looking at the door and then went to the dressing room that she shared with several other women. There she was welcomed warmly.

'Great Christmas, Sally?'

'Lovely, thank you. You?'

Still reeling from the surprising dislike in Millie's voice, Sally was happy to make light conversation.

A day or so later Sebastian caught up with her as they were leaving the theatre.

'Let's see if we can find some hot food and then I'll see you home.'

Immediately Sally felt more confident. Every evening it was becoming more and more difficult to leave the theatre. Bombing raids had intensified, as the enemy seemed determined to destroy the capital completely. Each evening Sally wondered whether it was safer to hide in the theatre and risk being bombed there, or to go out into the street and face the possibility of being caught in an air raid on her way to the hostel.

'They won't come till later, will they, Sebastian?'

she pleaded, although she knew it was impossible to guess when a raid might begin. One night it might start as early as seven o'clock and last until two or three next morning, the next night it might not start until much later or, if the sky was clear and bright with stars, raids could begin very early in the evening and last, she supposed, until all the bombs were dropped.

'I have no idea, Sally darling, but what I do know is that we can't allow ourselves to live in fear. We must be sensible, not take foolish risks, but live as happily as we can. So, are you game? Shall we defy Jerry and find hand-cut potatoes deep fried in the best imported oil and served with something masquerading as the finest *poisson?*'

'In other words, smarty, fish and chips.'

He laughed. 'My way sounds better. And not rationed either, better still.'

His easy charm cheered her and she tucked her hand into his arm and, almost gaily, walked along beside him as he adapted his slightly longer stride to hers.

'I always meant to walk around this whole area, Sebastian; find out what's on the other streets. I sometimes find it hard to believe that I'm actually living in London. I want to see everything: walk along the banks of the Thames, picnic in the parks, go into St Paul's...'

He laughed. 'You can pray anywhere, Sally Brewer.'

'I wasn't thinking of praying, just seeing it, thinking of all the famous people who've been in there before me. London's amazing. Every street seems to have something famous on it or some great doctor or writer or painter lived there.' She stopped and looked up at his face. 'Are you laughing at me?'

'I was nowhere near laughing at you. I agree with you and was thinking about how much I take for granted. Tell you what, we'll plan an itinerary. Every free day we'll visit something.'

'Ouch.' Sally stumbled over a small obstacle, a tin lunch box that had lost its lid. Sebastian caught her around the waist so that she did not fall.

They stood like that for a few moments as Sally assessed the condition of her right ankle and Sebastian contented himself by holding her and enjoying the delicate scent of her dark silky hair.

'I'm fine,' she said after testing her foot on the ground several times, 'and if you're serious I'd love to walk around London with you.'

'I'm serious, believe me, but right now I'd better take you home. Probably better to prop it—'

Sebastian did not finish his well-meant advice as the thick foggy atmosphere was rent by the chilling sound of the air-raid warning. His arms were still around her. Sally pushed her face against his ancient cashmere coat and, trembling in terror, threw her arms around his neck. It seemed that only seconds later, the dull, shadowy city was full of a familiar droning sound. It accompanied the sharp trills of whistles as wardens and patrolling policemen tried to shepherd pedestrians towards the nearest shelters.

Sebastian looked around. 'We'll find a shelter, Sally. Trust me,' he said as he swept her up into his arms.

'Underground's nea...' came from the bulky shape of a helmeted bobby, but anything else he said was drowned out by the terrifying roar of aircraft directly overheard. In spite of herself, Sally shrieked and clung even more tightly to Sebastian, who made soothing noises as he stumbled along.

'The bastards,' he shouted, almost dropping Sally. 'They're after St Paul's.'

Sally struggled until he set her carefully on the ground muttering, 'Max needs both your little feet.'

'Never mind my feet, do something.'

Later Sally and Sebastian were to laugh together over what Sebastian called 'the silliest thing said by anyone on that ghastly night'.

'Do something, she says, as if I was being lazy, not trying hard enough. Do somsing, you fool,' he shouted in an appallingly poor German accent. 'Order zat Heinkel to go home zis very minute.'

At the time he said nothing and merely guided her as quickly and as safely as he could towards the nearest underground station. They stopped several times, ducking their heads each time as if that would make the slightest difference to the death-dealing monsters prowling above them in the night sky. They would choose to drop their cargo where they were convinced the worst damage would be done and woe betide anyone below them.

'Not sure where we are, Sally; I always thought I could find my way blindfolded around London but the damned flames and smoke combined with fog and smoke...' He shook his head. 'No real idea, could be Blackfriars or St Paul's itself,

91

maybe even Bank. They could be after the Bank of England. Think of what that would do to international finance.'

'And if they destroy St Paul's? Oh, I feel so helpless, Sebastian. Couldn't we get out and walk to the cathedral? Maybe we could be helpful.'

He looked down at her. 'My brave little Sally. What could we possibly do? I'm a not-too-awful actor and you – well, you're a beautiful girl who will one day be very good. If you survive, Sally, if you survive. To walk out there into carnage is just too bloody stupid; we'd be in the way.'

They stumbled hastily along, others crowding around them and, with relief, made it into an underground shelter. Sally had automatically taken a deep breath as they entered. She would never like being underground where the walls and roof seemed to press down upon her, but she accepted that here was their best chance of safety.

She hardly cared where they were as long as there was some shelter, some relief from the relentless droning, from the chilling sound of exploding bombs. Explosions spoke loudly of death and destruction. Better to flock together like sheep or starlings and take comfort from the proximity of another human being. Better to sing, to proclaim 'There'll Always be an England', or to listen to that good-looking young fellow, who looked slightly familiar, declaiming speeches from Shakespeare's plays, mixing them up, quite hilariously, with bits from Ivor Novello or Noël Coward.

Sally saw the admiration in even elderly eyes as they looked at Sebastian. 'You're wonderful, Sebastian, absolutely wonderful,' she said.

'I know he's in pictures; seen him, I have. Even had a picture from a magazine pinned on the kitchen calendar. Can't think; it'll come.'

Sally listened and smiled. She could list Sebastian's credits for them but knew that for the petrified woman in the shelter, trying to remember them was so much better than wondering if the little terraced house or shop would still be there when the all clear sounded. It never occurred to Sally that her or Sebastian's could be the house that would disappear into a gaping hole.

They stayed in the underground until nearly five next morning. Sebastian had exhausted not only his voice, but also his long list of speeches and poems committed to memory. Others in the shelter had contributed in whatever way they could; children had slept; old men had tried, but at last it was over and they were safe to leave. They hesitated, like blind moles with their snouts at the edge of a hole, before taking their courage in both hands and stumbling out into...

'Bloody hell.'

'Jesus, Mary and Joseph.'

Startled exclamations rang across the landscape of flame and smoke, the noise of fire engines, the sudden thundering of stone on stone as parts of exhausted buildings collapsed. A sudden silence fell, followed almost immediately by joyful shouts.

'It's still there; they didn't get it.'

'It's on fire,' came a voice filled with horror.

'No.' Sebastian's tired voice still had authority. 'Trust me. Those flames are behind the cathedral.'

So it proved. St Paul's Cathedral, that magnificent Wren creation, had sustained damage, but its world-famous dome still stood defiantly among the burning ruins around it.

Eyes stinging from the clouds of drifting acrid smoke, Sally and Sebastian began to walk. Again Sally stumbled over some debris and clutched at Sebastian's coat. 'I feel dirty, Sebastian, and I'm chilled. I'm going back to the boarding house for a bath and a change of clothes.'

He patted her hand protectively. 'The theatre's closer, Sally. We're already late and we have only two days of rehearsal left. We'll find the Red Cross or the WVS – remember the blessed WVS turned up at the theatre – and I bet we'll find them at this disaster zone.'

They encountered a WVS tea van almost immediately.

'See, Sally, the WVS are out with their vans. If it's true that they're at every underground station almost before the all clear has stopped sounding we should suggest to Max that we do a fundraising concert for them.'

Sally took the roll with its scraping of – probably – home-made marmalade; the WVS, like housewives all over Britain, expected that soon jam would join the growing list of rationed goods. He handed her a cup of tea and she was surprised by how quickly she finished it.

'Probably the best cup of tea I've ever had,' she said. 'What do they put in it?'

'Relief,' he said. 'And a sprinkling of brotherly love. Come on, let's take the cups back and make our way to work.'

Sally stayed where she stood for a moment, somehow unable to move.

'Come on, old girl. We're alive and we're needed.'

Still she stood. 'I'm terrified, Sebastian. Look around. Oh God, it's terrible. There must be people lying dead or injured all over London.'

He shook her until her eyes filled with tears and then he held her tightly against him. 'We have a job to do, Sally. Sobbing in the street won't help anyone. The injured, the bereaved – they need cheering up. Our remit, remember, is to do our level best to raise the morale of our fellow man – or woman. Come on, Sally, square shoulders and let's do what we're good at.'

He took her hand and almost pulled her along, tripping over unnoticed, unexpected debris; a door, which they managed to avoid, a chimney-pot, bricks, two leather-bound books, large and small fragments of sometimes still-burning wood, and bizarrely, a well-used frying pan with a fried egg welded to it by even greater heat than that which had originally cooked the egg. Each sad sight only added to Sally's grief. Had Sebastian released her hand for a second she would have taken flight but, mercilessly, he clung to her, ignoring her sobs.

They reached the old theatre to find only Max and Lalita in possession.

Sally was both frightened and delighted to meet the *répétiteur*, although she was unsure what the word meant. She was also very much looking forward to meeting a Mexican as she had no real idea of what a Mexican woman would look like, all her knowledge of the country having come from American cowboy films. She had expected that she might be of medium height, plump with tanned skin, shiny, long, black hair, and flashing dark eyes. Lalita was tall and slender, her skin was lightly tanned and her thick, dark hair was fastened into a gleaming knot at the back of her head. Her eyes were as blue as Sally's own. Probably somewhere in her fifties, she retained some of the stunning beauty she must have had as a young woman.

'Thank you both for coming,' said Max gravely. 'We have discovered a Primus stove, two bottles of beer, some rather stale bread and three sausages. I suggest we eat, drink and be as merry as we can be until the others arrive – if they do. If they don't arrive, Lal will work with you, Sally darling; I want to turn you into a nice wee Scotch lassie for a heather-in-the-hills number.'

Lalita's skills were more than adequate to the task. First, she questioned Sally as to her knowledge of Scottish accents, pointing out that they were many and varied. She learned that Sally had spent only a few days in Scotland and that her knowledge of accents was taken from wireless broadcasts.

'I can say "Och aye the noo," she told Lal who laughed.

'Best forget that one, Sally; we're not doing pantomime. Now, vowel sounds. Repeat after me...'

And so began a gruelling crash course, repeating or trying to repeat the sounds that Lal was making. She had taken French at school and so could 'roll her r's' quite well but had to learn how to modulate them. In the limited time available Lal strove to teach Sally to create a sound that could be recognized as vaguely Scottish.

Two hours later, both were exhausted but rather pleased with Sally's new accomplishment.

Despite the traffic restrictions, almost every member of the troupe had managed to reach the theatre, each and every one with alarming, often hair-raising tales of their difficulties.

'A miracle; no other word for it. St Paul's is still gloriously there.' Sybil Tapper, choreographer and former ballerina, born, brought up, and trained in the city, brought the latest news.

Even those who were not Londoners by birth felt the symbolic power of the cathedral's survival.

'One in the eye for old Hitler; this failure must dent his pride, but I wouldn't call it a miracle.' The company's pianist, Sam Castleton, grey with fatigue under his smoke-grimed face, told them of the hours he and others like him had spent helping the fire service by carrying buckets, wash-basins, anything that could hold water, from any source they could find, forming immense human chains of men, women and even children from every stratum of society. All night they had fought, passing the containers from hand to hand until the water reached the fires that were bursting out in various parts of the great monument.

'Poor old Thames must be near bone dry, and the buggers have hit water mains. God knows how the hospitals are coping.'

Max stood up and clapped his hands loudly so as to still the chattering. 'No point in starting anything now. I want everyone home before dark.

Go over your pieces at home, try them out in the shelters if we have another night like last night, and tomorrow, if you judge you can't be here by ten at the latest, don't even try. We'll do a show with whoever turns up. Now go.'

'Come on, Sally, you look as if you're about to drop.' Sebastian surreptitiously examined Sally as she allowed the wall to support her. She was deathly pale so that her beautiful blue eyes seemed larger and brighter than ever. They made him think of cold spring water coursing down the stream at the bottom of his late grandfather's orchard. The sun made each clear droplet sparkle and somehow the greyish stones on the bed of the stream changed colour, now green, now blue, and then neither green nor blue. One day, he vowed, he would gaze into Sally's lovely eyes and discover what colour they actually were.

'Come along,' he repeated, for all the world like an exasperated schoolteacher dealing with a re-calcitrant pupil, 'I'll get you home somehow and there must be soup. Grandmamma swears by soup.'

Sally was not listening; he doubted that she understood one word but she pushed herself off the wall and turned towards the door, unable to do anything but what she was told.

'See you tomorrow,' he yelled. 'New Year's Eve. Who's for the Savoy?'

'Do shut up, Seb,' the others yelled back in unison but Sally smiled and that was all he cared about. He heard her wince with fatigue as he opened the outside door but she recovered.

'All right?'

'Yes, thank you, Sebastian.'

He put his arm around her as a prop. 'Lal worked you too hard today.'

Lal? That was it. She would ask now – anything to take her mind away from the terrifying events that were taking place all around her. 'Sebastian, what exactly is a *répétiteur?*'

'What lively questions you do ask. It's the brilliant person who repeats everything for the singer or the actor. He/she is a voice coach, and accent coach, but the most sought after are those who are also stunningly good musicians. If a singer or a dancer is having trouble with a particular phrase, the *répétiteur* plays it over and over until the performer sings or dances or speaks it properly. Invaluable. Some focus on opera or acting; some are all-rounders, like Lal, who can sound as if she's never left the East End of London one minute and become a sophisticated Russian princess the next.'

'I never realised it was all so difficult.'

'Nothing that's worthwhile is easy. But perhaps today, two hours of concentrated Lalita Cruz was overkill.'

She tried to smile. 'No, Sebastian. She's amazing. I appreciated so much individual attention.'

'Which Max is getting now.'

'He doesn't need...' began Sally and then, aware of Sebastian's meaning, blushed.

'You didn't hear the door lock behind us? You didn't wonder how they managed to reach the theatre early and to find a Primus stove, not to mention sausages?'

Sally said nothing. Too much had happened

99

and, at this particular moment, all she wanted was to get to her boarding house and fall into bed, preferably after a hot bath.

How dark it was. Not that daylight in London was a patch on the clear air of the Kent countryside she and her friends had loved to cycle through. In London one always had to peer to find the kerb of a pavement, and now, after all these fires, buildings collapsing in a cloud of dust, it was always dark. There was little or no traffic running. Rubble was being cleared from roads and pavements, frighteningly close to Little Church Lane, where Mrs Shuttlecock's house was; police and firemen were still much in evidence. Sally's breath caught in her throat.

'Have they worked all day too, Sebastian?'

'Probably. But they may have a rota system – two-hour breaks or whatever. They're not automatons.'

Sally desperately wanted Sebastian to accompany her all the way to her boarding house but his sensitive remarks about the long hours worked by the rescue services reminded her that he too had been awake through the fraught hours of the air raid. She straightened up. 'I'll be fine from here; it's not too far. You should get home before there's another air raid.'

He pretended to be hurt. 'How can you not allow me to play knight in shining armour? Grandmamma will be delighted to hear that her strenuous efforts paid off. I'll deliver you to your door in one perfect piece. Then I'll trot off home feeling rather pleased with myself.'

What could she say?

'Then let's hurry; you must be home before sunset.'

He took her hand and together they walked as quickly as they could, avoiding rubble wherever possible. What a prolonged battering the city had suffered!

A heavy layer of smoke and dust hung over the approach to Sally's street. Foreboding filled her as she turned onto Little Church Lane. The bus stop was still there outside the garden gate. The pole leaned precariously, almost pointing to the rubble-filled crater into which the boarders' house and the garden, which only yesterday had boasted the last of a fine show of Michaelmas daisies, had fallen. Sally turned as if expecting to find the house on the other side of the street. Houses did stand there, some windowless, two without front doors, most without chimneypots. These looked as if some giant hand had swept them off the roofs, tossing them down to smash to smithereens on the road.

'Sal...' Sebastian tried gently.

'Know the people in the 'ouse, miss? Them as lived there, I mean? Mrs Shuttlecock 'ad lodgers and none of 'em survived – far as we can see. Rotten luck.' A police constable, his kind but tired eyes looking out of a prematurely aged face, had appeared from one of the surviving gardens.

'Watch 'er,' he croaked, hours of smoke and dust having filled his throat, but Sebastian had already caught Sally before she fell.

'Miss Brewer was a resident of number eleven,' he said. 'Last night she was caught in the raid on St Paul's and sheltered in the underground.'

101

'Everyone?' asked a tremulous voice.

'All as was in the 'ouse, miss. I'm so sorry, but it's lovely for me to cross one off my list.' He licked the point of his pencil and crossed out 'MISS SALLY BREWER'. 'Any family, miss? They know you're safe, do they? And the 'ousing officer'll find you a place for the night, washing things an' that.'

'Miss Brewer will stay with me, Officer, and will be able to contact her parents from there. It's all right, Sally, I have a ridiculously large flat.'

Sally scarcely heard him. She was numb, felt nothing. She could smell death and destruction, though, and so when Sebastian put his arm around her and turned her back towards the centre of London, she stumbled along beside him. He was talking, but she seemed to have no understanding of his words.

After a while they stopped. 'I'm sure your parents wouldn't be too thrilled with this hotel, Sally, but you need a brandy.'

Sally's mind was still full of the noise of destruction and her nose with the smell of cordite. She walked with him to the bar, oblivious of the looks of disdain on the faces of some customers.

'Brandy, two,' Sebastian ordered tersely.

'Looks like she's already had enough,' said the barman. 'You'll want a room?'

'Don't be offensive, and bring the brandy in clean glasses.'

'Yes, yer lordship, at once yer lordship,' answered the barman sarcastically, but Sebastian did not react and simply watched him wash two glasses and half-fill them with brandy.

Sally coughed as the unfamiliar liquid ran down her throat.

'Drink it, sweetheart. We still have quite a walk unless we can find a taxi.'

Sally straightened her spine and sipped again. Sebastian saw the colour slowly return to her face.

'Sally, there must have been a tremendous loss of life in London last night and I don't know, but it is just possible that, by this time, your parents have been told to expect the worst. Do you have a number for them? We'll try to find a call box; I have some coppers in my pocket.'

Sally was shaking her head but whether in denial of the situation or acknowledgement that her parents had no telephone, he had no idea. He squeezed her hand and walked on, hoping against hope that a taxi would magically materialise but there was only emergency traffic.

'Some of the underground trains might be running, Sally. Shall we–' he began but she pulled herself out of his arms.

'No, no, I couldn't. Never again, never.'

'I live in Mayfair, Sally,' he said, but as she said nothing and merely stumbled on he decided that either she scarcely cared how far she had to walk or had no idea where Mayfair was.

'Let me at least hold you up,' he said, slipping his arm around her waist and, in absolute silence they continued their trek. She had wanted to see some of the sights of London and that night she passed several of them, completely oblivious of their beauty or fame.

At last they arrived at Hays Mews and the inaptly named Mansion where his flat was situated.

'Rather a lot of stairs, I'm afraid.'

Still she made no sound and wearily they climbed three flights of stairs and Sally almost fell in head-first as he opened the door.

'I think you should sleep for a bit, Sally. I'll put a match to the fire, make some cocoa, but if you can tell me the name of anyone you know in Dartford who has a telephone – the police would do – we'll ring them and they'll pop over and tell your parents that you're safe.' Sally was not so fraught that she did not know that a visit from a uniformed policeman would shock her parents and she cudgelled her brain. 'The vicar, Mr Tiverton,' she said at last. 'We're not the most regular attenders but he does know us. I hate to ask but they'll know about the bombing now, won't they?'

'The world'll know, darling,' he said, and then turned his attention to his telephone.

It took only a few minutes for him to be connected to Mr Tiverton, who was relieved to know Sally was safe and, when Sebastian handed the phone to her, assured her that he would visit her parents with the good news immediately.

'Tell them I'm staying tonight with a friend from ENSA, Mr Tiverton, and I'll be down to see them as soon as I can. The show must go on,' she said, heard him say, 'God bless you, my dear,' replaced the receiver and burst into tears.

Immediately Sebastian sat down beside her, enfolded her in his arms and rocked her back and forth until at last she recovered.

'Oh, dear Sebastian, what would I have done

without you?' she said looking up at him, smiling, her eyes sparkling with tears. He looked down and, as he had dreamed so often, lost himself in those shimmering pools. He held her closer. She relaxed against him and he stroked her back, as if she were a baby.

'Oh Sally, Sally...' his voice was a moan.

She raised her head, aware that every nerve end in her body was tingling with both fear and excitement. He would kiss her now, she knew it, just as Rhett Butler had kissed Scarlett O'Hara, and...

'Good Lord, Sally, look at the time. What am I thinking of? Sleep, you need sleep. Max will kill me if you're too tired tomorrow – today.' He stood up abruptly and his movement was so unexpected that Sally almost fell back against the cushions. 'You take my room. There is a guest room but when it was last aired, I haven't the foggiest.' He was leading her to the door. 'See, the door on the right is the bathroom and the bedroom leads off it. Everything you might need is there, except a nightgown...' He stood looking at her for a moment. 'Tell you what, while you're washing I'll nip into the bedroom and find you a clean pyjama top.' He was moving restlessly from one foot to the other as if he were about to start running. 'Good night, Sally.' And then he kissed her. At least, his lips brushed against her face.

Sally stood for a moment, almost dazed and then a tidal wave of embarrassment washed her through the open door of the bathroom. She closed the door and allowed it to hold her up-right until the nausea churning in her stomach had calmed down. She moved to the mirror and examined her face. Tears began to stream down her cheeks and she turned on a tap to hide the noise of her sobs. What had gone wrong? What had she done, or was there something she had not done? She had been so sure. From everything she had read or heard, she had been positive that he wanted, that they wanted…

Now she wanted only to run from the flat, to never be seen again by Sebastian. Dear God, what did he think of her? She needed to get away but where could she go?

She splashed water on her face, rubbed her fingers across her teeth and tentatively opened the door to the bedroom. It was empty. A nondescript blue pyjama jacket lay on the dark maroon counterpane that covered the large bed. The room lay in shadow as it was lit only by a small bedside lamp. The room was almost as large as the drawing room where they had been sitting and Sally hesitated for a moment as she looked towards the door.

No, no need to look for keys. She would be left alone.

A light knock woke her. Sally, who had climbed into the comfortable bed expecting to toss and turn all night, was surprised to find that she had slept soundly.

Sebastian was outside. 'Are you all right, Sally? I've made coffee, rather weak but it's hot.'

'I'll be there in a minute.' She hoped her voice did not show her utter dejection.

'Take your time. I'm ready to leave; bathroom

and kitchen are all yours.'

Less that fifteen minutes later, wearing the same clothes as she had been wearing for the last two days, Sally was in the kitchen. There were two cups and saucers on the table; one containing cooling coffee. Sally forced herself to drink it but could not think of trying to eat the slice of bread on the matching plate. And then Sebastian joined her and there was an awkward silence.

'We're running late.' They said the words together and although neither laughed, they did manage to smile.

Wordlessly they communicated that, until they had done their day's work, they would not talk about Sally's homelessness. The reality of war had become even more real yesterday but, in their own way, they were soldiers and, before weeping over what was lost, they must do their best to brighten the lives of needy others.

When they arrived at the theatre, they said nothing of what had occurred. 'Sorry we're late, Max. Talk later,' said Sebastian tersely, and Max looked at their faces and growled, 'Transport will be here in about thirty minutes.' He looked at them again. 'Get yourselves something to eat and drink and then find Lal and have her do something with Sally's face and hair. I won't ask, but you look like hell and you're no romantic lead either, Seb.'

Fourteen hours later, when they had returned from a base on the south coast, having done three back-to-back shows, he called them into his office.

'The last of my Christmas sherry,' he said, handing each a small glass. 'Now tell me what's going on.'

'You poor kid,' he said when Sally, with encouragement from Sebastian, had finished telling him about the bombing. Max jumped up and hugged her. 'Thank God you're alive. Your family? They know you're not hurt?'

'Yes, thank you. Sebastian phoned the local vicar who went to see them.'

Max waved his arm towards the large black telephone on the immaculately tidy desk. 'You can use this, Sally, or tell them to ring you here. Emergency calls only, of course. My God, your clothes ... everything you own, poor kid. Thank heavens the costumes and shoes are all here.' He looked slightly embarrassed. 'Apologies, sounds awful, but I have to think of finance. The NAAFI funds us, you know, and they've been incredibly generous, but their purse is going to be empty very soon with all the demands that have been made on it.'

He stood up; Sally and Sebastian got to their feet and all three moved to the door and then stopped in a huddle as Max thought of something else. 'You do have somewhere to stay?'

Sally blushed furiously. She had absolutely no idea what to say. Sebastian could not want or expect her to return to his flat? But a whole day had gone by and she had done nothing about finding a hostel or a room. Her brain went round and round, conflicting thoughts and feelings confusing her.

'For as long as she wants, Sally is welcome to

108

stay with me, Max.'

Max, much older and more experienced, stared at Sebastian for a long moment before saying, 'That's fine. None of my business. Would have contacted the housing officer had something been needed. But what about replacing clothes, Sally, and your ration book and any other important papers? The WVS or the Red Cross will know how to go about it, and I'm sure the other girls will help out till you can get back to Derby. No shops open tomorrow.'

'Dartford,' said Sally automatically.

Max smiled. 'Knew it began with a D. Now be off, my children, and we'll expect you here bright and early tomorrow. Another day, another base, another show, or, in this case – and I hate to break it to you since you signed on with a contract that said two to three shows a month – another four shows.'

Sally and Sebastian left the theatre in silence. They had more important things to think about than how many shows they did. As the door closed behind them they stood looking at each other in some embarrassment. Sally found that she could not meet Sebastian's eyes.

'I have two bedrooms, Sally,' he said. 'Last night I wanted ... but ... just let me say you'll be safe with me, in every way, for as long as you want to stay. In fact, you would be doing me a favour. As soon as the Housing Office, or whatever it's called, hears that I have an empty room they're likely to house one or two large foreign gentlemen on me, neither of whom will speak English, and I always feel such an ass when I can't understand people. Grandmamma always thought that if she shouted loudly enough, people would understand. They don't, you know, and it must be very exasperating for them. If you were to become my official lodger three problems would be solved immediately, one for you, one for me, and one for some hapless foreigner.'

'My parents would be horrified.'

'Need they know? I mean, God knows I don't want you lying to them or getting yourself all upset. But it's already next year and you need to find a bed.'

Sally wanted to burst into tears. Being away from home and having nowhere to stay was like being without anything to anchor her. None the less she tried to smile. Something told her that the events of last night would not be repeated, or would they? And what exactly were her feelings for Sebastian? It was all so confusing.

'A lodger, paying rent, until I can find something? Max thinks it won't take too long.' Another realisation struck forcibly. 'But Max is right, Sebastian, my ration book is gone. I can't even provide my share of basics.'

He tucked his arm into hers. 'They'll issue you a new one. Now Happy New Year, Sally. Let's go home and celebrate with cocoa.'

FIVE

January 1941

The New Year was here, not quite brand new but still very young. Could they say that it was now the third year of the war? Sally, although both physically and mentally exhausted, had lain awake in Sebastian's guest-room bed for some time before her body gave in and allowed her to sleep. She relived the air raid, the rubble-strewn walk to the boarding house, the unbelievable horror of seeing an enormous pit of debris where her temporary home had been, where several people she had known, had eaten and laughed with, had waited with in line for their turn in the bathroom, were dead. But most of all she had relived those confusing moments with Sebastian. The feelings danced through her, reminding her, making her wish ... for what?

Growing up, she and her friends had giggled when they thought of love, of sexual activity.

'Sounds horrible,' Daisy had said.

'You'll never catch me doing anything like that,' their friend Grace had agreed. 'It's bound to hurt like blazes.'

Would they say the same now that Daisy was writing letters in which the name Adair appeared almost more often than any other, and poor, orphaned Grace, now totally alone in the world, seemed to miss someone called Jack?

At last Sally fell asleep.

Sebastian roused her next morning with a very good cup of coffee. 'I've had a once-over wash and so there should be enough water if you want a quick bath.' He smiled at her from the door as he prepared to return to the kitchen. 'There's a new toothbrush in the top left-hand drawer in the bathroom. Call it a New Year's gift. Now, hurry.'

Sally hurried and soon they were on their way to the theatre. Green Park tube station was not far away and trains were running. Between trains and walking, they arrived at the theatre in good time and were surprised to see two huge army lorries sitting outside the stage door.

'First-class transport,' shouted one of the soldiers as he stood smoking a cigarette. 'Especially for you, darling.'

Sally smiled. Sebastian frowned. The soldiers laughed. 'Happy New Year, smiler,' they shouted, but Sally and Sebastian had already entered the theatre.

Sally was surprised and touched to see an embarrassingly large pile of clothing on her area of the make-up table.

'Max had a word,' said Sybil, her long blonde hair spilling over her shoulders as she spoke, 'and almost everyone's brought something. The chorus girls clubbed together, money and clothing coupons, and they intend to buy you brand-new unmentionables – just have to say size and colour – but I've seen some of their knickers and, if were you,' she teased, smiling at Sally, 'I'd go with them when they're shopping. There are several nighties,

112

some blouses and jumpers, two skirts and a fur coat Lalita says is too young for her, whatever that means.'

Sally was so surprised that she was completely unable to take it all in. She glanced at the heaped clothing, including the splendid fur coat. 'All these things for me. Oh, how very kind you all are. I can't begin to... I don't know how to thank you.'

'Lend us the fur for special dates,' shouted one of the chorus, but Sybil was not finished.

'Have a dekko at the clothes; some of it may not fit, although if it's too big we can do something; have a weep – which you need, by the look of you – put on the fur and we're off to the seaside.'

'The seaside. Oh God, not again,' was heard from several sides.

'Happy New Year,' shouted Max, and the tension lifted.

Outside they found that one of the lorries had already been loaded with the huge, clearly labelled wicker baskets – costumes, scenery, accessories, scripts, music, wigs, make-up, everything and any-thing that the group would need for four shows, one after the other. Larger pieces of scenery had been tied to the inside of the vehicle.

'Anyone see a label saying tea urn and sand-wiches?' ventured a new member of the chorus.

'Don't need it, love; the NAAFI does us proud and it's New Year's Day. Plus, since – if you haven't forgotten, and you shouldn't have – our uniforms are on the way, that means we are, each and every one, service personnel and entitled to use the Messes.'

113

The company moved to the second lorry where Max stage-managed a decorous 'climbing in'. It went well, no pushing or struggling to find a comfortable seat, until a delighted male voice rang out from the waiting line, 'I say, what lovely knickers.'

A girlish squeal followed the comment and then Lalita's voice restored order. 'Next time I tell you, "Best wear trousers," maybe you'll take notice. Now get in and sit down.'

There were no comfortable seats on the lorry. Several wooden benches provided room for almost everyone, and the more experienced had thoughtfully provided themselves with an extra sweater to sit on.

Sally sat quietly, lost in memories. She pictured her parents and her Dartford friends as they gathered together to think of the loved ones who were not there to celebrate with them.

I'm thinking of all of you, she vowed tearfully, every minute.

She tried to picture her parents and especially their faces if she told them that the kind friend who had offered shelter to her was a man. That wasn't too awful; it was wartime and some things just had to be done differently and accepted. But she could never tell them all that had happened, and knowing she was deceiving the people she loved most in all the world was a heavy burden. Max had promised her a day off just as soon as he saw a space in their overflowing calendar; she would visit her family then, but in the meantime she would try to find lodgings that her parents would find acceptable. In the short term, Sebastian's flat was a wonderful – and luxurious –

refuge, with lovely carved cornices and ceiling roses. The curtains were of material that Elsie Brewer might never have dreamed of owning, and, in one room, there was a beautiful piano that Sebastian said was a baby grand. In another, the most incredible bookcase, with glass doors that allowed the real leather covers of the rows and rows of books to be seen, stood between two windows that almost reached the ceiling.

Sally gave a small sob as she admitted that she would hate to leave, not because of the lovely things, but because every time she saw Sebastian her heart seemed to do such peculiar things. She faced the fact that he had awakened something within her. Did she love him? That night, those few minutes on the sofa, she had been sure that she did. Surely her feelings would not have been so strong if there was no love there? She could ask her oldest friends but it wouldn't be easy to write what she meant in a letter.

She was so lost in thought that she almost fell off the bench as the lorry braked at the gates to the military camp. Fairly primitive dressing rooms had been prepared for them and the theatre was in the gym. They peeked in as they passed.

'My God, the 'ole bloody battalion's coming,' Humph Peters, their comedian, and excellent show-opener, informed them, 'and, as always, bloody comfy seats in the front row for the hofficers and gentlemen, if there is any.'

Max strode up to him. 'Peters, you're usually very funny and I'm delighted to have you with us, but I have heard you swear twice in one sentence, and that's twice too many. There are ladies present and, believe it or not, the odd man who doesn't like swearing either.'

'Yeah, very odd.'

Naturally, Humph opened his act by telling the audience that his boss had told him off for swearing. 'So you'll understand if I can't say...' and he proceeded to tell them all the swear words he was not going to use.

The audience, and most of the cast waiting back stage, were soon laughing hysterically.

'So,' he went on as the laughter died down, 'when you 'ear this noise,' and he proceeded to make a very loud, disgusting sound, 'you'll 'ave to decide for yourself wot word I couldn't say. Sorry, but we're all in the army, right, and we does what the brass tells us.'

He was a huge success with the mixed audience and Sebastian, who was on next, was worried about his reception.

'*Hamlet,* after all that,' he whispered to Sally. 'They'll throw rotten tomatoes at me.'

'Without thinking, Sally laid her hand on his arm and blushed as she felt herself tremble. It was obvious from the way he looked at her that Sebastian, too, was moved.

'There are thousands of men who appreciate good drama, Sebastian, and many of them are out there. Besides,' she said as she tried not to look into his eyes, 'there are lots of young women in the audience. They may or may not like Shakespeare, but every single one of them will love you; hundreds of them will have loved you in *Goodbye, Mr Chips.* Go on, cheer up the girls.'

Sebastian whispered, 'Thank you,' and kissed

her gently on her brow and then he walked out onto the knocked-up stage. There was a quiet round of clapping.

'I was going to recite "To be or not to be" from *Hamlet*,' he began, 'but as I was laughing at our Humph I thought, those are soldiers out there. What do they want with a man who can't make up his mind half the time – and I bet nobody had to tell him off for swearing.' That started a roll of laughter. When it subsided he continued with his impromptu script. 'So I thought we'd better have a soldier king who knew just exactly what he needed to do ... and five gets you ten he could swear like a trooper.'

When they stopped applauding and stamping their feet, he recited the famous 'Once more unto the breach, dear friends' speech from *Henry V.* It brought the house down and when he had finished the rest of his prepared programme, many stood up and cheered as he left the stage.

Max was there to congratulate him. 'Well done, Seb; we'll put that into the programme after Humph's dissertation on early English swear words. Now, off you go, girls, knock 'em dead.'

The group of attractive well-matched chorus girls, dressed in extremely short, red, white or blue skirts with co-ordinating low-necked sleeveless blouses, cart-wheeled, one after the other, onto the stage, accompanied by loud whistles and cat calls. Sally stood in the wings, aware of and encouraged by Sebastian's presence near her, but now she worried less about her personal life than her performance. Her knees were knocking and she felt sick. This was so different from hours of rehearsal in a theatre, and properly lighted dressing rooms with wardrobes and full-length mirrors. Besides, she did not really want to be applauded because she was pretty. She knew that she did not have a great singing voice, nor was she a superb dancer, but the audiences – mostly male – seemed to like to hear her.

Or did they merely like looking at someone in a pretty dress?

Sally knew she was more than pretty. All her life she had been told that she was beautiful; she took her looks for granted. Thanks to Lal's terrific coaching Max was, at last, giving her a few very small, walk-on parts, but never anything challenging, no dialogue. Even today he had spoken not about speeches but about new songs for her: some of the American favourites that were being made popular by the wireless.

'"The Nearness of You", Sally, lovely tune and, sung by a beautiful girl in a pretty dress, a show stopper, or do you know "I've Got My Love to Keep Me Warm"? Ladies will love that one. We'll find the words and music. And trust me, that's a difficult one to get right,' and he had gone, leaving her both pleased and disappointed.

She sensed someone behind her. 'Think of something really lovely as you walk on, and smile. That's all you have to do to win over the audience.' With a smile of encouragement, Sebastian edged her gently towards her entrance position.

The clapping and cheering for the dancers' performance died down, Sally heard Max announce her and, just then, she caught sight of a uniformed sailor near the end of the second row. It had to be. No, it couldn't be

Jon, Just Jon. She smiled. Her whole face lit up – had she but known it, she had never been so beautiful, and every man in the audience reacted. There were whistles, thunderous applause, even cheering. Startled, Sally stepped back but looked towards the sailor and felt disappointment. He was nothing at all like Jon, other than that he was a man, about the same height and build, and was in naval uniform. The disappointment was surprisingly painful.

The small orchestra started to play. In the most unprofessional way, Sally missed her first entry. The music started again and suddenly Sebastian, still in his dinner jacket, was there, gliding with her around the stage, the perfect couple. It was not in Max's script. They danced until the end of the first play-through, then Sebastian made an almost indecipherable gesture to the conductor and withdrew, dancing effortlessly backwards to disappear through the curtain and Sally started to sing perfectly the moment her first note was played. She sang through the number, 'I Get Along Without You Very Well' – every word pulling at every heartstring – and her next number, and the last, but requests were shouted, not only from the back seats but also from the front.

Leave 'em wanting more.

Who had said that first?

Sally had no idea, but she was a professional and knew that another act was waiting in the wings and so, like Sebastian, she withdrew backwards but, unlike Sebastian, she smiled and blew kisses until she disappeared through the curtains.

Backstage an argument over Sally's wardrobe was going on between Lalita and Sybil, while the carpenters and technicians, every one a serving sailor, arranged the scenery for the next act, a piece from a play. Sybil paid them no attention, probably because this group were known to be meticulous and thorough in their work, but continued to state her case.

'Be bold, Lal, the lemon was beautiful; she looked absolutely gorgeous.'

'Blue, a pale blue, like a spring sky. With her hair and those eyes–' She got no further for Sybil interrupted.

'Lilac, the palest lilac we can find. Look more closely, her eyes aren't blue; at times they're almost lilac. I saw the exact colour once at Sadler's Wells. The Lilac Fairy in *The Sleeping Beauty* – maybe they still have the dress or will know where they accessed the material. I'll find out as soon as we get back to London.'

'They won't share info with us. You know how bitchy some professional actors and other artistes are being about ENSA.'

As experienced professionals, Sybil, former prima ballerina, now a renowned choreographer, and Lalita, an internationally known *répétiteur*, had seen arguments from all sides.

'And do not say, "There's a war on",' begged Lal as Sybil made to speak.

'*Lo siento mucho*, darling, but that is exactly what I was about to say. So, Sadler's Wells deals in classical high performance art; we too are dealing in high performance entertainment – I've just signed a girl from a professional company.

The dockers and the factory workers – and the miners, if we can get near them – have as much right to experience everything as the military. How on earth will they learn what they like and what they don't like if some sodding bigot is telling them that they're not clever enough to appreciate a Mozart piano concerto? Dinner on me at the Savoy Grill if I don't come back with loans of lots of goodies.'

'Done.'

They closed their discussion on the perfect colour for Sally's next glamorous gown and rejoined the group of actors who were waiting for their call. Max had decided that a scene from *A Midsummer Night's Dream* would go down extremely well on this base. Sally had longed to be given even a tiny part, but had tried to hide her disappointment when the cast list showed a professional actress called Sylvia Stone was to play Thisby. Sebastian was Prologue. The part of Pyramus was given to Allan Fordyce, a formerly out-of-work actor who had been delighted to be accepted into ENSA after having been refused permission to join the army. Like many actors, his dreams had been of playing Hamlet, King Lear, even Macbeth, but although he had graduated from a recognised acting school, he was not leading-man material. Max had seen him in a few productions and thought his forte, though Allan hadn't recognised it himself, was comedy. So far Max's instincts were proving to be correct.

Sally liked Allan. He was quiet and unassuming and had fully participated in the group's work. For this production, they themselves had created the scenery, the wall through which Shakespeare's love-lorn characters were to peek at each other. Every time any member of the cast passed the wall the rest of the company in the room heard a loud, 'Oh, wot a luverly wall.' It never failed to make them laugh and Max ignored their frivolity. In the middle of air raids, several of them had carried on singing, dancing, playing the accordion or even turning somersaults to amuse frightened people in the shelters. Whatever made them happier, as long as it was legal, was perfectly acceptable to him.

The scene brought the house down, as did every other performance they put on that day.

'The strangest New Year's Day I've ever lived through,' admitted Sally as, back at the theatre they climbed wearily out of the lorry. Four shows. A few of the experienced professionals, who remembered moaning about having done both a matinée and an evening performance on the same day, made a New Year's resolution never to moan again.

'Come on, Sally, let's get home.' Sebastian held out his hand for her bag and, for a second, she held it, realising that she had to make a decision.

They spoke little on the way to Sebastian's flat.

'Drink, cup of tea?' asked Sebastian, and Sally refused, explaining that she was too tired even to drink tea.

'Me too. There should be enough hot water for a bath. Give me a minute to clean my teeth. I'll probably fall asleep before I even get under my covers. 'Night, darling.' He made no move to touch her but went quickly into the flat's generously sized bathroom.

'Good night,' Sally called after him as she moved to the guest-room door to undress. *Good night, darling.* Such endearments, she was learning quickly, meant absolutely nothing in this new world of hers.

Sally woke to the smell of toast. When she had freshened up and dressed, she found her landlord in the kitchen, obviously ready to leave. 'Two minutes, Sally; I'm afraid breakfast is one slice of rather-stale toast and half a cup of Ovaltine.'

'Wonderful. I'm still firing on all the good food the bases gave us yesterday.'

He smiled. 'That's the British spirit, Sally. Wear the fur. It's rather frosty outside.'

They left the building, the warmly dressed Sally still eating her slice of bread.

'Hope we don't meet anyone who knows Grand-mamma,' said Sebastian. But Sally could see from his face that he was teasing. 'God knows what she'd have to say about the company I keep. Women eating in the street! Whatever next?'

That was the atmosphere they managed to maintain for the next few days. Work kept them busy and they were alone together only when they returned to the flat. Sally had made it clear that, since her replacement ration book had not yet arrived, she would pay for the food they bought. That solution disturbed Sebastian who had been brought up in the sure and certain knowledge that man was the provider, but Sally was adamant. She paid or she left. She had even considered asking Sir Seymour to allow her to camp out in a dressing room but since she scarcely ever saw him and had never heard him speak, she could not summon up the courage.

For her Scottish routine Sally learned to dance a Highland Fling and recite a funny and slightly risqué piece of modern poetry in her newly acquired Scottish accent. She was given an afternoon off but instead of going home as she wanted to do, she asked her mother to meet her in London and to bring with her some of Sally's winter clothes. Sebastian assured her that it was perfectly fine for Elsie to be invited to the flat but Sally, full of self-loathing, told her mother that the flat was too far away, and took her to a Lyons Corner House, which was a first and a treat for Elsie.

If Elsie thought that her daughter was rather uncommunicative about her living arrangements, she said nothing, but Sally was not herself during their entire meeting. Aware of her own reticence Sally tried to sound upbeat and talked about the people in the company, their accomplishments, their experience, and their kindness. She explained words that Elsie did not understand such as 'choreographer' and 'répétiteur', and only stopped when her mother's eyes glazed over.

She asked about her friends and their families and heard again all about how Megan Paterson had been killed in an air raid and that Grace was working on a farm in Scotland with some Polish land girls.

'I'm sorry, I did mean to write and tell all about Daisy in the WAAF, too, since you never get home so we can have a good old natter.' Elsie sounded rather hurt but this time, instead of feeling sorry for her mother, Sally was slightly annoyed.

'I wish I had time to come home, Mum, and I wish I had time to sit down every day and write letters. I don't but it doesn't mean I don't care. I care very much and I'm absolutely thrilled for Daisy, doing so well. But please try to understand. If we're not performing, we're rehearsing and if we're not rehearsing we're discussing what we'll do next.'

'It's no time at all when the trains are running,' Elsie continued as if she had heard nothing that Sally had said. 'You could bring some friends with you; I'd make this new beef loaf I've tried out on your dad. Really tasty. You'll never believe it's a tin of corned beef and some onions; it even looks fancy with a top of sliced veggie, potatoes and carrots, nice combination.'

Sally tried not to lose patience. 'It sounds lovely, Mum, but Mrs Petrie doesn't expect Daisy home every week.'

'Daisy isn't in London, and besides, she's in the real Forces.'

That hurt coming from her mother. 'So am I, Mum. I'm on the stage, singing and dancing, yes, but it is certainly an important part of the war effort. Perhaps we don't man machine guns or fly planes but in our little way we help raise morale and that's very important. Mr Churchill's very pleased with us and, believe you me, the journeys are no fun. We travel in army lorries. No one in the army's ever heard of cushions, and there's usually so little room for all of us, plus our costumes and musical instruments, et cetera, that we're crushed like sardines in a tin.'

'All right, love, but you know your dad misses

you something awful. You were with him almost every night in the cinema, you and the twins and little Grace, and now you're all gone. We're going to try to get one of them phone things but all they said was, "There's a war on. Any idea the number of broken lines we're trying to deal with? New customer; you'll be lucky."'

'I hope you reported him.'

'It was a her, and no, I didn't tell her off. Everyone's under pressure, love, and you're right, it is easier for me to get away for a few hours but maybe you could send your dad a postcard when you're somewhere out of London. Remember what he was like when you went off on school trips? Oh, he would like a postcard once in a while.' Bravely she tried to smile. 'You know how he liked to stick them up all over the projection room or my kitchen wall.'

Sally was angry with herself that she had not thought of such a simple solution. Her father missed her and she certainly missed him. 'I'll start tomorrow, Mum. First post office I pass, I'll buy some stamps and then I'll always have one handy.'

Sally was in tears and full of self-loathing when Sebastian met her at the station – having promised to carry what he knew would be a heavy suitcase – but only once Elsie's train was well on its way to Dartford.

'Good Lord, Sal, what on earth's the problem? You should have brought your mamma to the flat and given her lunch.'

'I lied to my mother, a deliberate lie. Have you the least idea how I feel?' she asked hysterically.

'They sacrificed everything for me – everything – and I repay them by...' She could not express herself in words.

Sebastian could and did, and the conversation developed into their first row.

'Good Lord, Sally, stop being such a child. Isn't the flat good enough for your mother?'

'Don't be such a fool. The flat is beautiful but it's a man's flat.'

He tried a little humour. 'A man who is obviously in training to become a monk. For heaven's sake, there's a war on; people find shelter where they can and are grateful for it.' He reached out his hand to her but she ignored it. 'Damn it, Sally, I shouldn't have said that; I didn't mean ... oh blast. As it is, we're living like brother and sister. You are completely at liberty to show Mrs Brewer your virginal room. I've told you that you're safe with me. Call yourself my war effort.'

'I can't stay with you, Sebastian; it's against my principles.'

'Well, I'll move in with him, love, and you can 'ave my share of the bed I share with my sister who never gets home before three and then she reeks of drink and God knows what else.' Several interested passers-by had been pretending not to hear as they slowed down to savour every word of the little scene being played out in front of them, and one couldn't resist joining in.

Sebastian turned to the woman, beaming his handsome smile. 'We're actors, love, just doing a bit of ad lib. Thanks for getting into the swing with us. Come along, darling,' he said quietly to Sally. 'Who'll come to the theatre if we give the

127

plot away here?'

This time Sally had no option but to take his extended hand and walk with him. 'You're very generous and kind but I can't. I'll find a hostel.'

'Not tonight, you won't, unless you really enjoy the underground experience.' He saw her shiver. 'Come on, let's get this damned heavy suitcase home before my left arm is as long as my left leg.'

Sally stayed on at the flat, helping with the limited cooking and cleaning that was needed. She still felt that she had lied to her mother but in fact she had said nothing at all about her arrangements, except that she was sharing a flat with a friend, which was true.

Mum never asked so she must have had an idea. If Sebastian was a girl, I'd have told Mum everything about her, and the flat, but all I said was it's a big flat and I have my own room. I have to tell them and I must try harder to find somewhere else to live.

As for thoughts of love, she persuaded herself, with some justification, that her dreadful experiences of that day, the ghastly reality of the burned-out house, the knowledge that several people she had known were now dead, had made her reach for intimacy. She would be careful not to get so close again. What Sebastians's rationale was, she had no idea.

But ENSA ensured that they were constantly travelling and on the few days that Sebastian and Sally did stay in the flat together, they were usually so exhausted that often they collapsed, fully dressed, on their beds and slept like logs till Sebastian's alarm clock woke him and he woke Sally.

One evening they were returning to London after performing near Chichester, many of the troupe dozing, when the world around them was suddenly full of menacing, muffled roaring. The sky was a speedway of death-dealing aircraft. Yet again the city was the target of an air raid. Heart pounding, Sally thought of her friend Rose, who worked at Vickers, but wanted more than anything to be a driver in the ATS. Occasionally Rose delivered groceries in the family van and Sally prayed that Rose was safe at home where her family had a specially prepared room where they sheltered during air raids. Thinking about one twin made her think of the other. Hadn't something been said during those precious hours when her mother had visited about Daisy staying with a WAAF friend in a London apartment and going to the theatre with the friend's father? Sally hoped that if Daisy was in London, that she and her friend were safe. Was it safe to be in London on any night these days? She vowed that she would write Daisy a letter or just a postcard – had she sent the twins a Christmas card? Had she sent anyone a card?

It never occurred to Sally that she herself received few letters or that, like her, her friends had no time for writing anything but the most important letters.

The drivers of the ENSA vehicles were obviously experienced in air raid situations for all lights had been turned off and the vehicles separated so as not to form a worthy target. When every aircraft had passed over and all were engaged in yet another attempt to flatten London, Sally peeped out and found that their lorry was off the road and under a tree in a field, not that the tree afforded much protection as its leaves had long since fallen.

Complaints and worries began once it was obvious that the planes had gone to richer pastures.

'How long will we be here?'

'We're sitting ducks, for Pete's sake.'

'Helluva lot safer than driving on accompanied by what looks like the entire German air force.'

'Call of nature.' Everyone recognised Humph's voice. 'I'm gettin' out. Those of a delicate constitution—'

He got no further. 'Stay where you are, everyone,' Max instructed. 'The military will decide the best course of action. Try to rest. It won't be long. We would have been ordered to scatter if there had been the risk of strafing or bombs being dropped. The blighters will junk unused bombs on their way back.'

Max was right. The military drivers had been ordered to find safer routes, ones that were less likely to be under the path of any aircraft returning to Germany. One by one, the engines were started and, rather than converging, the lorries took individual paths to an army base as far away as they could get from London.

'Join ENSA and see the world.' Max tried to cheer his tired, disgruntled company.

'Thanks a lot,' said one of the dance troupe, 'but I'm waiting for the luxury yacht you promised.'

'After the war, God willing.' Max smiled at her. 'Let's hope not too much damage has been done.'

130

SIX

The raid had destroyed most of Bank underground station, killing a large number of people.

Later that day, having worked hard for several
hours, some of the ENSA artistes took a trip to
Sadler's Wells to view some old costumes and
props they'd been told were going spare. On the
way back they passed the latest scene of destruction and were astounded by what they saw. An
enormous crater had been created where a busy
station had stood. Entire buildings had disappeared.

'Was it planned, Sally, to bomb the station
where they knew there were so many lines and so
many underground shelters, or did they mean to
hit the Bank of England?' Sebastian, usually so
controlled, was shaking as he pointed out the
Bank's great edifice that stood undamaged no
more than a few steps away. 'The smell, the mess,
the dust, the unbelievable destruction. They're
still looking for bodies and I heard a policeman
say he doubts they'll ever find out how many died
down there.'

Sally looked at the piles of rubble and twisted
wires that had been Bank underground station.
She had always hated being down there and could
scarcely believe in the genius of the engineering
feat that had tunnelled down, down and even further down into the bowels of the earth. Any time

she had been compelled to use it, she had felt like a trapped rabbit or a mole – it seemed so dark, so claustrophobic – but the people who had slept there night after night had seen it as a place of refuge. Surely they had believed that it went so far into the bowels of the earth that the enemy could never find them. But they had.

A few of the men walked with great care a short distance around the hellhole that stretched from one pavement to the other of the famous Threadneedle Street. Sebastian spotted some twisted steel stairs liberally coated in sawdust, sawdust that had obviously soaked up ... he could not even think the words, and turned away, anxious that none of the young women should see. For a moment he thought he could not breathe; there was no air around him and then he remembered those who had fought for breath just a few short hours ago in the fumes and dust, and he managed to pull himself together. Near him two policemen carried a stretcher. The broken bodies of the dead were being brought up as gently and in as dignified a manner as possible. He signalled to Max.

'We are in the way here, friends,' said Max. 'Let the professionals get on with their jobs and we'll get on with ours.'

As quickly as they could, not speaking, heads down to watch the uneven ground beneath their feet, the company returned to the theatre.

'Rehearsal stage, three minutes, and if anyone can find Millie Burgess, yell loudly. Tell her we'll need her today.'

The cast dispersed to change into rehearsal clothes and hurried to the appropriate stage.

Sally, who very much wanted to see a trained ballerina dance – even if just a few jazz steps – was pleased to see Millie approaching with some of the others, who were talking animatedly.

'What is it today, Max, *Tristan and Isolde* or Tommy Trinder?' someone asked.

Before anyone could yell, 'Trinder, please, Max,' a succession of soul-destroying screams rang out and Millie stood, tears streaming down her face, as she uttered one scream after another. The cast looked at her. It was obvious that no one had the slightest idea of what to do.

'Don't stand there gawping, you idiots. She's had a shock. Brandy and a blanket or coat, now, quickly.'

The lightly accented voice stopped and there was the sound of a sharp slap, followed by a gulp and then complete, shocked silence from Millie.

'Meet Lalita at her finest,' whispered Sebastian.

'You don't need to tell me how wonderful Lalita is, Sebastian.' The generous gift of a fur coat was keeping Sally very warm on uncomfortable journeys in army lorries.

'It's over, *querida,* and you are quite safe.' Lalita was talking quietly to the distraught young woman.

Max had rushed back from his office with an almost empty bottle of brandy. He poured the contents into a teacup, which he handed to Lalita. 'Sorry, that's all there is, Lal; haven't bought any since '39.'

Lalita ignored him as she took the cup and held it to Millie's lips. 'Drink it. Now. It's medicinal and we have a show to prepare. Good girl.' She turned to Sebastian. 'You look like hell,' she said without emotion. 'Finish what she doesn't drink, make yourselves comfortable and join us on stage when you're feeling better.'

She shepherded the rest of the group up to the main stage where Max, Sybil, the choreographer and – too often – teacher, and Jessie Dunbar, the conductor, sometimes accompanist and right-hand woman to Sam Castleton, the company's senior pianist, waited for them.

Sally tried to concentrate but, for some reason, her mind was on Sebastian back in the dressing room with Millie. She wondered why the former ballerina had screamed so horrifyingly at whatever the group had been saying – obviously it had something to do with the night raid. There was trauma there but if Millicent did not choose to share it, there was surely nothing that Sally could do or say to help her.

'Pay attention, Sally.' Sybil's clipped tones brought her back to the work she should be doing and she forced herself to think of nothing but where her feet should be.

The session was exhausting but just as everyone was feeling that no more could be tolerated, Max called a break.

'Take ten minutes. Sorry,' he lifted his hand like a traffic policeman. 'I know, I know, I'm hardly the soul of generosity but today was just a little different. Back on schedule tomorrow.'

Sally wrapped her thick woollen scarf around her shoulders, picked up her bag and headed out. She planned to find something either already prepared or something to cook later for the evening meal but was brought up short when she remembered that, as yet, she had no food coupons.

'Let's go off on an adventure.' Sebastian was behind her. 'If we walk briskly, which will certainly be good for my poor cramped legs, we could get to Covent Garden market. A fellow in the Balladeers said he bought a rabbit sausage, which was delicious, and rabbit isn't rationed so no coupons.'

Sally thought of a little bunny rabbit, a white one. No, even if she were starving she could not eat a bunny rabbit.

Sebastian had developed an extraordinary knack for knowing exactly what was going through her head. 'He had it with a cup of mashed potato, chopped cabbage and grated carrots, all mixed together.'

'Sounds better than bunny rabbits,' she said, and hurried to match his longer stride. 'How is Millie?' Asking any question made it easier not to speak about their personal situation. She had made a few enquiries about finding a hostel but so far there were no vacancies.

Just seeing him, talking to him, makes me happy. Am I in love with him? Does he love me? How do I know?

Better to forget that embarrassing incident.

He took her hand. 'She'll be fine, Sally. Afraid too many frightful things have happened to that young woman lately and one more ghastly bombing was just too much. Max is taking her home and he'll encourage her to take a few days off to rest. Mind you, I'm not sure that being alone all evening is the best thing for a distraught young widow.'

135

'So she lives alone?' Sally asked, a note of jealousy in her voice.

Sebastian did not seem to notice the jealousy. 'Yes, poor kid. When she married they bought a little flat and, since she has nowhere else to go and it's their home, as it were, she's staying there.'

'Goodness, how did you find out all that? Not even Max seems to know a thing about her; she's hardly the most talkative of people.'

Sebastian stopped suddenly and, paying no attention at all to Sally's question, looked around. 'Good, I thought so. The shop I was told about is, I hope, just down this lane and, if bunny sausage doesn't tempt you, I believe they have a delicious sideline in hot soup. We could take some home for tonight and heat it up in a pot. Good meal, no cooking.'

'You are amazing, Sebastian,' said Sally, and it was not his ability to find food that she was talking about. She was, however, perfectly aware that Sebastian saw nothing odd in what she had said.

'I know,' he said trying to sound modest, 'and where you're concerned, I do try to please.'

Sally smiled, trying to laugh and sound at ease. 'When did Millicent tell you all this?'

'All what? That she lives alone? Tea break, I suppose. Soup?'

Sally gave in and accepted a cup of soup. Sebastian also bought two rabbit sausages and another cup of the soup.

Fifteen minutes later, having, according to Sebastian, disgraced themselves for ever in the eyes of legions of the Brady family by sharing one cup of the soup while walking along the street, they returned to the theatre where they found that, not only had boxes of uniforms arrived but also that the scripts to be studied were lined up on a table.

'I know you want to have a peek at your glamorous new perfectly fitted uniforms but we'll have a read-through of the new ideas now,' said Max, pointing to the semi-circle of chairs on the stage, 'and I expect you all to be word-perfect by the beginning of February. We do have to beg for transportation to a camp near Grimsby as we have three shows there, one after the other, on the Saturday; big base, but first I think we need to talk about Millie's blow-up this morning. Needless to say no one is ever to bring up with her what I'm about to tell you. Some day she might want to talk, but in the meantime I expect you to treat her as you treat every other member of the company. If I'd known any of her tragic history I wouldn't have jumped down her throat the other day but when I apologised to her now, she said – and I want you all to listen carefully – "I am a professional and expect to be treated like every other professional."'

'In other words you've got permission to yell at her, Max.'

'I'll yell at you in a minute, Humph. Millie met her husband when they were students at a very prestigious ballet school. They became professionals in July 1939, married and danced for a few months in Montpelier – south of France, Humph – where they were hailed as the outstanding new couple; ballet loves to marry two dancers or, at least partner them. They returned to London when war was declared and Patrick insisted on enlisting. He was at Dunkirk. Millie heard that he had given up his place in a lifeboat to another lad, saying he could swim like a fish and would just carry on swimming or treading water till he found another boat. Problem was all the men in the water, hanging on to anything they could find, an oar, a piece of wood, were being strafed by planes. Patrick reached a small boat and had just been pulled aboard when he and almost everyone on the boat, and in the water round it, were shot.' For a moment Max found it difficult to continue. 'The death and destruction last night was just too much for her, and I could cut my tongue out. His body was never repatriated.' He could say no more.

'Poor kids,' could be heard from all parts of the group on stage.

Sally remembered the question Millie had asked Max. No wonder he looked so awful. She had not been looking for a foreign holiday but an opportunity, perhaps, to find her young husband's grave. But mention of Dunkirk reminded Sally of Sam Petrie, her friends' oldest brother.

Rose always thought I was sweet on Sam but it was little Grace who loved him, Grace who is now in the Women's Land Army and who, according to Mum is working on a farm in Scotland. Oh, Sally, how often do you have to remind yourself to write to your friends? But if anything had happened to Daisy, Mum would have told me. I'll stop worrying.

She looked around the group. There was complete silence and almost everyone was looking down at the floor. Sybil, who had been one of Sadler's Wells' greatest soloists, stood up. 'Millie's a professional and so are all of you. To work.'

It was a very subdued company who rehearsed that afternoon. Those who were not used to the life of the everyday actor were becoming bored with the constant repetition of the parts they were playing. When they were allowed to sit in a huge circle and read and digest the suggestions for a new show they brightened up considerably. Sally smiled quietly. It appeared that Max was as clever at directing people as he was at directing actors in a play.

And at last it was time to hand out the uniforms.

'Each person is responsible for any alterations needed, and as quickly as poss, please, everyone. Good night.'

Each evening the entire company left the theatre with all speed but the rate with which the theatre emptied as everyone rushed home to try on their 'absolutely-not-made-to-measure' uniforms was quite remarkable. Sally was no different from any of the others, apart from Sebastian, possibly, who remained calm.

There was no time for supper. She tried on each piece before hurrying to Sebastian's bedroom where there was a full-length mirror. Sebastian, complaining that he was trying to learn a speech, was actually spending the evening running back and forth to give his opinion on the uniform.

'Hardly flattering.'

'Thanks, Sebastian, obviously some bright spark

139

said women need uniforms as well as men, and so we'll add a skirt. Problem solved.'

'Don't you think you're being a little harsh? The hat is quite jolly.'

Sally looked at herself in the mirror on the back of the wardrobe door and groaned. 'It's, it's so ... so flat. It looks like a scone with no rising agent in it.'

'How well put. Now my cap has rather a snazzy brim, don't you think?'

She ignored the cap that sat, with a definite air of panache, on Sebastian's thick hair.

'Jacket's not bad,' she said, 'although they might have invented a special colour for ENSA, instead of this ghastly khaki. I do like these things,' she pointed to her shoulders. 'Epaulettes, is it? And I don't want to hurt your feelings, Sebastian, but there isn't enough of you to fill that jacket. I suppose you could wear several vests.'

'No, but I hoped you could take a tuck in for me here and there, couldn't you?'

He laughed as he watched her turn pale at the prospect.

'I'm adequate with buttons but that's about it. Haven't they got a smaller size?'

'Yes, but I'm too long.' He laughed at her. 'Funny little Sally, haven't you ever heard of tailors?'

For a moment Sally wished that she loved Sebastian and that he loved her; real love, the type that led to a long, happy married life. She wondered if she was the only person who knew how much kindness, generosity, determination and steel lay beneath his humour, frivolity and very real charm. She had never liked a person more. How confusing it all was. Ridiculously, Jon's face seemed to hang in the air before her and her heart beat more quickly. For a moment she wished she had never met him. What was there about him that kept him in her mind – and heart? No, surely it was not possible to love someone she hardly knew. It was impossible to find the words that explained the difference between her feelings, her reaction to thoughts of Jon and thoughts of Sebastian.

'What are you thinking about? Once again I hear creaking gears complaining.'

'Nothing important.' She looked down at her folded uniform garments. 'When do we have to wear this lot?'

'Travelling. Must arrive at a camp or military base looking military. In the Officers' Mess before performances or before we leave, should the CO ask us to assemble so that he can tell us how wonderful we are.'

'I don't even know where to begin with the alterations. My mum can turn up a hem but she's not like Mrs Petrie, my friends' mother. She even made suits for her sons.'

'Splendid woman. We'll bundle them along to my tailor when I take mine. They make ladies' bespoke suits and so they must be able to alter.'

'It'll cost a fortune. A real tailor.'

'No, it won't, Sal. There's a war on and London tailors know that. They'll be thrilled to get us fit to do our duty as they are doing theirs.'

Sally said nothing but determined to speak to the tailor personally. She owed Sebastian too much already. The blouses – two – were silk and they fitted nicely. She rather liked the look of the greatcoat and was realistic enough to know that with her height, she could carry off such a military style. Her long slim legs looked good in the uniform trousers too.

'Excuse my familiarity, General, but they'll look better if – how can I put it? – the rear has the odd tuck too.'

Sally flushed with embarrassment but, looking in the mirror, she had to admit that there was rather a lot of material. 'You're right. We'll say the jacket, the skirt and the trousers. Everything else is fine.'

'You don't think the tie is a tad long?'

Sally put her tie around her neck and tied it before Sebastian could help. 'The tie is perfect.'

'As are you, Sally B.'

This was a conversation she did not want to continue. 'I'll parcel these up.'

Sebastian watched her walk away and there was sadness in his eye, which, of course, Sally did not see.

A few days later Sally was once more wrapped in Lalita's beautiful fur coat. She had, of course, told her parents all about the cast's considerable generosity, and although she had chosen not to wear it on the day her mother had travelled up to London with replacement clothes, she had admitted that she now owned a floor-length coat that just happened to be real fur.

'A fur coat? And in the safe there's a ring made of rubies. Oh, Sally, we're a working-class family from Dartford. Our kind don't get presents of fur coats and valuable rings.'

Sally had tried not to think of either the coat or the ring, but although the ring was easy to forget, the naval officer who had invited her to address him as 'Just Jon' invaded her sleeping, or her quiet waking moments more often than he should. After all, she had met him once, and then only for a few minutes.

Is a fleeting moment all it takes to change one's life for ever?

Millie, back with the company and prepared to dance at least once in each performance, had chosen to sit beside Sally in the lorry, perhaps because they were close in age.

'Imagine being a soldier and having to travel everywhere in this ugly old thing.'

The fact that she had spoken at all surprised Sally out of her reverie; she looked at the inside of their vehicle, trying to see it as she had seen it the first time. Bare floor, hard seats, canvas roof and sides. Military vehicles did not change. She was thankful that she had climbed in early enough to get as far away from the flaps in the back as possible. The draughts could be appalling and were even worse when they stopped somewhere for refuelling or what Lalita termed 'a break for comfort'. The flaps would be opened and inevitably two or three cast members would seize the chance to smoke.

'Those damn things ruin your throat,' Lal said at least once a day and Sybil would join her in assuring any dancer smoking that their lungs were as important as their feet.

143

'Well? Is Miss "oh you're so beautiful" too pretty to talk?'

Millie had expected a reply.

Sally looked at her in astonishment. 'I'm sorry, I was thinking about the inside.' Since she felt like crying because of Millie's remark, she laughed instead. 'My mum would do wonders with some pretty swags of fabric.'

'And some carefully selected cushions.'

'To match the tie-backs.'

'Absolutely.' Millie bowed her head for a moment. 'I'm feeling rather low right now, Sally; it's not you.'

Sally smiled. What could she say? She remembered her father's words on her first day at her senior school: 'Keep your head down till Christmas, Sal, and you'll learn how the land lies.'

'Bold colours, I think.'

Millie agreed and the remainder of the journey was even pleasant by war standards.

Sally had never been to the North-East. She thought her friends Daisy and Rose Petrie had mentioned one or two towns, but Grimsby, which they passed through on their way to the base, had not been one of them. The lorries drew up at the quarters set aside for the ENSA group and almost immediately the carpenters started to put together a makeshift stage.

Sally and Millie could hear the banging in of nails as they made their way across an extremely muddy field. 'Hope it doesn't snow,' moaned Sally. 'It's going to be a nightmare walking back across this in evening dress.'

'Spare a thought for me in toe shoes. I've promised to do a solo, Sally, just to see how classical ballet goes down with the chaps. But I'm an old hand at crappy theatres. Wear Wellingtons, bundle your skirts up as much as possible and carry your heels. They might have laid some boards if we had an audience of paying guests – or perhaps they needed all their spare wood for the stage.'

'There is a war on,' they said together and giggled like schoolgirls.

'Yes, we're fighting in North Africa now. Wouldn't that be nice? Hot sun instead of cold, wet snow, sand everywhere, fleas ... bound to be fleas.'

'Exactly, and not a drop of water,' Sally added.

'And soldiers, and airmen and nurses; they'll set up hospitals for the wounded, and don't people get ghastly things like dysentery in hot countries? We could give them a show, go out on a troopship or something.'

'And come back with dysentery.'

'Worth it, Sally, to feel we've done something really splendid with our lives. I really believe those troops need a laugh or a bit of leg or one of Humph's risqué jokes more than the ones based at home.'

Still talking, they reached their quarters. It looked like a hospital ward, with evenly spaced iron beds each with sheets, a clean pillow and a coarse grey blanket. 'We've displaced some men,' said Sally.

Millie threw herself down on a bed and even that action was graceful. 'We'll make it up to them, Sal.' She sat up again suddenly. 'Do you actually know any soldiers?'

145

'I have friends with brothers. One is a POW, captured at Dunkirk, and another brother was killed by a sniper. She herself, my friend Daisy, she's in the WAAF.'

'Then put their faces in your mind when you're performing. Do it just for them.'

Sally could not ask Millie if that was what she did. Besides, she was sure she already knew the answer.

The first show went well; one or two blips with lighting or scenery but everyone, audience included, was quite used to that. The blips were fixed by the time the curtain rose on the second performance.

Peeping from the wings, Sally saw that several branches of the services were represented; there were even soldiers and aircrew from foreign countries. What would they make of British humour, she wondered, and that was when she saw Jon. Her heart seemed to flip right over in her chest and an entire Amazon forest of butterflies took flight in her stomach. She looked at him each time the makeshift curtain opened or closed, afraid and almost sure that she was mistaken, just like the last time.

'What's so fascinating, Sally?' Sebastian, attractive, kind, generous and gentle – in fact, every girl's dream – was standing behind her and could see the audience much better than she. 'Counting heads for Max, love?'

'No, silly really, but I think, that is, I thought I saw someone I knew, someone from Dartford.'

'How nice. It's possible, you know. You're from Dartford and you're here and who knows where

146

you might sling your hammock before this war is over? Which one is he?'

'How did you know it was a man?'

'The intense look of rapture, my dear.'

Sally had no time to confirm or deny his supposition as the Three Balladeers and a Trumpet had finished their surprisingly clever and funny performance and were bowing their way off the stage.

The chair on which Sally now reposed, Sleeping Beauty-style, was wheeled onto the stage. Sybil arranged the skirt of Sally's lemon gown in as attractive a manner as possible. The curtain went up, the small orchestra began to play a waltz, and Sebastian, astounded, saw the beautiful girl. Elegantly he moved towards her, bent down and kissed her. She, Sleeping Beauty, awoke startled, but allowed herself to be helped up by the handsome man. To thunderous applause they waltzed round the stage and then obeyed the director's order to 'Exit, stage right.'

Sally had to wait through two other acts, the always popular chorus girls and a group of five very clever jugglers wearing Elizabethan costume, whose act consisted of gently tossing one tennis ball back and forth to one another. Somehow, their looks of fierce concentration or perhaps the doublets and their exaggerated arm movements made the simple scene extremely funny. They gained even more applause than the Balladeers.

The piano was rolled on and Sally, in slacks loaned her by a WAAF, a blouson loaned by a sailor, and an airman's cap and nonchalantly worn scarf, strolled onto the stage amid the usual

147

whistles and catcalls. She sang several songs made famous by such luminaries as Gracie Fields and Vera Lynn, several light numbers from well-known American films, and ended up with the popular 'Come and Have a Drink at the Victory Arms'.

The audience, especially the large male contingent, clapped and whistled. Sally paid no attention but looked for Jon. If he ever had been there he was gone now. Sally remembered her job and ran off blowing kisses all the way. The first person she met was Max.

'Good girl, Sally, leave them wanting more.'

'Max, I'm not a great singer. I want to act.'

'I'll let you know when and if you're good enough. Now, you can either go, grab a cup of tea and change for the finale, or go to my room where I'm told a naval officer is waiting to see you.'

Sally looked at him. *Don't get excited, Sally, maybe it's Phil Petrie, although Phil's not an officer, is he? Wouldn't that be nice?*

'You're sure? Did he give his name?'

'I did ask. He said, "Say it's John, just John."'

'Jon.' She could scarcely breathe with excitement and scarcely heard the directions Max was giving her. She managed to prevent herself from throwing her arms around him – that was not how she wanted to impress the director – thanked him and hurried off.

Down one corridor, turn left or was it right? No, left and the second door on the right was the one assigned to the director.

Sally arrived at the door just as it opened and her disappointment was painful. It was not Jon

148

but another officer, older, heavier, shorter.

'I'm sorry,' she said as she tried to force back the threatening tears.

'Not nearly as much as Commander Galbraith, ma'am. He had no sooner spoken to your director than he got a telephone call and had to run – and I mean run – but he shouted back, "Ask her to talk to Maudie."' He looked at her questioningly.

For a moment Sally stood silently and then she awarded him her most beautiful smile.

'Mean something, Miss Brewer?'

'Yes, thank you. It certainly does.'

Sally smiled again and, with mixed feelings, returned backstage. *Maudie, Maudie, that's Maude from the shop. He must mean – what – that she'll give me his address. Oh, please let it be that she'll do that, but when will I get back to Dartford to ask her?*

Max met her in the corridor. 'Well, that didn't take long. Old friend?'

'Actually no. Just a chap I met once in Dartford. Just wanted to say hello.'

'You don't look overjoyed, Sal. Something wrong?'

'He had gone by the time I got there.'

'Poor girl, I'm dreadfully sorry. He did come across as a really nice chap, certainly seemed to have all the time in the world. He laughed and said he owed you a decent cup of tea.'

And Sally remembered the ghastly little café and the waitress who had almost thrown the tea at them. She was disappointed not to have seen him but she was happy too and smiled brightly at Max. 'Not your fault, Max; there's a war on, they

149

tell me, and he had to go. He left a message.'

'About tea?'

'No, sir,' said Sally with a cheeky grin, and with a lighter, happier heart she left the director and returned to her dressing area to prepare for the next show.

Conscious of her promise to her mother, she took one of her newly bought collection of picture postcards of Rural England out of her handbag and sat down to write a few lines to her father.

Dear Dad,

I'm doing a show 'oop north' as our very funny comedian says. Still not acting but I do recite poetry, and Max, our director, says I sing quite well. Miss you and Mum lots.

Love, Sally

'Sally, are you asleep?' Millie had thrown open the door. 'Come on, you're late for debriefing.'

Sally was amazed at how long it had taken her to think up two lines that would please her father. 'Sorry,' she said and ran.

Max, Lalita, Sybil, Jessie Dunbar and Sam Castleton, who was in overall charge of musical requirements, were very pleased with the reception the company had received in the North-East. When they were all assembled next morning, before loading the huge green monster of a lorry that was at their disposal, Max announced that, after much discussion, caused by the positive reception to one or two of the more high-brow acts, they had de-

150

cided to rework the entire programme.

'Some ENSA companies only do straight theatre and they're not always well-received; got to be sure of your audience. Now, I'm not saying, as had been said in some of the lighter press, that the lower ranks can't appreciate Beethoven, or classical ballet, or plays that are more literature than light entertainment. We think we're doing a nice mixture but...' He stopped talking and looked at the company. 'Anyone got any idea what I was going to say?'

There was an embarrassing silence for a moment or two and then Humph raised his hand. 'I watch the faces,' he said. 'Only way to really know how my idea of humour is going over. Three shows, three different lots of lads. To be honest, some of them didn't think much of me and some didn't think much of the play, but another audience looked to me, just some of them, mind, that they might have liked a bit more of the Shakespeare, or maybe instead of Millie dancing more or less like an "almost-ready-for-stardom chorus girl" – not that you ladies aren't well worth watching – some of 'em might have liked something like *The Dying Swan*, something really beautiful, and your lot can play anything, can't they, Sam?'

The leader of the musicians nodded.

'The dying swan, what on earth's that?' asked Allan Fordyce.

'Surprised an educated man like you not knowing, Allan,' Humph said with something very like a smirk. 'It's the most beautiful piece of classical ballet I ever saw in my life. Bet you do it beautiful, Millie.'

Max, with his glance swiftly moving from face to face said, 'Thank you, Humph, very well spotted. Your ability to read faces is part of what makes you such a good comedian.' This last was heavy with sarcasm as Max had been reading Millie's face while Humph had been speaking and had seen her close her eyes as if that might shut out the word 'dying'.

'I certainly was thinking we might strengthen our classical offerings and I'll discuss your suggestion with the team. Anyone else have anything to say about the audience reception, their participation in the sing-along or your own particular performance? Any suggestions at all?'

'Lunch,' called one of the dancers and everyone laughed, thus lightening the atmosphere. Max was not the only one who had been observing Millie.

'Bit early,' laughed Max, and the suggestions and observations began to come thick and fast from members of the company.

Sally said nothing during the sometimes heated debate. She had seen Millie fight to keep tears at bay. Mention of anything dying was just too much, but she didn't blame Humph. He had meant no harm. She had never heard of *The Dying Swan* either and was ashamed that she was surprised that a man like Humph had. *Just shows, you can't judge a book by its cover. Maybe I'll ask him – or I could ask Sebastian.*

Once more she had returned to the problem of living in Sebastian's apartment. Try as she might, their relationship was not the same as before she had moved in. Being out on the road was actually a relief, for she rarely saw Sebastian alone and he rarely sought her out. If anything, he seemed to be spending any free time he had talking to Millie. A small spear of jealousy went through her and made her angry with herself.

Why am I jealous? Because he's my friend. Childish Sally. Millie needs friends too. And she needs Sebastian more than I do. I shouldn't object to their little chats.

She determined to concentrate on her performance and to criticise every note or every step, but all that filled her mind was the face of a smiling sailor and a verbal message, and she yearned to be at home in the little house next door to the cinema in Dartford.

As close as Dartford was to London, the chance of having a few hours to get there and back seemed particularly slim. She had been able to go home for a few hours over Christmas; most of the company, including Sebastian, had stayed to entertain and so Sally was determined to ask no more favours.

Their costumes and props were packed and loaded with military precision and the company headed back to London. Mentally and physically exhausted, Sally and Sebastian returned to his lovely flat. Sally changed into her night clothes and went into the kitchen to see if there was at least one tin of soup in the depleted larder. Luxury. She unearthed a tin boasting that it contained, not soup, but Phillips Delicious Beans, opened it and called to alert Sebastian, who was splashing around in the bath.

She had just finished heating the beans and

dividing them between two small bowls when the air-raid alarm sounded. Sally banged on the bathroom door, yelling, 'Air Raid,' as loudly as she could and rushed to pick up her gas mask.

Few people forgot their gas masks these days as huge signs all over London and, no doubt, the rest of the country assured them, 'Hitler will send you no warning – so always carry your gas mask.'

There were no important documents for her to save this time as none had, as yet, been replaced. The originals lay at the bottom of a huge pile of evidence of broken or destroyed lives in another area of the city.

And then Sebastian, his ancient cashmere coat over his pyjamas, was there with the fur coat Lalita had given her. 'Put your shoes on and come, now, Sally.'

For a moment she wondered if she could pick up the plates of rapidly cooling beans to take them to the nearest shelter but Sebastian grabbed her hand and pulled her along, stopping only to pull the door closed behind him.

'Not that closing the door will make a wit of difference if we get a direct hit,' he said almost cheerfully, and she realised that once again he was making light of something so as not to worry her.

'I'll reheat them when we get back,' she said with a smile

'Brave girl,' he said and kissed her cheek. It was the first time he had been at all intimate with her since that night she first stayed and she took comfort from it. She could never be his lover but she hoped that they would always be friends.

They were not the only oddly dressed couple making their way to the shelter. An elderly man carried his tweed coat over his arm while wearing what Sally and Sebastian decided naughtily was his wife's second-best fur. She was wearing a magnificent full-length mink. As it opened to allow her to see where to put her feet they saw what is commonly called 'a king's ransom' in jewellery around her wrinkled neck: diamonds, sapphires, even emeralds, and strands of creamy pearls that Sally later decided were the only things in her entire life that she had ever coveted. The owner pulled her coat firmly around her as if she thought Sally and the obviously young and strong Sebastian might wrest some of them from her.

'I'd rather have my baked beans,' said Sebastian pointedly to Sally and they unconsciously decided to sit as far away from the frightened couple as possible. That was not difficult as the shelter had filled quickly with local residents, most, but not all, in their night clothes.

They were barely seated when the all clear sounded and, gratefully, the residents of the flats made their ways home.

'My grandmother would take pictures of my dad with her to an air raid shelter,' said Sebastian as they climbed the stairs.

'None of you?'

'Well, I'm – so far – still in good health. My father was a casualty of the Great War.' He rushed on as if he did not want to talk too much about his family. 'What would your parents take?'

'No real idea; their wedding photograph and my christening one, I suppose. Why, I don't know. I look like a squeezed sausage in frills.'

'You couldn't look like a sausage, squashed, squeezed or otherwise, if you tried, Sally. Ah, here we are and all safe. I think I'm a tad tired for beans. You go ahead but I think I'll leave mine for breakfast.'

Sally felt exactly the same and a very few minutes later they were both sound asleep.

The ENSA programmes were being welcomed and enjoyed whole-heartedly all over Britain. As more and more countries were swept up into the war, discussions began about the possibility of taking ENSA units overseas. Every day British civilians read foreign names in their newspapers or heard the strange names on their wirelesses. In July they read that Britain and the USSR – and Ernie Brewer was not the only reader who had to look up in an old school book to remind himself what country those letters represented – had signed what was called a mutual assistance agreement. Neither nation would enter into a separate peace agreement with Germany.

'I'm sure it's a fancy name for Russia,' said Elsie as she scraped margarine on her morning toast.

Ernie disappeared and returned from Sally's bedroom carrying a much-used geography jotter. 'Union of Soviet Socialist Republics,' he read out to Elsie, who said simply, 'Exactly, Russia.'

'Can't win with women,' complained Ernie as he sat down to enjoy his toast.

A few weeks later newspapers announced that British forces had invaded Iran, a country with massive oil supplies, much needed by the Allies. Their remit was to protect Iran's railways so that quantities of war materials, including oil, could be safely transported.

Ernie and Elsie brought out Sally's old geography notebook again and again over the weeks and months.

It reappeared as the appalling story of the murder, by German troops, of thirty thousand Jews outside a town called Kiev, in a far-away place called Ukraine, leaked out and into British newspapers.

'If this is true, then all the stories about extermination camps in Germany might be true too,' suggested Ernie.

'Nobody would treat fellow human beings like that,' said Elsie.

'If they didn't think the people were fellow human beings, Elsie love,' said Ernie, sadly, 'they just might.'

SEVEN

During the spring of 1941, Sally and other members of the ENSA company were discovering that there were two main arguments over the possibility of ENSA companies taking their programmes overseas and each was valid. Exhausted military personnel, wherever they were, needed and deserved rest and some fun and in the absence of anything else, Forces units were trying to handle entertainment themselves. After all, hundreds of actors, singers, comedians and musicians had not tried to avoid enlistment or conscription but had joined up as soon as war was declared. All were prepared to fight but also to do whatever they could to lighten the burden of their fellows, and so many of them formed small entertainment groups within their own squadron or battalion. The other valid argument was that it was exceedingly dangerous to bring civilian groups, no matter how talented or how welcome, into combat zones. Transportation, too, was costly and many voices said that if much-needed money was going to be spent on sending entertainment to war zones, it should be used to send the best entertainers.

'And that's not us,' Max told his company gloomily. 'Some of you were great and one or two of you are getting that way but we have to face facts. It's the George Formbys and the Vera Lynns and,' he added with a small bow to Sybil and Millie, 'the Sadler's Wells quality dancers that will be sent.'

And so, as they waited to hear what the powers that be would eventually decide, Max and others like him rewrote their shows and accepted as many invitations as they could possibly squeeze into their engagements diaries.

A visit home?

'Maybe next week, next month, just as soon as you can be spared.'

Sally, with a very guilty conscience, continued to

live in Sebastian's comfortable and elegant flat. She began to relax into a fraught-free platonic relationship with Sebastian and a pleasant, slowly-growing friendship with Millie, who was also re-building her life under the influence of Sebastian's easy humour. Often all three of them spent their free time together and could be found at Sebastian's flat, the girls reading magazines like *Woman* – especially if there was a story in it by Millie's favourite author, Lyn Arnold – sharing a tin of Pascall's Saturday Assortment, or playing fiendishly competitive games of Freddie the Fox – the game of choice – Snap or Tiddlywinks.

The few hours spent relaxing with their childhood games were welcome breaks in their heavy schedules. At least they were for Millie and Sally, and Sally sometimes found herself thinking that if she had time to play Snakes and Ladders then surely she had time to write home. Sebastian behaved as if he were enjoying himself but then it was sometimes difficult to tell what Sebastian really thought – he was so polite.

Easter Sunday, 13 April, found the company being driven into Portsmouth where various units were preparing to go overseas.

'We're planning a send-off these boys will remember all their lives or, at least until they get home again,' Max told his weary and rather grubby troupe after they'd endured a particularly long and tiresome journey. 'Everyone, get cleaned up and into costume as soon as possible. Wish we had an Easter egg for every one of you but we'll think of something, and the navy's promised a hot meal as each act walks off-stage.'

No one particularly cared what would make up the navy's idea of a hot meal.

'Anything's better than the cardboard sandwiches and cold tea we had for lunch.' That complaint was heard from several dressing rooms.

Sally and Millie shared a shower, and then put on the underwear each would need for her first appearance.

'I need to limber up, Sally. Sorry, but I'll need all the space.'

'No problem. I'll pull on something casual and go and have a close look at the sea. It is the sea, isn't it?'

'Of course. You didn't think those huge ships could be moored on a pond, did you?'

'Very funny,' said Sally as she saw Millie's head appearing out from between her knees. 'I'll leave you to your idea of fun.'

Sally looked at her watch and, aware that she did not have too much time, hurried out and tried to find a high point from which she hoped to be able to see the sea. She was hurrying down a neat path pointed out to her by a sailor when she heard a voice she recognised.

'Miss Petrie?'

As she turned, her heart seemed to skip a beat.

'Hello,' was the only word she seemed capable of uttering. Her mouth had gone quite dry.

'Sally?' His voice was tentative.

She smiled a glorious smile that lit up her lovely face. 'Yes, Jon, it's me; I'm with the ENSA company.'

There was something different about him. He looked taller and, never heavy, he now seemed to be thinner. But few of the military personnel she had met were on the heavy side; probably all that exercise.

He walked towards her. Yes, he was thinner even than he had been a few months before. His face was rather pale and no, could that be a streak of silver in the thick, straight, brown hair?

'May I say you look absolutely lovely?'

The lads in Dartford never gave compliments like that!

'Thank you.'

'With ENSA? When we met first I thought you were a student.'

The ring. He had suggested she sell it to make student life more comfortable.

Somehow she knew that he was not thinking about the ring. 'I was and I wasn't. When war was declared I was just about to start training and the school – a very minor one – closed. The owner, however, very kindly had me hired as – what are they called – the person who does whatever needs doing?'

After a few moments' thought he suggested, 'Slave,' and they both laughed.

'Have you time to chat? We could have coffee in the Officers' Mess and you could tell me all about it.'

The Officers' Mess. Something else to write home about, and to share with my three best friends. And we would meet when I'm in the most casual of clothes and am wearing absolutely no make-up. Yet he says I'm lovely.

'Tell me everything,' he ordered as soon as they were seated at a round table covered by a starched pristine white cloth. A tall slender vase held some daffodils, many still in bud. Coffee was served in what Elsie would have termed 'best china' and they drank the delicious brew as they chatted.

'I have to get changed soon, Jon.'

'I know, there's never enough time.' He reached over and touched her hand, which was resting on the table.

Every nerve in Sally's body tensed. She looked up and blue eyes met brown. 'Jon,' she said and smiled. 'Dear Jon.'

'Sally,' he said. 'I'm memorizing everything I see.'

Now his hand held hers and the coffee cooled in the cups.

Time passed more quickly than either thought possible. Sally tried to compress all her experiences into a few interesting words and Jon made a carefully edited list of his. But the idyll had to end. At last they stood up to leave for the theatre and he looked down at her. 'You never got to Dartford. It's not too far away and if you'd been here yesterday I could have driven you home.'

'To talk to Maudie?'

He laughed. 'No, but she is a darling. She was my nanny; actually the only member of my family – if I can claim her as family – still alive. I had telephoned to ask her to give you my name and address.' He looked at his watch. 'We must go, Sally, or you'll be late.'

They left the Mess and half walked, half ran to the theatre, where he stopped at the door. 'Do you ever have time to write letters? I'd love to hear about the theatre and when I may expect to see you with Olivier or, even better, Gielgud?'

She had no need to think. 'I have time, Jon.'

He took a white card out of his pocket. 'That's my military address. You write first and I'll answer whenever I can and when you will know where the company is likely to be.'

For a moment there was a silence as if time itself stood still. Then he stooped and kissed her very gently, his lips soft on hers. 'I can't stay for the performance, my so very dear Sally; this is a busy night for me. Goodbye, my dear. Write to me.'

She stood and watched him stride off and then, as if there might be some sign, she touched her lips. It was as if he had never been. But there was the card. She looked at it for a long moment. His name, his rank, his ship but no address. Then, very carefully, she put it in her bag for safety.

She almost jumped when Sebastian somehow materialised before her.

'I didn't know you had a friend in the Senior Service? None of my business, of course, but Sybil is looking for you everywhere. She wants to teach you a few moves so that you can work with Millie.'

'You're joking.'

'No. The management is a tad worried that Millie might not manage and so a young, tall, statuesque vestal virgin, suitably undraped, of course, will be there to help her out.'

'You're not joking; you're simply out of your mind, and Sybil has lost hers completely. I'm the fairy guard, remember, with two left feet and as for *en pointe*...'

She had no time to say what she had been about to say about professional dancers thinking nothing of humiliating amateurs by asking them to do something of which they were totally incapable, for Sybil, looking as innocent as if she could not possibly have overheard Sally, had joined them.

'Sally, do leave the logistics to your elders and betters. I want you on stage in rehearsal mode before I've finished talking to you.'

Sally almost, but not quite, made it.

'Right, stand on that chalk mark. Seb, you on that one. If Millie gets through, and we hope she does, that's all you'll do, Sally, apart from hold up a few rather elaborate urns. Seb, you are about to enter the world of classical ballet.'

Both Sybil and Sally laughed at the horrified expression on Sebastian's face. 'You told me I'd be a statue.'

'Dear boy, of course you're a statue but at one point, the statue will allow the ballerina to hold his hand while she executes some rather nifty turns. Just wait, Sadler's Wells will be calling out for you at the end of hostilities.'

'Very funny, I'm sure. Now what will happen to my urn if I have to hold it and a tiny but aston-ishingly well-muscled young woman at the same time?'

Sybil awarded him an extremely frosty look. 'I sent the naval engineers a rough drawing and those boys made urns any theatre in London would be proud to own. And don't worry, Sally, they may look like the real thing but there isn't an ounce of metal in them; they weigh less than nothing.'

Millie arrived wearing a top, a rather short skirt, and ballet tights, apparently made of a tightly knit cotton, like but somehow very unlike the rather thick stockings Sally's mother wore. Strangely enough they had no feet but stopped at her ankles as if they were glued there. Sally noticed that Sebastian's eyes, like the tights, appeared to be glued to the perfect body revealed by the unusual clothes.

Millie carried two pairs of ballet shoes, one pale blue and the other black, and two knitted tubes that closely resembled the sleeves of a large woolly jumper.

'Right, we'll start. The commander's lending us a pianist as Sam isn't too familiar with the music.' She waved and a young naval rating appeared. 'This is Josh Fitzwilliam and, Josh, this is our cast.'

Millie looked at the young man. 'Dear Lord, can you sight-read Tchaikovsky, young man? You don't even look old enough to be in the navy.'

To Sally's surprise, the pianist bowed to Millie. 'A great honour, madame, and trust me, I'll manage.' He smiled, went over to the piano and softly and surely began to test it. For a few minutes while the 'dancers' took their positions, his hands wandered delicately over the keys or furiously chased each other up and down the keyboard. Sally stood transfixed, her weightless urn on her left shoulder. Never had she heard music like that before.

'Intro,' ordered Sybil, and the music changed. It was soft and gentle as April rain, and Sally felt soothed and comforted as somehow it appealed

165

to some basic human need.

And then Millie was there, floating, drifting thistledown. She seemed to leap in graceful bounds across the stage. Next she was on her toes, spinning here and there, finishing in front of Sebastian, who stood like a guard outside the King's palace. Possibly she had whispered to him, for he held out his free hand, which she grasped as, perfectly balanced on one toe-block, she bent over, stretching her graceful arm towards the stage while her free leg rose behind her, higher and higher, straighter and straighter, until her toes pointed to the sky. In a second she had straightened, both feet were on the ground, and she skipped off the stage.

There should have been tumultuous applause but this was a rehearsal and, apart from, 'Wow, fabulous,' from 'the water carriers', there was nothing.

Millie returned, pulling the sleeve-like tubes over her legs to keep the muscles warm. She pulled on a much-stretched grey cardigan as she walked to the piano. She looked furiously angry, ignored everyone but the pianist, who was looking over some of the other music on the piano, and shouted, 'What the hell are you doing in the navy?'

Josh Fitzwilliam stood up. 'My duty, Mrs Burgess. I simply obeyed the call-up,' he answered gently.

'Your duty is to give the world your music.'

'Oh, but I will one day. I'm twenty years old and have been studying music since I was three. I promise you I won't forget such training in a few years. Perhaps, even as a sailor, I will have opportunities like this again; I promise you that I'll look for them. You have joined ENSA, madame, and so you know how important it is to take music, beauty and laughter to serving men and women. Much better than pills, don't you agree?'

'You are a fool,' she said, and ran from the room.

'Explain, Sybil,' ordered Max, who had just joined them.

And Sybil did.

Josh did not appear to be either surprised or shocked. 'I had heard rumours and am deeply sorry for her, madame. I appreciate her concern but I know what I have to do.'

'See if wardrobe can find you tails for the performance.'

'No, madame.' His tone of voice told Max and Sybil clearly that he would not change out of his naval rating's uniform. 'I prefer that the audience notice only the dancer—' and then he smiled naughtily at Sally – 'and the beautifully moulded statue.' He bowed and was gone.

'That kid will go far,' said Sebastian.

'Pray God, it's not to the bottom of some ocean.' Sybil picked up the urns and, her eyes full of unshed tears, walked quickly off stage where she immediately began to rehearse the next part of the programme.

'You're awfully quiet, Sally,' said Millie much later that evening as they sat together enjoying the delicious hot meal the navy had prepared for them after their performance. Sebastian, for once, had joined a men-only group in the Officers' Mess.

'Nice to be without our mother hen,' said Millie. 'Didn't you think the entire crew had ramped up tonight? And that lovely boy could be onstage at the Albert Hall instead of risking his life like this. But, young men... The best have ideals, don't they?' She straightened her spine as if determined never to allow it to droop again. Already she had spent too much time weeping over brilliant lives cut short. 'Weren't you pleased with the overall performance?'

Sally, who had managed to avoid thinking of Jon while the show was going on, was now full of worry. They had met again, but oh so briefly. They had agreed to keep in touch. And now he was gone. His ship, a battleship, was going to war – somewhere. The card gave only his name, his rank and the name of the ship. How would a letter find him?

'Sally?'

'Sorry, Millie, my mind wandered; so rude.'

'My mind used to wander like that too,' she laughed and, in spite of her own unhappiness, Sally was thrilled to hear it. Had Millie laughed even once since she had joined the company?

'I do agree with you about tonight. Being with someone more gifted or capable tends to make people perform better. I found that at school. Perhaps we instinctively try harder when we're forced to perform beside someone who is so much more talented. I loved the ballet, by the way. You looked like my favourite scrap when I was a little girl. A fairy with gossamer wings and a dress made of bluebell petals. Tonight you were

168

the fairy but without the wings.'

'Sweet thing to say, Sally, but dancers of the ballet, men and women, do have wings.'

Sally looked at her in some confusion.

'We call them legs.'

They both laughed. Another natural laugh from Millie, thought Sally.

'That's it; you looked as if you were flying; it was so beautiful. I kept thinking how much my mother would have loved it. My family don't know anything about ballet or great music or any of that stuff. Now I wish we did.'

'Hear me preach, Sal. That's what's so wonderful about the Arts; they can be enjoyed and appreciated at any age. I'm glad Sybil forced me to dance; it brought beautiful memories – horrible ones, too – but the good outweigh the bad. Ballet looks so incredibly beautiful but there are real sods in the ballet world as well as everywhere else. Patrick was totally without guile, though. I loved him so much. I thought I would die when I heard that he had been killed. I prayed to die. How could I live without him? But it got worse because...' She stopped for a moment, too distraught to carry on. Then, making a visible effort, she continued, 'It got worse because it was a mistake. Patrick was never at Dunkirk. He was stationed at the UK Forces Headquarters at a place called Arras in the north-east of France, a few miles from the Belgian border and, as it happens, not too far from the port of Dunkirk. It was almost his first posting and he had been there no more than a few months when the German army retook the area just before the retreat from Dunkirk. I'm praying that Patrick was interred where he died because there is no doubt at all about it, my friend, my beautiful Patrick died at Arras. I have his identification tags and a few of his personal belongings, including the last letter he received from me.' She was silent for a moment as her hand rested lightly on her breast. 'I keep it with me always, Sally; it's stained with his blood.'

What could she say? Sally tried desperately to find just the right word but nothing perfect occurred.

Millie seemed to sense her feelings of inadequacy. 'I'm sure it was chaos, dead and dying everywhere, but surely, probably, someone would have dealt with the bodies, wouldn't they? They wouldn't just leave them as they fell, would they?'

The picture Millie had painted in her mind was so frightening that Sally rushed on, 'How could that have happened, Millie – that you don't know where Patrick is buried, I mean? I'm so sorry.'

'It was all explained to me. After all, it was a ferocious battle; the place was overrun. Sensible to care for the injured first, I know that, or getting the able soldiers out of danger. I don't know whether they retreated or fled or what happened; they may have been among the men who sought safety at Dunkirk. Real life isn't like at the pictures, Sal, is it? But nothing is really, is it?

'You're right, Millie, films are just stories, made-up dreams. But we'll get to France; that's your dream and we'll make it come true. Trust me, somehow we'll get there.'

Millie's eyes filled with tears but they were not tears of sadness. 'You and Seb and, yes, Max, Lal

170

and Sybil, too, have all helped me, Sally. Patrick was with me tonight, I could sense him. Do you think I'm crazy?'

Sally had no idea what to say. Did Sally mean that her husband had come back from the dead? That was impossible, wasn't it? Or had Millie experienced a vision? Words came eventually. 'I don't think you're crazy. I was brought up to believe in something or someone greater than we are. Who knows what He can do?'

'You two are in trouble. Why aren't you both in bed?'

Sebastian, the mother hen, was there and he was angry.

'We were late having dinner, Seb, and we did justice to it, as I'm sure you did to yours.'

'Of course I did, but we are leaving for Southampton at four thirty tomorrow morning. It's after eleven now and all these men have to clean up and get to bed too.'

'Sorry, Sebastian; sorry everyone,' Sally called across to the dining-room staff.

'Any time, ladies, sling your hammocks here any time you choose.'

Sebastian gathered up his charges and, still apologising profusely, Sally and Millie were practically marched out in front of the grinning kitchen crew.

'I want to talk to you, Sally,' Sebastian said and he sounded angry still. 'Some example you two set tonight. You know the rules. Clean up after the last performance, eat, and go to bed, not leave a good hour between eating and cleaning your teeth.'

'We were having a very important conversation,' ventured Millie.

'I'll bet, and did it feature a good-looking sailor?'

Millie laughed again. 'Jealousy rearing its ugly head, Seb?'

'Oh, go to bed,' he snapped.

The girls, both aware of and grateful for his caring, stayed quiet and he walked with them to their quarters.

'Good night, *mein Führer*,' Millie called after him as he left them at their door.

'Don't, Millie, he has been so unbelievably good to me.'

They crept in so as not to wake the two others from the company who had been billeted with them.

'Teasing is good for him,' whispered Millie, 'but honestly, Sally, I will never forget his face when he thought he was going to be forced to wear ballet tights.'

They were stifling their laughter as they fell asleep.

There was no conversation at all next morning; there was either absolute silence or an occasional surly grunt. Only the military personnel, scrubbed and polished and perfectly dressed, moved around smiling happily as they served a breakfast of porridge, some type of heavy rye bread and scalding cups of tea that Millie swore she could dance on without sinking.

But at last they were packed and once more climbing into the huge military vehicles, finding the first available seat and sitting down, closing their eyes and going back to sleep.

Sebastian's low voice woke Sally. 'He kissed you. Is he in the habit of kissing people he scarcely knows?'

Sally rubbed her eyes like a child. 'For heaven's sake, Sebastian, I hardly got a wink of sleep all night. Two of those hoofers snore like you wouldn't believe. I was up rolling them over every hour on the hour.'

He hung his head, 'Sorry, Sally, you're right; it's absolutely none of my business. I just thought that as we're friends, you might tell me that you're involved.'

'Involved? I know him as Jon, Just Jon. Stop looming over me. Sit down on the floor and I'll tell you...'

'That he means nothing to you?'

'To tell you about how we met. In fact, I've only ever met him twice,' she said, and she was now as annoyed as Sebastian. Why should he feel he had the right to ask about her private life? But then Jon's voice asking her to write to him came into her head and she wondered if Sebastian, who was her friend, her adviser, her saviour, deserved the truth.

'Do you remember when we met?'

'How could I not?'

'The blue cloak.'

'He gave it to you?' He hesitated before saying, 'You looked wonderful in it.' As always, Sebastian's innate kindness took control and he tried to praise her.

'Oh, Sebastian, how could he give me such an expensive gift? First of all, I had never met him at

173

that point, and secondly, my father would have been livid. No, I bought it in a second-hand clothes shop. This damn war has them opening up all over the place. If you'll stop interrupting I'll tell you the story.'

When she was finished he looked at her, his expression a mixture of affection, pride, understanding.

'And where's this fabulous ring?'

'In the safe at the cinema.'

'Good God, Sally, if it's at all valuable, put it in a bank vault. I don't actually know what guarantees they give these days with regard to arson, bombing, etcetera but it's bound to be better than the local picture house.'

'I'll discuss it when I have a chance to get home. To be honest, I very rarely think of it.'

'You told me you had promised to write to him. Rather difficult if you don't know who he is.'

Sally stood up. 'Are you calling me a liar or do you think I'm stupid?'

In an instant he was on his knees beside her, one hand capturing a dark strand of shining hair and winding it round his finger. 'Of course not; merely jealous as hell.' He sat down again and seemed to make a conscious effort to cheer up. 'I'm lucky enough to see you every day. Of course you must write, but a letter addressed just to John ... John who?'

'Sebastian, naturally he introduced himself when we met.'

'And you did ask the name of his ship?'

A beaming smile lit up Sally's face and she decided to tease him. 'No, I didn't ask the name of the ship, but it's all right because he gave me a little card with the details and he said something like, "This is my military address and letters should reach me." How super, I'll tell him about you in your new role in the ballet.'

'Thank you, but I can survive adequately without the publicity, and you are still avoiding telling me his name.'

'It's Jonathon Galbraith, but I think of him as Jon. I'll show you the card when we reach our next base.'

'But surely it's in your purse?'

'Yes,' she whispered, 'but in case you haven't noticed, it's dark, and no, don't look longingly at the flaps. Everyone in the path of a blast of cold air will want to throw you out onto the road.'

Knowing this to be only too true, Sebastian sat down again on the inhospitable floor and eventually fell asleep, his head against Sally's knee. She looked down at him with sincere affection. Because of him she was living as she had only ever dreamed about.

Her home was an expensive London flat with a delightful man who seemed to ask nothing of her. She paid a token rent, a few shillings less each week than she had paid in the boarding house. Sebastian was the kind of man her father would term 'salt of the earth'. I can't take, take, take forever, Sally decided. He's been different lately, very careful not to be too close. She laid her hand on his head and he sighed in his sleep. Why could she not feel again the overwhelming need and desire that she had felt the night the boarding house had been blitzed, nothing left but rubble and some exhausted broken Michaelmas daisies? She had clung to Sebastian, ready to do anything. But he had behaved like the perfect gentleman he was.

Although she had thought then that their relationship might develop, she soon found that her feelings for Sebastian had changed, and Sebastian was wise enough to see that.

Why had they changed? Was it Jon?

He was kind, he was handsome but he was still as far as she knew, a married man. More importantly he was not someone with whom her parents would feel at ease. They might just have coped with Sebastian, for to them he was merely another actor – she stroked his dark hair as she looked down at him – but Jon? No, it would not do. She would write, as a friend, to a friend in the navy who must be anxious for news from home. In a month or two, he would be too busy, overwhelmed with letters from his family and friends, and he would forget her.

She would keep the cloak and possibly even the ring, but she would never wear either, locking them away somewhere so that nothing could ever remind her of him.

She knew that Sebastian would not forget that she had Jon's card and when they arrived in Southampton she did not wait for him to ask to see it. He deserved that much.

'Look, Sebastian, here's Jon's card. He's a lieutenant-commander, whatever that means.'

Sebastian, sitting at a table in the Officers'

Mess, took the little rectangle and looked at it. *Lieutenant-Commander Jonathon Galbraith, RN.* The name of his ship, *George Francis,* was in the bottom left corner, but of course that gave no indication of the ship's whereabouts.

'How do letters get to him, Sebastian? My friend Daisy's brother is in the navy and it takes weeks, even months, to get letters to him or from him. They have nothing for weeks and then two or three arrive on the same day.'

'Probably that will be the same for your Jon. No difference in mail pick-ups for the ranks.' He looked at the card again, even turning it over to see if anything was written on the other side. 'Very modest, but possibly that's naval etiquette.'

'What do you mean, etiquette?'

'Are you telling me you really don't know who he is or his family?'

'I told you I only met him that one time in the shop and then at the naval base.'

Sebastian looked at her. After a moment he smiled. 'He could have written, "Family owns half of Kent and a place up in Scotland." I suppose it could be called a farm. It could be seen as boasting, writing that on your address card.'

'Are you telling me the truth?'

'As I know it, darling. Blame it all on Queen Victoria. She bought a castle in Scotland and, lo and behold, any English family with a bit of money bought a wee *placie* too.'

'Did yours?'

'Good Lord, no. Great Grandpapa liked the sun. I hear it never stops raining in Bonnie Scotland. We stayed in Ceylon. Explains why I'm

177

fussy about my tea. You called him "Just Jon", Sally. Why was that?'

'The nice lady in the shop was saying his name and he interrupted and said, "Jon, just Jon."'

'I like your Just Jon, Sal.' Sebastian took a deep breath and decided he was on a hiding to nothing if he didn't face up to reality now. 'You have Uncle Sebastian's blessing,' he said, adopting an Oscar-winning magnanimous smile.

She looked at him sternly. 'Are you hiding something from me, Sebastian? I do know he's married – I bet that surprised you – and I now know that he lives in the Dartford area. With an accent like his, and jewellery like the ring, he has to be one of the families who have their tea delivered by Petrie's Fine Teas.'

'Your friends?'

'Yes.'

'After the war I shall demand that they deliver my tea too.'

Did he ever take anything seriously? She turned her back on him. 'I'm going to write a letter.'

He smiled and Sally could only smile back. His smile would melt ice.

'Say hello from me,' he called, and she walked out, slamming the door behind her. A table, a piece of paper and a pen. Sally sat in the billet she was sharing with three others. How to begin?

Hello, Jon,

I wonder where you are. I have seen more of England since I joined ENSA than I have ever seen before, although my family did go to the Empire Exhibition in Glasgow. I know that's in Scotland but it's Britain as well, isn't it?

If you do get this and if you do want to reply, it would probably be better to send a letter to me at the Theatre Royal, Drury Lane, although I think the postal address is Catherine Street. I was living in a theatrical boarding house but it got a direct hit one night. I was lucky because I had taken shelter when the raid started. For the present I'm staying with a friend but...

She could not explain. If she did Jon might think badly of her or would he be male and practical and say, 'Very sensible.' Her father, she was sure, would be very male and a very angry father at the same time. 'How could you, Sally? Get the first train home today or I'll come up and fetch you.' She could just imagine it.

She got up and looked at herself in the mirror and knew exactly what Max would think of her tired pale face. What had caused those great dark circles under her eyes?

She had not lied but neither had she told the truth about her living arrangements. She would, one day, have to tell her parents the whole truth, but if she found lodgings quickly, she could give everyone her new address with a clear conscience.

Happier, she finished the quick note.

...I'm looking for somewhere else.

They're calling me to rehearsal. I'll tell you all about the programme next time I write.

How should she finish it? Love, Sally. No, far too forward. She hardly knew him.

Hope all is well,
  Sally

There, that was perfect.

EIGHT

City followed city, one church hall looked remarkably like another church hall, one hospital ward more or less like any other. As summer followed spring and then the wind began to hint of autumn and winter, it seemed to Sally that overcrowded hospital wards were filling with more and more injured military personnel or civilian casualties of the raids. Injured children were especially difficult to entertain, not because they were a bad audience but because Sally's heart went out to each and every one. She wanted to somehow 'make it better', as her mother had used to do with a warm hug whenever she had hurt herself as a small child – and she saw that she could not.

'This is obscene,' she yelled at Sebastian who, with his long legs stretched out on an ottoman, was trying to catch up with the newspapers. He longed for detailed accounts of cricket matches but instead read of 'Food Facts for the Kitchen Front' or horrors perpetrated in country after country.

'Humph's latest bawdy ideas of humour, Sal?' He knew perfectly well that she had grown up

180

enough to let the company's comedian's desperate vulgarity sail over her head but he hoped – and failed – to make her laugh.

She stood there before him like Lady Macbeth ringing her hands. 'This bloody war,' she shouted and he winced, never having heard her use the word before. 'What kind of creature thinks up these atrocities? There were maimed babies in that ward today, Sebastian – babies, blinded, deafened? What type of human being is relaxing at home tonight, satisfied with what he's done? And what good did we do? Catching a glimpse of my neckline does nothing for a baby.'

He stood up and pulled her, struggling, against him. 'Stop it, Sally, I haven't even begun to try to hold you still.' He waited until she calmed, rested her head on his chest and began to weep. 'You must believe in what we're doing or leave us. Nursing...?'

'I tried a first-aid course once. I can't even put on a bandage.'

'Thank you for telling me. Should I need it, I'll be sure to seek aid elsewhere, but, Sally, my dear, dear girl, your smile helps, because even babies know you mean it. And no, you're not Vera Lynn but those babies loved your lullabies. A soothing hand, a quiet lullaby; they're reassuring, really they are, and it's the same for the men. Hold a chap's hand, smooth his hair out of his eyes, smile directly at him, no matter how disfigured he is. That's really hard. Even we supposedly big, strong chaps find that hard. Sometimes just being there is enough. You wait and see, when you're famous all over the world the exhausted postman

181

will be struggling up your stairs with fan mail and lots of them will say things like, "You've no idea how special having my hand held by a beautiful girl made me feel." They'll be telling their children they knew you before you were famous. Even the dashing Lieutenant-Commander Jon will be claiming friendship – or more. How's the mail between London and "somewhere at sea"?'

'No idea.'

'Poor girl. Keep writing to him, Sally. I'm absolutely sure he's writing to you.'

Heartened, she smiled at him. 'I don't deserve you as a friend, Sebastian.'

Did he look at her rather sadly? 'Silly Sally,' he said, 'we'll be friends for ever.'

Her heart swelled with love, affection, appreciation – she didn't know quite what, perhaps all three – but she remained close to him. He kissed the top of her head and held her away from him. 'It is an absolutely despicable fact, Sally Brewer, but if one has money in this city, even with a war on, one can get anything. Come along, find something pretty to wear and we'll dance the night away at the Savoy or the Waldorf.' He assumed an affected voice. 'Choose, Flavia, choose.' It was a line from a skit he'd seen once and had used several times, each time successfully.

Sally was unused to dancing the night away at exorbitantly expensive hotels and she had never heard of the Waldorf, but the Savoy had featured in films she had watched over and over again.

'Which is your grandmother's favourite?'

'No idea, but she had her coming-out dance at the Savoy, and so the Savoy it will be. Actually

I'm glad you chose it; they have a superb dance orchestra. Go, Cinderella.'

Sally ran. To wear, to wear? What was good enough for the Savoy? And then she pulled open her hardly unpacked suitcase, which served as a wardrobe, and removed her favourite lilac dress that should, by rights, have been hanging in the costume wardrobe at the theatre.

'Oh, please, don't let me spill anything on it or have some great clod-pole of a man stand on the hem,' she begged, but there was no answer. She was content with hoping that the question had been heard.

'Bring your gas mask, Sally, in case the wardens stop us.'

'Stop us?'

'You can't walk to the Savoy. My car is in a garage a few streets away. With any luck it will start. God knows when I last used it. I'll ring our "jack-of-all-trades" while you finish primping.'

'I'd forgotten you had a car; actually I was never sure it was yours.'

'It wasn't. It was Grandmamma's, saving young ladies from cads and bounders for the use of.'

'Something terribly wrong with that sentence.'

'I know but I'd much rather you didn't try to correct it. Fearfully boring, lessons in grammar as one drives to the Savoy.'

'If the car starts.'

Nothing happened when Sebastian tried. He tried again and then help came from the garage attendant. 'I'll give her a good old crank, Mr Brady, and you coax her gently and don't run over me.'

183

The 'good old crank' was administered, the engine hiccuped into life and the attendant jumped to the side.

'Thanks, Dmitri, you are a prince among men,' called Sebastian. 'And he could be,' he said in an aside to Sally. 'Came over in the Russian Revolution, highly educated, speaks about seven languages and is a wizard with numbers. Checks all my accounts for me; finds mistakes all the time.'

'Someone's stealing from you? How awful.'

Sebastian laughed. 'No, if anything I'm stealing from me. He says I'm always in too much of a hurry and I don't take enough care. I've tried to get him a better job but he says he's perfectly content. Actually, I think he's writing a book, *The Orloff Family History* or *The Truth about the Russian Revolution;* neither would surprise me. I gave him a type-writing machine last Christmas. He wept buckets. Russians are so emotional. Good, here we are. No, don't get out. We'll go straight to the door and the staff will park her.'

A few minutes later Sally, feeling like a princess, was walking up the Savoy's beautiful staircase, breathing in the scents of pots and vases of exotic plants and flowers. When they reached the restaurant a table was found almost immediately. Sally was stunned but excited and the tiniest bit guilty. The world was at war and she, like every other woman in the crowded room, was beautifully dressed.

'Champagne?' asked Sebastian, and, trembling with excitement, Sally nodded. The wine waiter and Sebastian had a discussion that she did not understand at all and then the waiter left.

'Let's dance while he's digging it out, Sally, and then you'll have to decide what you'd like to eat. Their smoked salmon is delicious. I hear it comes down from Scotland – how, I don't know.'

'Swims,' she suggested, and he laughed.

He took her arm and led her out onto the floor, which was already crowded with couples of all ages and all nationalities. Not for the first time, Sally wished she had studied harder at school. She was almost sure that she heard a couple speaking French but they were speaking much more quickly than her French teacher had spoken and a one-day trip to Calais had done nothing for the learning process. Just then two beautifully dressed couples took to the floor at the same time and, for the moment, the language question flew right out of her head.

'Sebastian, don't look, but is the man beside us – no, don't look, he'll see you looking – is he someone I know?'

'How can I tell if you don't let me look, Sally? But yes, he is; he's in the Cabinet and the woman with him is the wife of some ancient baronet. Sally, stop trying to lead. The place is full of famous faces, or should I say infamous faces? There are very important meetings and discussions going on as well as rich people out to enjoy themselves. The difficulty is to differentiate between them. That rather smartly dressed woman is an American journalist and the man with her is with the BBC. You'll have seen both of them on Pathé News. Wouldn't it be fun to eavesdrop but alas the powers that be would not approve. That beauty at the best table is Vivien Leigh, you'll know, of course, and I expect you've noticed Clementine Churchill talking earnestly to that dull-looking man. I gather Mrs Churchill is a tireless woman – and she needs to be. And over there, among the *jeunesse dorée,* I do believe there are at least three Mitford sisters.'

Sally was almost quivering with excitement. Part of her was saying, 'I can't believe I'm here with all these people,' and another part was saying, like Sebastian's grandmother, 'Your mother would not approve.'

'I won't let it go to my head, Sebastian, but I think I know how Cinderella felt at the ball.'

He squeezed her tightly for a heartbeat. 'Is it a happy feeling, Sally?'

'Definitely.'

'Good, let's go. I want food.'

'Are there foreigners on the dance floor?' she asked as they stopped dancing and made their slow way back to their table, threading their way through tables where elegant couples sat, crystal glasses to hand. Without exception, the women were dressed in glorious gowns; their necks and arms glittering with jewels, and delicate but more often cloying perfumes hanging in the air around them.

'Apart from Americans? London's full of foreigners: dignitaries, politicians, diplomats. Why do you ask? You don't object, do you?'

'Don't be silly. I was trying to recognise languages.'

'Now, as for me, I was too busy coping with trying to find out who people were and who they were with – and all without looking at them, plus dealing with fancy footwork.'

'Mine or yours?'

He laughed again as the sommelier appeared to open the champagne. When he had poured the first two glasses and wished them a happy evening he went off to his next table and Sally sipped.

'Good?'

'Incredible.'

'I know that only the few idle rich can afford these prices but believe me, Sally, the luxury hotels are very important to the war effort. Many of those people on the dance floor are here for important discussions. They don't sip champagne all night every night and their dining out usually has real purpose. As a general rule, it's the hosted who are important, not the hosts.'

He changed the subject after they had ordered a light meal of smoked salmon and smoked duck, which they shared. 'Were Grandmamma here she would be glaring at some of those overdressed women; not glaring exactly – because glaring is rude – but her displeasure would be palpable.'

'Why? I've never seen anything like this before. Some of the jewels must be priceless.'

'Exactly, and according to the ladies wearing them, each piece once belonged to the late, lamented Marie Antoinette. Why anyone would think such provenance is something to lie about, I cannot imagine, but then I am a mere man. But back to Grandmamma who often told me that, as she was being prepared for her formal presentation to the King – not this one – her own grandmother told her that before leaving the house for an engagement a lady should examine herself in a mirror, back and front, and remove something; a bracelet, a flower.'

'I'm sure your grandmother was always perfectly dressed.'

'I agree but look at the rather large lady in the purple satin.'

Sally looked. 'Her jewels are fabulous.'

'Too much. Reminds me of a rather vulgar Christmas tree, pre-war, of course. Dangle, dangle, dangle and even more glitter.'

'Oh, you are in a snippy mood, and a tree can't be vulgar; that's a people thing. All I can think of is that I've had real champagne and, would you believe, I have most definitely developed a taste for smoked duck. My mother will be surprised.'

'Not so much as your developing love affair with the finest of French champagnes; now that *will* surprise her. Let's dance off some of your *joie de* bubbles.'

No one wanted to sit out while Carroll Gibbons and his Savoy Hotel Orpheans were playing. Sally stood up. Conscious that people were looking at her, she walked gracefully with Sebastian to the dance floor. Her silken skirts swirled, then settled themselves around her, and she smiled, wondering if the admiration or envy in some eyes would still be there if it became known that the dress was borrowed – and without permission. Sebastian held her close, enjoying the dance, for she now moved effortlessly; the former 'fairy guard' who had not been allowed to dance was now the belle of the ball.

Champagne continued to flow, and everyone

who had been able to find a place on the crowded floor was creating memories as they moved to one of the world's greatest dance bands. War was raging all over the world, bringing misery, death and destruction to countless numbers of people and yet, here in this English bubble of perfection, music was playing, and no one was hungry or thirsty. Fear had to be there, though, hadn't it?

'This has to be a dream,' decided Sally as once more she allowed Sebastian to guide her round the ballroom in a foxtrot. She was living a dream. She closed her eyes and allowed the sounds, the scents and the atmosphere to soak into her. She was drifting away when Sebastian's voice brought her right back to the present.

'I'm so devastating that you're falling asleep – and at the Savoy, of all places. Really, Sally, one only sleeps here if one is inebriated or if one has booked into a vastly expensive bedroom, and you, my darling, are neither drunk nor in bed. Mind you, there are air-raid shelters here, complete with beds and maid service. I'm sure you won't wish an air raid on us and so, Cinderella, let's be on our way.'

They picked up Sally's evening purse, which she had left on the table and were moving through the still-crowded tables towards the doors when a voice stopped them.

'Do forgive me, Mr Brady, Miss Brewer, my name is Cedric Arnold – ah, I see you recognise it,' he said looking at Sebastian. 'Could I prevail on you to sit with me a while? I have a proposition for Miss Brewer, not that I wouldn't be interested in your *après la guerre* career if you're not still with

189

the West End wolf, Mr Brady.'

Sebastian held out his hand. 'Behold big tooth marks, Mr Arnold. I'm sure Miss Brewer would be happy to talk with you but perhaps not tonight as we have three shows tomorrow.' He turned to Sally. 'Sally, darling, Mr Arnold is a very success-ful theatrical agent and he's obviously interested in representing you.' He looked at the agent for confirmation.

'Absolutely. I see at least two other agents look-ing rather cross that I seem to have approached Miss Brewer before them – I've been waiting all evening for the opportune moment. May I sug-gest that I ring you tomorrow, or better still that you ring me at a convenient time, to set up a meeting?' He took a card from the breast pocket of his cream silk waistcoat and handed it to Sally. 'Until tomorrow,' he said.

Having no experience of theatrical agents, Sally looked at Sebastian for guidance.

'If there's a moment between rehearsals, I'm sure Max will allow a telephone call, Mr Arnold,' Sebastian said.

'Max? Not *the* Max?'

Sebastian nodded. 'Yes, Max, the great white Hunter.'

'How droll. I'll concede that the great Maxi-milian discovered this enchanting creature...' he turned to Sally, 'but even he will agree that such talent needs the best agent.'

'I'm representing her for now, and will see that she has time to make some calls tomorrow.'

'Calls? Plural?'

'But of course. You did say you saw other circling

sharks. Good night, Cedric.'

He cupped Sally's elbow in his hand and walked with her out of the room.

'What did you mean – representing me, Sebastian?'

'Nothing. Arnold's good and he represents some famous names.' He rattled off several that Sally had seen in films. 'But if he thinks others are anxious to have you on their books ... well, simply, he'll cut you a better deal.'

'Wow, Sebastian, everything is happening too quickly.'

Sebastian stopped. 'Sally, you are the only person in the world who calls me Sebastian. Why? Seb's fine.'

'I've never known anyone called Sebastian before and I think it's a lovely name.'

'Even when you've only had cocoa?'

'Even then.'

'Then you may continue and, yes, things do have a habit of staying dormant for far too long and then jumping up. I believe you'll be all right with ENSA. I may be wrong but I doubt that even Arnold could get you more money or more time off at this moment. When the war is over – that's a different story.'

'I've already had a raise. I got £4 a week last year and this year...'

'No one's business but yours, darling. I'm delighted your worth has been recognised, and talking about agents reminded me of something I wanted to discuss with you.'

'Can't it wait till tomorrow?'

He helped her drape the beautiful fur around

her shoulders. 'In the summer you must bring up the blue cloak. Devastating, but perhaps better with white.'

She said nothing and so they waited silently until his car had been brought round.

'Thank you, Sebastian. I can't wait to write to all my friends and tell them that I dined at the Savoy; they'll be thrilled for me.'

The uniformed doorman held the passenger door open for her and she slid across the seat. 'I've just remembered something. Daisy, probably my best friend, well, I'm sure Mum said in a letter something about plans for her to stay with someone she met in the WAAF. They were going to a play and then her dad was taking them to the Savoy or maybe it was the Ritz. Oh, wouldn't it have been fun if we'd been here when Daisy was? I mean, perhaps we could all have had lunch. You'd like Daisy; everybody does.'

'Sally, darling, if she's the teeniest bit like you I will adore her, but for now, could you please stop talking. I'm worried that your vocal chords will wear out. Happens, you know.'

She stopped immediately and, almost instantly, fell asleep.

Dmitri, still awake in the parking lot, found the situation extremely amusing. Sebastian was calculating how much strength he would require not only to carry the tall slender Sally wearing a fur coat that weighed twice what she did all the way to the Mansion, but also to get her up three flights of stairs. 'I carry her to the Mansion, Mr Brady. Then you carry upstairs and I keep closed my eyes.'

'Very funny, but I would be grateful.'

The Russian picked Sally up as if she weighed no more than a small child and set off, Sebastian beside them wondering if it would have been better for the men's roles to be reversed. Dmitri was obviously extremely fit and his chore should have been the stairs. Luckily, Dmitri did the stairs as well.

Sally slept through the entire proceedings and never did discover that a man who might have been a deposed Russian prince had carried her, not only from the car to the flats, but also up three flights of stairs, before laying her down on her bed as gently as if she was a baby. Instead, next morning, she apologised to Sebastian, who waved her thanks aside.

'Let's get to work,' he said, 'and, next time, remind me to feed you *before* I ply you with alcoholic beverages to which you are not accustomed.'

Sally buried her head back into the pillow. 'Was I drunk?' The words could hardly be heard.

'Not what I would call drunk, Sally, and it was my fault; you drank two glasses of champagne very quickly and on a very empty stomach. The fault was mine,' he repeated, 'I should have taken better care of you. It won't happen again.'

She sat up and noticed that thankfully she was still wearing the evening gown. Very carefully she climbed off the bed. 'Please go away, Sebastian.'

'Water's better than warm,' he said, and went off to see if he had enough coffee to make her a cup.

He did, and by the time they set off to the theatre she was feeling much better.

'Did anything happen last night?'

'I can't believe you're asking me that.'

She had no idea what he meant and then realisation dawned and she smiled. 'I'd trust you anywhere, Sebastian Brady. I meant, maybe it didn't happen, the agent person.'

'Oh, yes, your first encounter and it won't be the last. Arnold is good, don't know if you remember that I told you that.'

'Course I do,' she answered vaguely. 'I'm supposed to ring him.'

'Sally Brewer, you sound as if you've just been sentenced to eleven years before the mast. You're an actress, or will be when Max and the others have finished with you; you're also rather lovely. One of the best known agents in the business has shown an interest. Ring him but, to be frank, I wouldn't sign a contract with anyone at the moment unless you're thinking of leaving ENSA.'

She looked at him as if he had lost his mind. 'Leaving ENSA? Why would I do that?'

'It's possible that an agent could get you a better paying job, even a film role. Whoever your agent is, Sally, he or she will be entitled to a percentage of your earnings, ten per cent, possibly even twenty. Twenty per cent of nothing isn't much, and you'll earn nothing with ENSA – except a world-wide reputation. And, bear in mind that coaches like Sybil, Lal and Max don't come cheap and they're coaching you out of nothing but a belief in your ability and in ENSA's motives. Talk to Max.'

But Max was always busy and the days went by.

Sally wrote to Jon.

Did you get my letter? I hope so. A friend Sebastian Brady took me to the Savoy and it was such fun. They have such a good band or should I say orchestra? They're called Orpheans, and no, I haven't got the spelling wrong. Haven't a clue what it means. Perhaps you have heard them and know. They do play on the wireless sometimes. Some of the actors around me, like Sebastian, have been to university. Sometimes I think my parents were right and I should have gone to university but Sebastian says, 'All knowledge is there in books, read,' and I do read when I'm backstage and have a minute. I'm reading plays, of course, but I do enjoy a good murder.

She stopped and reread what she had written and she wondered if the whole letter was too frivolous? Murder stories? Would a man like Jon, an officer in the Royal Navy, read stories?

Sally took a deep breath and decided to finish the letter. He would either answer or he would not.

At the Savoy, a theatrical agent stopped me and asked me to ring him. He's interested in representing me.

Quite exciting really, but I don't know. I don't need an agent while I'm working with ENSA. I'll ring him and tell you the result in my next letter.

Sally

If there was a next letter, she thought as she made her way to Max's office to see if he was available and, if he was not, if she could use the telephone.

Max was not there but Sybil and Lalita were

sitting together at his desk, piles of documents before them. Sally explained what she wanted.

'Use the telephone – we'll pretend it's an emergency – but don't take too long. It hasn't stopped ringing all day and these–' Sybil indicated the neat piles of papers – 'are applications for positions that we just don't have at the moment. All require reading and answering.' They bent their well-groomed heads over their papers and began to read.

Sally watched them for a moment. Many, perhaps all of those applications were from qualified, possibly highly experienced artistes. She picked up the telephone and dialled Cedric Arnold's number.

'Mr Arnold, I'm very grateful for your interest but I'm not ready to work with an agent. Thank you very much but, at the moment, I prefer to work with ENSA. Perhaps when this war is over...'

She hung up just as he was getting into full stride. Had she ruined her career for ever? And then she realised that, really, she did not want to work with Cedric Arnold. He reminded her – very slightly but enough – of Elliott Staines.

She was about to close the door behind her on her way out when Lalita pulled it open again. 'Sorry, Sally, but we found this letter under a pile of these damned applications; only came in the last few days, though, otherwise we'd have seen it.'

Sally almost grabbed the slight envelope. Only one person in the world would write to her at the theatre. 'Thanks, Lal, no problem, thanks,' and, clutching the letter to her, she sought refuge and privacy in the ladies' lavatory.

She locked herself in the cubicle and opened the envelope.

Dear Sally,

How lovely to receive a letter from you. Most of the letters I receive these days are from lawyers. Lawyers don't make jokes in letters. I thought once about becoming a lawyer, more than once really, but I inherited property when I was very young and had I been a lawyer, I would have been writing letters about roofs, and drainage, and yields et cetera to myself.

I love sailing and I love the navy. Would be perfect if we weren't at war but I joined the navy straight from university and have had some glorious times, so can't complain.

I take it you always wanted to be an actress, or is your career an accident of war? Too many of the young men sailing with me are only here by accident. It was the same before the war – perhaps they joined the navy instead of going down the mines or working on a farm – but there were compensations. Once, when I was a very junior officer, we sailed through a school of whales, and what a joy it was to watch the sailors' faces as those enormous creatures seemed to play games for our enjoyment. Now we watch for mines instead of whales.

Enough of that. Tell me which plays you like, what parts you've played and what parts you would like to play. We have quite a collection of books on board and perhaps I'll be able to read the plays and talk about them with you.

PLEASE write again,
Jon

197

I will, I will, oh, dear Jon, I will. She reread the letter several times. It saddened her that Jon had talked of 'young men' as if he himself were old, but she remembered his face, his smile, his thick dark hair. He was older than she was, she knew that, but he seemed more of a contemporary than an older man. Sebastian was older and yet seemed younger at times. Was it responsibilities and duties that made one old? Jon was married, too. Was his wife writing to him? Oh, she did not like to think of that, and she certainly couldn't ask him.

Still sitting, she heard the main door open and a voice call, 'Sally, are you in there? We have work to do.'

It was Sebastian.

'This is the ladies' room, Sebastian. Go away. I'll be there in a moment.'

And since she only had to unlock the door and walk out, she was.

NINE

Jon's ship was torpedoed as it approached Gibraltar. It sank in minutes with what at first was termed a complete loss of life; crew and soldiers on their way to a battlefield that none of them would ever reach. The cruel sea around the sinking ship was full of dead and dying men. Soon telegrams were being sent to every corner of the British Isles and mourning families read the chilling words 'Missing, presumed dead'. Sally, of course, did not receive a telegram and so she continued to write her short letters and waited, trying hard to be patient, for another letter.

It was Sebastian who eventually told her of the disaster. He had read of the tragedy in *The Times* but, seeing Sally's lovely face smiling happily across a room, for a few days he had been unable to say anything and, of course, no one else knew of her relationship with a British sailor.

Watching her writing her letters, her paper propped up by a book on her knees, her face relaxed always into a gentle smile, Sebastian fought for courage. The bad news had to come from him and it had to be before she saw or heard something. A friend or a member of her family might make a passing remark in a letter – 'Shame about the sinking of the *George Francis*. Some fellow from Dartford was on it, a Lord Hedges.' Oh, no, he could not allow that to happen.

First he told Millie, who had suffered as Sally would suffer. A woman, he had decided, would be better able to comfort her.

'You tell her, Seb. Dear God, I had no idea, too wrapped up in my own misery, I suppose. You tell her and I'll be there to help you hold her.'

But Sally did not fall apart. She listened quietly to Sebastian as he told her one Sunday at the flat, and then she stood up and said with great dignity, 'Thank you. I need to be alone now.'

They expected her to go to her bedroom but she walked to the front door, lifted down what she always called 'Lal's coat', slipped it on and

199

went out.

'Go to the window, Seb, quickly, and see which way she goes,' Millie urged. 'We need to follow her.'

'She won't do anything silly,' he said as he came back into the hall. 'She won't.'

'Come on,' she handed him his coat – she was already dressed for outdoors – 'the shock she's just had, she wouldn't notice if a plane landed in front of her.'

For almost three hours they followed Sally as she walked and walked and walked, staying just that much behind so that they could keep her in sight, hoping that she would not turn her head to look behind her.

She did not and eventually she stopped. She stood on the edge of the pavement and stayed there. Sebastian, aware of the constant flow of London traffic, was terrified that she intended to throw herself in front of something but Millie thought differently.

'I think she's just realised that she has no idea where she is; she's little girl lost, Seb. I think maybe we can coax her to come home. You go, just take her hand and see what she does.'

He was full of doubt, but he did as Millie suggested.

'Sally, Sally, my dearest girl.'

She did not try to pull her hand away. Instead she said, very quietly, 'He's dead, Sebastian. Just Jon is dead.' He dared to pull her into his arms away from the traffic and she put her head against him. 'I love your cashmere coat,' she said.

'Let's go home, Sally. Millie's here and we could

have tea together.'

Sally walked between them like an automaton, saying nothing and neither did they speak. Seb knew a quicker way to return to his flat and so they did not take nearly so long to get back.

'What now?' Sebastian was at a loss as Sally stood still in the hall, not even moving to take off the heavy coat.

'Sally, I think you should have a little nap,' suggested Millie, although it was already almost nine thirty. Since Sally said nothing, Millie took control and propelled her to the room Sebastian indicated.

Less than half an hour later, Millie returned. 'She's out like a light, Seb, or perhaps she's pretending so as to get rid of me. I got her undressed and into a nightie but, speaking from experience, she'll probably be awake all night, maybe till she cries herself to sleep.'

'Should I do something – get her a drink, make her some tea?'

'Leave her alone, Seb. She'll let you know if she needs you.' Millie picked up her coat. 'No, you need to stay here,' she said as Sebastian protested that he could not allow her to walk through London so late in the evening. 'I'll be fine, Seb; my legs are lethal weapons.' She tried to smile. 'Get some sleep, if you can, and I'll see you both in the morning.'

Whether or not Sally had slept or stayed awake was never found out. Next morning, Sebastian found her, fully dressed, in the kitchen, attempting to grill three slices of bacon. It was the enticing smell that had woken him.

'Sally...' he began, but she held up her left hand, the right being busy with the grill, and said, 'Slice the bread, Sebastian; one slice is enough for me.'

He understood the unexpressed order and never mentioned Jon unless Sally mentioned him first. It was some time before she did.

Over the next few months Sally often smiled at memories of her young self – what a great tragedienne she had been, all wasted on her family and friends probably because there had been, she was glad to admit, no tragedies to grieve over. After all, a broken fingernail or a snagged stocking was less than nothing when compared with death and destruction.

Now loss was real and Sally's mind and heart refused to believe it. She was, she told herself, a member of ENSA – and therefore she had work to do. She did it. But when night fell and she was able to escape from Sebastian's concerned cosseting she lay on her bed, too tired to wash, too lethargic even to undress and put on a nightgown, and the tears came. Eventually she would fall into an exhausted sleep.

Sebastian, Millie, and others who cared about her, saw that she did not eat but seemed to survive on cups of tea. Sebastian bought champagne and she looked at him as if she believed that he had lost his mind.

'A celebration, Sebastian?'

'Good God, no, dear girl. Champagne is known to be a restorative. You're losing weight, Sally. Sybil and Lal are concerned. Max has been asking them if they think you're coping.'

'Of course I'm coping. That's what women do.

We cope.'

'Please, eat something, a little soup. I have a fresh egg. I'll scramble it for you or how about a soft-boiled egg with toast soldiers?'

'I am eating; I'm perfectly well.'

He kneeled down on the carpet beside her chair in what he called the drawing room, and looked up into her pale, drawn face. 'Sally, your uniform is hanging on you. Your lovely face has no colour, not even your lips, and your beautiful eyes are...' He had been about to say 'dead' but quickly managed to change that to, '...have lost their sparkle. ENSA performers need to sparkle, Sally.'

'I have some eye drops.'

'The real, natural, beautiful Sally is the girl the servicemen queue to see. Perhaps you should take a few days off, and I'm sure I have enough petrol to drive you down to stay with your parents.'

The reference to her parents distressed her. 'No, I'm perfectly well. I don't want my parents to see me like '

He stood up, walked across to the telephone table and picked up the receiver. 'I'm going to ring your vicar, Mr Tiverton.'

He got no further. A trembling Sally was at his side. 'No, please, Sebastian. I'll do it, damn it; I'll eat your stupid egg but I'm perfectly well, perfectly well,' and she burst into tears and fell into his arms.

He held her, patting her back as if she were a child. 'There, there, it'll be all right, Sally. Soft-boiled egg, then?' He held her away from him and heard a slight giggle.

'Anything's better than your scrambled eggs.'

'That's my girl.'

She ate slowly, stopping occasionally as if to swallow was difficult. Sebastian watched her and when she had finished the egg and a little of the toast he said, 'And now a hot bath, a clean nightie and sleep. Can you do that on your own?'

Sally slipped into the almost hot bath and in doing so, saw her body properly for the first time since the news of the sinking. 'You're scrawny, Sally,' she told herself, 'just skin and bone.' She closed her eyes and stayed quietly, letting the scented water lap around her. *Did you slip under, Jon? Was it gentle? No, you fought, didn't you? I could slip under, I would, but there's Sebastian. Hardly a decent way to say thank you. Oh, please God, Jon has to be alive. I will not give up. I will not.*

She got out, dried herself and put on pyjamas and her pink dressing gown. She cleaned the bath and hung up the towels to dry and then she went to find Sebastian. He was in the kitchen, listening to the wireless.

'I'm sorry, Sebastian,' she said, taking his hand and squeezing it. 'I don't deserve you.'

Over the next days, weeks, months, some good news was broadcast. It appeared that an unknown number of survivors – many of them badly injured – had been picked up by other ships in the area: an American aircraft carrier, a British destroyer, a German U-boat and two supposedly uninvolved fishing boats about which no details were given.

'Who cares which flag they're flying?' Sally cried – her words probably repeated by grieving women all over England, 'just so long as they ferry the men to safety.' But no news reached her that Jon was among the rescued, and she continued to grieve, knowing it was unrealistic to raise her hopes and unbearable that they should be dashed.

A Dartford paper had printed a small piece on the tragedy. That was when Sally found out what Sebastian had successfully hidden from her: Jon's full name and title.

The paper reported that Lieutenant-Commander Jonathon Erskine Galbraith, Lord Hedges, was missing after the sinking of the *George Francis*.

Sally, tears streaming down her cheeks, read the the cutting, which her mother had sent her. A casual picture of Jon at a cricket match was published to illustrate it. Sally looked at it for some time and decided that it was probably a few years old. Jon was smiling and looked so young and so happy that she felt the photograph might well have been taken before the outbreak of war. She read the small piece again and, no, there was no mention of a Mrs Galbraith or a Lady Hedges. Would she, wherever she was, have received a telegram telling her that she was probably a widow? Sally's heart went out to her. She and Jon must have loved each other at one time, and maybe they might have been reconciled.

All Sally had to prove that she and Jon knew each other was a short letter, and somehow she knew that the Royal Navy would need a great deal more than that before they told her anything at all.

She sent a picture postcard to her father. He

would enjoy the photograph of rose beds in a London park.

Dear Dad,
Thank Mum for the newspaper cuttings. I met Jonathon Galbraith at an ENSA performance. He's the man whose wife lost the ruby ring. Please send me any more news of him if you can. Maybe Daisy's dad would know, or Alf Humble.
Love you,
Sally

She was sticking a stamp on the card when she realised that, since her mum had suggested that she send postcards to her dad, she had written nothing to her mother.

'She'll know they're meant for her too, won't she?' she asked Sebastian.

'Wouldn't put a bet on it, Sal. Touchy creatures, women.'

'You would know,' she teased, and her voice sounded almost as light and easy as in the time before Sebastian had told her of the sinking. 'I'll write her a girly letter telling her all about my clothes.'

He wanted to hold her, to tell her not to try so hard, that she didn't need to pretend with him. He set his mind to thinking of ways to help her recover.

'Do you mind if Millie comes for tea this evening, Sally?' Sebastian, looking decidedly guilty, was hovering at the door of the dressing room.

'Of course not – and it's your flat, Sebastian.

Entertain whoever you want to entertain.'

'It's not exactly like that, Sal. I wanted both of us to invite her and to have a nice chat, well away from the company, the theatre, noise and crowds and speeches to learn.'

'Sounds good. What do we have for tea?'

'Bread and cheese.'

'The chef at the RAF station gave me a tomato. We could have toasted cheese with thinly sliced tomato on top. Definitely up to the Savoy's standards.'

'Absolutely. They'd be proud of us.' He waved, which was unusual, and went off, closing the door behind him.

What is he up to? thought Sally as she continued to remove her stage make-up.

An idea occurred to her and, startled, she stopped, one side of her face a completely different colour from the other.

Millie and Sebastian? No, surely not. They're friends. He's just a kind, caring person and she needs someone kind and caring. Are they? Do they? Or does he want her to live with him? If so, they won't want me there. Perhaps they'll go to her flat... Oh, shut up, Sally. Millie is still mourning her husband and all that Sebastian has done is issue an official invitation to tea.

She could not forget, however, that already Millie had spent time with them over the past months and, several times, had stayed for tea. What was different about today?

I'll find out soon enough.

Millie brought her bacon ration with her and

both Sally and Sebastian remonstrated with her. 'We can't take your rations, Millie. Goodness, we get so little bacon these days. You have to keep yours.'

'Actually, I'm not generous. I don't eat bacon; my grampa had a smallholding when I was a little girl and he had a pig. Pigs have piglets and I loved them; baby pigs are so sweet. They followed me all over the place. Mind you, it wasn't a very big place, a medium-sized field, I suppose you'd say. Imagine my horror when I found out the piglets were Sunday breakfast and their mummy was Christmas dinner. I don't eat bacon and I don't eat pork.'

'Don't think I'll be able to eat it again either,' said Sebastian.

'Don't worry about him, Millie. He'll feel like that until he smells your rations being grilled for his breakfast or his supper and he'll forget all about the poor little piggies.'

'How well she knows me,' Sebastian said to no one in particular as he accepted the packet from Millie and popped it into the kitchen's small refrigerator.

The three of them feasted on toasted cheese and grilled tomato, prepared by Sally and Sebastian, but mainly Sebastian who was quite accomplished in the kitchen, and they listened to the wireless for a while before Sebastian insisted on escorting Millie home.

Sally cleaned up, ironed a blouse for the morning and went into her room to try to learn a speech before bed. She heard Sebastian return and was surprised when, instead of passing her door on his way to the bathroom, he knocked.

'Hello,' she called out.

'I've got something to talk over with you. If you're not already in bed, do you think you could spare me five minutes?'

'Be right there,' she called.

She got off the bed where she had been trying to write from memory the speech she was supposed to be able to recite perfectly next day. As a schoolgirl she had found that writing down anything she wanted or needed to know by rote was the surest way of committing it to memory.

Pulling her old dressing gown over her rather schoolgirly pink pyjamas, Sally left her room and went into the living room where she curled up on Sebastian's elegant sofa and waited for him. He came in a few minutes later and she smiled quietly. To an outsider they would look like an old married couple, she in her comfy dressing gown and Sebastian in his tailored tweed dressing gown with the legs of his blue and white striped pyjamas showing underneath.

'Cocoa?' he asked, but she shook her head. Whatever he had to say she wanted it all out in the open.

He sat down across from her. 'I told you I've been chatting with Millie in the last few weeks. You know that she lives in a small flat that she had been buying with her husband; his parents gave them the down payment as a wedding present. She's finding the payments difficult – she's not making a fortune as a member of ENSA – and can't approach either set of parents as she feels that all four have been too good already.'

So that was it. He wanted Millie to live with him; of course he did. Everyone could see what good friends they had become.

I won't cry. I'll find somewhere else. And really it's much better that I find another place.

Sally felt as if a large block of ice had somehow reached the pit of her stomach and refused either to melt or to move. But she would not show him how hurt she was.

'I can't really see how it will help her financially, Sebastian, but of course I'll leave. Max will contact the housing officer for me. There are other hostels in London and one of them will have a space, surely.' She stood up, preparing to start packing but Sebastian had inserted himself between her seat and the door; she was hemmed in.

'Good gracious, what are you talking about, Sally? What a girl for jumping to conclusions – always the wrong ones, incidentally. Who said anything about moving? I wanted to talk to you before I mentioned anything to Millie because, of course, what you want comes first. You are my number-one lodger. If you would kindly stop jumping ahead before you've heard a word of my extremely carefully thought-out plan and listen, we could discuss the problem the way old friends should.'

She felt a tear escape and trickle down her cheek and brushed it away. 'Sorry, please tell me your plan.'

'It's simple, as far as I see it. Millie's had too many setbacks already, wouldn't you agree?' He took her agreement for granted and carried on.

'She wants to keep her home but she can't afford the payments. What if – and this is where I thought I'd been absolutely brilliant – she came to live with us? This is a large flat; we could work out sleeping and wardrobe arrangements. Millie could let her flat; oodles of people looking for accommodation in London. With the monthly rent, she should surely have enough to make her mortgage payment and pay me a little. I don't need it but I'm sure she's like you – annoyingly independent – and we three could carry on, the Three Musketeers. As landlord, I could throw my weight around and make sure you two do all the housework. What do you think?'

'About your plans for the housework?'

'No, about asking Millie to join us? Come on, Sally, I really didn't set out to be a landlord – for one thing, Grandmamma would not approve – but surely your parents would be happier if there was another woman here.'

Sally remained quiet. She had never known anyone like Sebastian before. What was he getting out of their arrangement? What would he get out of sharing his beautiful flat with not one stray but two? She knew, or thought she knew, how much she had disrupted his life and yet here he was, prepared to make even more changes. Unless of course, he was falling in love with Millie.

'What is going through that beautiful little head of yours? I've told you before that one can hear the wheels grinding.'

'I was wondering what your grandmother would think?'

'Grandmamma? She would see countless opportunities for seduction and be furiously angry.' He laughed. 'Sally, there's a war on. I have room and you need somewhere. And Millie? She's a little wounded bird. I'd like to help her and that doesn't involve, what shall we say, an intimate personal relationship. But I need your help too. If we ask her and she accepts, then you two might have to share a room. My bedroom is the largest room in the flat and so the ladies could share that and I'd move into the guest room, or, if you need separate bedrooms, I'm quite happy to doss down on a sofa in the living room.'

'You're too long.'

'Bless you. I was hoping you'd say that but it really doesn't matter, Sally; we spend so little time at home these days anyway; it's not much more than a place to keep the clean underwear, and have the occasional nap. Look, let's get off to bed. You think over what I've said and let me know in the morning.' He stood up, bent over and kissed her forehead, then went out quietly. A moment later she heard his bedroom door closing.

Sally stayed on in the lovely drawing room for some time. She liked being alone there; its quiet elegance always made her feel happy. She knew how lucky she was to have Sebastian as a friend. In this room she had wondered once or twice about what marriage to him would be like, to be the mistress of this beautiful room with its piano that surely their children would learn to play, as Sebastian had done. They too would admire the paintings – watercolours, Sebastian called them – and she and Sebastian would encourage them, a boy and a girl, equally clever and enrolled in good schools, to read the special books in the bookcase and not merely look at them through the glass.

That short-lived dream had died and for a brief multicoloured bubble of time Sebastian's face had been replaced by that of Jon. The rapier-sharp blade that was never far away cut into her again and she curled up on the sofa and muffled her tears in a cushion. She had loved the yellow and pale green cushions from her first sight of them.

'Regency stripes,' Sebastian had told her. 'Grandmamma loved everything to do with Regency furniture and soft furnishings. I think I'd prefer the room to be a tad more modern; it's all a teeny bit shabby but I'm too lazy to do anything about it and there is a war on. Redecorating isn't exactly top of my to-do list.'

'I think it's perfect,' Sally said.

'Bless you, my child. That was exactly the right thing to say.'

She cowered closer to the cushion, remembering every word of the conversation and also the tiny dream she had had of sharing a beautiful room, not unlike this one, with Jon. But Jon was missing, presumed dead. She could see that written on every face that approached her, telling her not to give up hope. Rather than hope, perhaps in vain, would it not be better to fear the worst, to accept the pain? And who was she to grieve over another woman's husband anyway? Millie accepted the loss of her darling Patrick for she knew only too well that there was no hope.

Patrick was dead. Their dream was ended.

But Sebastian wanted to help Millie and she could help too. Of course, Millie must move into the flat. Sharing Sebastian's flat would help her continue to have part of their dream, hers and Patrick's. She would keep their home.

How long had she huddled there? She was cold and stiff. 'Stupid Sally,' she scolded herself, for if she caught a cold and could not perform, one of the qualified people on any one of the lists that Sybil and Lalita were making would take over from her. Her absence would never be noticed. The tiny place on the ENSA programmes that read 'Sally Brewer' would be erased and another name inserted.

Sally forced herself to sit up and then to stand. The light was still on, but the blackout curtains would keep that a secret from ARP wardens or prowling German planes. She turned off the lamp, opened the door and crept out, closing it soundlessly behind her.

She stood in darkness for a moment, trying to remember just how far down the corridor was that part of the ancient wooden floor that loved to give away secrets by groaning as if in pain. She misjudged it and the floor announced her presence. She stopped, hardly breathing, but heard nothing. Sebastian had to be asleep.

Sebastian lay listening and wondering how he could comfort her. He had tried once but ... the moment was lost and now their friendship was the most important thing to him.

Sally reached her room, her special, precious private space. Soon it would be hers no longer.

Could she sleep each night on Grandmamma's Regency cushions? No, it would not be allowed.

'Be more than grateful for all he has given you, Sally,' she said and, opening the door as quietly as she could, she slipped inside and went to bed where she lay sometimes sleeping but more often awake as the noise of exploding bombs, screaming wounded sailors and roaring waves invaded her dreams.

'The bathroom's all yours,' Sebastian's voice pulled her from her nightmares, 'but drink this coffee first. Essence, I'm afraid, but the best the chef could do this morning.'

'Sack him,' she said, trying to pretend this was a usual morning. 'Ten a penny down the Labour Exchange, guv.'

'Fifteen minutes. Any longer and you can face Max on your own,' he said, and was gone.

They reached the theatre just in time for Sebastian to hold the door open for Sybil.

'Good God, Sally, you look as if an entire army of brigands has had its wicked way with you. What has she been doing, Seb?'

'I beat her twice in a row at Snakes and Ladders. Some people just don't know how to lose gracefully.'

'My dressing room now, Sally.'

Sebastian shrugged and Sally grimaced but followed Sybil through the theatre to her dressing room.

'Sit down in front of the mirrors and don't look at yourself. You're liable to have a heart attack.'

Sally said nothing but did as she was bid, apart

215

from not looking in the mirrors – she had seen her face already and knew the worst.

Sybil came and stood behind her, examining the face in the mirror very thoroughly. 'I won't ask anything, Sally, but we all know that you have had major bad news. It's only our business if it affects your abilities.' She bent down and thumped a heavy bag onto the table. 'This is, I suppose, damage limitation. Had you gone all the way through theatre school, make-up lessons would have been part of your curriculum. The secret of perfect *maquillage*, make-up, for day wear, is to apply it so well that it hides evidence of life's blows and so cleverly that everyone looking at you wonders whether or not you're wearing any at all.'

Twenty-five minutes later Sally stood up and smiled at the vision revealed in the mirrors.

'Unfortunately the young, happy Sally will be washed off at bedtime,' said Sybil. 'Try to sleep, Sally. That really is the best medicine. Have some cocoa, or Ovaltine, even a cup of China's blessed tea, but no alcohol. Makes you sleep, certainly, but you'll look hellish in the morning.'

'Thank you,' Sally said quietly, and walked to the door.

Sybil held her arm as she passed. 'Remember, Lalita and I are here and we've heard everything and been through most if not all of it. Another day I'll really do those eyes of yours. You'll be amazing on film; the camera will adore you. Now go.'

Sally went.

TEN

Dmitri, Russian prince or accountant or night watchman – whatever he was – discovered that the large bed in the flat's main bedroom was, in fact, two single beds put together, and he and Sebastian spent a happy afternoon taking them apart.

'*Voilà*,' announced Sebastian to his new flat-mate, 'all modern conveniences.'

Millie had been thrilled by the invitation to share expenses at Sebastian's flat but had felt the need to put up some token resistance. 'It's not fair disturbing you both like this. I'll manage something.'

'Thanks to the multitalented Dmitri, you're not disturbing anyone. We have a bed each; Sebastian won't ruin his back curling up on the sofa, and his wardrobe is far bigger than the one in the guest room so there's plenty of room for our clothes. I hope I don't snore.'

'No problem; I'll put a pillow over your head. But I have to admit that Patrick said I sounded just like one of my grandfather's pigs.'

Sally managed a slight laugh as it was obvious that Millie was trying hard to sound light-hearted in a vain attempt to show them how well she was handling the loss of her own place. 'I'll leave you to unpack. I'll be in the kitchen. We usually listen to *The Kitchen Front* while we're preparing supper;

so far we haven't tried anything that's been suggested but we do like Freddie Grisewood.'

Millie assured her that she would join them as soon as she had put away her clothes and toiletries. 'I'm a hopeless cook, Sally, but quite good at washing dishes and general tidying.'

'Afraid I'm not much good either, but don't worry. We'll manage. Sebastian isn't creative but for basics he's really quite good.'

Sebastian was in the kitchen fiddling with the radio knobs. He continued until the announcer's voice sounded clearly. 'Good. Millie settling in? You're sure you don't mind sharing, Sal?'

'Of course not. I used to envy my friends, the twins I've told you about. Must be nice to have someone to talk to.'

'I thoroughly enjoyed being a spoiled only child. The entire world revolved around little me. Probably that's why I became an actor; couldn't bear the adulation to dry up.'

'You do talk nonsense.'

'I know, my darling, but it beats trying not to talk about the things we have on our minds.'

She sat down heavily, the words 'he can read me like a book' chasing through her head. 'It's the not knowing for sure if he's dead. If only he had been rescued I wouldn't care how badly he was injured. I keep in mind what you said once about looking straight at the wounded men. We've had lots of practice, haven't we?'

'Ssh.' Sebastian had heard Millie coming along the corridor.

'No need to treat me like porcelain. I think I've proved I won't break.' Millie joined them at the table. 'I wanted to ask you if you'll be here at Christmas, Seb, both of you or either?'

Sebastian looked up at the calendar on the kitchen wall. It showed a picture of Notre-Dame Cathedral in Paris and under the picture was the French word, *Mars*. 'Golly, shame on you, Sally, not noticing that it's November.'

'I thought you liked the picture and I know it's November of 1941. You're more than a year out of date.'

He took down the calendar and made as if to throw it into the rubbish bin. Both girls jumped up. 'Seb, we're asked to save all paper for the war effort.'

'I will be here for Christmas,' said Sebastian as if nothing had happened. 'Probably we will all be here.' He opened the pantry door, showing Millie a box with the words 'PAPER' written across it and deposited the calendar inside. 'I shall miss that view of Notre-Dame,' he said sadly as he sat down again. 'One does get used to things and, by the way, since you are both paying me hefty rent, you shall each have your own key, if there's enough metal lying around for new keys to be cut, and then you may come and go as you please. Sorry, Sally, I should have thought of that before. I do have at least one spare key; it will be in my cufflinks box.'

'Where are your cufflinks?' Millie was fascinated.

'In the shirt drawer, of course. Where else would they be? Now let's listen to old Freddie and then, omelettes, do you think?'

Sally put out her hand and grasped Millie's

219

slender wrist. 'They're from powdered eggs; completely tasteless.'

'There's a war on, ladies, and with another resident we will now be entitled to nine pints of milk a week – lots of cocoa, yum yum. As we are also entitled to one packet of powdered eggs each every four weeks that's the bountiful total of three delicious packets a month. Omelettes or scrambled eggs, ladies? Choose.'

'Tasteless omelette, or tasteless scrambled eggs,' said Millie. 'Come on, Sally, pretend we're lucky to have such a varied choice.'

'It's going to be all right having Millie here,' Sally decided as, later that evening, she took her turn to have a hot bath and hair wash. Yes, it was going to be all right.

When she was finished in the bathroom, she returned to the large bedroom she was sharing with Millie. 'I need to write a letter to my parents,' she said. 'I'll go into the living room so as not to disturb you.'

But Millie assured her that she herself had to write to her own family and to Patrick's parents to let them know of her possible plans for Christmas. 'Quite frankly, I don't think I could bear to go to either set of parents this year, Sally. Mine try too hard to be casual and Patrick's parents are just so devastated by his loss, they're barely functioning. It's left me feeling I'm lacking somehow; I'm not nearly enough to help them. I'm just Millie and I took Patrick away from them. Poor darlings, watched me like a hawk for weeks after ... after, hoping I was preggers, I suppose. A baby might have been some consolation. I'm going to ask Max to send me somewhere. What about you?'

'I'll go out to events if Max needs me but I'd like to go home; perhaps my chums will have leave and we always have such lovely fun. You could come with me; you'd be made very welcome.'

'Not this year, Sally, but thank you. Now let's get our letters written.'

They piled the pillows behind their backs and sat up, their writing pads on their thighs and began to write. Sally wrote a short note to Daisy asking if it could really be true that she was learning to fly. The sheer wonderment of such an achievement filled her with happiness for her friend. But she did not ask Daisy if her father had a customer called Galbraith or Hedges. She remembered picking strawberries at Old Manor Farm, and hearing that a real lord owned that farm and others in the area, but she could not remember his name – if she had ever heard it. She could no longer put off giving her parents her address.

Dear Mum and Dad,

I'm sitting up in bed writing letters. Millie Burgess, who's a war widow, is doing the same in the bed next to mine. It's rather like Daisy's room, twin beds, little rugs and, in this room, two comfy chairs. The flat is owned by Sebastian Brady; you remember the actor who kindly drove me home from London and who has helped me get into ENSA. He has very kindly taken Millie and me as his lodgers.

**That's the address at the top of the page. **

We pay rent and we all clean and cook together and, most of the time, we're working together. Millie is a

221

ballerina; she's wonderful. Sebastian's room is on the other side of the flat. Next time you come up to town you must see it – the flat, I mean. You'd love the curtains although Sebastian says they're old-fashioned. Millie and I like them.

You haven't sent me anything more about Jonathon Galbraith. Please, Mum, if there is anything in the Dartford papers, send them to me.

The Dartford papers? For some reason as Sally wrote those words down, she seemed to hear Jon's voice. 'Talk to Maudie.' Maudie... Of course, his former nanny would know any news because she knew everything about the family, and if she was not listed as a relative she would certainly know the people who would be given information about Jon's fate.

I must get to Dartford, or would a letter to Maudie at the second-hand shop reach her? Maybe it would be best to try to see Maude at Christmas... She dipped her pen in the ink and finished the letter to her parents.

Apart from anything else, there is the ring to think about. Even if I knew who to talk to about it, I would feel better. Mum, I don't know about Christmas yet but I want to be home with you and Dad so badly. I've asked Millie to come with me but she's saying no, and I think that's because she thinks she'd be in the way but I'll ask her again if I find out for certain.
Lots of love,
Sally

Having finished two letters, put them in envelopes, addressed them and stuck on stamps, Sally put away her notepaper and it was only then that she saw that Millie was already sound asleep.

Next morning, Millie was busy in the kitchen when Sally, overjoyed to find the bathroom empty, hurried in to wash. Sebastian was at the door as she came out.

'Millie's cooking something. Terrifying thought. Be an angel and have a look.'

'I will when I'm dressed.'

With that Sebastian had to be content.

'Porridge,' Millie said with pride. 'We have lots of milk. See, I've scooped the cream off the tops of three bottles and so we can each have a little cream. Doesn't that look good?'

Sally looked and had to admit that the bubbling porridge looked absolutely perfect. 'I thought you couldn't cook.'

'I can't, not Beef Wellington or Chateaubriand. Patrick liked his protein.' She was quiet for a fraction of a moment before continuing. 'This is just porridge. Wish we had some brown sugar or syrup.'

'My dad used to say that if you put sugar on your porridge, you would fall asleep on the beach in the summer. We have salt on ours.'

'Sounds awful, but each to her own.'

'That looks good. When did you do it, Sal?' Sebastian had arrived and was peering over their shoulders.

'I didn't. Millie did it because porridge isn't cooking.'

'I see,' he said, and it was obvious that he had

no idea what they were talking about.

'Remember your letters, Millie,' said Sally a few minutes later as they made their way out.

Millie was checking the seams on her stockings. 'Oh, for just one pair of silk stockings. I don't think I've seen any at any price all year.'

'Manufacture was banned this time last year,' said Sally, hoping that mention of 1940 would not bring that distraught look into Millie's eyes. 'You should go barelegged – in the summer at least – your legs are so good, and, if you need to look dressed, just draw a seam down the back. What do you think, Sebastian?'

'About Millie's legs or legs in general? Ladies do not walk around bare-legged, or so Grand-mamma would say. It's unseemly,' he added, and they all laughed at his unintentional pun.

'What have you three been up to?' Sybil and Lalita had reached the stage door just before them. 'Good to see everyone looking so much better. Millie, be sure to give Max's secretary your new address – absolutely vital that we know where everyone is, and families should be kept informed of moves. We're using the stage this morning, so off you go and get into rehearsal clothes.'

Sally was delighted that she was now sophisticated enough to know that wearing rehearsal clothes did not mean – or usually did not – that they were rehearsing. It meant simply that they were to wear clothes in which they were comfortable and in which they could move easily, should they be asked to move. The dancers usually wore tights and leg warmers, the men, actors, musicians, et cetera tended to turn up in loosely fitting trousers and open-necked short-sleeved shirts, while the women, apart from the dancers, wore either shorts or a skirt and a blouse. Almost everyone tended to throw a sweater or cardigan across the shoulders, tying the arms together in front.

'We're as much in uniform,' Sally decided, 'as soldiers and sailors.'

Again she experienced a shaft of real pain as the word 'sailor' conjured up an image. *How can I contact Maudie? What was the name of the shop?*

'Wake up, Sally, you don't want to hold us up. I warn you that Max is not in the best of moods.'

The reason for Max's ill temper was made very clear to them when they assembled on the stage.

'Good news first. I have refused to accept any events on Christmas Day. Sybil, Lal, Sam, Sebastian and I will do a few hospital visits; none of us has family waiting at home. The rest of you will have Christmas Day off. Those who have some distance to travel, speak to me and we'll see how many days we can let you have. Priorities to those who had no Christmas leave last year. The requests keep coming in and we'll prioritise them too, but there are several companies operating out of this theatre and so we can pass requests over to them. I have to warn you that we'll be doing quite a lot of travelling next year and at least one gig is in France.'

He stopped talking as excited chatter broke out.

'France? But they're fighting there. Won't it be dangerous?'

'There's a war on. Of course it will be dangerous but Jerry is dropping bombs on us here. Not much difference, far as I can see.'

'Bit more glamorous, *la belle France*.'

'If you lot didn't make me want to cry, I'd laugh,' Max growled. 'There is nothing remotely glamorous about travelling in choppy seas on a troopship, or sitting on your backside on the floor of the belly of a transport plane. The accommodation we've had so far is a suite at the Ritz compared to some bombed-out old church in a muddy field in France. I'd ask Father Christmas for Wellington boots and some woollen underwear.'

'I have them already,' said Millie quietly.

'Sebastian, didn't the idle rich go to France to toast themselves on the beaches all day and to gamble, glass of bubbly in hand, all night?' shouted one of the Balladeers.

'We did indeed. Blasted war has ruined our playground.'

'The beaches must still be there.'

'It's possible they're not quite what they were,' said Max. 'Millie, I'll see you in my office at morning break. Sally, I'll have a word with you now.'

Sally could guess that Max was assuring Millie that she would be taken to France, but why did he need to speak to *her?* What could she have done wrong?

She hurried after him.

'Yes, Max?'

'Sit down.'

She sat down quickly.

226

'I've had a call from a chap called Arnold who says he has some work for you.'

'But he can't have, Max. I told him I wouldn't sign with him because I wanted to stay with ENSA until the war is over, honestly I did.'

'So I'll tell him you don't want to be photographed for an advertisement campaign?'

'Gosh.'

'And you certainly don't want a forty-five-second slot in a morale-boosting film starring Noël Coward?'

'*The* Noël Coward?' Sally's face had gone pink at first and now Max saw it grow paler and paler and he took pity on her.

'Sorry, Sally, I'll explain. The photographic session – you in a uniform holding some cleaning product all military should be using – is to be shot in London and will take less than a day. Your mother or other responsible adult should be with you. The filming might take a few days and so we'll have to dock your wages but even that small job will pay well. The film studios have their own chaperones so no worries. Arnold will contact you here, but these things take time so don't expect to hear more for a while yet. Well done, Sally; they're not even auditioning you. Arnold's judgement and, of course, your growing reputation were enough.' He leaned over his desk and shook hands with her. 'Congratulations. Pity Coward doesn't need you to speak but if you're going to have a first film role, standing beside the great man is just about the best place to start. You will get what's called a still from the film, possibly the two of you side by side. Directors and producers will lap it up and one would look rather nice in this office. "ENSA star stars with star",' he finished, and was delighted to see her smile and blush.

Sally was absolutely dumbfounded. She had thought she was to be reprimanded for something and instead golly, such news. An advertisement, for newspapers or magazines, she thought, but had been too unaware to ask, and 'a few days' to capture a short scene in a film. What would her mother say?

'Thank you very much, Max, and may I tell Sebastian and Millie?'

'Of course, but don't broadcast it. Jealousy takes root very quickly in a theatre's fertile soil.'

Sally hurried out, passing Lalita on her way in.

'The little Brewer tell you her good news, Lal?'

'No, do tell. Lovely that someone is hearing tidings of great joy.'

Max filled her in on the two offers, finishing with, 'And what do you think of that?'

'I'll try to ensure Sybil's allowed to do her make-up for the ad campaign. She doesn't make nearly enough of her eyes.'

'And the film? Noël Coward? What does your Machiavellian mind make of that?'

'Rather surprised. Possibly he doesn't know she's with ENSA. Arnold knows he doesn't think much of us and so he probably didn't mention her involvement or...'

'Or?'

'"The play's the thing" and he doesn't give a hooha.'

'Well, there's a new word for my growing Spanish vocabulary.'

'I made it up.'

'I know, darling, but you make them up so well. Kettle on?'

At the lunch break, instead of going to get some food with Millie and Sebastian, Sally asked Sybil for a sheet of paper and an envelope, and stayed in the dressing room to write another letter to her mother. How amazed Elsie would be to have two letters in the same week.

Dear Mum,

You will never believe my news. I'm going to be in the papers; it's a product advertisement. I'll be promoting a cream or polish or something like that which cleans up oil and grease. I have to wear a uniform – no idea which one – and be photographed with the jar or tin – and Max says the company will pay me. They told me to bring you with me on the day of the shoot – a shoot's what they call taking pictures or filming. I don't know which date, Mum, but it is to be soon and you'll get expenses so that's nice, isn't it? And my even bigger news? Will I be nasty Sally and not tell you or nice Sally? All right, nice Sally. I'm going to be in the pictures. Yes, the dream is beginning to come true, Mum. Noël Coward, yes, the real Noël Coward is making a film and, for some reason he wants me – I think wearing a naval uniform – standing beside him as we look out to sea or something like that. I'll be in the film for exactly forty-five seconds, yes, that much, but it will take two or three days to make sure it's exactly right. I don't need a chaperone there because the studio has their own chaperones for under-age actors.

You will come, won't you, and you can meet Sebastian and Millie. I'll let you know immediately they give me the dates.
Love,
Sally

She had felt her heart lurch as she had written 'naval' and by now tears were threatening to fall. However exciting these new opportunities, she felt a huge emptiness undermining her, sapping her fortitude. What was the point of any of this when the man she loved was missing, presumed dead?

The man I love. With some wonderment she acknowledged what she'd allowed herself to think and everything became clear – she loved Just Jon.

'Would you like to tell me all about it?'

She had forgotten that Sybil was working at the desk.

Desperately Sally reached for a handkerchief but she had forgotten to pick up one before they left the flat. 'Damn, damn, where is Sebastian when you need him?' she mumbled as she sniffed loudly and tried to wipe her eyes with the sleeves of her cardigan.

'Here.' Sybil pushed a delicate lace-edged linen handkerchief into her hand. 'Bet it's prettier than Seb's.'

Sally tried to smile. 'Much.'

'I won't pry, Sally, but if I can help in any way, I will. Seb's been herding you and Millie like lost lambs lately. It's not prurient interest, child. We could say that you're part of our company and what weakens you weakens all of us – seems totally selfish, but at least I won't gossip.'

Sally looked at Sybil's amazing ballerina face, the nose and cheekbones sculpted as if by a master. 'It's all right, Sybil, really. If I get home at Christmas, even just for a few hours, I can do something. That's all it would take, a few hours.'

'Didn't Max tell you the company is not working on Christmas Day or do you have so much on your mind that the good news didn't penetrate?'

Sally flushed, annoyed at her own stupidity. 'He did tell us; I'm sorry.'

Sybil's beautiful hands waved in the air, dismissing Sally's worries. 'Can't think of anyone who doesn't have a blocked mind occasionally. Now listen, we can get you home today if there's a family emergency.'

Sally shook her head. 'No, my parents are fine; it's just ... a friend. Oh, Sybil no one will tell me anything because I'm not a relative,' and she started to weep again.

Sybil soothed her as if she were a child. 'Tell me about him, Sally. If I can help I will.'

And so the whole story spilled out. Sally sniffed loudly when she had finished and blew her nose on the lightly scented handkerchief. 'Oh, dear, I've ruined it; I'm so sorry. If I could talk to Maudie ... maybe. I don't know but I'll try. He said, "Talk to Maudie" but that was for her to give me his address and then we met anyway.'

That made no sense at all to Sybil but gamely she carried on. 'Why don't you ring her? Does she have a telephone?'

'I don't know. The shop might.'

'Good start. Where's the shop?'

'In Dartford, on the High Street, but I can't remember what it's called; it was a second-hand clothes shop.'

'WVS?'

Sybil patted her back, then quickly pushed Max out as he started to enter his office with a, 'Ten minutes, Max. Emergency.' By the time Sally had mopped her eyes again she was aware of Sybil speaking to someone on the telephone. '...Yes, Dartford, second-hand clothes shop on the High Street, WVS.'

Sybil picked up a pencil and scribbled and then Sally heard, '...You are so kind. That is most helpful. Thank you.'

Sybil looked across at Sally, smiled encouragingly, then turned back to the telephone and dialled.

'Good morning, my name is Sybil Tapper. I'm with ENSA at the Theatre Royal in London... Well, how very kind of you to say so. I'm trying to get in touch with a volunteer named Maudie... Oh, that's absolutely splendid. Thank you.' She put her hand over the receiver. 'Sally, the lovely Fedora – enchanting name – is bringing a Maude from the storeroom. Here.' She handed the receiver to Sally. 'I'll go and pacify Max.'

A few minutes later, Sally heard, 'Hello, Maude here, what can I do for you?'

Sally thrust back threatening tears. 'Maude, Maudie, it's Sally Brewer. I really need to ask you about Jon Galbraith...'

232

ELEVEN

Elsie and Ernie Brewer thoroughly enjoyed their Sunday afternoon strolls through the park with their friends, Flora and Fred Petric. Then, tired but relaxed, they would treat themselves to a nice cup of tea. They had caught up almost completely with all the doings of their children, including Grace, who was not their child but who had always been treated like one of their own, and the various war reports or rumours that came to them in the local newspaper or on Pathé News. Elsie had kept the best piece of their news until, enjoying the autumn sunshine and the changing colours of the leaves, they made their way home.

'Come on, Elsie, spit it out,' Flora teased. 'So help me, all afternoon you've looked like one of the Humbles' hens preparing to lay an egg, and I can't wait another second to hear. Is Sally walking out with that young actor chap?'

'Oh, better than that. Now promise me you won't tell a soul.'

Since, over the past twenty years or so, those words had been uttered by each mother fairly regularly, Flora and Fred nodded their heads vigorously.

'Our Sally's going to be in pictures.'

'Oh, Fred, isn't that wonderful? Elsie, love, tell us all.'

So Elsie told Sally's news to her friends, who listened wide-eyed.

'Noël Coward, the actual Noël Coward?' Flora was beaming with admiration. 'Ernie, you'll order the film for Dartford right away, won't you?'

'You know I will.'

'How did you manage not to spit that news right out, Elsie? I'm sure, if I had news like that, everyone in Dartford would hear me shout.'

'I know, like you shouted out when our Daisy went to learn to fly a plane,' Fred laughed. 'Tell her how thrilled we are, Elsie, and oh, wouldn't it be nice if they was all home for Christmas.'

The old friends chatted a few minutes longer and then as autumn showed its sharper teeth, they said 'cheerio' and went home, all still talking.

The Brewers continued to talk about Sally's news, at least Elsie talked and Ernie listened as the cry of wonder and amazement at their daughter's success went on and on.

'Wouldn't it be lovely to have her home for Christmas?' he asked as Elsie stopped for breath. 'If Grace gets down, maybe it'll be like before the war with them all running in and out and making a right mess of this living room.' His voice was full of joyful anticipation.

Elsie didn't want him to look forward too much; disappointment would be hurtful. 'Just remember Grace was allowed home for her sister's funeral. Can't expect to get Christmas leave two years in a row, not during a war.'

'You're right, love, and we don't really know about Sally, do we? And the ballerina girl, poor girl, widowed so young. We've room for her, right, pet, if she comes?'

'We'll make room, Ernie.'

'It isn't Jon, it isn't Jon. Isn't that fantastic? I mean I'm terribly sorry for the poor dead sailor but he isn't Jon.'

After her telephone call with Maudie, Sally had rushed to the stage where the company was waiting for directions. Some were exercising, some vocalising, and others just 'milling'. Among these was Sebastian. She had pulled him out into the wings.

'Tell all, quickly, Sally. Max will be here bullying us in a minute.'

'I never bully,' came Max's voice from just behind Sebastian. 'Mind you, I could be persuaded to start. Tell him your good news, Sally, and then back on stage for rehearsal.'

As Max's head disappeared through the curtain Sally smiled, a heart-breakingly lovely smile, and shouted, 'It isn't Jon.'

'That is good news – but who told you?'

Patiently he waited while Sally told him all about Sybil and her telephone calls and then, at last, the telephone call to Maudie. 'And Maudie knows because?'

'She was Jon's nanny when he was small. You probably had a Maudie too.'

'A Clara. She smelled of lavender and sometimes peppermints. Sally, Maudie isn't a relation, a relative, is she?'

'No.'

'Then she wouldn't—'

She held up her hand. 'Just listen, Sebastian.'

He listened.

'His wife was listed as next-of-kin, as was Miss Maude Cooper. Jon wasn't really sure where she went when she left him; he told me it was either the United States, a place she had always wanted to visit and there had never been an opportunity – since he was away at sea most of the time – or Malta where she was born. Well, it was definitely Malta. The people who send the telegrams, the War Office is it, then contacted Maudie and they sent her the photograph. The poor chap, she says, is very like Jon but it isn't him.'

He put his arms around her. 'Oh, my darling Sally, she wants it not to be Jon as much as you do. Don't you think she's seeing what she wants to see? His book of poetry was in his pocket.'

'He was wearing a gold watch on his right arm.'

'Lots of people do. My father wore his wedding ring on his right hand because he was left-handed and his wedding ring ruined his squash grip.'

Sally had not the faintest idea what a squash grip was and neither did she care. 'Jon was ... is left-handed, as it happens, and he did wear his watch on his right wrist but he was ... is allergic to gold and always wore a leather strap and a metal watch of some kind, but never gold.'

'That does sound rather convincing, Sally, but if this poor fellow isn't Jon, isn't it likely that...?'

'Jon drowned or was killed. Yes, that seems likely but Maudie doesn't believe it and neither do I.'

'Oh, Sally, "this way lies madness". Maude was his nanny. If she's the slightest bit like my Clara, she loved him as if he were her own child. She wants, needs him not to be dead.'

'I won't give up until they find him.'

'Hundreds of men went down with the ship. Their bodies will probably never be found. Ships are being sunk in every ocean or sea in this tortured world, planes are being shot down. A huge army of waiting women is being formed.' He stopped, unable to think of any word that would help her, but, as a friend he could not patronise her with false hope.

She looked at him and the look was one of grim determination. 'I won't just wait, Sebastian. I'll look.'

For an insane moment the most appalling thought crossed his mind. She meant to throw herself into the Mediterranean.

Sally saw his look of fear and recognised it.

'Dear Sebastian. Don't worry; I found him before and I'll find him again.'

Every sailor picked up from the *George Francis* by the various battleships had been returned to Britain, except for those rescued by the German ship. Eventually the families of those men heard that their husband, son, brother was in a prisoner-of-war camp somewhere in German-occupied territory, but all the details of the living had been handed over to the Red Cross. Jonathon Galbraith, alive or dead, was not listed among them. Survivors rescued by the American or Allies' ships were now in British hospitals, at home with their families or – such was the need for manpower – back on duty.

Sally and Maudie appeared to be becoming firm friends. Once a week, Maude would ring the theatre and either talk to Sally or, if Sally was working, she would leave a message; and, as often as she could manage while travelling from factory to hospital or church hall, Sally would find a telephone box and ring Jon's former nanny.

One night, after a late rehearsal, she dialled Maude's number. It was answered almost at once as if Maude had been waiting for her call.

'Sally, how lovely to hear from you.'

'Sorry to be so late, Maude, but I...'

'No dear, there's no more news, good or bad, and I don't mind when you ring. I don't seem to sleep much these days.'

'You must try harder. If Jon, when Jon comes home, he'll need you.'

'Good girl. He is not dead, Sally; he may be wounded, dreadfully wounded, but I'll, we'll take care of him.'

'Chin up! There's still hope that Jon's in a hospital somewhere,' said Sally, trying to be brave for Maude's sake as well as her own. 'If his identification tags have been lost or he's too severely injured to speak, then no one will know who he is. We have answers from all the ships...'

'Except the fishing boats.'

'Yes, Maude, let's pin our faith on the fishermen.'

The beeps sounded and they terminated the call. Next time, there had to be good news.

Sally had nagged at Maude like a playful puppy hanging on to a child's toy. She conceded that Maude was right; she must wait patiently. She now completely understood why Millie wanted, needed, to get to France. She knew that her young husband was dead; he would never return to her but she had to see his grave, to lay flowers on the patch of French soil that held all her dreams, to sit on the earth and talk to him, tell him how much she loved him and missed him, and to assure him that she would never forget him.

Sally's hopes lay in the limited information that had been given by the captains of the fishing boats that had picked up both bodies and injured sailors and, according to their secretive captains, taken their sad cargoes to their home ports. It seemed that one boat had returned to a port in Corsica and the other to Malta. But how could Sally, an actress living in London, find out anything more? It all seemed impossible, yet surely it was here that her only hope lay.

It was a Sunday afternoon, the first afternoon in some weeks that the three flatmates had had to themselves. Free to choose to do whatever they felt like doing. And so, of course, they did nothing; they dressed casually, and with their faces clear of the slightest trace of the heavy 'flexible greasepaint' they used for performances, they looked remarkably young and fresh. They peeled potatoes and an onion Dmitri had brought them from his victory garden and then they made potato soup. It was a far cry from the meals they often enjoyed on military bases, and was nothing at all like the meals they occasionally shared in hotels, but they enjoyed it tremendously.

'Doesn't this make you think of Sunday afternoons before the war, Sebastian?' asked Millie.

'Golly no, a hundred times better. Grandmamma always had the same coven of ancient *grandes dames* to afternoon tea on Sundays. All widowed, poor old dears, but so excruciatingly boring.'

'Boring? Then they weren't a coven,' Millie pointed out seriously.

Sally thought of Sundays in Dartford. Sometimes, a church service with her parents, but more often reading the papers and peeling the vegetables, then lunch and off to the park or on a cycle ride with her three best friends.

Did we ever pass Jon's home or cycle on his land?

'Would fishing boats go out during a raging battle, Sebastian?'

Sebastian and Millie looked at each other over Sally's bent dark head. The message in their eyes was the same. Will she ever come to terms with this? They had discussed Sally's inability to let the matter drop several times.

'As far as I know, she met him only twice, Millie, and for just a few minutes each time,' Sebastian had explained. 'I simply can't understand it.'

But Millie, who had first become aware of Patrick when, in rehearsal, she watched his taut, muscular body leap effortlessly through the air to land at her feet, the naughtiest smile in his dark eyes, was well aware that sometimes a moment was all it took to change one's life for ever.

Eventually, it was Sebastian who answered Sally's question. 'Highly unlikely, I would say, Sal. Possible, of course, that they had already been in those waters; I mean, "geography needs care", as my old form master was rather too fond of saying, but I don't think Corsica is a tremendous distance from Gibraltar. The Corsican boat could have gone out a few days before and ... gosh, I don't know, got caught in bad weather and so didn't make it back to port before the battle started. Malta, though, is a heck of a long way from Gib. Could the fishermen have heard the guns and thought, "We're part of the British Empire and should try to help out"?'

'No idea,' Millie contributed to the conversation. 'Maybe they were smugglers – after all, if those poor islanders are unable to replenish supplies because of the U-boats, then no doubt black marketeers are doing a roaring, if exceedingly dangerous business. Could they have been gun runners? Possibly even spies? For what it's worth, I think they were up to no good, got caught up in a battle, had some decency and, instead of disappearing, tried to help. Corsica's French, isn't it, and that would make them allies; Malta is British.'

'I think Millie's right,' Sebastian said. 'Corsica and Malta should be on the side of the Allies and so anyone picked up by fishermen from those islands would most probably be safe.' He managed to stifle the word 'initially', which is what his tongue seemed to have formed itself to say and, of course, if Millie was right and they were not fishermen at all ... he did not want to contemplate that scenario.

241

Sally jumped to her feet with excitement, her face suffused with healthy colour for the first time since Sebastian had told her of the sinking. 'Jon's there, I feel it. He's on one of those islands. May I use the telephone, Sebastian? I'd like to ring Maudie. She'll be thrilled to hear there really is hope Jon's still alive after all.'

While Sally went to the telephone, Sebastian and Millie moved to the kitchen where they could speak quietly and have a slight chance of not being overheard by Sally.

'What are we going to do, Seb? She's going to want to try to get to one of those places. Allied soldiers aren't stationed there, are they? We couldn't possibly take an ENSA programme, could we?'

'I don't know the answers to any of your questions. I do know that Malta is being blitzed into nothingness. Some of the nobility have huge tunnels under their homes, constructed during the time when Turkish armies were invading Malta, and the people are taking shelter there, but if by some sheer madness, a fishing boat from Malta took survivors from a British ship there, what on earth would they do with them?'

Sally overheard the last comment as she replaced the telephone receiver. 'They would take care of them and they'd contact London and find out how to get them home.'

Neither of her flatmates wanted to remind her that the people of Malta were struggling – often without success – to feed themselves.

'How was Maude?'

'She brightened up, I think. I know you two are sure that I'm wrong but isn't it worth clinging to

242

even the tiniest bit of hope?' As she spoke she looked at Millie.

'I have no hope, Sally.'

'Yes, you do, Millie. Not that Patrick will miraculously walk in that door but that we'll get over to France. I know we will. Somehow, whatever we have to do to reach Arras, we'll do it, and you'll see ... you'll see.' She turned to look directly at Sebastian, who was obviously finding the conversation difficult. 'We will help, won't we, Sebastian, in whatever way we can?'

'Sally, of course if we are sent to France we will do our utmost, but it's a huge country; even if we do get there we might well be stationed nowhere near Arras.'

'Quite right, Sebastian, but the one thing we can do is never give up hope so that we're ready should the chance arise. I'm going to work really hard to improve my abilities so that when the Government finally decides that our company should go to the front, I'll be good enough and Max will select me. You two are brilliant and don't even have to worry about being good enough.'

But as Max was fond of reminding the company whenever the subject was raised, there was no money immediately available to send them overseas just yet.

Two days later, the concert party had a lucky escape when they were strafed while on their way back to London from an airfield in Suffolk they had never before visited, and where they had given three back-to-back performances. They had come under fire before but this attack was so

243

intense they could almost believe that it was personal. Luckily there had been a few minutes' warning. The road before them had been completely clear and then, almost out of nowhere, had come a motorcycle dispatch rider.

'Get off the road, get off the road,' he shouted – and he was already hoarse – 'split up, split up, incoming aircraft. Get away from the railway line; probably bombs.' He was past them in a screaming blur.

His last few words were whipped away by the wind but the driver had understood. It was well-known that the Luftwaffe targeted railway lines, bridges, roads, any means of communication or transportation they could. Up until then it was unlikely that anyone in the lorries had been particularly concerned that their route was parallel to a major railway line. All over the country railways and roads followed the same routes, usually the shortest possible distance between two points. Most of the company had been attempting to sleep but the shouts woke some, and the rest were woken very roughly when the transport vehicles began to turn and swerve all over the road as the drivers followed their prearranged orders for evasive action. Baskets of props, costumes and musical instruments rained down on unlucky cast members who had been thrown to the floor. Sally and Millie, already on the floor, were saved from injury when a huge hamper that seemed destined to hit them burst open, burying them under a load of painstakingly washed and ironed costumes.

They began to struggle and then lay still, holding their breath as what sounded like hundreds of small stones rattled against both the ground and the lorry sides. The lorry stopped suddenly with rather a loud crash, but fortunately stayed upright.

There were screams, some of fear, some of pain, and then a loud explosion.

'What was that, what was that?' Sally felt bruised and battered, but she knew that she was otherwise unhurt and that somewhere with her, in the intense dark, was Millie, but where?

I won't panic; I know she's here. I was touching her just a moment or two ago. But that must have been a bomb. What did it hit?

She began to crawl blindly, feeling around under the blanket of materials. 'Millie, Millie, please be all right, please...'

Then she heard Sebastian's voice. 'And what about poor old me? Come on, Sal, there's a good girl. Millie crawled over here and she's dazed but all right. They tried to blow us up, the swine. How on earth they missed any part of the convoy, I cannot imagine. Blew a ruddy great hole in some poor farmer's field. Perhaps Jerry isn't as rigid about eye tests as our air force. Let me help you down.'

'I'll catch her, Seb,' came Max's voice from beside Sebastian and she emerged from under the costumes to see him reach up to help her out to join the others.

Even in her distressed state, she was conscious of Sebastian's calm – and Max's for that matter. Could anything rattle their quiet determination in any situation?

'They're off to miss more sitting targets, thank

God, and we've been stopped by banging into an overturned transporter. Just as well it was here or we would have ploughed straight through that wall and into the river. Nice night for a swim.'

'Who's in the lorry?' Sally asked, her heart was beating rapidly. Although several company members were walking around looking rather dazed, there was no sound at all from the crashed vehicle.

'Hold my hand, Sally?' The trembling voice was Millie's. 'Casualties? We must have sustained casualties.'

'The piano's a gonner, and the double bass.'

Millie's gasp was audible.

'Instruments, Millie, not people.' Max, sporting evidence of a bloody nose and with what was already turning into the king of all black eyes, had finished checking each lorry. 'Thank heavens you two girls are all right. It will be some time before our Sebastian will attempt an arabesque, Millie; his right ankle's swelling up like a balloon.' He turned to where the tall slender shape that was Sebastian was now leaning against the overturned lorry. 'We've been damned lucky, Seb; no serious injuries. Bruises, cuts, a few sprains, I think, and one or two obviously trying to deal with shock. The lorries and our equipment bore the brunt. Damned capable drivers, but had the blighters dropped more bombs... Can you climb into the cab, old chap?'

Sebastian winced. 'Rather heave myself up onto the tailgate.'

'Nonsense, Sebastian,' said Millie forcefully, 'the foot must be elevated, not dangled from the back of a lorry. Sally took a first-aid course. You'll bandage him up, won't you, Sally?'

Neither nurse nor patient looked convinced.

'Just get it done,' ordered Max, 'and by the time I give the order to move.'

'I'll do it, Sally,' said Millie, relenting when she saw Sally's face. 'Sprains are a daily risk for dancers and so I've done it a lot.'

'What if it's broken? It's getting awfully fat. Does it hurt really badly, Sebastian?'

'I'll live, Sal. Would you be an angel and follow Max. I'm not sure that he realises he's bleeding. See that he's all right, please. Much good I am – this damned ankle. I'll find something to lean on and come after you.'

'You'll do nothing of the sort; that ankle might be broken, Seb.' Millie seemed glad to have found someone to look after. 'Sally is perfectly capable of checking on other injuries.'

Sally took a quick breath. She rather hoped that Sybil or perhaps the incomparable Lalita had already cleaned up Max's face – or any other injuries sustained by company members – before they found out just how hopeless her first-aid skills were. But she owed it to them all to do what she could. She straightened her shoulders and breathed in and out a few times. 'Good, I can do this,' she said and began to walk among the stranded vehicles, determined to find Max and to clean his face, no matter how bad it was.

'And no matter how badly anyone's hurt I will not faint, I will not,' she said without realising that she had spoken aloud.

'Of course you won't faint,' said the somehow

still immaculate Sybil. 'I've cleaned Max's nose-bleed – if you were looking for him – but two of the Balladeers have cuts and someone has been violently sick over some of the costumes. Be an angel, Sally, cuts first – there's some clean water in that bottle over there – and let me know if any-one is still bleeding when you've cleaned them up. Clean cloth and a bit of pressure should do it. And if you could just get that ghastly mess off the Ugly Sisters' ball gowns before it sets, I'll be in your debt.'

Sally, finding it hard to breathe since the smell was so awful, attended to the cuts sustained by the men first.

'What caused this one?' she asked looking at a nasty cut on the younger man's forehead. 'Doesn't look as if you banged it.'

'He's the luckiest bugger in England tonight, love,' said the older Balladeer. 'Me too, I sup-pose, being so near him at the time, but that track was made by a bullet. Came through the canvas and ricocheted off the French horn. No wonder he were sick.'

'No wonder,' said Sally, as she tried and failed to find a smile.

'He should have it made into a brooch for the wife. See how close you came to losing me.'

They both laughed and now Sally managed to smile with them as she dabbed gently at the long cut.

'She'd probably rather have the bullet, Sid; threaten to use it next time you and me stays too long in Blackpool.'

That remark really made them laugh and Sally,

now desperately cleaning up the vomit, wondered at them. Was this humour the Blitz Spirit, which the newspapers spoke about? One or possibly both of the men had been very close to death just a few minutes before and here they were laughing.

'You're the prettiest nurse we've ever had taking care of us, isn't she, Sid?'

'I'm nowhere near being a nurse; I did take a first-aid course and I was a complete failure. My friend, Grace, tiny little person like Millie, she could deal with anything.'

'Good for Grace. But, trust us, Sal, you should write to her now and say, "Graduation was delayed but have now passed with flying colours."'

And they laughed again.

Max was discussing the safest route to London with their military drivers. He knew the company were exhausted and wanted to take the quickest road home.

'Not a good idea. Jerry likes to drop excess cargo to make his plane quicker on the way home.'

'So we don't go the obvious way?'

'That's right, Mr Hunter. Any planes still airborne will be anxious to score as many points as possible as they go home. Wouldn't like to be the Jerry who has to tell his boss that he couldn't hit any part of an entire convoy of army vehicles in the middle of a main road.'

'And they know which trunk road we're on.'

'Right, so, we've had a good look at our fuel tanks and we figure we've got enough to let us do a little sightseeing. We have scouts out but a motorbike can't outrun a plane.'

'I know you'll all do your best. Maybe we'll grab some sleep.'

A week later, the frightening incident had been banished to the 'unpleasant memories' folder. Sebastian, still limping badly, was out with Max and a few others at a male-voice lunchtime event at St Barts. Sally and Millie, wearing their most casual outfits and with their hair wrapped in scarves, were having a 'tidy up while we get ready for Christmas' day.

Millie finished very quickly and since Sally had offered to do the week's ironing, began again to talk of her hopes of paying her respects at her husband's grave.

Sally realised that she had begun to iron a very delicate silk blouse and, since, at the same time, she was trying to give Millie her undivided attention, was paying little or no attention to the hot iron. With a shriek of anguish she lifted it up just in time to avoid a scorch mark or possibly even a huge iron-shaped hole.

Millie was so involved in her planning that she seemed unaware of Sally's near miss.

Sally put the blouse aside while she waited for the iron to cool. She looked through the clean-clothes basket, picked up the kitchen tablecloth and began to iron it.

'Did you hear our revered landlord this morning when I put the tea-stained one on the table?'

Millie shook her head. 'What was it? Some wise words from this terrifying grandmother of his?'

Sally laughed and was delighted to hear Millie

join in. 'Indeed it was. Grandmamma had standards, Millie, standards. If we lower them, the
enemy has won.'

'Not sure I'd have liked his grandmother; the
woman has a lot to answer for, I think. But never
mind that. I hope you told him to iron the clean
one himself.'

'Never thought of that but I'd love to have told
his grandmamma to iron it; frightening woman.'

'She was an angel, Sally Brewer, one with the
highest standards which, I have to admit, she was
able to indulge because she lived in the era of the
servant class.'

Sebastian had returned, obviously in time to
hear at least the end of their conversation. 'But,'
he continued, 'being not frightening but formidable, she would have worked out how to do it.
"Needs must," she used to say. Now fill me in on
your morning's chatter, if it didn't all involve
household chores.'

And Sally did. She finished by telling him that
she hoped to persuade Millie to go to Dartford
with her.

'Great idea, Sal, but I have to tell you both that
if Millie prefers to stay here, Sybil and Lalita are
happy to make use of her.' He laughed and turned
to Millie. 'If, of course, you want peace and quiet,
then Dmitri and I will stand at the end of the moat
and fight them off.'

'Dmitri?' So far Millie had not met this enig-
matic character.

'Russian aristocrat, accountant, writer and car
mechanic, Millicent. According to him, you are a
ballerina and therefore must be cherished.'

251

'Sweet man. But, Seb, you appear to be empty-handed and did you not agree to arrange supper this evening?'

'You'll break his heart if he discovers that your main interest is food.'

'He's Russian. Aristocrat or not – he'll understand.'

'Very well. Come along, ladies, and I'll show you what we have to go with our non-rationed rabbit sausages.' Sebastian ushered them, like ducklings, ahead of him and into the kitchen. '*Voilà.*'

'Where on earth did you get that?' The girls had been muttering about rabbits but Sebastian's second surprise caused them to question him in unison.

Sebastian handed Millie the bottle that claimed to be claret. 'Dmitri,' he said. 'He helped another of the residents with his car in return for this. My clever Russian prefers what he calls "Wodka" and, since he has a friend who had a bottle or two to hand, I gave him a little remuneration and he gave me the wine.'

'Is this black market, Seb?' asked Millie.

'Shouldn't think so, darling. Alcohol isn't rationed; it's merely dreadfully expensive. Of course, French wines are becoming more and more difficult to obtain; between bombing raids and U-boats. I hope the vineyards are safe but why should they be, if ordinary homes and wonderful historical buildings are not?' Sebastian pretended to sigh. 'Those of us who have developed a taste for lovely French cheese with a glass of the right vintage are doomed.'

Millie stood up quickly. 'Don't make stupid

jokes, Seb, doomed? What do you know about being doomed?'

'Bad taste, Millie, sorry. Now let's cook the sausages and serve them with some lovely mashed potato. We'll have a glass of wine, and I'll tell you what we were given to eat in the canteen or whatever it's called at St Barts.'

His basic decency saved the situation, and since he pleased Millie and of course Sally by discussing the area around Arras and making suggestions as to where there might eventually be a British base at which ENSA could perform in relative safety, the evening was spent quite happily.

Next morning, glad to be out in reasonably fresh air, they walked to the theatre.

'Well, what?' asked Millie.

Completely mystified, both Sally and Sebastian looked at her. 'Well, what what?' they asked in chorus.

'Food, you know how much food interests me. What food, Seb?'

'Oh, at the hospital? Sorry, I forgot. It was an amazingly not-bad pie, called Woolton pie.'

'Woolton? It had wool in it? Whatever next?'

'Ha ha, you are both side-splittingly hilarious. We'll get Humph to twinkle around on his toes and you two can do the comedy.'

'Sometimes, we'd be better,' said Millie in a matter-of-fact tone. 'Go on, Seb, tell.'

They were forced to hesitate at a wide water-filled hole in the pavement and Sebastian helped Sally across. Millie refused his help and, with a joyful laugh, soared across not only the puddle but also a section of pavement in a perfect 'split leap'.

'Good Lord, Millie, how did you do that, and from a standing start, too?'

'Seemed a good opportunity to see if I could still manage.' She looked measuringly at him, a mischievous smile on her face, 'You could too, Seb. If you start now, I'd say in six or seven years, if your dodgy ankle holds up, you'll have mastered it.'

'No, thanks. My pelvis, and no doubt other parts of my rather splendid body, weren't designed for the ballet.'

Sally was still looking at Millie in wonder. 'Even in uniform, that was beautiful, Millie.'

'Thanks, but it wouldn't have been if I'd been wearing my uniform skirt; passers-by would have received quite a shock. Now go on, Seb, and tell us about the pie. If you say it's really good we could try it at home.'

'Keep up politically. Do you two read nothing but girlie magazines?'

Sally frowned sadly at him. 'Sebastian Brady, I'm not sure you meant that.'

Suddenly aware of what he had said, Sebastian laughed. 'Sorry, ladies, women's magazines. The pie was basically a mixture of vegetables, heavy on potatoes and cauliflower, turnips and carrots, all readily available in the British victory garden or in your local greengrocer's. Was there an onion? I can't remember; everything tastes good with an onion, don't you agree? The vegetables were cooked – in some sort of stock, I suppose – and then put in a pie dish with a lovely pastry top, brushed with a little egg, or perhaps a little margarine because, after baking until the pastry was cooked, it came out all golden – just like Mummy used to make, at least Sally's mummy, I bet. Our old chum, the chef at the Savoy, created it and named it in honour of Lord Woolton who is...' He waited unsuccessfully and then filled in, 'Head of the Ministry of Food.'

'Sounds stodgy; I'd rather have the vegetables raw, except the potatoes.'

'I dream of oranges,' sighed Sally. 'Tinned things just aren't the same.'

'Papayas,' said Sebastian. 'Has either of you ever tasted papaya?'

They shook their heads as they walked. 'Haven't even heard of it,' said Sally.

'Ceylon,' mused Sebastian, 'my childhood, the most incredible fruits grew in our garden: bananas, pineapples, mangoes, papayas. Best tastes in the world, I think; I remember the first fresh papaya I ever had, so tasty, and pomegranates. A pomegranate is so beautiful, lovely red-gold skin, slice it in two and you have two bowls of glistening seeds, like edible rubies. My Senegalese Clara said that the fruit grown in Ceylon both cured and prevented illness. Look at me, never so much as a bad sniffle, ever.'

'Then, next time you're there, Seb, you must pick some for us.'

'We'll all go,' promised Sebastian, 'when this damned war is over.'

TWELVE

Sally had tried very hard to persuade Millie to go with her to Dartford for Christmas but Millie was adamant – if she went anywhere at all, it would be either to her parents' home or to that of her in-laws.

'You're so kind, Sally, and I do thank your parents for a very genuine invitation but – not this year. I would add nothing to the party and might dampen everyone else's pleasure. Another time, perhaps. We could do Christmas shopping together, though; something special for Seb. Any ideas?'

'What's a war bond? There was a bit on the wireless about sensible gifts this Christmas. I wrote down a few things that were suggested. War bonds, whatever they are. Flasks to take to the shelters; that's not a bad idea – Max broke his a few days ago.'

Millie looked up from restitching the hem of her uniform skirt, which she had somehow caught on a packing case. 'Max? Do we have to buy gifts for everyone?'

Sally laughed. 'Of course not. But if anyone was to give Max a gift, then a new flask would be a good idea.'

'Patrick's parents' flasks are ancient, Sally. Two new ones might be rather nice. What else was suggested that's not too expensive?'

'The only other thing I wrote down is a sleeping bag. It was suggested for use in the shelters too.'

'Can't see my mum in a sleeping bag.'

'Does she bake?'

'Yes.'

'So does mine and I thought I'd buy her some nuts; in one of her letters she was complaining about the price of nuts and the difficulty of getting fruit for cakes and Christmas puddings, things like currants. What if we went to Fortnum and Mason and if they have a pretty box of nuts and dried fruits I could buy one for Christmas.'

'And then she uses her present to make you a cake?'

Sally frowned thinking that Millie was probably right. 'Hm, does sound rather mean – let's forget that idea, although I will buy some just to take. Have you been to a place called Jackson's of Piccadilly?'

'The tea shop?' Millie was staring across the room. 'Not a bad idea, Sally. I haven't been there in years and I think it does much more than tea now. Cups,' she said, and Sally saw that she was looking at exquisite and probably valuable porcelain cups in Sebastian's display cabinet.

'Super idea, but I couldn't begin to afford anything like that.'

Millie stood up and folded the mended skirt. 'Those are antiques but we could go to Jackson's for some tea and, who knows, perhaps they sell lovely tea cups or teapots. My mum has a weakness for teapots.'

Immediately Sally began to feel guilty. The

Petries, her parents' oldest friends, sold fine teas. She could not possibly go to another outlet, no matter how historical or famous.

'We'll buy a book for Seb,' decided Millie, unwittingly making Sally feel better. 'We'll find out what has to be read this Christmas, and if Jackson's sell china, I'll buy one pretty cup and saucer for my mum, cigarettes for Patrick's dad and hankies for his mum. That one of yours must have cost a fortune, Sally, where did you get it?'

For a moment Sally could not recall an expensive handkerchief and then she remembered Sybil's handkerchief, which she had washed and ironed so carefully and tried to return to its owner who had gently pushed it away. 'Keep it, child, I have several.' The handkerchief was at the bottom of her underwear drawer, being saved for a special occasion.

'Sybil gave it to me.' She said no more and Millie did not ask.

'Hankies make a nice present and I'll think of something for my dad. First free time, Christmas shopping it is,' said Sally, 'and I must buy cards too. I won't have a friend left in the world soon if I don't keep in touch.'

'Real friends understand; look at me. I've stayed away from everyone since I lost Patrick and my genuine friends have found me, but I still think I'll stay here this year. Just can't handle "Deck the Halls."'

On the Tuesday of Christmas week they were given a two-hour break and, having had lots of fun making lists, reading book reviews and seeking advice, they went Christmas shopping.

'These books have been suggested for Seb,' said Millie. '*Mildred Pierce* by someone called James M. Cain, but there's too much female hysteria, according to the review I read, though the writer has a good reputation. Then there's *Blood, Sweat and Tears* by guess who?'

'Not the foggiest.'

'Sally Brewer! The PM, Winston Churchill. Seb's a great fan, isn't he? Seems an ideal choice.'

'I'm not sure, Millie. Originally, he was, but his praise has been somewhat less enthusiastic this year.'

'By the way, none of my business, of course, but is there some reason why Seb isn't in one of the services?'

Sally thought before answering. Sebastian's business was his own but Millie had seen her own husband give up his career and then his life serving his country. Perhaps she had a right to know why a seemingly able-bodied young man had not been compelled to enlist. 'He did try to enlist, wanted to fly, but he was rejected; some inner ear problem.' She would not add that Sebastian's failure – as he saw it – was, she believed, the reason he drove himself so hard for ENSA.

'Poor Seb. Thanks for telling me; I'm sorry I asked; I really should know Seb well enough by now not to have doubted.'

'Yes, you should,' said Sally, 'but I wondered too, just at first. Now let's get on with finding him a gift.'

'*Little Town on the Prairie*, Sally, the latest by an American writer, lovely, happy books; that's my intellectual level.'

'It's for children.'

'I've read one of her books before; fascinating, possibly based on truth, and definitely not just for children.'

'Then I'll buy a copy for you for Christmas and you can pretend you're surprised.'

'Oh, Sally, I can't believe it.'

Millie's eyes had filled with tears and Sally tensed, wondering what on earth she had said that could possibly have upset Millie. 'Sorry, Millie, did I say something wrong?'

To her surprise, especially since they were standing in a large department store, the usually undemonstrative Millie threw her arms around her. 'No, absolutely not. Patrick used to say that, every birthday, every Christmas, every anniversary, first time we danced together, first time we ... well, never mind, just every anniversary. He was the world's worst gift buyer, definitely a chocolates-or-flowers man, and he never could think of anything original. His mother and I used to leave big hints and eventually he would say, "I'll buy you the silly book" – or whatever else it was that had been hinted at – "and you can pretend to be surprised." We miss that, his mum and I, Sally, so thank you.'

'You're welcome,' Sally smiled as she answered but she was thinking that sometimes friendship was like trying to put one's feet on the only safe place on an ice-covered lake. One false move and you fall through. But, she decided, if Millie wants a children's book for Christmas then she shall have it.

There was a buzz in the stores that was not wholly connected to Christmas. The news of the Japanese attack on the American fleet at a place called Pearl Harbor was on everyone's lips.

'They'll be in the war now with men as well as all the aid they've been giving us. Britain won't have to hold the fort alone now.'

Even billboards announced that 'THE YANKS ARE COMING', and excitement and euphoria managed to lift the spirits of a nation wondering how to celebrate Christmas and keep their families warm this first winter since the introduction of coal rationing.

Sally and Millie enjoyed their few hours immensely and Sally, who had been conscious for some time that she wore only her uniform or the clothes the company had donated to her, went shopping but instead of a new dress for Christmas, she bought as much chocolate, which wasn't yet rationed, as she could afford. 'I'll put it in a basket and leave it for everyone. All I did at the time was say thank you.'

'No one expects anything, Sally.'

'I know but I feel better. Now, Jackson's. I think my mum would love one of their lovely red tins; she keeps buttons in tins, threads, pins. Maybe they'll sell one without tea but if not, I'm sure Mrs Petrie will understand.'

Eventually, after much discussion, they bought Sebastian the latest book by A. J. Cronin, *The Keys of the Kingdom.*

'All the other writers, apart from Mr C., are American and this year we definitely want to buy

British,' said Millie.

Sally, agreeing wholeheartedly, smiled as she hid her purchase of a little book called *Little Town on the Prairie* in her handbag.

Later, as they wrapped their gifts, Sally's thoughts flew to past Christmases, five Petrie children, Grace, herself and, at some point during the day, Stan, Rose Petrie's best friend, the Humbles from the farm, Miss Pritchard if she wasn't having Christmas lunch with the vicar and his family, and anyone else who was lonely. No, perhaps Millie was not quite ready for quite so much fun and laughter.

'You'll be welcome in my home whenever you choose, Millie, and you're used to sleeping in the same room as me so sharing at our flat wouldn't be a shock.'

It was Wednesday, Christmas Eve, and Sally, full of excitement and expectation, was on the train to Dartford before it occurred to her that Millie might well be looking forward to a room to herself – even if it was only for one night.

She heard someone blow a whistle, and the train, groaning as if it objected, was now beginning to move. Dartford. She was going home and for the first time in her life, the town now meant more than family and old school friends. Jon had lived here too. All the time that Sally Brewer had lived in Dartford, so had Jon and she had not known him, had not been aware of him. Had they passed each other on the street? Had he ever enjoyed a Sunday morning stroll in the park, or, was it more likely that owners of country estates walked around their own grounds? Had he taken his wife to see a film in the cinema where she occasionally sold ice cream? Maudie would answer all her questions, if Sally could somehow speak to Maudie without worrying her parents. She remembered her parents' reaction to the ring. What would they say or do or feel if they knew that their daughter was ... *say it, Sally, say it* ... in love with a ... sailor ... all right, all right, she tried to quieten her conscience – in love with Jonathon Galbraith, Lord Hedges?

Her joy dissipated. For the first time she saw how stupid she had been even to think about Jon, to dream about him. He did not love her, he could not. Never had he said the slightest thing that would make her believe he did not love his wife still. She had left him; he had not left her. And now Jon was missing. His face swam before her, thick dark hair brushed back from his forehead, his eyes, almost cold as he discussed the ring and then warm and gentle as he asked her to write but always, always, an underlying sadness. For a moment she felt that the emotion building inside her would explode.

He will be found... Feverishly Sally went over and over her short meetings with Jon, the words they had spoken, the letters they had written. She closed her eyes and felt a tear escape and run down her cheek. Afraid that others would follow, she wiped it away with her hand and sat up straight.

Nothing had happened. Nothing that could be regretted had been said by either of them. 'He was kind and generous to me; he was lonely and asked

263

me to write to him and I did. That's all there is to it, but he's a friend and I'll never give up hoping he'll be found – for Maudie's sake; that's what friends do.'

She could almost feel herself changing as the train whistled and shunted itself across Kent, the driver, the engineer and the guard more alert than ever as they watched the sky. Sophistication was falling off her as if she was shedding a skin and the nearer she got to Dartford, the more excited she became. All her old friends, she felt sure, were going to be there. She had had no time to write to Grace or to receive a reply. Perhaps Grace would be sharing her room. She had certainly spent a lot of time with the Brewers last year when her sister had been killed in the raid.

I'd love to spend some time with Grace, and hear all about farming. Sally looked at her fingernails and decided happily that they were very elegant and obviously totally unsuitable for digging potatoes or milking cows. *No, farming would not have appealed to me at all.* She looked out through an unprotected square of glass in the carriage window and pictured shy, quiet Grace dealing with large, lumbering cows.

Who would ever have thought that Grace would become a land girl? A nurse maybe, a secretary in an office certainly, an office where her work would be as neat and tidy as Grace herself.

I'll make a New Year's resolution now. I will use daylight travel time in the lorries to keep up with my friends. Maybe Millie will too; she'll write to the friends who have kept looking out for her and caring about her. Sally laughed out loud and became aware of unfriendly looks from two dowagers on the opposite side of the carriage. 'If they recognise me, they don't like me, and if they don't recognise me, they still don't like me.'

She awarded them a special smile. *Poor things, being grumpy just because someone laughed.* 'Happy Christmas, ladies,' she said. 'Isn't it wonderful to be going home for Christmas?'

'You should be in the services,' said one of the dowagers, 'doing your duty.'

Should she reply? Tell them that she was in ENSA and often worked seven days a week, that she had spent nights on the floors of uncomfortable lorries or in almost tumbledown buildings with nothing but a coarse blanket for a cover, that she had dressed herself up in a pretty dress and gone out to entertain battle-scarred troops without so much as a cup of tea to revive her after a long, sometimes frightening journey?

No, she would not.

'Decorations. Come on, everyone, we are going to make these the best decorations in Dartford. Where's your dad's silver paper, Rose? Your mum says there were huge sheets from a tea box.'

Rose produced the sheets, some scissors, and glue and in no time at all they were sitting on the floor, where they had sat so often as little girls, and were cutting the sheets into strips. When the strips were done, the girls cut them into equal-size pieces to be shaped into links as the decorators intended to string both the Brewers' and the Petries' front rooms with shining silver chains. Christmas was going to be even more wonderful than she had hoped. For the first time in ... none of them could remember when they had last been together but that made them even more determined to be as happy as possible while they could. The extra special icing on the Christmas cake of pleasure was that a Christmas card, simply informing his parents that he would be home soon, had arrived from Sam. They already knew he had escaped from his POW camp and now they learned he had somehow reached the north of Italy. The card had been delivered by the local Roman Catholic priest who would only say that it had taken a long and tortuous journey. Flora, hearing in her head the words 'Careless Talk Costs Lives' could not contain her joy. Last year had come the news that her youngest son was dead and her eldest in a POW camp. But now, a year later, he was on his way home somehow and she would be ready for him.

'Such a pity I can't keep a piece of this ham for him,' she was heard saying several times over the holiday. 'He'll not have had much food to eat this year.'

'Don't fret, Flora,' said Fred, 'our boy's coming home and today all our girls are here. Let's enjoy every speeding minute.'

Sally wept unashamedly as the train drew out of Dartford Station. Her break had been sheer delight except that there had been no sign at all of Maudie who had, no doubt, gone somewhere for Christmas, perhaps even to stay with Fedora.

How stupid of me. I should have telephoned her before I left London.

The totally inadequate overnight bag she had brought with her was stuffed full of her Christmas gifts: among them a hand-knit cardigan from her mother in a pale peach – such a lovely change from khaki or green – a box of very good quality white notepaper from the twins, complete with instructions that had made everyone laugh and Sally groan with embarrassment – 'This is notepaper. It is to be used for writing to friends and family REGULARLY' – a jar of scented hand cream Grace had bought in Boots the chemist. It had a pretty picture of a lily of the valley flower on the label and the words *Muguet de Bois* underneath. Sally knew the words did not translate as 'lily of the valley', but as 'something' of the woods. She would ask Lalita for the exact translation. Her favourite gift, though, was from her father. It was a small but elegant metal folder with the words 'Stamps and Diary' etched into the front. Inside was a small red holder with a book of stamps tucked into it, and a tiny engagement diary for 1942. The writing on each page was so small that she had to strain to read it, but apart from a space for every day of the year, there was information on everything from Bank of England Dividend Rates – which was of absolutely no interest to her – to the names and birth dates of each member of the Royal Family, which she was delighted to have. So far she had written nothing in the engagement diary. That will come, she thought. Some day soon I'll write 'Off to France' on one of these little blanks. But first I have to contact Maude.

Assuming that she would be very likely to meet Maude during her short stay in Dartford, Sally had made the excuse that she needed to do private last-minute shopping and had run up to a favourite shop, Horrell and Goff's, where she had found a scented drawer liner, so ladylike and just right, she thought, for a lady like Maude. The unopened package now sat on top of her suitcase, accusing her of not being properly prepared.

I know, I know, she told herself over and over. I should have telephoned and made an appointment. I could have invited her for Christmas tea. She would have enjoyed meeting Miss Pritchard; probably she already knows her. And why did I not ask Mum to invite her to visit us? She could have told Mum just how wonderful Jon is, how kind, how caring.

Before she could worry any more about what she should or should not have done, the train stopped.

'Oh, no, not again.' Groans and moans were coming from all sides.

Sally tried to see out of the taped-up windows but since it was already almost four o'clock, it was too dark.

'Where's the guard?'

'Where's the conductor?'

'Why have we stopped?'

Questions were flying from all sides but no answers came.

And at that moment, just as if a thick blanket had been dropped over them, they were in darkness.

That was when the screams started, loud, piercing, hysterical screaming. Sally was grabbed suddenly by a middle-aged woman. 'I want to get off the train,' she hissed into Sally's face as her hard fingers clutched Sally's arm painfully.

Sally looked at her. No, it was not one of the nasty women who had travelled down with her. *Another one. Just my luck.*

'Someone close to the door will open it,' began Sally who was unable to continue as the terrified woman gripped harder and tighter, and screamed even more loudly so that now the carriage was full of chaos. Children, frightened by the screams, began to wail. Sally could vaguely hear an official voice but it was impossible to make out what was being said. What was it the instructor had said about hysteria in that long ago first-aid course? She had not the faintest idea and so she relied on instinct. She shook the woman who seemed determined to draw blood from her arm. 'Let go and be quiet,' she said as firmly as she could.

Sally tried to make out the features of any other worried passenger and then, realising that her fellow passenger had let go of her arm, she slipped out of her best 'out-of-uniform' shoes and climbed up onto the long padded seat.

She clapped her hands as loudly as she could and shouted, 'Quiet, please.'

To her great surprise the shouting stopped and an almost eerie silence, punctuated by sobs from small children, took its place. Sally felt rather silly, standing in her stockings on the seat.

'You tell 'em, love,' shouted a burly man who had just pushed open the door to the corridor, allowing a little light to enter the crowded coach. 'I'll have a look out here and see what's up; some-

269

thing on the line is all, I bet. Can't hear no dratted planes.'

The hysteria inside the coach had abated somewhat and, with the door held open firmly the people in Sally's carriage could hear that there was similar panic further down.

'It's blasted Jerry up to no good again. We have to get off; they're going to blow up the train.'

At that announcement from a youngish man, the carriage once more rang with screams and shouts and even blows as people, including the woman who had grabbed Sally, pushed and pulled in their haste to get out. Sally had noticed the young man as she got onto the train, wondering idly why he was not in uniform, but making no judgements as several valid reasons immediately sprang to mind.

The corridor was now filled with frightened, often hysterical people, many of whom, just the day before had celebrated the birth of the Prince of Peace. Sally, feeling decidedly silly, climbed down from her bench, groped around for her shoes and slipped them on.

'Now then, now then,' came the very loud voice of authority. 'What's going on here then?' The conductor, carrying a large torch, was pushing his way through the heaving mass of people, scolding as he went. 'I told yous there was a slight hiccup, bit of a scare on the line up ahead, but the disposal boys's got here and it's nothing but some poor blighter's laundry got dropped off the bridge. There, told you,' he finished as the light went on. 'Bit of a scare, understandable, but wasn't no need to panic now, was there?'

'We heard nothing, not a word, I shall be

writing to my MP.'

'You do that, love; sure he's got all the time in the world to answer you. Too busy yelling, half of you, and so I'll tell him if he shows his nose.'

And off he went to the next coach. Sally sat down and again turned her face to the window as if she found the pattern of lines of tape fascinating. She did not want to look into the faces of the women across from her.

With a shudder and then a jolt, followed shortly by another, the train began to move gently away, picking up speed as it went. Sally closed her eyes, heard the familiar comforting sound of the whistle and sang her repertoire of new songs in her head until they arrived in London.

THIRTEEN

Max was in an absolutely foul temper, not a good sign and especially not on New Year's Eve. 'Those of you who had Christmas leave, tell me that you have done everything I asked you to do.' He stood looking into every face and watched some flush a little, some look quietly proud of themselves and some look slightly worried. Sally was definitely in that group. Before Christmas Max had announced that they might be going overseas and those who wanted to be selected for overseas work were asked to make a will.

'We all know that we're probably in danger here rather often, but the powers that be feel that there's more need to be organised if undertaking work in areas of active conflict. It's not tempting fate, it's simply a sensible precaution.'

He seemed to be looking straight at Sally who had deliberately avoided the unpleasant task. 'I did mean to do it but I haven't got anything to leave anyone anyway.' Immediately she saw a picture of her hand showing the beautiful ring. What was she to do about that? She could not wear it; Jon had bought it with love in his heart, not for her, but for his wife. Were she to wear it, she would think of her...

'Your parents are your next of kin, Sally, and would inherit.' Max's deep voice broke into her thoughts. 'That goes for several of you, but just in case there's something you would really like your best chum to have, make a will. Did anyone do it?'

Not a hand went up.

'Christmas, Max, too busy.'

'Excuses, excuses. By next Monday, ladies and gentlemen, or I'll be looking for new blood. And, by the way, we are recruiting. I think we need our own little orchestra. Can't possibly move a group like Geraldo's orchestra, but we need something slightly grander than we have; we need wood-winds and strings, if anyone knows an experienced player? We were sent some "I'm available" letters earlier but mainly pianists, a guitarist, two drummers.'

'Guitar's a stringed instrument, Max,' shouted one of the Balladeers.

'How kind of you to point that out.' Sarcasm dripped from Max's voice but then he smiled. 'I don't particularly want soloists, but a classically trained guitarist who could do any and all musical styles would be a godsend. Lal, Sybil, look up his details, please. If he's good then he could add something to our little group. We're still looking for a few violins, a cello maybe.'

'Double bass is a really versatile instrument, Max,' put in Sam, who rarely spoke, 'everything from great classical–'

Humph interrupted him, 'All the way up to the latest jazz.'

Everyone laughed.

'All right, smarty, get the feelers out and please, not your second cousin twice removed who had violin lessons when he was ten and played at the village fête. We want musicians. Think Henry Hall, Lou Preager, Geraldo. I want new comic routines; sorry, Humph, remember that the radio broadcasts carry your jokes to every military base we have, all over the world. The troops don't want to hear it all over again when we turn up in person. New dance routines, some new speeches or readings, Seb. Have you heard or read anything by a chap called Dylan Thomas, a Welshman? Sir Seymour thinks he'll be great some day and we want to be up to date with the latest thing.'

Sebastian was forced to admit that he had never heard of the Welshman, 'and anything that I do find would probably be better read or recited in a Welsh accent. That'll take me a few days to work up.'

The company went to their rehearsals grumbling a little but also excited. They knew they had to move on and what better time to be trying something new than a new year?

Sally had hoped that she was safe with her programme, or that she would be offered a speaking part in something, anything. She had her date arranged for the advertisement photographs, her mother having agreed to come up to London and to meet Sebastian and Millie if their schedules allowed, but that wasn't until the spring. It meant that she was available to travel with the company to perform on two bases in Scotland.

Train journeys continued to be a nightmare, continually delayed or cancelled. She could remember every moment of her fairly short journey back from Dartford and had several times woken up dreaming that the train was being attacked by German aircraft. How much more dangerous it would be to travel almost the entire length of the United Kingdom. Somehow travelling up in a convoy of lorries did not seem quite so dangerous.

But you've been in a lorry that they tried to bomb, she told herself. More than once.

'Perhaps it's just that a train is a much bigger target and I won't know a single person on it,' she confessed to her friends.

'We're at the beginning of the fourth year of this war, Sally. It has to be over soon. The Americans will be here to help before long, and they're a huge power; they'll scare Jerry,' Millie assured her. 'Just you wait and see.'

'If Max sees the "Cleaner" campaign pictures and I do get this chance with Mr Coward, maybe he'll give me something, just the smallest part – the maid, the cleaning lady... Oh, I do so want to be an actress. I'm not a Vera Lynn or a Beryl Davis.'

'Approach Max then, ask Lal to have a little word, but don't put your singing voice down.'

But Max was adamant. 'You're not ready, Sally. You're a beautiful girl with a great figure and the men love just looking at you.'

'I'd still look the same as an actress.'

'Not a good sales pitch. Looks have zilch to do with ability; you have ability. I'm upping the ante, Sally, and if you work hard, you'll improve and, one day, perhaps in a month or two, maybe less, who knows, I'll find a few words for you to deliver – onstage. Now go away and see if you can sing and act at the same time. I want to hear you deliver, "Mad About the Boy" and I want your body singing too. The delivery needs more than a little ooh-la-la; you can do it.'

Sally had not the slightest idea what he was talking about and he could see it written on her face. 'Sally, you have to relax, let go of your inhibitions; use those fabulous "Come to bed eyes" of yours. It's not a simple little love song; it's certainly not a sweet little girl song. It's a woman's song. Go find Lal; if she could get brainless tenors sounding wonderful, you should be a walkover. Sam will play it for you, listen to him play it; the music should tell you what to do. Go.'

Since there was no sign of either, Sally looked for Sebastian and found him in a huddle with two actors and a playwright. They were obviously very busy and so she turned away and began to walk back to the rehearsal area where, she decided, she was eventually likely to find Lalita. Sebastian caught up with her.

'Problem, Sal? Tell Uncle Sebastian.'

'You're not nearly old enough to be my uncle, and I don't want to take you away from your work.'

'I'll always have time for you, Sally, and, believe me, I could – legally – be your uncle even if I were younger than you are. I know, I know, sounds impossible but when we have time to play I'll show you how. Now tell me, who stole your chocolate?'

'What are you talking about?'

'I am trying to cheer you and failing miserably. Tell me your problem and we'll return to the chocolate later.'

She told him about her orders from Max. 'I don't know what he means, Sebastian. I sing or speak with my tongue, teeth and lips and, of course, my diaphragm. What else does he want?'

'Sex.'

'You're insane.'

'Sally, that number is a sexy song and I think you equate sexiness with vulgarity. They're not at all the same thing. You're used to singing sweet little love songs. Your voice is pleasant, not great, but pleasant on the ear. You look fabulous – when you're not frowning as you are now. Watch out, the wind will change and your face will stick like that.'

'Stop talking nonsense and tell me what else I need to do.'

'Have you seen Carmen Miranda in films?'

Sally smiled. 'Of course, she's fabulous. How does she keep all that fruit on her head?'

'Too bad there's a war on; there's no chance of

a bunch of bananas for you but she doesn't need them to be sexy. She projects the mood of the song with her gestures, her facial expressions, her moves, her eyes and you have to do the same.'

'I'd die of embarrassment.'

'Then you'll never make an actress, Sally.'

She rounded on him. 'That's all I want to be – an actress. Perhaps I should have stayed in Dartford; at least they were giving me parts. I could have been in a Noël Coward play instead of dressing up like a doll in pretty dresses and singing love songs. I'm not a singer.'

'You've forgotten that ENSA with the songs and the pretty frocks has given you experience, exposure and, Sally, my darling, an advertising campaign and an appearance plus a credit in a film.'

Those home truths deflated her. 'Oh, I don't mean to be so ungrateful but I want my parents to be proud of me.'

'They are.'

'Sebastian, have you the slightest idea how difficult it was for my parents to send me to a fee-paying school, to allow me to stay on there preparing for a university education while my friends were out at work? And then after all that and when I'd been accepted at a university, I refused to go because I wanted to act and they allowed me, and now what do they see?'

'Their beautiful daughter doing important war work. Sally, don't negate everything we're doing. You can see the faces in the audiences change; strained, tired faces relax, smile, laugh. Now, I want you to listen as often as possible to the Forces request programmes. Maybe some chap will ask for "Mad About the Boy" and you'll hear how a pro sings it.'

'How a pro sings what, Seb?' They had not heard Lal coming in.

'The song Max wants.'

'Quite a change for you, Sally, but you're an actress, you can do it. Play it for her, Seb.'

'Sorry, Lal, my skills aren't up to that. Christmas carols by the fire are more my style.'

'Just as well I'm here then, Seb.' Sam Castleton had followed Lal and now he sat down at the piano and began to play. There was no music in front of him.

'I'm sorry but I don't know the words.' Sally could see her career dissolving before her.

'I have it in the office. Now watch and listen.' Sam played the song again but this time, Lal sang to his accompaniment. Her voice was husky but true and, as she sang, she moved around the room, using her hands to reach out to people – some who were not there but with whom she was obviously communicating. Sally thought she was absolutely wonderful and found herself responding and wondering how Lal managed to be sexy without being vulgar at the same time.

'Next time you're free, come along to the office to pick up my copy. Seb won't take long to learn to play it and you just try to remember Lal's performance when you're rehearsing it.' Sam's gentle face relaxed into a smile. 'Relax, Sally, you can do it and everyone knows it but you.'

Somehow an endorsement from Sam made Sally feel as if she could master almost anything. One or two of the chorus occasionally uttered

278

snide remarks: 'Max's little pet' or, more wound-ingly, 'At the Academy they always said a girl needed a hell of a lot more than big blue eyes; seems they were wrong.'

She tried to ignore remarks that she assured herself came from jealousy.

'Thanks, Sam. I'll try.'

'Great,' said Sam. 'If I'm not in the office, the music with the lyrics is on the bottom shelf of the little music cabinet. Help yourself.'

She thanked him and Lalita and left the rehearsal stage, deciding to go straight to the musicians' office to pick up the music. Tonight, New Year's Eve, she would learn to sing the song – with some ooh-la-la, whatever that was.

Sebastian had other ideas.

'We're not staying in on New Year's Eve. Don't panic, Sally; I'm rusty but I do sight-read and when we have some free time tomorrow, I'll play it for you. Meanwhile, think Lal and ooh-la-la.' He dissolved with laughter. 'Poor little Sally, if you could see your face. *"Quelle horreur"* is written all over it. Come along, we'll put on some glad rags, Millie too – high time she was out on the town – and we'll party.'

'Where?'

'No idea. Not the Savoy, we'll go to a night club – such decadence.'

Sally said nothing. She would enjoy going somewhere different with Sebastian. Her spirits had lifted. It might only be a cup of rather stewed tea at a WVS van, but Sebastian had an innate ability to turn the simplest piece of tin into pure gold. How different life in London was from her restricted life in Dartford. This war was changing everything and she could see that despite the privations, the danger and destruction, some changes were for the better.

'We are visiting a veterans' home tomorrow, aren't we?' she asked at last.

'Due there early afternoon. We can bring in 1942 with the sincere and solemn hope that its coming will also bring the end to the bloody war, and still be bright-eyed and bushy-tailed to cheer our heroes. Go alert Millie.'

Millie was limbering up on stage and Sally watched her, waiting for an opportunity to interrupt her practice. If Millie saw her she made no sign as she went through what seemed to Sally to be the most amazing contortions. She followed these with dazzling pirouettes and then small jumping steps across the stage, ending in some split-leaps. She was not out of breath; she did not seem to be sweating or stressed at all. Sally wondered what Millie would look like in the traditional ballerina's tutu and decided that she would be absolutely beautiful. Millie was not beautiful; in fact she was rather plain with no distinguishing features, but Sally decided that, even in rehearsal clothes, Millie was fragile thistledown flying across the stage.

'Gosh, you're fabulous, Millie, absolutely beautiful.'

Millie laughed. 'You're sweet, Sally. One of these days I'll take you to Sadler's Wells.' She gave Sally no time to reply. 'Did you want me for something?'

'Sebastian wants us to go home, put on some

280

glad rags and go to a night club; you will come, won't you?'

'To welcome the new year, Sal? Well, it has to be better than the last two, hasn't it? Give me ten minutes and I'll join you in the green-room.'

London on New Year's Eve was not beautiful. The smoke and dust that enveloped this most historical of cities made it virtually impossible to see the ground under one's feet. Oh, for this war to be over, for London's lights to shine again, for London's bells to ring again.

'Will cities in Germany be as dark as this, Sebastian?'

'It's dark all over the world, Sally.' Sebastian, his cashmere coat open over his dinner jacket and starched white shirt, seemed to have no difficulty in finding his way along the streets.

With Millie holding one arm and Sally clinging to the other as she tentatively picked her way down unrecognisable streets, Sebastian walked on happily. 'I was an English Springer in a past life, girls, trust me.'

And they did.

They passed others who picked their way slowly or attempted to hurry, fearing that at any moment a plane spewing death would roar out of the sky, but none did.

'Come along to the shelter with us, ladies,' suggested two young men who had already opened – and sampled – the bottles of whisky or beer they were carrying. 'Come on, bring the posh bloke; we'll teach him how to give you lovelies a good time. We got decorations up and we're having a party with dancing. Everybody welcome, except Jerry.'

'You're very kind, but no thank you,' Millie said quietly.

Sebastian pulled Sally and Millie even closer. 'Happy New Year, chaps, and thanks for the invitation but my friends prefer to be above ground.'

'Chaps, 'ear that, Charlie, according to the posh git, we're chaps. Your loss, ladies. The best party in London tonight'll be down our shelter. There's lots of us there. Great booze – we been saving for months – and food.'

'I'm sure it will be a terrific,' said Sally, as she pushed Sebastian, who looked as if he might be ready to fight, backwards. 'Have a great time, and a happy and safe New Year to you both.'

Muttering darkly about toffs and la-di-das, the young men swaggered off.

'You all right, Millie?' asked Sally. 'Beer talking; no harm in them.'

'Apart from the fact that they're not in uniform.'

'Soldiers get leave, Millie, let's just forget them.' She hugged Sebastian. 'Come on, Sir Galahad, it's getting late; where shall we go?'

'There's the Embassy Club on Bond Street; I haven't been but Max went with Sybil and enjoyed it. Or, we could take the underground to Covent Garden. The Opera House; it's operating as a night club for the duration and they have a terrific orchestra. They probably play "ballroom" as well as all the bang-up-to-the-minute dances from America.'

'Sounds lovely. What do you think, Millie?'

282

'I'm so sorry, but I just couldn't go to the Opera House–' began Millie.

'Dash it, Millie,' interrupted Sebastian. 'How insensitive of me. I should have thought; too many memories. So sorry.'

'It's all right, Seb, and don't feel badly. I thought I could manage but it's just that it's New Year's Eve...'

She left the rest unsaid but the others understood. Millie was not alone in having memories of other times. Sally too was thinking of times before the war when New Year's Eve meant that the next year was something to be welcomed, when with her family and her friends she found that lovely memories flooded in, bringing joy. She feared that Millie's memories, instead of cheering her, only made her mourn for what was lost.

'The Embassy Club, Millie? Some champagne, a little supper?'

Millie's eyes had filled with tears, obvious even in the poor light. Her voice shook when she spoke. 'I'm spoiling the evening. I'll go back to the flat, Seb, and welcome you both back next year.'

'No,' said Sally at the same time as Sebastian said, 'Absolutely not.'

'I'm ruining the evening. Please.'

'We're friends, Millie, and friends spend New Year's Eve together. Whatever we do, we'll do it together. I've just thought of something that I haven't done since I was a schoolboy and I always loved it.'

They looked at him expectantly.

'Just say if you don't like the idea and I'll abandon it, but when I was very small Grandmamma and I went to the steps of St Paul's on New Year's Eve. There was hardly a space on the steps – so many people did the same – but someone always made room for my grandmother; she had a wonderful effect on people. There was chatter and singing and we listened out for Big Ben to toll the hour and then we sang "Old Lang Syne" and wished one another a Happy New Year – people we didn't know and would never meet again – but there was such warmth and comradeship and then we went home – Grandmamma had her car – and I was allowed one sip of champagne from her glass before I went to bed. Such joy.'

'Then that's what we'll do, Seb. Right, Sally, are you up for singing "Old Lang Syne" as Big Ben brings in 1942?'

'Best idea yet, Millie.'

Sebastian, who had been slightly embarrassed as he allowed his memory to spill out, took the girls by the hand. 'Come along then, my little musketeers, all for one and one for all – and I happen to know where a nice bottle of bubbly is keeping cool.'

They reached St Paul's less than fifteen minutes before midnight. On this third New Year's Eve of the war, there was room and more for them, as Londoners chose to celebrate in the shelters or remained at home. Air-raid wardens could be seen scanning the skies just as they had done every night of the war and would continue to do until the final all clear was sounded.

At last the great clock began to toll away the old

year and count in the new. 'Bring world peace in with you,' shouted an elderly man from the steps.

'Here, here,' shouted many voices, and then it seemed that everyone in the crowd grabbed the hand of someone near them, known or unknown, joining together in a wish for world peace as they sang 'Old Lang Syne'.

FOURTEEN

January 1942

'Sally, Sally, is that you? It's Maude here – in Dartford.'

Sally's heart definitely skipped a beat. 'Maude, hello, yes, it's Sally.' She stopped talking and held her breath, thinking that somehow that would control the excitement that was setting every nerve end on fire.

The pent-up breath exploded as she heard Maude crying out to her, 'He's alive, Sally, Jon's alive.'

Max, who had called Sally to take the call in his office, helped her now into his own chair. She was, he suspected, very close to falling down. 'Be calm, Sally, take your time. I'll be just outside but I'll send in Seb or Millie, if you like.'

She squeezed his hand. 'No, thank you, Max; I'm fine, really.'

He left the room and she picked up the black receiver from where she'd left it lying on his desk.

'Jon's alive, Maude. You're sure this time?'

Crying and laughing, Maude explained. 'One of his friends in the Admiralty rang me up, Sally. As far as I could understand it, the French Resistance rescued him and a fellow officer. They were picked up by a fisherman who looked after them in his home, although there seems to be some doubt about where the home was – one of the islands off the coast of France or France itself.'

'Maudie, is ... is he all right?'

Maude's voice was full of joy. 'Jon wasn't injured but the other chap was. A doctor in the nearest village looked after him and, although everyone there knew about them, their presence was kept a secret from the Nazis. Seemingly, they've been in France all this time, unable to get word through to the authorities, and the Resistance fighters have been trying to get them home. It's so exciting, but rather frightening too. It seems the Resistance has contacts with a group here who drop our people into France and sometimes the plane lands and picks up people to take home, too.'

Sally thought of her friend Daisy, now a pilot in the Air Transport Auxiliary. Daisy was in love with a Czech pilot who was flying with the RAF and he, Tomas, flew missions into occupied countries. So much bravery everywhere.

'I know, Maude, they're splendid people, but Jon is all right? You're quite sure? Where is he now? When can we see him?' The questions came thick and fast.

'I don't know too much at the moment. The

chap wanted Jon's family – and really that's just the two of us – to know he'd been rescued. They suffered terribly from exposure; I don't know how long they were in the water before the fishing boat found them. He is in a military hospital but again according to the chap who rang, it's mainly to be checked over. When he leaves the hospital he'll be debriefed and that can take a few days.'

'Where is he? May I see him? I'm sure I would be given leave to go with you. Oh, Maude, I don't know why I'm crying.'

'Hear me weeping too, Sally. It's relief, dear. And the answer to your questions is, I just don't know. This old chum, a Commander Livingston, will keep me informed and, of course, I'll ring you immediately, but for now I think we should thank God and do the jobs we've been given until Jon himself contacts us. He loves you, Sally; I'm quite sure of that, and so he'll ring or write when he's able.'

He loves you, Sally. The words stayed with her, ringing in her head long after Maude had disconnected. Love had never been mentioned between them. Ridiculous to think of it. How often had they met? Had they even spent as much as an hour together? How many letters? She had written many, sending them out like little doves of peace to be tossed by the winds, hoping that somehow they would reach him. How many had she received from him? One single letter. Had he written letters that had been lost?

He loves you.

Maudie knew him, but could he love someone

287

he'd scarcely met?

Yet the image of him was fresh in her mind, as if she had been constantly reminded of him. She wondered what had stoked that memory. Sebastian's kindness? Sam Castleton's gentleness? She realised that even a uniformed sailor, glimpsed quickly in an audience, had reminded her of Jon, had kept her memories, her growing feelings, alive.

She hoped that something, perhaps nothing more than a song, had reminded Jon of her.

In February, when it seemed that the country was at its coldest, Max's company set off for what he termed 'the wilds of Scotland'. Sebastian and Millie, who had some experience of Scottish cities, hoped he was joking.

'Edinburgh's lovely, Sally; small, when you compare it with London. At the top of the Royal Mile is Edinburgh Castle, my favourite castle – unless I remember Heidelberg, which was Patrick's – and a few steps from the castle there's a super old concert hall, quite round, if I remember correctly, where my lovely Patrick partnered me for the first time. *Giselle* was the ballet, quite beautiful. We will all have to go and see the sights and walk and walk and walk.'

'But we won't even see Edinburgh,' sighed Sally, seated in the lorry next to her.

'No, we're going to be on the other side of the country,' Sebastian pointed out.

Since it was virtually impossible to see any of the Scottish countryside, the three friends – and most of the company – settled down with their own thoughts and memories. They were all in uniform with their heavy coats on top and a few lucky ones, including Sally, who had fur coats wore them on top of everything else. The hardier souls were content to stop there but many cast members also wrapped themselves in their blankets.

As always Sally's thoughts turned to Jon, who had been released from hospital and was according to Maude, somewhere in Portsmouth. Jon himself had contacted neither of them.

'It's the debriefing thing, Sally, don't take it to heart. The Navy needs to learn everything that Jon experienced, everything he can remember. It seems the fishermen who rescued them can't be traced. Jon's colleague is still receiving medical attention at St Thomas's, where they seem to be doing fabulous work. Let's not forget the first doctor; it's thanks to him that he's alive and will make a full recovery.'

'But why can't the fishermen be traced?'

'I don't know, Sally. I'm telling you everything I know. All I care about is that Jon is alive. He'll tell us everything when he comes home.'

What beautiful words, 'comes home'.

Sally had told Sebastian and Millie the good news. The three of them were in the kitchen, drinking cocoa, the night before a trip north. Millie and Sebastian were full of rational explanations for the fishermen's disappearance.

'They could be in *le Maquis,* the resistance movement, Sally, and simply not want to be found, or they might have been smuggling, not fishing, when they rescued Jon and his colleague.'

'Smuggling what?'

'Sally Brewer, there's a war on; ammunition, food, wine, animals, anything... You say Maude told you Jon was found in the south of France, but didn't you hear earlier about some Corsican fishermen?'

'Yes, there were rumours about fishermen from – possibly the south of France, Malta or Corsica.'

'I'd forgotten about Corsica,' confessed Millie. 'Wasn't Napoleon born there?'

'Yes, but completely irrelevant at the mo, Millie. There's *maquis* – with a small m – on Corsica. I believe it's the Corsican-French word for the scrubland that covers the island. Maybe there's also a *Maquis* with a capital M on Corsica and our friendly fisherman works with them. Can't remember reading much about the island recently but it is French and therefore quite likely the inhabitants dislike Herr Hitler as much as France itself does.'

Millie had doubts. 'But why must they be found? Perhaps they simply don't want to be found.'

'Apart from to thank them, they are the only people who really know what happened out there in the Mediterranean,' explained Sebastian. 'They didn't spend hours – dear God, maybe even days – floating in cold water as Jon did, and that exposure must have taken a lot out of him. You've been told that he wasn't injured as in shot, blown up, but he's lived through one hell of a traumatic experience. Isn't that one of the things the medics found after the Great War – interior scars, for want of a better word?'

Sally burst into tears. 'What are you saying?' she sobbed. 'That Jon's not all right?'

Sebastian held her in his arms, patting her back as he did so. 'No, I'm not saying that. I'm sorry, Sal. All I'm saying is that Jon survived a terrible experience and he has to be given time to come back to full strength. The navy will give Maude an address as soon as the debriefing is over. It may already have happened.'

Millie stood up and took Sally's hand. 'Your turn to wash up, Seb. Come on, Sally, bedtime if we want to be bright-eyed in Bonnie Scotland tomorrow. Jon will tell them everything he can remember and when they're quite sure he can't remember anything else, they'll tell him to ring Maudie.'

'Sebastian washed the tea dishes, Millie,' Sally said later as she reached over to switch off the lamp that stood between the beds.

'I know; won't do him any harm to do another lot. Night-night, Sally.'

In early afternoon they pulled into a bleak airbase for refuelling, both of men and machines, and never, decided Sally, had potato soup been more welcome or more delicious. The sun was shining brightly outside the canteen window and that gave them a false sense of warmth for when they stepped outside the canteen the wind, 'straight from the Arctic', according to Millie, threatened to blow away everything. There was a shout as one of the dancers lost the blanket that she had refused to leave behind in the lorry and several of the men, including Sebastian, went haring after it, helped and hindered by the wind. Eventually the blanket snagged itself on the blocks holding a

Spitfire in place and was recaptured with much merriment.

'Anything else you'd like to drop, darlin'? We'll be more than happy to chase it for you.'

They were not scheduled to put on a show on that particular base and so, blanket recovered, they walked out to the waiting lorries.

'That was a nice little break,' Max assured them. 'Great hospitality and the chaps got a good bit of welcome exercise too. I've thanked the station commander and promised that we'll try – don't groan – that we'll try to put on a show for them, as a small thank you, later in the year. They say Scotland's lovely in the autumn. Now all aboard and if you can sleep, do so. Next stop, two shows back to back.'

Three hours later they stopped at a naval base on the River Clyde. The wind was not quite so fierce now and nothing was blown away as they followed their hosts to the quarters allotted to them, two large Nissen huts each with the most wonderful black stove that belched heat.

'Pick me up here when the war's over,' joked Humph. 'I'm not leaving this hut until then.'

'There's Scotch in the Officers' Mess,' said the naval rating who had directed them.

'Amendment, amendment, pick me up at the Officers' Mess when the war's over.'

Everyone laughed and, of course, Humph used his new joke in his performances.

Sally, her mind full of worries that Maude might be trying to telephone her that very moment, tried to think of nothing but entertaining the troops. She dressed carefully, allowed Sybil to apply make-up to her already expressive eyes, walked onto the basic stage the airmen had happily built for them, and smiled. The men had started to clap and whistle as soon as she appeared but when she smiled many started drumming their feet and cheering.

She held up her hands and immediately they were quiet. 'Thank you, gentlemen,' she said, immediately wishing she had called them 'boys', 'I've worked so hard to learn a new song' – and then, delivered with a demure pout – 'just for you.' She accompanied this last remark with a pointing finger, 'And you and you and, all of you,' she said, 'but I can't sing if you make too much noise.'

She turned to Sam who was leading the small band that he had put together, and which was playing for her. He smiled, raised his baton and – music, and no more demure Sally Brewer.

'Mad About the Boy,' sang a very confident Sally as she walked down into the audience, making eye contact with various men seated there. By the time she reached the end the room was in uproar.

'That wasn't too bad,' Max greeted her as she eventually – with one last thrown kiss – walked off-stage.

'Actually, I thought it was very good,' said Sally, and she smiled happily at the director before hurrying off to change for her next appearance.

'I didn't realise Seb was such a fine pianist,' Max said as he and Sybil stood watching the show and noting audience reaction. 'He's really got Sally performing.'

'He isn't; that's not where his genius lies. You

were watching Lal just now, every sultry, smouldering glance, every movement of those hips. The girl can act, Max. Maybe time to think of a vehicle.'

'Possibly. We could try her out in France but not a word till I find the right material.'

Unaware that her fate was being decided, Sally continued with both her new and old routines until the last curtain call of the second show. Then they congregated in the Officers' Mess, where Sally became the honey pot around which the wasps gathered. They had had a lecture from Max on how to handle military adulation. 'Be friendly, but not involved. Bear in mind that most of these men are new to a military life; many will never have been away from home before, unless to a Boy Scout camp and almost all will have at least one wife or girlfriend waiting, we hope faithfully, at home. Girls, be very careful never to be alone with anyone. Move around the base in groups. Understood?'

'They're boys, Max.'

'They're not. They're soldiers or sailors or airmen, most of them have grown up very, very quickly. And if it makes you feel better, be assured that "No fraternising with the ENSA company" is exactly what their commanding officers have said to them. Smile, say hello, but keep your distance.'

Sally, who was finding it very difficult to keep her distance from men of all shapes, sizes, ranks and ages, was delighted to be rescued by Millie and Sebastian, and as a threesome, they were able to stay chatting until finally Sally confessed that she was exhausted. She wondered if Millie had found it difficult to once again be in a group where she was singled out for admiration. This type of event must have been part and parcel of her life as a professional ballerina and a number of the men, and not all of them officers, were delighted to meet her and to talk about classical ballet.

'Did you enjoy the evening, Millie?' Sally asked as they were preparing to get into the very tightly covered iron beds.

For a few minutes there was silence and Sally worried that she should have kept quiet and then Millie smiled. 'Pain and pleasure, Sally. I hadn't realised how much we rely on the admiration of the audiences. We – and I'm putting actors and singers and dancers together now – work so hard to make a routine, a number, a step, perfect. We think, hope, pray even, that we've mastered it but it's not until someone waits for us in the cold outside a theatre and says, "That was super, Mrs Burgess," that we know we've done it. I didn't realise how much I missed that.'

'Will you return to the stage when the war is over?'

'The time it's taking, I'll only be fit for the wicked witch in *Hansel and Gretel*.'

'Nonsense, you're exquisite on stage,' said Sally boldly.

'Thank you, Sally, and since we're throwing fulsome congratulations around, didn't you raise your game tonight?'

'I've never been so pleased that my parents were safely tucked up in bed in Dartford.'

Laughing, they fell asleep.

Impossible to sleep late on a military base.

'Some idiot was outside our window playing the damned bagpipes before dawn even cracked,' Millie complained to Sebastian as she blinked sleepy eyes in the canteen.

'We are in Scotland, Millie. It was reveille, Scottish style.'

'Dear God, Seb, it sounded like cats being tortured, and as for the brawny Scotsman bellowing out commands...' She stopped, lost for strong enough words.

'Have a nice strong, hot cup of tea, and we can follow that up with Scottish porridge, but for heaven's sake, don't put sugar on it. We don't want to be frog-marched out.'

'Very funny, I'm sure,' said Millie, taking a sip of tea. 'Oh, delight! Strong enough to dance on, as Patrick used to say, just the way I like it.'

'Good, well, get a move on. I think they're warming up – I use the term loosely – the engines, and we will be departing before your porridge bowl meets the soap suds in the sink.'

'Sorry I'm late.' Sally, dressed for the long journey home, had arrived. 'And if you're worried that I'll keep you late, Sebastian, all I want is a nice cup of tea.'

'No food?'

'Last night's "supper in the Mess" – doesn't that sound sophisticated? – will still be with me when we reach our next stop. I'll be lucky to get into the lilac dress tonight. The portions reminded me of my oldest friend's mother, a lovely human being,' continued Sally as she drank her tea. 'She had three sons before the twins were born and until they were sixteen or so Mrs Petrie always gave the girls the same amount of food as she gave their great hulking brothers. Fine for Rose, who's tall and naturally thin, plus an incredible athlete, but poor little Daisy is your height, Millie, and hated all that food on a plate. Her mother was convinced that her small daughter had to be delicate, because her build was so different from that of her twin or their brothers.' Sally smiled at a pleasant memory. 'She's so delicate she's now in the ATA ferrying Spitfires.'

Millie was fascinated. 'She delivers Spitfires to airfields? A girl?'

'I'll explain the ATA in the lorry,' promised Sally and since Millie had finished her porridge, they called out their thanks and goodbyes to the staff and headed, half grudgingly, towards their transport.

Soon the three friends were seated on a wooden bench in their lorry waiting for everyone else to load. By now, the same people always sat together; only the very few loners looked desperately for spaces once everyone else was accommodated. The musicians sat together, the actors sat together, the soubrettes sat together.

'When you think about it,' Millie said, 'It's actually quite sensible to sit with your peers; then everyone can discuss the performance and make suggestions for improvement. There's really little else to do except sleep – and even that's debatable on these lorries.'

'How did you travel before the war?'

'With a ballet company, do you mean, Sally?'

'Yes. We do always get such a warm welcome from the troops, but the travelling and the accommodation is pretty basic, isn't it?'

'In some cases stars do travel differently or separately from the rest of the company, I suppose. Max, Sam, Sybil and Lal all travel in a lorry just like us, no special seating, no being whisked from place to place in expensive chauffeur-driven cars, no private railway carriages – I've been on one of those in the US, amazing. We had a butler, a chef and a valet. One dancer had her toy dogs with her and the butler walked them whenever we stopped. And the food ... the Ritz in a railway carriage. I could have become used to travelling like that. Patrick always said as long as the lavatory flushes and the bed linen is clean nothing else is important and so far, my friends, that's what we've had.'

'So no complaints, Millie?'

Millie remained quiet and, in her mind, Sally ran over the accommodations they had shared in the past year.

'There was the Nissen hut with mould growing on the walls.'

'And the loo that wouldn't flush.'

'Remember the beds with the bedbugs – it's funny now but we were scratching for weeks, remember, Sally?'

'Bed bugs are never going to be funny, Sebastian. We may be officers on paper but some of the "real" officers don't see ENSA like that. We're entertainers and too many people still have Victorian ideas about our morality – or lack of it.

Besides, most military bases just don't have accommodation suitable for a sudden visitation from a large group of people. Each and every base or hospital has tried, I think, to make us feel really welcome, even the ones who sort of mumble, "Tommy Trinder, or Vera Lynn or Laurence Olivier or whoever, is with you, isn't he, she?" And of course, that person was going to be housed with the base commander, not in a Nissen hut with snow coming down the chimney.'

'You never told me you were in that hut, Sal.'

'No point; besides it was winter and it was one night. Do ballet companies have a pecking order, Millie?'

'I suppose. Primas had the best rooms, the corps de ballet the worst, but we figured those in the better rooms had earned it and one day, maybe, with lots of hard work, we might just make it to a private suite at the Ritz. War's a great leveller, though, and I imagine companies will all crowd together in the same hotel. I heard a whisper that the great Ninette de Valois is going to work with ENSA, arranging the travel, et cetera for dancers. She might not put a fledgeling ballerina and a prima in the same room but they'll be in the same boarding house or hotel.'

'Good Lord, we've talked so much we're in England.'

The lorries had stopped and, peering out through the rear curtains, the friends could see that they had arrived at an army base that was known to them.

'We must be refuelling,' said Sebastian, 'and Sally, isn't this the place where it snowed both inside and out?'

Sally did not answer as she was busily engaged in watching a long procession of fairly small vehicles winding its way across a vast expanse of moorland.

'Glory be,' said Sebastian. 'Ladies, stand up and welcome our American cousins. Those green things crawling all over the hills like ants, are Jeeps, American made and American driven.'

'He's right, Sally,' came Millie's voice, almost squeaky with unaccustomed excitement. 'I hope they're staying for lunch.'

The Americans were not only staying for lunch but also for the foreseeable future. Of the ENSA company only Max, Sybil, Lal and Sam were invited to lunch with the base commander, his senior officers, and the senior American officers. The rank and file were given lunch in the canteen but the two groups were under strict orders not to mingle.

'We're on the same side,' fumed Sally. 'What do the brass hats think we're going to do or say?'

'They don't care what we say; they're afraid some soldier boy will tell us something. The Yanks are keeping their plans very close; I doubt even Max will be any wiser when he rejoins us,' Sebastian speculated.

That proved to be the case. Max admitted that the four of them had enjoyed an exceptionally good lunch but conversation had been very general. Common mistakes in a common language seemed to be an important point of discussion. Woe betide anyone who did not know that the hood of a car and the bonnet were the same thing, that a sidewalk was a pavement, that Monday through Friday was a more sensible and shorter way of saying Monday to Friday both days included.

'Lalita was in her element,' said Max proudly. 'By the time we got to dessert, not pudding, they had no idea what nationality she was or which state of the United States of America was her birthplace. Two officers from Arizona asked her which part of New Mexico she was from and she said, "The second part," and that made some, of them laugh.'

Sebastian looked puzzled.

'Mexico, Sebastian,' whispered Sally, 'the second part of the name New Mexico.'

And Millie laughed.

Two hours later they were back on the road 'like itinerant beggars', said Sebastian, but this time the conversation was very different. Discussions of future performances were perfunctory at best, as everyone wanted to talk about the American invasion, but they were amazed by how little had been learned over lunch.

'Come on, Max, the colonel must have said something,' stated more than one company member.

'Yes, he said they were setting up bases in England and Northern Ireland and were planning manoeuvres, but what they intended to manoeuvre I haven't the slightest idea. He assured us they would be self-supporting as far as possible but whatever they had to source in Britain, they would buy. That promise, I would imagine, will

301

be received warmly by any local shopkeeper, not to mention pub landlord. And that's it, folks, as our new cousins say, read the newspapers, listen to the wireless. They'll tell us when they're ready.'

With that they had to be content.

FIFTEEN

Spring 1942

There were two pieces of good news waiting for Sally. Not only had Maude telephoned with the update on improvements in Jon's health, saying that he was now allowed to have visitors, but her friend Daisy had written a brief note to tell her that Sergeant Sam Petrie, escaped POW, had arrived home and was with his parents and family. Sally could not wait to share her news and went looking for Sebastian. He was onstage in the rehearsal studio working on a scene from *Hamlet*.

She made to leave the studio but Max called her. 'If you're free, Sally, be an angel and feed Seb his lines; my Ophelia hasn't arrived yet.'

Sally took the script. Ophelia. How absolutely wonderful; she found herself hoping that Sylvia would be later still, not so late that Max would be absolutely furious – he could be quite frightening when riled – but late enough for Sally to have a chance to show the director what she could do. *Hamlet* was one of the plays she had studied at school.

'Don't panic, Sally, doesn't matter if you fluff a bit. We're not doing the whole scene, only the conversation between Hamlet and Ophelia. Take it as read that Hamlet has delivered the great soliloquy and he's just about to break Ophelia's heart by telling her to become a nun – or worse. Most of what she says is short but just read each last line to jog Seb's memory and tell him what he's supposed to say next. Are you all right with that?'

Sally was not going to panic and was annoyed that Max had assumed that she would. 'I know the play, Max, acted the second gravedigger at school.'

'Then you'll know he's not in this scene. Don't try thinking for me.'

Sally was about to say that she had no intention of thinking for him but he cut her off.

'Onstage now, both of you. Hamlet is talking to Ophelia, Sally; he can hardly do that if he's onstage and she's skulking around in the stalls.'

Annoyed, Sally walked stiff-backed up the steps. 'I wasn't skulking,' she told herself, 'and what a nasty word to use.' She looked down at Max and wondered what he had to smile about and then she forgot everything as she attempted to make sense of a small part of Shakespeare's great play. A few minutes later, she was not onstage at the Theatre Royal but in a large, cold stone-built castle in Denmark. Was it summer or winter? She could not remember and vowed to reread the entire play later. For now, she decided that it was late spring. She looked at Sebastian, who smiled reassuringly at her and she began:

'*How does your honour for this many a day?*'

Sebastian replied and after what seemed like five minutes, Sally heard, 'Thank you, Sally; that was helpful. What did you think, Seb? Still a bit to go?'

'I'm there, Max and...'

He stopped as the door opened and Sylvia Stone, the experienced actress who was to play Ophelia, slipped into the room somewhat shame-facedly. 'Sorry, Max, Seb. Slept badly but it won't happen again.'

'Right, we'll start at the beginning, as much as you can without the cheat sheets, Seb. Thank you, Sally.'

'Thank you, Sally' was short for 'Go away, Sally, we don't need you any more.'

Sally managed to smile as she left. She walked back through the theatre reliving the experience of actually standing on the stage of the Theatre Royal, for five minutes, Ophelia to Sebastian's Hamlet. Sebastian will tell me the truth about my delivery, even if he was concentrating on remembering his lines. She got back to Sam's studio lost in a delightful dream of playing the part of Ophelia onstage, not dressed in her uniform shirt and skirt but in some sort of Danish regal garment. No, the gown wouldn't be regal. Ophelia was a young girl and not part of the royal family. Something white, perhaps, in a soft floaty material.

'What are you doing, Sally? You almost knocked me down.' Sybil had appeared in the door of her office.

'Sorry, Sybil, I was daydreaming.'

'Something nice, I hope.'

She could not possibly tell Sybil, of all people, and instead said, 'Wonderful news, Sybil, two lots. A friend's brother, who was a POW in Germany, has just arrived home. So exciting; he's such a super chap.'

'Well, that is incredible news but surely the Germans didn't just release him?'

'No, it's all really exciting. He escaped from a working party, somehow made his way to Italy, where he worked with the partisans for a time, and then, and I've no idea how, he made it to the south of France ... and arrived home a week or two ago.'

'Lovely, it's like a novel or a good play. A little love interest there, perhaps?'

'No, not Sam. He was like a big brother. Lots of my school friends were really keen on him, in fact on all of the Petrie brothers. But there is another of my close friends who is, I'm quite sure, very special to Sam and, goodness knows she deserves some happiness.'

'And the second piece of good news? Your splendid naval officer, I'm sure.'

Sally felt her cheeks redden with embarrassment and excitement. 'It's wonderful, Sybil, just wonderful. I may be allowed to see him. His old nanny is going to see him this weekend. Maude will let me know how he is and whether...'

She could not continue. So many doubts. So many worries.

Sybil patted her. 'Of course Jon will want to see you, Sally. Everything will be all right, even if it takes time. I'm sure of it. Now you'd better change out of that skirt; trousers will be fine.

We're trying a new number, something big; you'll have the solo; two or three of the tap dancers – if any of them can sing, that is – will back you up, all of our male dancers, even if we have to rope Seb in; he's quite a good hoofer. I'm sure you know it; "Chattanooga Choo Choo".'

'The incredible Glenn Miller. Golly, are you sure?'

'Go change, Sally. Jessie's waiting for you.'

Sally had worked a few times with Jessie, Sam's assistant, and she hurried to get ready.

The first words Jessie had spoken to Sally in some time were, 'You know the lyrics?'

'Not perfectly. I have sung along when it's on the wireless but I'm not sure that I'd be completely accurate.'

Jessie pointed to a copy lying on the piano. 'Can you read music?'

'Not exactly.'

'That means no, then. Fine, read it to me, as far as you can remember, in the same tempo as you've heard it sung on the wireless.'

It seemed a strange request but Sally was not a musician and had no idea whether or not this was usual and so she went along with the request. She opened the booklet, took a calming breath and began to read. Once or twice she found herself out of breath but she finished and dared raise her head to look at the pianist. Jessie made no reference to her reading, merely saying, 'Sit down in that chair and read it again.'

She did as she was told.

'Much better, *Brava*. Do you know what the difference was?'

Sally had not the slightest idea.

'When you were sitting, Sally, your feet were never still. You moved your legs, your body, to the beat you were hearing in your head. You were feeling it and feeling it makes all the difference in singing and in acting.' She handed Sally the sheet music. 'Now take the song away and learn the words and if you're practising while you're washing your smalls, move your feet.'

It was Sally's turn to wash the supper dishes that evening and she stood at the sink, apron around her slender waist and felt the beat.

Millie, who probably knew what she was doing, said nothing, but Sebastian watched her for a moment and then said, 'I like the wiggling, Miss Brewer, but what on earth are you doing?'

'I'm feeling the beat for my new show piece.'

'Interesting, but wouldn't it be better if I played it for you or—' he looked at his watch and made a face – 'we turned on the wireless.' With two neighbours in their eighties, Sebastian never played the piano after eight o'clock in the evening.

Millie smiled. 'If old General Fitzallan could see our Sally wiggle, Seb, he'd be asking if he could turn the pages for you, no matter how late it is.' She turned to Sally. 'Wouldn't it be wonderful if you are to take Chattanooga Choo Choo to France?'

'I wish we did have a date, Millie, but Max did seem really sure that we're down at the bottom of the list.'

'Hey, come on, Sal, we're nowhere near the bottom.'

'Sorry, Sebastian, but I only meant as far as

funding for overseas tours is concerned. If Vera Lynn agrees to go, money will be found. Only right, I suppose.'

'Are you still as happy to go overseas, Sally?'

Sally flushed. 'Why wouldn't I be?' she asked. 'You're thinking about Jon and whether or not he's able to have visitors, but even if he is, maybe he doesn't want me as a visitor. Maudie hasn't contacted me about visiting Jon. I wouldn't be surprised if he's forgotten all about me. He was so kind to me once and because he was lonely he asked me to write but maybe when he had time to think about it, he realised that it was a mistake.'

'Sally Brewer, he realised nothing of the kind. Was it ENSA or the feeble old actor in Dartford who stole your self-confidence?'

'Neither. I am self-confident but I am also not so conceited that I can't see where I need improvement. Sybil and Millie and you, Sebastian, are improving my dancing, but Nellie Melba couldn't turn me into a singer, which is fine as I have no desire to be a singer. I'm an actress.'

'Positively spoken. Now let's have a run through of the train song.' And making what he thought were train noises, Sebastian led the girls into the front room. He had just opened the keyboard when the telephone rang. 'Drat it, who could that be?'

'Only one way to find out,' Millie pointed out and Sebastian answered the telephone.

'Of course, one moment, please.'

He held the receiver out to Sally. 'For you, Sal. Come along, Millie, back to the kitchen.'

Her heart was beating so strongly that Sally felt the need to put her free hand on her heart to calm it somehow. 'Hello,' she said somewhat tentatively, 'Sally speaking.'

'Jon here.' A moment of silence and then he spoke again. 'How are you, Sally?'

'Jon?' Now it seemed as if her heart had stopped altogether. Everything appeared to have stopped; she was even holding her breath. She coughed and all was normal. What should she say, what should she ask? So many questions were in her mind.

He answered one before she had asked it. 'I'm very well, Sally, and so glad to be home.'

Home? The word could mean so many things. Home as in back in England. Home in his house in Dartford. 'Where, Jon? Are you still in a hospital?'

'Afraid so but it won't be long before they discharge me. I'm perfectly well. Got one or two events mixed up – so much to remember. I did try to make a diary of sorts in my letters to you.'

Tears began to slip down her cheeks and she tried to brush them away with her free hand. 'I'm so sorry, but I didn't get any letters.'

'I know. Emmanuel didn't pass them on. Difficult for him. It's not as if he could simply take them to a post office. When can you come down? God, I'm sorry. You may not even want to come down or you're probably too busy.'

'I will never be too busy to see you, Jon. I'm sure I will be able to travel. Is there a day for visiting or a time?'

He laughed and she liked the sound. She had never before heard him laugh.

'It's not that type of hospital. Maudie came down on Sunday because she and Fedora keep the shop open all the other days of the week.' He gave her the number of the hospital so that she could ring him when she had managed to make an arrangement. 'And I won't mind if it's too difficult at the moment, Sally, just knowing that you will come is wonderful. I have so much to tell you.'

Suddenly the line went dead. Sally kept the receiver against her ear, waiting, waiting, holding her breath to make sure she was as quiet as could be, but could hear nothing. She managed to re-place the receiver and then she curled up in as small a ball as she could make against Sebastian's grandmamma's Regency cushions.

Millie found her there sometime later. 'All right, Sal? Was it Jon?' She handed Sally her handkerchief. 'Now had I known I would need to do this – bearing in mind that you never have a hankie when you need one, I'd have taken out a pretty one today.'

Sally sniffed and sat up. 'I'm fine. It's just that Jon was talking and the line went dead. He didn't say goodbye.'

'Nothing in that, Sally; it happens all the time. Interruptions to the line, or pip pip because the person on the other end has run out of money – modern hazards. Just think of the miracle of actually hearing a voice out of that piece of black Bakelite? How is he?'

The young women sat for some time talking quietly until Sally had told Millie everything that Jon had said.

'Our lovely landlord is making toast and cocoa, possibly for the last time now that electricity's rationed. It'll be chocolate next and then how will we survive? Hasn't cocoa got something to do with chocolate? Let's join him.'

Sebastian, too, was able to reassure Sally. 'Tomorrow you should be quite open and talk to Max. He understands about love, Sally. If we have a free day coming up you could get an early train...' He stopped. 'No, wait, I have a better idea. Trains have two speeds at the moment, slow and stationary. I'll check with Dmitri about how much petrol I have. I'll drive you down – my God, what am I saying? Where is he? Must be by the sea. Please don't say Truro or somewhere like that. Millie, you come too. We'll leave Sally with Jon and we'll find a cosy seaside pub and, if we're lucky, have an almost pre-war lunch.'

'Hayling Island, but I didn't have time to ask him where that is.'

'Portsmouth. What do you think, Millie? Are you up for "The sea! the sea! the open sea!"?'

'The sea? No. The cosy seaside pub, absolutely.'

And so it was settled.

Max assured Sally that what she did in her own time was not his affair. He checked the engagement diary, and since the company had no commitments, other than rehearsals, on the following Tuesday he wished her well. 'Hope you find your friend in good health.'

'Sebastian and Millie will come too. Is that all right?'

'Not if I have an emergency request, Sally, I'll need them. Best I can do, I'm afraid.'

311

Sally thanked him and was on her way to the door when he called, 'By the way, Sal, learn Ophelia's lines – Sylvia's expecting a baby – not announcing to the company just yet but she may well take some leave soon. If she does and you're up to it, I may slot you in somewhere but you'll have to be really good; Lal can always fill in.'

Sally managed to leave the room calmly but as soon as she had closed the door behind her she hurried to the ladies' room, turned on a tap to deafen the sound, and shouted 'Yippee' not very loudly.

'Good news, Sally?' To her embarrassment Sybil had joined her at the basin.

'Yes, thank you. Jon rang and I'm going to see him.'

'Lovely.' Sybil finished washing her hands, walked to the door where she turned. 'When I got my first major role, I found a chimney and shouted "Hallelujah" up it as loudly as I could.'

Sally could hear her laughing as she walked away. 'I haven't actually got it,' Sally told herself. 'Max has no favourites. If I'm not good enough, I won't get it, but this is the closest I've been.'

Millie and Sebastian were not free after all on Tuesday as Max accepted an invitation to perform at a local military hospital. Sally, very grateful that he had not cancelled her free day, dressed carefully in a light-weight woollen panelled skirt in green and black and which came to just below her knees. With it she wore a long-sleeved green silk blouse buttoned right up to the neck, the loose sleeves buttoned tightly at the wrists. Her shoes were black, flat, soft leather walking shoes, laced and tied with a small bow – suitable only for strolling in gardens or parks. She curled her hair into the popular sausage curl on the forehead and tied the rest back with a black ribbon but deciding that the colour might remind him too forcibly of death, she replaced it with a green one borrowed from Millie. Happy with what she thought of as her "secretarial image" Sally boarded a train, which went fairly slowly but steadily all the way to Portsmouth. She got out at Portsmouth and looked around the very busy station, wondering how on earth she was going to find her way to the hospital. She was just about to join the long, snaking line for a taxi when she heard her name called. A sailor whom she had never seen before was walking towards her, holding a placard with her name on it.

She waved to him. 'Are you looking for me? I'm Sally Brewer.'

'I know, miss. Saw you at an ENSA concert, wearing the loveliest frock – told my missus all about it. Commander Galbraith's compliments, miss. He's sent me to bring you to the hospital. Taxis are as rare as hen's teeth these days.'

A few minutes later Sally was being driven through the gates of the naval medical facility, where she saw a tall, slim man in naval uniform standing outside a beautiful old building built from some kind of warm red stone. It stood foursquare at the top of the driveway, the naval officer just in front. Jon? No, Jon's hair was dark and the hair that peeped out from under the hat had a streak of silver above each ear. As the car came to a halt just at the foot of the steps, he moved to where it was and opened the door. 'Sally?'

'Jon?'

'Yes, it's me.' And he held out his right hand to help her out of the car.

They stood looking at each other. They did not fall into each other's arms and kiss. Jon gripped Sally's arms, held her away from him for a moment and then kissed her gently on each cheek. 'Thank you for coming. You look ... absolutely wonderful.'

They stood for a moment, Sally still in Jon's grasp, looking at each other until eventually Jon said, 'They're giving us lunch in the Mess, Dover Sole. I hope you like sole.'

'Yes, thank you,' said Sally rather demurely.

'There's so much I need to tell you, Sally, so much I want to know about you. Shall we lunch first and then, if you don't mind walking – it's not too windy today, is it? – we could stroll around the grounds, quite pretty actually with daffodils and some rather splendid tulips; reminded me of tulips I saw in a park in Paris before the war. Ever been to Paris? Oh, don't answer that, Sally. I'm so nervous I'm babbling.'

'It's all right, Jon. It's me, just Sally,' and he smiled then, a smile that, as it had done once before, a lifetime ago, changed his face into that of the much younger man he really was.

He took her hand and they made their way to the Officers' Mess and they ate the beautifully fresh fish, drank a little white wine, and chatted. When they had finished lunch they walked outside and began to follow a path that wound through and around the garden.

'May I hear all about you or should I tell you what happened?'

'You can learn all there is to know about me any time, Jon. I'd rather learn about your wonderful rescue.'

'I'll start at the beginning then, and if it's too frightfully boring, I'll shut up.'

'It won't be, Jon. Tell me everything. My train doesn't leave till six forty-five.'

'Very well. I wrote it all down during the debriefing, piecing it all together. I remember the second half of our experiences perfectly well. We were in the south of France then, and I know exactly where we were and what we did, but it took me some time to recover from being – I don't know how long – several hours at least in the open sea, and so my memories of the weeks we spent in Corsica, for that's where we were, are sketchy at best. The important things I remember; that Emmanuel was one of the finest men I've ever met, and he and his cousin Jean-Jacques risked everything to save us.'

'Go ahead, tell me the whole story, Jon,' said Sally.

'Dear Sally, that would take much too long, but I'll start at the beginning. I was married, you knew that, and when I asked you to write to me, I knew that I should explain, but I found I could not talk about Luisa, my wife, or my failed marriage. I felt an attraction to you the moment you said, "Hello, Just Jon." I wanted to laugh. You were so normal, and so little in my life had been normal for such a long time. I forced myself to

315

believe that it was better that you meet someone suitable, perhaps Sebastian or someone like him, and that doing the things that young people who like each other do, seeing a film, or watching a play, you would fall in love naturally and would eventually forget all about me. In the meantime, though, I would receive your letters and pretend we were in another time, another place. I castigate myself for my selfishness. I was a married man and I was a serving sailor in a war and should have been thinking of nothing but my duty to my King and my country. But your letters were like clean fresh air blowing across my fields and I treasured them.

'When we were torpedoed I would imagine that any of us still capable of thinking thought only of how to survive. How any of us escaped is still a mystery and a miracle. They blew us up, Sally, up in the air like a firework at a Guy Fawkes party. I felt nothing and after the first boom as the torpedoes hit, I heard nothing; I was deafened. It was so eerie, the sky darkened by thick black smoke and the sea by oil and blood, and I remember the taste of both in my mouth. I suppose that, for a time, I was unconscious, because I remember being surprised to find myself being pitched and tossed at the whim of the waves, and hearing absolutely no sound at all, not the slapping of waves against debris and, frighteningly, no voices or shipping sounds carried on the wind. I managed to turn round several times; I was looking for my ship, for the other Allied shipping that had been there – how long ago – but they had gone, every one. Dear God, the thoughts that race through one's head at such a time. They are all lost, I remember thinking, and I am the only man left alive in this sea. How long will I last or will it be a kinder death if I simply turn over and let myself drown? How long was I unconscious, and am I conscious now? I had as much power over my body and my survival as the pieces of driftwood that floated past me, or the bodies that were bumping against mine. I recognised several: the captain, three seamen I'd known since they first joined up, Cookie, and then a wave threw a slight body on top of me and it was Ben Templeton, one of the junior officers. I grabbed him, not knowing what I was going to do with his body but not wanting to let it go. His eyes were wide open and I could see his mouth moving but no sound came and I thought that perhaps he was dead and some nerves were still reacting. I was very clinical about it; helped me to avoid thinking about drowning and never seeing you again. I seem to remember trying to shout but heard nothing and supposed I had lost the power of speech too.

'The next thing I remember was waking up in the bottom of a boat, a fishing boat, for the smell of fish permeated both the planks and the net carefully draped over us to prevent us suffocating. Ben was beside me; his face was pale and his eyes were closed but someone had bandaged his head with a lady's silk scarf, a bright green one, which looked strange on a sailor's head. I had not noticed an injury; perhaps the waves washed the blood away from me.

'Still I could hear nothing, but the boat was moving and I thought, I should be able to hear something, the engine, the prow cutting through the water, something, and I accepted that I was deaf, but alive, and so more blessed than my comrades. I think I wept then – me, a grown man – but the tears were not for me.

'The fishing boat, with its odd catch, was moving, and a man was beside me pulling me up to a sitting position. I'm ashamed to say that, for a fraction of a second, I thought he meant to pitch me over the side for if he was German, a deaf and dumb prisoner of war would be no use to him. Perhaps he saw my fear for he pulled me closer to his chest and put a bottle to my lips. His lips were moving but I could not hear what he said. The message from the bottle was clear and I drank and began to cough and choke as some red-hot liquid ran down my throat. He took the bottle away; he was laughing and obviously telling the pilot what was happening for I felt him laugh again. The alcohol had gone from burning to warming and I began to feel better. He gave me another drink, looked at Ben, said something and disappeared.

'We did not put into a port but to a small secluded bay. It was very dark. Several men appeared from a cave and they stood around talking and gesticulating, disagreeing too, I think from the angry faces. But then one large man walked back into the cave and eventually came out leading an old mule, which was harnessed to a cart. We were taken to a house; Ben was carried in and I'm pleased to say that I managed to stumble in mainly on my own. The lady of the house made hot drinks, which I later learned were from herbs in her garden. Quite delicious. They had put Ben in a rather splendid wooden bed, like the Daddy Bear's bed in the fairy story, and he was stripped and washed, put into a clean if somewhat coarse nightshirt, and our rescuer, Emmanuel, held him up and helped him sip the drink. My inability to communicate was frustrating and the fear that it was permanent was terrifying. I think they tried to calm me and Madame gave me bread and hot soup. The curtains were drawn, I assumed because it was night, but as I finished my meal, a man was admitted. He smiled at me but went straight to Ben and began to examine him. The green bandage was taken off his poor head, and for the first time I saw that the fair hair on top of Ben's head was matted with blood. He was given quite a large dose of whatever fiery liquid I had drunk on board and after a few minutes, the doctor, for he was obviously a highly trained medical man, cut his hair and washed and sewed up an ugly gash on the top of his head. I don't think Ben cried out but I could hear nothing. When the doctor was finished with Ben, he examined me. I have no idea what he said but I too was stripped and washed, dressed in, I think, Madame's nightwear, for I'm sure that Corsican men don't often embroider little flowers on their clothes. Those dear people had one nightshirt or nightgown each and they gave them and their bed to us, for Emmanuel picked me up as if I was his child and set me down beside Ben. More fiery liquid, not from the original bottle and I fell into a deep sleep. I'm not sure how long I stayed in the bed but it was some time. Shall I go on?'

319

Sally smiled. 'Of course, I want to know every-thing but could I ask you something?'

He nodded.

'When did you learn the name of your rescuer?'

'That night. He wrote it down for me and we communicated like that for some time.'

'Wonderful.'

Jon looked at her, smiled, and continued. 'The doctor, who also wrote notes to me – which we burned by the way – came every day, and he ex-plained that he was sure my deafness was temporary and that my speech too would return. Dear man, that gave me hope. Emmanuel and Jean-Jacques were fishermen and each owned what we'd call a smallholding. Several times they would have visitors during the night. Smugglers, I thought originally, but it turned out that our rescuers were *Maquisards*, members of the Cor-sican Resistance. They wanted us off the island because they feared for our safety, and obviously for that of their families. Emmanuel has two children and Jean-Jacques's wife had a baby while we were with them. Their captain was in touch with the French Resistance on the mainland and they hoped to get us to France, thinking that it might be slightly more likely that a rescue could be effected from there. In the meantime, Ben got better and better and I became quite useful. My hair and beard grew – what a scruffy chap I was – and since I could neither speak nor hear, everyone thought I was both helpless and harmless and so I was allowed to wander around the island. Eventu-ally my hearing and speech began to improve, so slowly that sometimes I thought I was doomed to live the rest of my life in a kind of hazy world, but eventually they were restored – such a relief. I told no one but Emmanuel and the doctor and so, hearing everything but appearing as if I was still mute, I became even more useful. Ben recovered – months had gone by, winter was setting in, not that it's bad in the Mediterranean – and together we worked with the *Maquisards*. Tragedy there, eventually, when Emmanuel's small group was ambushed by a German patrol and shot. They were looking for us too, and Jean-Jacques, stout fellow, decided there was nothing for it but to row us across to the south of France where we were picked up by the *Maquis*. We worked with them till we were rescued – end of story.'

'There must be so much more to tell, Jon. Have you written it all down?'

'Most of it, in those letters to you that you never received.'

'How tragic. I would have loved to have read them. And their content must have been vitally important to you.'

'They were never sent, Sally. Emmanuel took them to the local priest who read them. Stupidly, in my early letters I named names and so the good Father hid the letters instead of attempting to pass them on to agents who would have tried to get them to you. More tragedy if they fell into the wrong hands.'

'And are they still with the priest?'

'He too was a *Maquisard*, Sally; he disappeared the night Emmanuel died and we don't know where he is.'

'How very sad.' What else could she say?

Jon pushed up the right sleeve of his uniform jacket, and looked at his watch. 'It's time, Sally. Bob will see you on to the train.'

He took her hand and together they walked back towards the main building. Jon stopped beside a great tree whose branches screened them from the road. 'May I kiss you, Sally? I have wanted to for such a long time.'

In reply she put her arms around his neck and he bent his head to kiss her. Desire such as she had never before experienced swept through her and she responded to him with as much passion as he was showing her.

'Will you come back to see me?' he said when he could speak. 'I don't know when they plan to let me return to duty but that's what I want, what I know I must do for the boys who were lost. My dearest girl, I need to return to active service but will you wait for me?'

He released her and walked away a few steps and then returned but he did not touch her. 'My wife is another tragedy of this war, Sally; she died in one of the ghastly attacks on Malta. Had she survived we would certainly have divorced; the proceedings had already started, but I do regret her death. There, you know all my secrets. Will you write to me and perhaps, when you're free, come to see me again?'

'With all my heart, Jon.'

Sally wrote her first letter that night, sitting up in bed, propped up with pillows. Jon had asked for more personal knowledge, for instance, the date of her birthday, her favourite flowers, colours, food, everything she could think of that would allow him to see something of the first twenty years of her life. She felt there was little to tell; she liked primroses and roses, her colours were lilac or yellow, and as for food, she could eat anything except liver and she did not like blackcurrant jam. She wrote of primary school where she had made friends with the Petrie twins and the orphan, Grace Paterson. She said that she had loved English, French and history at school, had loathed maths and science of any kind. She enjoyed reading novels but that more than anything she loved films, moving pictures, and, since her father was the projectionist in the cinema next door, she saw almost every film that was sent to them.

She wrote too of how wonderful it had been to see him and that she longed, with all her heart, to see him again soon.

She read her letter over and thought it terribly boring but she knew that it was important to be completely honest.

Next morning, with some trepidation, she posted it on the way to Drury Lane and decided to forget all about it.

It did niggle away at the back of her mind but since they were recording a performance to be broadcast on the BBC Forces Programme, she was kept very busy. She was surprised when Lal took her aside after the broadcast rehearsal.

'You know that it's highly unlikely that Sylvia will be with us in Europe – Max did speak to you about it?'

Sally tried to appear calm and professional.

323

'Yes,' was all she said.

Lal smiled. 'This afternoon we want you to deliver Ophelia's speech from Act Three; terrific practice for you. Now we'll spend some time working on it.' She looked at Sally, who had tensed up. *'Con calma*, Sally; in some ways radio is more relaxing that an actual appearance. After all, you don't need to be in costume; no one can see you, but the voice, the delivery, is more important than ever. All right, ready to try?'

'Yes, please, Lal. Thank you.' Sally was filled with excitement and apprehension in equal measure. Ophelia's great speech on the wireless; Jon could hear it. *Oh dear, I should have thought of my parents first.*

They worked until Sybil called them to come back to the studio. 'We're ready to go, Sally. Is she ready, Lal?'

Lalita smiled and nodded. 'Absolutely. A believable fragile Ophelia takes to the stage.'

Praise from Lal, who was herself more than qualified to portray Ophelia, gave Sally an enormous boost. She went into the studio in a relaxed and confident manner that was obvious to technicians, directors and eventually listeners everywhere there was a British outpost of any kind. But when the recording machines were finally switched off, it was to her Hamlet that Sally turned.

'Sebastian, I didn't let you down, did I?'

He hugged her, an obviously very brotherly hug. 'Had any other woman asked me that, Lady Ophelia, I'd know she was fishing for a compliment, but you, little doubting Thomasina... You

324

were very good, Sally, thank you.'

He turned to Lal, who was busy sorting out scripts on a small table. 'Well done, Lal.'

'Everyone worked hard on this, especially Sally, but we have to remember that she is squeezing years of study into months.' She picked up her files. 'Come along, Sally, I think we deserve a drink. If you'd agree to pay, Seb, you may join us. We'll find Millie on our way out.'

There were four envelopes on the carpet when Sebastian opened the door that evening and ushered his flatmates inside. One was addressed to Millie, two were obviously business letters for Sebastian and the fourth was an unstamped envelope with 'Sally Brewer' written on it in small, very neat letters.

Sebastian picked it up. 'Someone delivered this by hand, Sally, but who? Only residents with keys can get in the front door.'

Sally had opened it. 'It's from Jon, she said, 'but he said nothing about coming up to London.'

'Might have been at the Admiralty – unexpected orders,' suggested Millie. 'What's he say, Sal?'

Sally unfolded the sheet of white paper and read it silently.

My dear Sally,
You are probably still on your journey back to London, but I had to sit down and write to you straight away to tell you how very much your visit meant to me today. I know the world would say that we don't know each other at all but I feel as if you have been

an important part of my life for ever. The world would say, 'Nonsense', but I hear what my heart is telling me and I believe it. Even though a ghastly war is still raging and I am here and you are there, I hope to see you often.

A colleague will post this or drop it into your flat. I only wish I could deliver it myself.

Jon

She finished reading, folded the paper and returned it to the matching envelope. 'A friend dropped it in but I have no idea how he got in.'

'There will be an explanation. Probably gave it to Dmitri. Everything all right?'

A broad smile lit up Sally's face. 'Yes, thank you. Everything's fine.'

SIXTEEN

May 1942

The date for Sally's first appearance in an advertising campaign arrived and, of course, it was on a day when she had arranged to go to see Jon, who was still living at the hospital. It seemed to Sally that he spent most of his time poring over maps of Corsica and France and trying to dredge from his memory every name, every meeting, every action of *le Maquis*.

'There were deaths and disappearances, Sally, and so they are looking for clues, coincidences –

I don't really know. Once they're sure that nothing important is hiding in my head, I'll be back on duty – on a battleship, if I'm lucky.'

Ben Templeton had been returned, not to active duty, which he wanted, but to an office job.

Now, on a beautiful spring day, Sally walked quietly round Berkeley Square, trying to decide what to do. Her tortured thoughts walked with her. *I want to see Jon. It's been three weeks and I want to see him so badly. A photograph for an advertisement isn't going to do much for my career. What will happen if I ask them to find someone else? There are bound to be hundreds of pretty girls who would be only too delighted to take my place.*

As always she discussed her problem with Sebastian and Millie.

'You're out of your mind, Sally. You're at the very beginning of your career and to ruin your reputation this way is insanity.' Millie was adamant.

'But Jon needs me.'

'He'll understand, Sal. You miss one visit. It's not as if he's desperately ill. Physically he's absolutely fine, from what you say.' Sebastian looked at Millie for moral support.

'Seb's right, Sally. Of course you two will miss seeing each other but it looks as if you'll have the rest of your lives to look at each other.'

Sally, only too aware that no matter what Maudie had said, Jon had never actually said the words 'I love you', was still unsure. Sometimes, when she was with Jon or talking to him on the telephone, she felt that he had stopped himself as if he was about to say something and had then decided that he had better not. 'We're not any-where like that yet, but surely giving up one little job to visit an injured serviceman won't hurt my career?'

'Every agent in the business will be told that you can't be relied on, Sally. Professional suicide. I've told you what I think – know, from experience – but it's entirely up to you.'

Sally was torn. Would Cedric Arnold, the agent who had offered her the job, refuse to represent her? Would he tell every other agent that she had backed out of a commitment? Was it possible that he would feel that her promise to Jon should come first?

'No, Sally,' she assured herself, 'he absolutely would not.'

She rang Jon from Sebastian's flat that evening and, just as the others had said, Jon was adamant that she keep her promise to the agent. 'I'm excited for you that you have the opportunity, Sally. Just wait, when I see the advertisement I shall proudly show it to all my friends.'

'And?' demanded Sebastian when Sally joined Millie and Sebastian in the kitchen where they were listening to the wireless.

'He wants me to do the shoot.'

'Of course he does.'

A week later, Elsie Brewer took the train to London to chaperone her daughter while the advertisement was being made. There was actually very little of the glitz and glamour that Elsie had expected. They were taken by car from Cedric Arnold's office to a photographer's studio on Piccadilly, where a production assistant showed Elsie to a chair, gave her a cup of tea and a newspaper, and took Sally off to change. Sybil had not been accepted as stylist or make-up artist by either the photographer or the film studio, and so Sally was left to the ministrations of the photographer's staff. Her face was made up quite heavily and after sighing because her hair was long 'and there really isn't time to cut it', the hairstylist wound Sally's hair into a fashionable roll, which he pinned at the back of her head, praying all the time that the Wren's cap they were using would still look particularly attractive perched 'on all that hair'.

It did.

Next came the dresser, who showed Sally two uniforms. 'Please put on the one you think will fit, Miss Brewer.'

Aghast, Sally looked at them. The uniforms were quite genuine but one was much too big and the other far too short. 'Neither will fit,' she said, wondering sadly if her modelling career had come to an abrupt end.

'I'll make it fit,' said the dresser, holding the bigger one out to Sally. 'Put this on.'

The length of the skirt was perfect but nothing else was near her size. The dresser walked round her a few times, pins in her mouth and a tape measure in her hand. 'You do stay lovely and slim, I must say. All the exercise you Wrens get, I suppose.'

'I'm not in the navy; I'm with ENSA and I'm naturally thin.'

The girl was unable to speak for the amount of pins sticking out of her mouth but she got behind

Sally and pulled and hauled at the skirt and jacket as she pinned great flaps of material together. Sally watched in awe as the front of the jacket and skirt grew smaller and smaller.

'Won't the pins show?'

The dresser removed the pins left in her mouth. 'God love you, no, pet. He'll shoot you from the front as you hold up your lovely tin of cleaning fluid. It's actually the product that's important, not the vehicle – you're the vehicle. Don't worry, the picture will be nice – he's good – and neither your gigantic bustle nor the pins'll show.'

And so it proved. Sally, wary of making any unnecessary moves, hobbled into the studio and was positioned in front of what looked like a giant bed sheet.

'Bit more lippy, Mildred,' said the photographer, and then he turned back to Sally while more bright red lipstick was being applied to her lips. 'Sorry about the pins, love, but I can't possibly afford a uniform for every size. You got a lovely figure, and face, don't make near enough of those come-to-bed eyes. Right then. Product, please.'

A tin of the product, a 'revolutionary cleaning agent', was brought in and put into Sally's left hand, which was manipulated into the exact distance from her face that the photographer wanted.

'That's it. Smile at it, ducky, pretend it's your fella.'

Sally lost count of the number of photographs he took. Her face grew sore from constant smiling and she had been startled by a despairing cry from the photographer at one point– 'Mildred, you've got lippy on her teeth.'

The lipstick was wiped off and they started again.

'Great. You're a natural, love. They'll send you one or two for your portfolio.'

Sally was unpinned and was delighted to get back into her own clothes. Her mother was waiting. 'What did it look like, Mum?'

'You looked lovely. Don't like all that muck on your face but Mildred says it will look perfectly normal in the photographs.'

Cedric had originally promised them lunch at the Savoy Grill, and Sally was keen for her mother to experience the service at the luxury hotel, but Cedric apologised. 'I have a client, Mrs Brewer, not a patch on your daughter for talent or looks but thinks she's the reincarnation of Sarah Bernhardt and the producer on the film she's mangling – apologies, making – is, according to Madame "an arrogant, talentless" and I won't repeat the third adjective she put before "oaf". I simply have to go and sort it out. Delightful to meet you, though, Mrs Brewer, and I'm quite sure we'll be meeting again very soon, and we'll lunch. Sally, *bisous*,' and he was gone.

'What a peculiar man, Sally. What on earth does *bisous* mean?'

'Just ignore it, Mum,' advised Sally, who could work out what the word meant. 'It's harmless, a stupidly clever thing that everyone in the industry understands.'

'I'm not going to tell your dad what that photographer had the cheek to say about your eyes. Where shall we go for a sandwich?'

331

'Sebastian's flat. I can't interrupt a rehearsal so that you could meet everyone but at least I can show you where I'm living.'

'I wouldn't be at ease in someone else's house while they're out, Sally, and I want to do a bit of shopping. Let's go to Covent Garden market. I always seem to find something nice on at least one of the stalls.'

Mother and daughter had a delightful time and when they finally sat down in a little café Sally decided that it was time to tell her mother all about Jon. She felt as if someone had turned on a tap or as if she had suddenly become a storm-swollen stream, for words poured out of her mouth. She told her mother everything and Elsie sat holding her daughter's hands and listening until at last the flood stopped.

'You love him, Sally.'

It was not a question but a statement.

Sally could only nod.

'And he's a naval officer who's been through a dreadful time but wants to go back to sea.'

'Yes, Mum. He feels it's his duty and besides, he loves the navy.'

'And he really is a lord.'

Sally rarely considered Jon's title. Discovering that he had one had been … not a shock, but a surprise and not a very welcome one, but Lord Hedges seemed to have nothing at all to do with Just Jon. 'Yes,' she answered her mother quietly.

Elsie shrugged. 'God alone knows what your father will say – if he ever has to find out.'

But there was no more time and they took the underground to the railway station. Sally was

332

really sad when she saw her mother onto the train that passed through Dartford but she felt, in some way, relieved of a burden.

'Tell your friends I'll meet them next time, Sally,' Elsie called from the train, 'and come home when you can. Bring them. I'll find something for them to eat.'

Sally waved until the train was out of sight and then, even though she had been given the whole day off she went back to Drury Lane where everyone was anxious to hear all about her experience.

'We should have warned the poor darling about the old "stick in some pins and shoot from the front" trick,' laughed Sybil.

'I didn't mind it actually,' Sally told them, 'not when he explained. It was quite sensible really, and now I understand the faint smell of mothballs. The uniforms were probably older than I am.'

'Wouldn't doubt it for a minute. All set to do it again?'

Sally didn't answer immediately. When she had been offered the job, she had been filled with anticipation and excitement; this was surely the wonderful beginning of her true career. But there had been no excitement. She would withhold judgement until she saw the photographs.

'Possibly,' she said with a smile.

She had to repeat everything later that evening for Millie and Sebastian, and then she decided that, instead of writing quick notes to Jon and to her parents, she would try to make up for the time she had been away making the commercial by studying Ophelia's speeches – just in case.

'*O, what a noble mind is here o'er-thrown!*' Sally read Ophelia's speech over and over again before standing in front of the bedroom mirror and, after convincing herself that she was Ophelia, reading the speech aloud several times, trying to convey the rejected girl's heartbreak for herself and for Hamlet, whom she loved. She was quite pleased with what she heard but was not so conceited that she thought it was perfect.

'I'll ask Sebastian to hear it and maybe he'll coach me, just in case, but not tonight,' she told herself, and so when Millie crept into the shared bedroom half an hour or so later, Sally was sound asleep.

Next morning they were reduced to drinking Camp Coffee, which only Millie really enjoyed, because their rations of tea had run out.

'I could have sworn we had a few ounces left,' complained Sebastian, who was looking in totally ridiculous places for the lost tea leaves.

'Oh, golly, it's my fault,' said Milly. 'I meant to ask you two but forgot.'

'Ask us what, Millie? A third of the tea is yours; you can do what you like with it.'

'I gave a few ounces to Sylvia. Tea seems to be the only thing she can drink in the mornings – that stays down anyway – and they'd run out. I'm sorry, I should have asked.'

'Couldn't go to a better cause. Let's not worry about a few cups of tea. It's my turn for the queues this week and I'll try to catch our grocer on a good day. We are out of almost everything.

Either of you got any soap?' Sebastian had found himself in the bath tub with only a brush.

'Yes, I can give you a bar, Seb, but it's perfumed.'

'Thanks, Millie, but I'll see what I can find.'

Sally was feverishly calculating just exactly what she had left from the small but important packages that had been in her Christmas stocking. 'Saved, Sebastian. I have a bar of Palmolive.'

'Which shall I choose? Palmolive or perfumed?'

They were still talking nonsense when they reached Drury Lane.

Sylvia, although three months pregnant and still suffering badly from morning sickness, was determined to remain with the company as long as she could.

Fate intervened, for that very morning when they had expected an early rehearsal, Max called a meeting.

'All I want is to hear that this damned war is over,' said Humph. 'I've a notion to slow down, go fishing, maybe grow sweet peas.'

'That'll be the day,' teased one of the band members. 'You'll be carried out, feet first, before you get round to slowing down.'

They were seated at the front of the auditorium and Max, casually dressed as always, walked in from a side entrance and looked at them.

'Well, it's come, my children...'

He was not allowed to finish as the bandsman who had been teasing Humph burst out, 'No, you're having us on, Max. The war, it's not over, is it?'

'Not so far as I know. The summons has come. We're off to the battlefields of *La Belle France*.'

Some excited chattering broke out and soon the noise was so deafening that no one could hear anyone speak. Max hauled himself up onto the stage and bellowed, 'Quiet,' at the top of his voice, and startled, the company obeyed him.

'We will be gone for at least three months, possibly a great deal longer. At the moment there is some doubt about exactly where we will be but wherever it is, this is not a summer holiday. There is a war on and there is fighting on French soil. Since no expense is being spared sending us to France, the Government wants value and so, if it gets too hot in France, we may find ourselves in Belgium, Italy or even Egypt. No one will be ostracised for not wishing to go and so I would like you to think carefully before committing yourselves. Please remember, you won't be able to change your minds and fly home after a week. I'll be given all the information we'll need and will make sure that everyone has a copy.'

'Passports? Inoculations, that sort of thing?' asked the leader of the Balladeers.

'I said I would pass on all the information about our travel as soon as it comes through to me. Everyone must think carefully, discuss it with family – if you haven't already done so. No one will think the worse of anyone who chooses to remain at home; there's still plenty of work to do in Blighty.'

'What happens if we find ourselves in the middle of a running battle?' That question came from several directions.

'We'll be evacuated as soon as possible. Now, can't do better than that, can we?'

Questions and answers went on for some time, and Sally and Sebastian sat and listened intently to both. Millie, on the other hand, was no longer listening but was aglow with pleasure. Her friends could see her excitement in her eyes and both knew just what this opportunity meant to her. They made a tacit agreement to watch her very carefully. She was so driven by her need to find Patrick's grave that it would be quite easy for her to get herself into a scrape.

It was only as the three of them were walking home that evening that Sally actually realised what working in France might mean to her.

She stopped in the street. 'I can't go; it's impossible. I can't leave Jon for three months, and besides there's the film.'

'You have dates for neither, Sally, in fact for none of the three. We have no date for France. Government wheels, et cetera, et cetera.'

'Sally, Jon may well be leaving you. Didn't you say he is trying to return to active duty? You won't be the first working couple separated by duty.'

They were still arguing – or discussing, as Millie preferred to say – all the options when they reached Hays Mews and the building that housed Sebastian's flat. 'Let's have something quick like beans on toast for supper,' suggested Sally as they climbed the stairs, 'and then we can make some kind of plan.'

'First, guess who queued for exactly sixty-three minutes to collect this week's bacon ration?' said

Millie. 'Looking at it, there doesn't seem to be as much as last time but I'm sure you two will still find it super tasty with the beans.'

'Well done,' chorused her flatmates.

'I hope you went through an entire exercise routine while you waited,' said Sebastian. 'What joy you must have brought to the exhausted masses. I do wish you'd been with me at Robinson's. Exhausted mothers and lots of children running around like little dervishes. A ballerina pointing her dainty little toes might have stunned them into silence.'

'Very funny. I actually spent the time going over and over Max's announcement. The date for France can't come soon enough for me.'

Sally tried to be cheerful. After all, she had dreamed of going abroad and the lovely news of her colleague's interesting condition had not slipped her mind. So far Sylvia had made no announcements or promises, and Sally tried not to hope that the actress and her husband were unlikely to be prepared to have her go off to a war zone. *If she decides to go I'll help her as much as I can but in the meantime, surely it's sensible for me to study her lines?* 'Why is it that human beings wait months, years, for something to happen and then everything happens at once?' Sally knew, despite her intentions, she sounded glum.

Sebastian said, 'I think there's a rather rude word for that, Sally, but–'

'Grandmamma would not approve of your telling us,' the girls said for him.

They had moved into the kitchen to prepare their evening meal.

'I'm sure there's nothing left to ration,' complained Millie as Sebastian separated the bacon slices.

'Sausages,' he said. 'To make us all miserable, they'll ration chocolate and sausages.'

'You are a hypocrite, Sebastian Brady. You nip down to the Savoy or the Cumberland when you fancy a treat.'

Sally stood up. 'I'll just find that soap, Sebastian,' she said, and quickly left the kitchen.

Sebastian looked stunned. It was obvious that Millie's remark was the last thing he had expected but he spoke calmly. 'Not fair, Millicent. I nip down, as you put it, quite rarely these days and, if I remember rightly, when I do nip down, I tend to take a chum or two with me.'

'Sorry, appalling idea of a joke, Seb. I was trying to get Sally's mind off all her problems. Poor kid. If life was perfect all three of her treats would fall one by one into her lap.'

'But life isn't perfect, Millie, as you know better than any of us. Now how about supper – in the Savoy or in the kitchen?'

Sally had returned with the large bar of green soap and so two female voices chorused, 'Kitchen.'

Having seen that Sally seemed free of her worries for the time being, Sebastian served the simple but delicious meal, the bacon slices for Sally and himself, not with the beans, which they had decided to save, but with some left-over macaroni cheese, one of Millie's particular favourites. Since there seemed to be a tacit agreement not to speak about the proposed trip, and no suitable subject of conversation presented itself, he switched on the wireless. It was the first time the three of them had felt even slightly ill at ease with one another and they listened to a news broadcast without the slightest interest.

'What on earth possessed me to make that stupid remark to Seb, the world's most decent, generous human being?'

They had washed and changed into nightwear and were laying out clean uniforms for the morning when the question burst from Millie.

'Tension, Millie, I suppose, but he knows you didn't mean anything.'

'It's still unforgivable.'

'We're going to France, Millie.'

'Please, please, let us be in the right region.'

'You won't do anything foolish if we're not? I've seen maps of France; it's a huge country.'

Millie, who had danced in France for several seasons, chose not to remind Sally of this. 'If you mean, will I wrap my undies in a handkerchief and start walking, no, I won't, Sally. If it's to happen, it will. What about you, leaving Jon?'

'As you said he's possibly going to leave me, but he's alive, Millie, and I will be grateful for that.'

SEVENTEEN

The next few weeks were frenetically busy for the company. Not only were they preparing for a three-month foreign tour but they were rehearsing and making appearances. They travelled to

Liverpool and to Portsmouth and visited several military hospitals, sometimes trying out new routines, new songs, and even new performers. With mixed feelings, Sylvia Stone had resigned and the company gave her a little party and collected money for gifts for the expected baby.

'A gas mask – for a baby? You have to be pulling my leg.'

Several of the older members of the company asked that their donation be used for anything besides the gas mask but most of the younger ones decided that since a gas mask, no matter how awkward or uncomfortable, might keep a precious tiny person safe or at least safer, it was well worth buying.

Lalita and Sybil managed to find exquisite hand-embroidered baby nighties in a small shop on the King's Road and together, the nighties and the gas mask lay on a table, the beautiful and the ugly, side by side.

'Rather like life,' said Max as he looked at them. 'Must have taken all your coupons,' but the two friends merely smiled.

The other gifts were practical: nappies, feeding bottles and safety pins. The young parents were absolutely delighted.

Jon had not returned to a ship but had come up to work in London at a desk job at the Admiralty. He stayed in a little flat he owned not far from Sebastian's. He and Sally spoke to each other or met as often as possible. One Saturday afternoon when Sally had no commitments she invited Maude to come up to town to join them for a walk in Hyde Park, but to Maude it was not a success. She no longer recognised London and seemed to feel every blow inflicted on her beloved capital city. When Sally and Jon took her to her train she hugged both of them warmly but said that she would not return unless to see Jon once more before he went to sea.

'Have you no time to visit Dartford, Jon, my dear? Surely you want to see the house?'

'Too many unhappy memories crowding out the good ones, Maudie. I've offered the old place to the Admiralty. They're going to turn it into a rehabilitation centre. They'll fill it with hope and courage, you'll see.'

The elderly lady stopped dead in the middle of the platform. 'Oh, Jon, what would you father say?'

'"Damned sensible", Maudie, is what he'd say; you know he would. The war can't last much longer and when it's all over we'll set it to rights together, the three of us.'

He was looking at Sally as he spoke and her heart filled with excitement. Perhaps because their meetings were of necessity so short and so precious, there had been no talk of the future. They were living in the moment and this was the first time Jon had said or written anything that had hinted at togetherness.

He took her hand and, side by side, they saw Maude onto her train.

'Damn it, but I hate saying goodbye to her these days, Sally.'

'Dartford has lived through its poundings, Jon. We must be positive.'

Suddenly he snatched her into his arms and

swung her around. 'Yes, we must. Let's go to...' he thought for a moment, 'the Ritz. It's closest. We can have dinner and we can dance, and everyone will recognise you and all the men will envy me and I'll feel like King Cockerel. That's the name of a cockerel I had when I was about seven. How that fellow strutted around, sticking his chest out and yelling his triumph.'

Sally laughed at him but glanced down at her clothes doubtfully.

Jon smiled. 'You're absolutely lovely, Sally. The Ritz will be honoured to have you.'

They took the underground and eventually climbed out at Green Park from where it was a short stroll to the Ritz Hotel. Sally noted the crowds of people with rolled-up blankets, flasks, and other assorted luggage, including a violin and at least two accordions. 'Those poor people must sleep here every night, Jon.'

'I expect they do, Sally, brave souls, but they'll make music before they go to sleep.'

They walked to the hotel where they dined and danced in surroundings so different from the ones they had just left and then, because neither wanted the evening to end, they walked to Sebastian's flat. 'Come in and meet them, Jon.'

'I'd love to, my darling, but it's much too late; another time.'

Sally took out her key and Jon took it and inserted it, and then he pulled Sally into his arms. 'Sally, you do know what I feel about you? I love you, and tonight I wanted nothing more than ... to love you.' He kissed her then and they stood like couples in love all over London and

343

they kissed and touched and murmured fevered promises. 'I love you, Sally, with all my heart.'

'I love you too, Jon, dearest Just Jon.'

He pushed the door open and handed her the key. 'Good night, Sally, my lovely Sally.'

She went in and closed the door as slowly as she could, watching his beloved face until she had to close it completely. 'Good night, Just Jon.'

She tiptoed in but the kitchen light was on faintly and she could smell cocoa.

'Well, we thought you were never coming in. Didn't you invite him in, Sally?'

'How did you know we were there?'

'Because you went for an afternoon walk in the park and never came home. We've been sitting in the window, peering through the blackout curtains for hours,' explained Sebastian.

'Quite dishy, our Jon,' said Millie.

'Yes, he is, isn't he?' agreed Sally. 'Good night. I'll see you both in the morning.'

'Oh, no you don't, madame. You tell us everything.'

'There's nothing to tell.'

'Nonsense,' scolded Millie. 'We want to know everything. It's your duty to tell us.'

'All right. We went for a walk, put Maudie on a train, went to the Ritz – yes, the Ritz – and had a lovely dinner...'

'We had beans on toast,' Sebastian interrupted her. 'Quite delicious.'

'And then we walked here but Jon thought it was too late to come in. And that's all. Good night.'

And by the time Millie had had a turn in the

bathroom and had climbed into her bed, Sally was – or pretended to be – sound asleep.

The next morning Cedric Arnold telephoned the theatre to announce that dates had been made for filming Sally's part in the propaganda film. 'Most of it has been shot already,' he informed Max. 'Mr Coward is an absolute wonder, unbelievably busy. He's here, there, and everywhere, but always has time to chat. What a wonderful opportunity for my little ingénue. This could be the beginning of her career. I have such plans for her.'

'So too has ENSA, Cedric,' said Max, 'and actually I can't say anything yet but I have a feeling someone else is determined to help her plan her future.'

And no matter how Cedric coaxed, Max, who possibly felt just a little guilty at his slight indiscretion, could not be drawn.

When Sally and her friends arrived at the theatre Max called Sally into the office and gave her the news. 'I haven't actually got three free days this month, Sally – he should have given us more warning – but I did promise and you will be given leave to take part. After all, it's good for the organisation as a whole. We're proud of you; you've worked really hard and who knows where this may lead – for your future. Well done, Sally, now off to rehearsal, if you can calm down sufficiently.'

Sally, who was quite sure that she was perfectly calm, smiled weakly and left the room.

The rest of the day flew past in an exhausting mixture of new songs, new dance routines, a costume fitting – and learning lines for several sketches. In the evening the company put on a show in a hostel that housed refugees and, for the first time, several cast members found themselves performing for an audience many of whom understood not one word of English. The performers in the skits and the comedians, used to laughter, clapping and stamping feet, were stunned to find themselves facing a mainly polite but unappreciative audience. The musicians, the dancers and Sally all earned grateful applause.

Lalita was invaluable, going around the audience chatting in French or Flemish, Dutch, even Polish.

'ENSA needs to recruit Czechs and Poles, Belgians, Dutch, Scandinavians, not to mention Spanish and Italian speakers,' she said. 'This language barrier is a huge problem, Max. These poor displaced people haven't a clue as to what's going on. Please God, this damned war will be over before they all learn English – and they *will* learn – but how can we cheer them up in the meantime?'

'Tell them to be grateful they're safe,' came the voice of one of the soubrettes.

Lal rounded on her. 'Put yourself in their shoes. Have you the slightest idea what these people have gone through?'

Embarrassed, the girl turned away.

'Language is certainly an enormous problem,' said Sebastian as they were on their way home later. 'Perhaps the embassies have lists of people who fit the bill.'

'Quicker to go to any opera house or concert

hall, Seb. There's hardly an orchestra in the country that could function without its musicians from other countries,' suggested Millie.

Inspired, Sally added, 'Land girls. The air force. They're full of people who've escaped from Hitler.'

'How are your land girls going to entertain, Sally?'

'Actually, I have a friend who's a land girl and a Polish girl worked with her, but before she had to flee from Poland, the girl...' she thought for a moment trying to remember the news at Christmas, 'Eva, that's it, her name is Eva and she was training to be a classical singer. I think the family who own the farm are sponsoring her at a prestigious London music school. There are probably other foreigners there too.'

'Lovely story, Sally, and great ideas. Pass them on to Max and Sybil tomorrow.'

'I know another refugee, a German one—' began Sally.

'Don't think we'll take kindly to German refugees, Sal,' Millie interrupted her.

'Why ever not? He's not an entertainer. He's actually a brilliant scientist working for the Government.'

They had reached the Mansion and there was an awkward silence, broken by Sebastian. 'I've heard of chaps like that, German but probably Jewish or something else that Herr Hitler doesn't like. I do think Lal, our resident linguist, will be thrilled with all these ideas, Sally. Enough for now, *mes amies*. Tomorrow is another day and I hate to be ungentlemanly but it is my turn for the bath. I'll be as quick as I can. Good night, ladies.'

'He'll be ages,' Millie said. 'Let's have a cup of tea.'

The telephone rang very early next morning. Sebastian answered it and called Sally.

'For you, telephone.'

Sally hurried to take the receiver. 'Hello.'

'Sally, it's Jon. Can you possibly get away for an hour or so today to meet me at the Admiralty?'

'I don't know, Jon. What is it?'

'Try, Sally. I'll be here all day. Just ask for Lieutenant-Commander Galbraith. Tell the Max chap that it's important. Please.' The line went dead.

She replaced the receiver and, still in her dressing gown, went into the kitchen. 'It was Jon. He wants me to meet him at the Admiralty.'

'When?'

'Whenever I can get away, if I can. Oh, what will I do if we're too busy?'

'We all have to eat, Sally. Go during a break. Is he leaving?' Millie spoke bluntly.

'I don't know; it's possible, I suppose, but there hasn't been any warning.'

'I hardly think they'll ask even a lord if it's convenient, Sal. What else could it be?'

Sally said nothing but turned and left the kitchen. The others heard her in the bathroom a few minutes later. Water was running but whether it was to wash in or hide tears, her friends could not tell. They made porridge and tea, had theirs while listening to an early news broadcast, and waited for Sally.

348

'Thanks but I'm not hungry,' she said as Millie offered her porridge but she did accept a cup of hot tea and sipped that slowly.

'Damn, but it would be so handy to have a banana in the refrigerator. Super fruit. You'll need to eat something, Sally.'

'Later,' she muttered.

She had not even finished the tea by the time they had to leave and she said nothing as they travelled to the theatre.

'Talk to Max now,' ordered Millie when they arrived. 'No point in putting it off.'

Sally, her face so pale that her large eyes looked even darker than usual, approached the office and met Max on his way in.

'Good heavens, girl. What kind of night did you have? You look like hell.'

Such harshness caused Sally to pull herself together. 'May I go to see a friend at the Admiralty? It shouldn't take long.'

He stared into her face. 'Well, you're no damn use the way you are. Go, and bring a prettier face back with you.' He walked into his office closing his door with a crash that echoed through the entire building.

Sally found her way to the Admiralty and, after waiting in an anteroom for four or five minutes, was taken to another room. The sailor who accompanied her knocked on the door, opened it, said, 'Miss Brewer, sir,' and invited Sally to enter.

Jon, in uniform, was standing at the window. He turned as she entered but stayed exactly where he was, his arms, in his smart naval jacket, behind his back. He made no move to touch her or even to approach her.

'Jon?' Sally knew that he was going away but waited for him to say it.

'Please, Sally, do sit down. I have so much to tell you.'

'You're going away.'

'That's only part of it. I have no choice, Sally, I have to go; you wouldn't expect me to stay even though I want to stay here more than I have ever wanted anything in my entire life. I'm needed.'

'I need you.' The words she had vowed never to utter had jumped out of her mouth before she could stop them. 'Sorry, sorry, I shouldn't have said anything. I didn't mean to embarrass you. Please go and I wish you–'

But he did not hear what she wished for him as he crossed the room, pulled her close to him and kissed her feverishly, her eyes, her nose, her lips. He breathed in the clean, fragrant smell of her as she raised her arms and put them around his neck, returning his kisses with as much abandon as he gave them. He held her as if his arms were locked around her so that he was physically unable to release her. 'Sally, do you mean that? You need me?'

'Yes,' she said simply. 'I need you. From the moment you stood there while Maude was trying to introduce you. Poor Maude, she didn't know whether to use your proper name or not and you said, "Jon, just Jon." I kept seeing your face and hearing your voice, even before we met at the naval base.'

He held her then as if she were a child, and for

a time said nothing and Sally stayed safely in the circle of his arms and wished that she could stay there for ever. But there was a knock on the door and at last he released her.

The same sailor was there but this time he carried a tray, which he put down on the table behind Sally. 'Coffee, sir, ma'am.' He saluted and left them.

'Be mother,' said Jon. 'Such a mundane thing to do, drinking coffee. Ordinary life does seem to go on.'

Sally poured coffee, which had the most enticing smell, and Jon sat beside her. 'Yes, Sally, I'm going away and I have no idea when I'll be back. *Déjà vu.*'

'You'll write?'

'Every day, if I can, and let's hope at least some of the letters turn up. I'll number the envelopes and then you'll know if one is missing.'

'And I will write to you and do the same.'

'And you'll tell me every little thing; what you're reading, what you're singing, what the weather's like – terribly important to the British. And, Sally, if you possibly can – and I know you'll be sent overseas soon – but if you can, will you see Maudie now and again – look after her for me?'

'Of course, but it won't last much longer, Jon, it can't.'

'When it does end, Sally, if... I'll leave the Service and go home to look after ... everything. I want you to be a part of that, the major part. But you have your career and I know you'll make films, be in plays and I'll be your biggest admirer.

351

I love you but right now I won't tie you down. I wanted to, dear God how I wanted to. At The Ritz, I thought how blissful it would be to take a room but life is too precarious. Ships sink.'

'Lightning never strikes twice, Jon; it's an old saying.'

He laughed and it was the joyous clear laugh of a happy young man. 'Darling Sally, ask any farmer about lightning strikes.' He held her to him again, this time as if he would never let her go. 'A lifetime isn't long enough to love you, Sally, but it's time for you to go. You have your career to think of. Tell me all about the film; we're sent all the propoganda stuff, which always seems a bit like coals to Newcastle, but this time I shall so enjoy watching it with the chaps.'

Again the measured knock. 'Miss Brewer's car is here, Commander.'

'Thank you. One moment.'

'I don't have a car, Jon.'

'The navy takes care of its own. I'll walk you out, my darling, but one last kiss...'

Sally stared out of the window as the car eased its way through London. A thick mist from the river allowed her to make out only ghostly shapes that seemed to hang in the air and not be rooted in the ancient soil of England. Against them all, though, she saw Jon's face as he waved goodbye.

EIGHTEEN

Early July 1942

The pain of Jon's absence was a million times worse this time. Sally felt even more sympathy for Millie as she tried to fathom what pain the death of the best-beloved must bring. It was impossible. She could not imagine anything worse than she was experiencing now.

She seemed to go through the days like a machine and even her appearance in an important British film did not excite her half as much as she had thought it would. On the first day of filming her tiny appearance she was driven to the studios and handed over to 'Wardrobe'. For Sally it was to be a second appearance in uniform, but this one had been made to measure and the tiniest adjustments were made on set. A very superior director walked and talked her through her few seconds of fame beside the great man but the set was the deck of a battleship and served only to remind Sally of Jon. She did the entire three seconds again but this time with a man in uniform who was the stand-in. Jon will find all this interesting, she thought. Next she went to make-up, where it took longer to arrange her hair and to make up her face than it had taken her to get to the studio.

Next she was posed beside the stand-in and

began to feel like a puppet as first she was positioned in one direction and then another while a man with a camera wheeled it to face her. He disappeared behind it and she thought he had gone but a voice from the other side of the room shouted out a comment or an order now and again.

'Try sad, Sally my angel, not scared. All right?' A little later: 'Better, but Zac, put your arm around her waist and pull her closer to you. That's it. Determined, that's it. You're off to war, prepared to give everything for your King and country. Good, but Angel, you're a Wren, you're both leaving but in different directions. Who knows what might happen? Look up at him, you may never see him again.'

It was only too easy to act that part.

The 'great man' was to be there later and so after standing on the deck, being ruffled by a gentle breeze from a strategically-placed fan, and turned this way and that, they 'broke for lunch'.

'She's not exactly an English rose,' she heard one man say. 'Perhaps we should bleach her hair. What do you think, fabulous with those dark blue eyes?'

'No, she's classy, just perfect.'

The shooting ended early as the 'great man' was suddenly unavailable. Sally was driven home and went through almost the same scenario the next day. More stills were shot, other places on the deck were suggested and tried out.

'You just can't take a bad picture, Sally; the camera courts you. You'll be great in movies. I know you want to do your bit with ENSA but have you planned for after? The war has to end and every studio will want you, even the ones in the States.'

Sally smiled. Once she would have been ecstatic, but she heard again Jon's words, his promises. She knew what she wanted to do after the war and although the theatre was still an important part of it, and possibly film too, it did not involve moving to America.

Home earlier than the others, Sally washed her face very thoroughly and, having changed into casual clothes, she went into the kitchen to prepare an evening meal. She looked in the larder, which must once, not too long ago, have been full of hanging hams, ripening cheeses, a freshly caught piece of fish on that cold marble shelf, jams and jellies and bottled fruits in serried ranks, but now there remained two eggs, a rather hard piece of cheese – which she thought she could turn into a sauce – if there was anything to serve with it, some potatoes and carrots and a tired piece of cabbage. Hardly ingredients for a feast or even a weekly supper at the Brewer house.

And I have had two super lunches and probably another one tomorrow; I'll have to do something.

Sally had never been taught to cook. Her mother had been so delighted to have a bright, talented daughter that she had encouraged her to study or, in her leisure time to sit in the projection room and watch the films with her dad. Now Sally looked at her ingredients and felt completely discouraged. 'But they must smell something tasty as they walk in,' she told herself, 'cooking can't be hard.'

She peeled the potatoes and the carrots, sliced the potatoes and cut the carrots into small pieces. 'An onion?' She wished now that she had spent more time in the kitchen with her mother and less with her father in the cinema. Sally seemed to remember that her mother had almost always used an onion in a main-meal recipe. 'When did I last see an onion?' she asked herself, and had no idea. Nor could she remember if they had fallen into the rationed category.

She fought with her desire to throw the cabbage away. It certainly was not at its finest but she washed it and cut it up, before putting it into a pot with cold water and some salt.

She layered the potato slices into a casserole and enjoyed herself sprinkling colourful carrot cubes on each layer. She whisked the eggs with some milk, grated the cheese, which was so hard that it took her ages, and she was not pleased when she snagged a nail on the grater. After attending to the nail she sprinkled the cheese on the top layer of the vegetables and then whispering, 'In for a penny, in for a pound,' she poured the egg and milk mixture over the top of the casserole.

Time was marching on and she remembered that her mother had always dotted potatoes with butter. The refrigerator contained no butter at all but there was a small block of margarine and she used that instead, saving a little for breakfast toast. Her watch informed her that her friends were probably making their way home and she turned on the oven at a lowish heat, turned on the gas jet under the saucepan and went off to lay a pretty table.

Not long after she had finished preparing what she hoped would be a beautiful and welcome surprise, Sally smelled burning. The cabbage pot was almost burned dry but the cabbage still resembled cabbage and she grabbed the handle and pulled the pot to the side. She yanked open the oven door only to be met by a wall of smoke, convincing her that the oven was on fire. She looked around helplessly. What on earth was she to do?

'Turn it off,' yelled Sebastian as he hurried across the kitchen. He propelled Sally out of his way, turned off the oven, and picking up a tea cloth, painfully manoeuvred the browning casserole out of the oven.

Millie joined them in time to hug Sally, who had burst into tears.

'I didn't mean to set it on fire,' she sobbed. 'I wanted to surprise you both.'

'You did, Sal, and it's not on fire, just a little browned.' Millie hesitated for a moment before asking, 'What is it, actually?'

Sally was on the point of more tears when Sebastian started to laugh. 'Oh, Sally, my angel, you are absolutely priceless.' He poked a fork into the dish. 'Whatever it is, Sal, it's redeemable. Just the top got a little...'

He started to laugh again and that, of course, made Sally angry. 'What it is, is every single thing we had to eat in the house, totally destroyed, everything, potatoes, eggs, everything.'

'You did put some liquid into the potatoes?'

'Of course, well, two beaten eggs and a little

milk.' Sebastian turned to Millie who was stirring the boiled cabbage. 'Any ideas, Mil?' he whispered.

'Don't fret, Sally, it was lovely to smell cooking when we were coming upstairs.' She glared at Sebastian, who looked as if he was going to laugh again. 'The top, the eggs, cheese and milk just got a little too brown, that's all.' She checked the milk in the refrigerator. 'We have plenty of milk so let's have a cup of tea while we moisten the potatoes and put them back in for a few minutes.'

'I shall scream if I have another cup of tea,' said Sebastian. 'And you really don't want to hear that. There's a presentable bottle of claret at the back of the larder. I was saving it for tomorrow but let's have it now and Sally can tell us all about her day; I, for one, am all agog.'

Since Sebastian had appeared in several films, both as a child actor and as an adult, the girls knew that filming was not new to him but his suggestion was typically generous.

'You are a fibber, Sebastian Brady,' said Sally, 'but the nicest fibber I know.'

'I'll fetch the vino,' he said, and went off, returning a few minutes later with the bottle and three of his grandmother's crystal glasses. 'Hey, it's a French wine. I think that's a good omen.'

They drank the wine and toasted one another and their hopes for the future, and the wine helped them find the burned potatoes edible. Sally told them all about her second long day and when they were washing up they broke the news to Sally that they were leaving for France in the middle of the following week; just enough time to pack and to inform everyone they wanted to know.

'Get a letter off to Jon first, I'd say, Sally, and since we have the weekend off to pack and say our goodbyes, you'll have time to see your parents.'

'What about you, Millie?'

'Hardly time to get up north, but I'll ring Patrick's mum and dad and I'll write to mine. You, Seb?'

'My favourite Russian will keep an eye on the place; he's completely trustworthy and I won't worry about it. The only thing Dmitri can't prevent is a bombing but no one has control over that. It's not as if we were popping over to the Med for a few days in the sun, is it, ladies? We have to invest quite a bit of faith in this expedition. We don't know what we're going to experience and we've no idea what we might see when we get back. We're on Peter Pan's adventure and it's probably best to think of it like that.' As if something had just occurred to him he stood up. 'I'll see you both in the morning. I'm going to see Dmitri now; no point in putting it off.'

Sally's car arrived for her even earlier next morning. 'His nibs's here, miss, and so best if we get you there as quick as.'

When they arrived at the studios, Sally was taken straight to wardrobe and make-up. Once again she scarcely recognised herself when all the make-up had been applied. 'Will my mother know it's me?' she asked the make-up artist.

'Trust me, Miss Brewer. The world will see – and recognise – your beautiful face. I'm merely accentuating what you have for these blasted lights, which absolutely leach all colour from you, honestly. Your mum won't believe you've got make-up on. I've done the greats, love: Anna Neagle, Margaret Lockwood, Vivien Leigh, you name her, I've done her and not one beautiful lady has complained.'

Sally remembered her favourite costume that had been bought because it looked like 'something Margaret Lockwood would wear'. It was still in her wardrobe, still wearable, still making her feel elegant and sophisticated. 'I won't either, thank you,' she said, and, seated before a mirror, happily watched the artist at work.

After make-up, the hairdresser got to work and then Sally was taken to 'Wardrobe', where she dressed in the perfectly fitted Wren uniform. I'll scream if it isn't filmed today, she thought as excitement built up in her stomach where it seemed as if millions of little wings were fluttering.

'Mr Coward, may I introduce–'

The director got no further before he was interrupted.

'Sally, how lovely you look and how terrif to meet you at last.'

Sally, finding herself face-to-face with Noël Coward, was speechless. He just could not be real – not *the* Noël Coward – but the man in naval uniform took her hand and his hand was definitely a warm, human hand.

'Now, Sally, we're not in a studio in greater London but on a warship and you and I are going to go up on deck so that I can have one last look at England. We'll gaze together for a moment and then you will go ashore to wait for me. I know it wasn't rehearsed but I want you to square your shoulders and walk away; the camera will follow you and when you reach the dock, stop, turn around and raise your hand. Can you do that? Can you pretend that someone you love is going to sea? Imagine how you would feel if you knew the man you love might not return. Can you do that?'

Sally was unable to say a word, but she nodded.

'Good girl. Let's get into position.'

From then on it was a repeat of the two days of rehearsal except that now the great man was there instead of his stand-in. They stood together looking out to the South Coast and then Sally did as she had been asked, squared her shoulders, walked down the ramp to the 'dock'. At the bottom she stopped, turned and lifted her right hand in a farewell gesture. She heard the word 'Cut' and then loud clapping.

'Told you, sir, she's a natural.'

Since Sally had received no further instructions, she remained where she was until the director himself walked down to fetch her. 'We'll look at it, Sally, but I think it's a take. Good girl. Come and have a break. Shot of something or a nice cup of tea?'

Sally wanted nothing and after a few minutes' wait she was taken to yet another room where something called 'rushes' was being shown. Everyone but Sally discussed them at great length. Sally was stunned by seeing herself actually in black and white on a small screen, but she was pleased to note that the make-up artist was right for she looked almost exactly like herself.

Both the star and the director were happy. 'Fantastic, Sally. We usually have to repeat and repeat.'

'I'm sure your next screen appearance will be much longer, young lady.' Noël Coward shook hands with her. 'Are you joining us for lunch?'

At that moment Sally could think of nothing she would enjoy less. It was just too much to take in. 'No, thank you, sir,' she said. 'The company is off on a European tour next week and I have a million things to do.'

They said goodbye with hugs, kisses and promises; the director himself walked Sally to her car. 'Welcome to the business, young lady,' he said as he opened the car door for her and watched her until she was seated. As the car drew away, in the mirror, Sally saw him still standing until they were out of sight.

The studio car dropped her at the Theatre Royal and Sally changed into rehearsal clothes and worked with her colleagues on numbers they were preparing for the tour. The few who knew where she had spent the morning said nothing until it was time to finish for the day and then Sally was bombarded with questions, which she answered as honestly as she could. Yes, Noël Coward had been wonderful. Yes, the director was pleased. And since food or lack of it was always a preoccupation in the business, Sally was stared at aghast as she confessed to not having joined the great man for lunch.

'What an opportunity you missed, Sal. Lunch

with a major director and a major star and you said no?'

'I'm sure they thought Sally absolutely splendid for returning to war work. It is a propaganda film, after all,' Max reminded them. 'And you did find out about stills, Sally.'

'The cameraman said stills would be sent out, Max, but probably when we're all in France.'

'To send on or not to send on,' said Max, 'that is the question. Think I'll not trust them to the vagaries of wartime postal services, Sal. We can look forward to a wonderful surprise when we return.'

And that was all that was said.

The next few days were unbelievably busy. Sally went down to Dartford on the Saturday and talked to her parents, who were both upset that she might be deliberately travelling into mortal danger. She tried to reassure them that the danger in France would be no greater than possible danger travelling in England. Her mother made up a parcel of clothes that might be useful as a change from uniform. She added a bar of soap, some tooth powder and a small container of shampoo.

'I wish there was more to give you, Sally. How will you manage for all that time in a foreign country?'

'We'll be fine, Mum; Sebastian speaks French and mine isn't too bad; it's all coming back.'

'That's something, I suppose, and you did get a prize for French in fifth form; never thought you'd be speaking to real French people though. Will you be able to write to us?'

'Yes, Mum. Our letters home will go with the military post. It will take longer than a letter from London but I will write as often as I can.'

'And you'll be home for Christmas?'

'I don't know. My first time in a foreign country; it's exciting.'

'I can think of another word for it, but if you must go we'll see you onto the London train. Can't you spend the night?'

'I wouldn't want to delay getting back, Mum, and besides Sunday travel is a nightmare.'

Saturday evening travel was not much better but at least her travelling companions, sleeping servicemen, were quiet.

The carriage was full but she felt completely alone and it was a pleasant feeling. An only child, even one with many close friends, she had often been quite alone and she had enjoyed those moments. She was enjoying this time now. She looked at the men, sprawled along the bench opposite her and beside her. Each had tried, it appeared, to fall asleep tidily but exhaustion had caused their limbs to relax and they lay bundled together like the puppies she had once seen on a farm near Dartford. Some bodies were controlled even in sleep, others lay, mouths open, limbs everywhere, a few snored, some making fluttering sounds, others full-throated rumbles. Sally felt immeasurably sorry for them. Had they been on leave and were now going into action? She counted them and wondered sadly how many empty spaces there would be on the benches the next time they were given leave. Perhaps Jon and the crew of the *George Francis* had fallen into exhausted sleep on trains on their last leave before their final voyage. Surely each and every one had been loved and missed as she loved and missed Jon, but so few would ever make another voyage. What a stupid thing was war. For the first time, she felt herself looking on the sleeping men with a feeling she recognised as tenderness. I hope they all come safely home, she thought as the train pulled into London.

The underground took her straight to Green Park and from there it was a fairly easy walk for her, even in the blackout, to Hays Mews. As she walked she told herself that in the past few months she had grown up immeasurably. The trip to France was not a holiday excursion. No, ENSA did not carry guns or drive tanks but they faced danger just the same. She knew that she would try as hard as she possibly could to bring some relief and happiness into the lives of the service personnel she would meet.

But let it all be over soon.

Sometimes she had to think very hard to remember what life had been like before September of 1939. Had there been a time when there were empty seats on trains? Had people always queued for hours for any small ration of meat the butcher was able to find? How deep had her bathwater been before the war and had she always had plenty of sweet-smelling soap and shampoo – oh, lovely fragrant shampoo that one had always taken completely for granted? Had her friends the Petries really collected her on the spur of the moment to drive down to the seaside to swim and picnic? Impossible to do anything without advance planning now, and there was certainly no petrol for a frivolous jaunt to the coast.

Millie and Sebastian hurried to the door when they heard her and Sebastian was annoyed. 'Why didn't you ring me? We'd have come down to meet you. The streets aren't safe these days.'

'It was fine, Sebastian, honestly, and besides, the only person I know who has a telephone is the vicar.'

'Ever heard of a telephone box, Sally? Anyway, never mind, we've saved two tins of sardines and we'll have sardines on toast for supper.'

'Make yourself comfy, Sal, while I do supper. Parents all right about the plans?'

'I can't say they're thrilled but they wished us well. Mum gave me some soap and even some shampoo, Millie, and we can share them. Everything all right with your families?'

'I left it rather late to write letters, which was probably a bit selfish – I couldn't bear the thought of my mum coming down to see me off. I imagine we'll be gone before either my family or Patrick's get their letters but I've made them as loving and reassuring as possible.'

'Did you say where we're headed, Millie?'

Millie turned at the kitchen door. 'I found myself unable to write the word "France".'

After their simple supper, Sebastian took an elderly atlas from a bookcase in the hall and they looked at maps of France.

'How strange,' said Sally as she looked first at the paper on which she had written down a few of the places where Max had said they might perform, and then at the map. 'Look, not only are these four towns or villages quite close to one another but they could be in alphabetical order; A, B, C, and D. Arras, Bayeux, however that's pronounced, Caen, and Douai. They're all in the north or north-west of France and not too far from the English Channel.'

But the only one that interested Millie was Arras.

Her grief and anger when Max told them that their visit was to be delayed indefinitely because France was under German control was tragic to witness. She withdrew into herself, working like an automaton but confiding in no one.

For the troupe it became every week a new venue, yet another uncomfortable journey, new routines to learn. Sally lost count of the number of the remade costumes she wore, the NAAFI canteens where they dined, the scratch suppers in Sebastian's kitchen. The year ended and the next year came in, bringing with it both the Americans and renewed hope. Every day Sally wrote to Jon and occasionally received a letter – carefully numbered. Each precious missive expressed his feelings for her. Sally treasured them, but at times she feared that the world would be at war forever. Would she ever see him again? Another year came.

'We'll know every church hall, theatre, and hospital in Britain if we don't get out of here soon.' Even Sebastian was complaining by mid-summer.

The whispers began, 'The Americans, Normandy, Omaha Beach...'

Then Max was there, smiling broadly. 'It's

time, my angels; we're off to France.'

Sally knew that sailing across the English Channel was often unpleasant as the sea could be boisterous and choppy; it didn't seem to her that it was much better to travel by air. The plane was a military one, not a passenger plane complete with fairly comfortable chairs and a smart steward. Indeed, it seemed to dip and rise on the wind much as a boat would dip and rise on the turbulent waves below. She was not the only passenger to be extremely relieved to find herself bouncing down onto a runway. Neither could they leave the airport, suitcase in hands, as easily as if they were arriving at a London railway station. There were endless formalities to be gone through and it was some time before they found themselves trundling across a rain-swept pathway, while the icy rain seemed to find as many ways of making them uncomfortable as it possibly could. They were in uniform and the rain trickled off their hats onto their hair and down inside their collars. There was some muttered swearing but mostly they walked in silent misery to the great military lorries that waited to take them to their first base.

Once on board, they huddled in damp and silent misery, incapable of changing the situation in any way and merely hoping that life would improve.

It did. Several hours later they were wakened from their restless dozing to find themselves in familiar surroundings. Nothing they could see told them that they were in France.

'We'll unload, get ourselves to our quarters, dry off a bit and Major McConnell here says that the best soup outside Bolton is waiting for us in the mess hall. Come on, everybody; we can't have the troops trying to cheer us up, and please, no one is to miss the meal; it's rude and also silly. We deserve a good hot meal and it's been prepared for us. Right, *bienvenue à la belle France.*'

'Can't see a bloody thing *belle* about it so far,' said Humph, but after his little grumble he set himself to doing as he had been told.

NINETEEN

Late August 1944, a Military Base in the Calvados Prefecture, North-West France

Sally was bitterly disappointed in her first sight of France. She had harboured ideas of how it would look: miles and miles of vineyards, for was not French wine famous? Even the Prime Minister had been known to praise French wines. And it was August. The fields around Dartford would be in the middle of a golden harvest. Where were the farmers? And there should be castles or *châteaux,* as they were called, exquisite buildings with lots of towers and windows, surrounded by parklands where lakes and ponds were scattered among soaring but disciplined trees, and flower-beds were aglow with colours and perfumes. There would be picturesque villages with ponds where ducks and geese swam and sun-tanned children paddled. They would have boats, or was it only English boys who played with boats? She didn't know but had looked forward to finding out.

The reality was very different. There were orchards, but bombs had blown great holes between the burned-out rows of apple trees. Occasionally she saw a few desultory apples hanging listlessly on broken branches. She did see castles, two with boarded-up windows and one where the windows were not boarded-up but blown out, and where broken fire-stained walls had crumpled into what might have been a moat. An unhappy silence hung over all three. The damage done by bombs and bullets to once picturesque villages was horrifying and in one village street they saw the rotting bodies of dogs, cats, and poultry. A cow, bloated in death, lay almost on the doorstep of a bombed church that, from the little that remained, Sally thought was possibly the same age as their lovely, historic church in Dartford. The smell of rotting flesh overwhelmed the perfume of the flowers that were trying so hard to bring some beauty into this sad land.

They had been in the north of the country for almost three weeks and Sally wished herself back in England. Jon would write to England. He could not know that she was in France, not yet.

They had done several shows and, as always 'the boys' made it all worthwhile; applauding everything, sending ear-piercing whistles after the dancers as, in their skimpy red, white and blue skirts and tops, they high-kicked their way

370

off the hastily erected stage, joining in when they sang old favourites like 'Roll Out the Barrel' or 'MacNamara's Band'. They listened attentively when there was a scene from a well-known play: Shakespeare, Shaw, Coward, Wilde; it did not matter, they loved them all, and the whistling and cat-calls when Millie danced were deafening.

'They're applauding my legs,' said Millie mildly. 'I wonder how many have ever seen a ballet.'

'I'd be more eager to know how many will go to a theatre now that they've had a taste,' said Sebastian. 'Of course they like your legs – what red-blooded man wouldn't – but you can't see their faces when you're dancing and we can. Most of them are simply spellbound.'

'Not so much as when Sally is singing.'

'Nonsense,' said Sally. 'I'm more normal, Millie, approachable, if you like, just a pretty girl in a nice frock; you bring us ... magic.'

'Well said, our Sally.' Sybil and Lalita had heard the last part of the conversation as they walked back towards the wings where Max was still standing. 'But you all bring magic and don't they need some magic here?'

Sally agreed with that. Their living quarters were basic and it was almost impossible to get enough hot water for a bath or to wash hair, especially long hair like Sally and Millie's. Again, the engineers did wonders and Sally was grateful but often she wished she was in Sebastian's beautiful flat with its airy rooms and its constant hot water. She remembered Lal's comment: 'Don't they need some magic here?' The soldiers' living quarters can't be any better than ours and they

371

have to go out on patrols, she told herself. No more complaining, Sally Brewer.

Next day they saw the first of many poignant reminders of the war. They had gone in a lorry to a small village nearby which was inhabited now by only a few elderly people and some mothers and children. Just as they approached the village Millie, who was looking out at yet another ruined harvest, called out, 'What's that on the side of the road? Damn it, it's behind us now.'

'We'll have a look on the way back, Millie,' said Max. 'Right now we want to do something for the elderly residents here. Youngest man in the village is about seventy-three or -four.'

The priest spoke some English, as did a doctor who was obviously much too old to be practising still – but was. Sebastian surprised most of the company with his knowledge of spoken French although everyone knew that Lal and Sybil were fluent. In no time at all the five were conversing like long-lost relatives while the mainly black-clad villagers and the rest of the performers listened and smiled occasionally at one another, both groups fully aware that only the villagers had the slightest idea of what was going on. Sally listened carefully to the conversation but grasped little as the speakers spoke too quickly for her. She would not give up, though, telling herself that she had allowed her knowledge of the language to rust and now she was cleaning it.

Well, that was an eye-opener, Sebastian told them when he came back. 'There are no able-bodied men left in the village. The CO, bless him, knew this, and the soldiers driving us have some supplies for them. Believe it or not, the villagers are insisting on giving us a barrel of cider in return and the colonel is saving it for Christmas, if they're still in this ... Damn it, I was going to say hole, but I mean friendly part of *la Belle France*. Sally, do you know *"Sur le Pont d'Avignon"?*'

'The words, yes. I seem to remember dancing to it when I was at Tiny Tots dancing school.'

'Right, you and I are going to walk back along the road and I'll go over it with you because you're going to sing it to these lovely people and, Millie, you know the melody?'

Millie nodded.

'Will you make up some steps and dance?'

'Of course, and I'll bring in all the children. Sally, you can dance with us, too; we'll dance in circles and the men, including our two lovely young soldiers and you, Seb, will bow and the ladies will curtsy.'

Sebastian hugged her. 'You are a genius.'

Three hours later they left the village and, looking back, saw most of the women and many of the old men in tears. The children who were still dancing together on the Avignon bridge stopped to wave wildly.

Not a word was spoken on the way back to the camp, every cast member too full of emotion and recently acquired knowledge.

Sally and Sebastian were glad to be quiet for they had passed the object that had interested Millie on their way in and had seen that it was a memorial of some kind, a pole stuck into the ground with a British soldier's helmet hanging on it. Some fresh and some withered wildflowers lay on the ground at the base of the little pole. Much better that Millie not see that sad little memorial.

The company stayed in the region, although not at that particular camp, for almost six weeks. The parched summer days eventually gave way to the first rains of the autumn. Moving around the camps became more and more difficult. Again, the engineers managed to lay some type of wooden pathways between tents and huts, especially the incredibly limited washing and lavatory facilities. Everyone had Wellington boots and they squelched their way around, evening suit trousers tucked into the boots and evening gowns lifted up by the hems as far as decently possible.

They moved to Douai, a town on the River Scarpe, and Sebastian hoped that he was the only one of their particular group who knew that Douai was probably no more than fifteen or sixteen miles from Arras, another town on the Scarpe, but more importantly, the place where Patrick Burgess had been killed and was probably buried. Were Millie to find out, he could picture her simply walking out of camp and heading north-west.

Of course, Millie was perfectly well aware how close they were to Arras. She too had studied the map and had every intention of getting there somehow. Fate had brought her so close but for now she was prepared to wait to see if it took her even closer.

They were doing a show for the garrison at the Douai camp and Sebastian was sitting in the tent he shared with Humph and Allan Fordyce when a soldier brought him a note from the colonel.

Startled, he read it and stood up. 'Golly, I've never been summoned by a colonel before; he wants to ask me a favour. What on earth would a colonel want with me?'

Allan was practical. 'You know the quickest way to find out, mate.'

Sebastian smiled wryly and went with the soldier.

The colonel was sitting at a desk, a large pile of documents in front of him. He stood up when Sebastian was ushered in. 'Apologies for disturbing your rest period, Mr Brady, but I have an enormous favour to ask of you and I do want you to know that you are free to accept or refuse.'

'Do my best to help, sir,' said Sebastian, who remembered feeling almost as nervous when he had been summoned to his headmaster's study.

'Feel a bit silly, actually, but I did hear you do the great Agincourt speech a few years ago.' He stopped and Sebastian waited.

'Do you want to hear it this evening, sir? I was going to do Hamlet but Henry can slot in perfectly easily.'

The colonel said nothing but handed Sebastian a book, which obligingly opened at the page where an elderly train ticket had been inserted. Each of the pages had a poem and Sebastian smiled. He was sure he knew which poem the experienced soldier wanted. 'Beautiful poem,' he said.

'You have a good voice,' said the colonel in some obvious embarrassment. 'It's one of my favourite poems and I'd love to hear you recite it, but it might not fit in with your plans.'

'It's perfect, sir; it will be an honour to recite it.'

'No need to say...'

'Of course not.'

'I'll get the book back later.'

'No need, sir. I know it well.'

He walked back to his tent thinking about soldiers and of others' impressions and preconceptions of them. Colonel Ingram was what was commonly called 'a man's man'; he was not public school, not elegant, but craggy like a much-eroded cliff, and he liked poetry. I'll give it all I've got, Colonel, Sebastian vowed.

Later that same evening, in his evening suit, his shoes almost as shiny as those of the soldiers, he walked across the stage to the microphone. 'Slight change of plan, ladies and gentlemen' – for there were nurses present. 'I'm not doing Shakespeare at this point in the programme but reciting the work of a poet who didn't publish much, if anything, other than the one I plan to recite, a poem that I think is one of the finest in the English language. It's by a young man always known simply as C. Wolfe, a young man who read the report of a military funeral in a newspaper and was so stunned by it that he wrote these beautiful and immortal lines: "The Burial of Sir John Moore after Corunna".'

There was absolute silence in the large tent when Sebastian had finished and then, as one, the audience rose and clapped until their hands and everyone's ears were sore. Sebastian, tears in his eyes, bowed, and walked off, but the clapping went on for some time.

Those backstage heard Max's voice: 'Get the girls back in, or Sally. Damn it, Seb, where did that come from?'

The skimpily clad dancers tapped their way onto the stage, the audience calmed down, and eventually the programme finished as it was supposed to finish.

As always, the cast were then entertained by the troops in the Officers' Mess.

'Read that poem in sixth form, Mr Brady, sir, absolutely superb.'

Sebastian coloured faintly. 'Seb's fine, glad you liked it.'

'I've never heard that poem before, Sebastian,' said Sally. 'How brilliant of you to remember it, actually on a military base.'

'Never heard that silence for an actor before, Seb; great compliment, but is it true? Was he real?' Millie was looking at him with huge eyes in a very pale face.

'Yes, Millie, it's all true.'

'What a ballet it would make,' she said calmly, for all the world as if they were strolling down Piccadilly. 'Are we going to Arras? It was on our alphabetical list.'

'I'm not in charge, Millie, and the venues change according to circumstance. Max is the one to ask. But, dear one, what do you hope to find?'

She looked at him and smiled. 'I don't ... hope to find anything, but Patrick died there and I must say "Sleep well". If we're not scheduled to visit, then I'll have to think of something else. We're so close, Seb, so close. Please, Sally, you'll help me, won't you?'

Sally looked straight at Sebastian. 'We can talk to Max; he has the schedule, not Sebastian, but we're on your side, Millie, aren't we, Sebastian?'

'I don't want either of you doing anything stupid, Sally, getting yourselves into danger. Talk to Sybil and Lal; they'll talk to Max.'

Sally and Millie looked immediately for the two senior women and found them involved in serious conversation with a few of the senior officers.

'Not a good time, Millie,' began Sally, but they had been spied by one of the officers who asked them to join their group.

An hour and two glasses of French wine – not from the barrel from the village, Sybil was delighted to point out – later, all four women walked back to their quarters together.

'Now's the time, Millie.'

And, for the first time, Millie opened up to someone other than her two best friends.

'You should have told us earlier, Millie; perhaps we could have worked from top to bottom instead of the other way round.'

'I'm sorry, Sybil; it's not you or Lal or Max, it's me, but I must and I will get to Arras, even if I have to walk.'

'That would be rather foolish since we're going there anyway, but listen to me, and listen carefully. I will not tolerate your putting yourself or anyone in the company in danger.'

'Of course.'

'Then a little more patience, child. We will do our duty in Bayeux and after that, we will travel on, according to the schedule, to Arras.'

With that promise, Millie said she was content.

A few days later Sally returned to her tent to find three letters: one rather crumpled and stained envelope and two blue aerogramme letters on her camp bed.

'Millie,' she shouted, 'It's Christmas. The postman's been.'

'Fab. Something from Jon?'

'Two – these blue airmail ones – and one from my dad. It'll be from both but it's his writing.' She examined the light-weight blue papers. 'A and B, clever Jon. What about you?'

'A fat one from Mum.'

'Lovely,' said Sally. She smiled across at Millie, took her nail scissors out of her handbag, slit the first letter open and settled down to read.

Somewhere at Sea, 4 July.

'Millie, would you believe it? Jon wrote this letter at the beginning of July. Where has it been?'

'At sea, obviously,' said Millie, and went back to her own mail. Sally followed her example.

My darling Sally,

We went ashore a few days ago and I tried to ring you. A pleasant chap at the theatre told me that you were in France. I hope you are well and enjoying the experience. I'm so sorry not to have had time to write before but we have been rather busy in one way or another.

We can be at sea for weeks and then we must put in at a safe port for refuelling, provisions, fresh water, et cetera. That's when we are able to pick up mail too and you can imagine how happy everyone aboard is to see that fat bag stuffed with envelopes.

Do you have a photograph of yourself for I would so

love to have one? Of course, I remember how beautiful you are; you are, after all, safely tucked away in my heart, but it would be lovely to have an actual photograph to talk to or to show proudly to friends. Why did I never think of it when we were together?

Next time we are ashore I'm sure there will be letters from you in the post bag. At the moment I am trying to picture you in France. Our radios keep us up to date with news and I feel that the France that you are seeing is not the country I knew so well as a student. When the war is over I would like to show you the beautiful little village where I lived for a year and introduce you to the delightful people who made me feel that I was part of their family. They visited me in 1938 but I haven't seen or heard from them since. I hope they are safe.

Occasionally we are able to listen to broadcasts from London, not only the PM but a few days ago we had Myra Hess, the concert pianist, playing in the National Gallery. Many of the lads had never heard a great pianist play before and it was a joy to watch them listening. She played Mozart and Bach, lovely way to start, don't you think, if you've never heard classical music. And, of course, we have catholic tastes and sat roaring with laughter – well, some of us as someone has to look after the ship!! – listening to Tommy Trinder. Two of the lads were actually weeping, a combination, I think, of fear and hope and memories. So, we send enormous thanks to each and every one of you in ENSA. Keep up the good work.

Jon, just Jon

The letter marked B was much shorter.

Darling Sally,

I forgot the most important part of my letter. I should have said this in dear old Blighty but I was afraid – of so many things; failure mainly. Sally, I love you as I have never loved before. I want to marry you when this war is over. There, I've said it. I can't tell you how much I wanted to take you to Bond Street, to a decent jeweller, to watch you choose a beautiful ring meant for Just Sally but we're at war and who knows what will happen? God willing, I will survive.

I asked Luisa too quickly and she accepted and I didn't realise that, poor child, she loved the title and only thought she loved the man. You are free, my darling, to be yourself with no ties, no burdens. I will never interfere with your talent or your career.

All my love,
Jon

Sally started to cry and immediately Millie was there with an affectionate hug. 'What's wrong, Sally? Is Jon all right?'

'He loves me and wants to marry me.'

Millie continued to hold and soothe while Sally tried to stifle her sobs. 'That's a problem?' Millie asked at last.

'Oh, Millie, he's so noble. He wants to marry me but he says I'm free. I don't want to be free. Damn it, he's reminding me of that idiot *Hamlet:* too much thinking.'

Millie tried very hard but eventually could not control her laughter. 'This education lark is a bit of a double-edged sword,' she said when she had stopped laughing.

'Sorry, Millie, what about your post?'

'Yes, one from Patrick's mother enclosed in Mum's. She's unhappy that I've gone to France. She's worried about me, poor dear, but can't understand why I'm dancing for soldiers in the country that, according to her, killed her son.'

'What can you say to that, Millie? Remind her that the soldiers are British.'

'No, it's not worth it. I won't even refer to it when I answer her. If I find anything in Arras, that will make her forget everything else – except that her only son is dead.'

'Let's hope we find something.'

Millie smiled. 'Dear Sally, you and Seb are such good friends. Patrick would have loved you both too.'

Nine days later they climbed into a lorry and headed north-west. They had hoped not to find the sad markers every few miles but they were there and added to Millie's distress. The first time she saw one she yelled, 'Stop, stop,' at the top of her voice and banged as hard as she could on the barrier between passengers and the soldiers. Everyone heard a disgruntled 'What the hell was that?' as the lorry slowed to a halt.

The military driver was at the tarpaulin. 'What's the problem?'

Millie made her way over the others, apologising as she moved to the back of the lorry. She poked her head out and came face to face with a rather annoyed driver.

'He recognised my legs as I climbed out,' Millie told them when she had climbed back into the lorry, 'and he showed me the marker. The helmets aren't all British; there are French and German ones too and he can't stop at them all but if he spots a British one fairly close to Arras, he'll "Gie me a shout", whatever that means.'

'He'll tell you,' put in Lal, the linguist.

But they did not stop again until they were at their new base.

It was not where Patrick Burgess had served but it was close. Max took the unprecedented step of coming to a female hut and sitting down quietly with Millie.

'I can't let you wander at will, Millie; there are mines in the area. We have to stick as much as possible to the camp, but be aware that your husband must have been familiar with this area. Can that be enough for you? He saw these fields, that river; he breathed this air.'

'Thank you, Max; I actually hadn't thought of that and it does help. I won't do anything stupid but the letter said he was buried where he fell. They sent me his identity tags – I have those but just to see what might be his grave...'

'I do understand; all your friends do, but take no senseless risks.'

Millie promised and their work of preparing for a concert began.

To make it as much as possible like a theatre performance at home, programmes were prepared and tickets were issued. The programmes were illustrated with small pencil drawings of dancers, of rather splendid imaginary curtains, much more like the ones that fronted the stage at any London theatre, and of uniformed soldiers.

Sebastian had had an idea. 'Who did these?'

No one he asked had any idea and he shrugged; he would think of something else.

Two days later he saw their usual driver working on the engine of a field ambulance and stopped to watch. The young man's intensity as he gazed into the workings of the great machine reminded him of Dmitri. 'You a mechanic as well as a driver?' he asked.

The soldier laughed. 'Not in a hundred years,' he said. 'This is what's called learning from experience. Name's Rowan, by the way, my mum's favourite tree.' He pointed to the open bonnet. 'You any good?'

'Afraid not. There might be someone in the company, though. People are always surprising me with their talents.'

They chatted together for some time as pieces of engine were removed, cleaned and returned, and Sebastian felt pleased that he could at least clean. 'How long have you been in the army?' he asked at last. 'Was it something you always wanted to do?'

'No, waited until my age group was called up and so I've been in seventeen months, one week, and, if I knew what the time was back home, I could give you hours and minutes.'

They both laughed and then Sebastian had to tell why he had become an actor and why he had joined ENSA instead of one of the services. He looked again at the young soldier and decided that he had probably been at university before his conscription.

'So you weren't studying engineering?'

'God no, I was at art school in Glasgow.'

'I thought I recognised a Scottish accent when you talked to Millie.' He looked at the young man with the oil-marked face and hands. 'You illustrated the programmes?'

'Light relief.'

'They're terrific, Rowan. I have a proposal for you...'

TWENTY

A few days later, when Sally returned from a visit to the village where they had first performed, she found a small parcel on her bed. It was addressed to her and had been posted in Britain, but there was no return address and no note inside, only two very dirty and water-stained envelopes. Jon's writing was on the envelopes and, startled, she sat down on the bed and opened one. There was no address, no greeting, but the writing, most definitely, was Jon's.

The island is so beautiful; it's mountainous and so the roads – such as exist – are very steep. We were being driven down to the sea a day or two ago and suddenly a great line of goats jumped down in front of us. The Corsicans didn't even turn a hair while the herd trotted across the road, no more than two inches from the front of the truck. I don't think I have ever felt my heart beat so quickly, and Ben, the other chap rescued with me, was sick, poor lad. I was sure we were

*destined to reach the sea the hard way, falling right
over the cliff edge but Emmanuel, the driver, laughed
at us.*

*But apart from the roads, I think I could easily grow
to love this island. You cannot believe how highly the air
is scented. The scrubland that covers every inch that
has not been cultivated is called* maquis *and is full of
the most beautiful wild flowers, trees and herbs. There's
heather, lavender, thyme, mint – oh I don't have
enough paper to list them. The people use them in their
cooking and we have tasted the most beautiful honey.
Our rescuer was a fisherman before the war and he still
goes out for fish when he can, and his wife pulls pieces
from several plants to add to her pots and such food as
we are given – and they share generously – is delicious.
You have probably heard or read the word* maquis.
*The Resistance movement in the south of France have
taken their name from the* maquis. *They are* le
Maquis, *because that's where they hide out. I tell you
it's all but impenetrable. The Corsican resistance
fighters call themselves* les Maquisards.

*It's going to be a long time before there is any oppor-
tunity to return home. Emmanuel and Jean-Jacques,
both* Maquisards, *will try to get us to France; they
feel that there may be more opportunity to be picked
up there. I don't know why I'm writing this letter.
How can it possibly reach you?*

The letter ended abruptly. She looked again at
the envelope. Where had it been to get into such
a state and who had sent it? It could not have
been Jon – unless he had completely forgotten.
He had, after all, been quite ill.

Sally tried to remember every word he had

386

spoken, all he had told her of his time in Corsica. Of course. Emmanuel was the fisherman and he had been killed, poor man, by a German patrol. Jean-Jacques was his cousin and he had rowed the two men they had rescued from Corsica to France. What a voyage that must have been.

She decided to read the other letter before going over all her memories.

Dear Sally,

As soon as I had given the messenger my letter I regretted having written it. I used names. How stupid. I am an officer in the Royal Navy and should be more alert. These fishermen and farmers have risked every-thing for us. That I could have been thoughtless made me squirm. I decided to be much more circumspect, to continue to write to you because the simple act of communicating with someone I care about is, in some way, a lifeline, even though I fear that you will not receive them. That worried me because, should my careless letters reach the wrong hands, it could bring even more death and destruction to these good people and this lovely island. But I need not have worried for Emmanuel is a wise man and he has the priest read my letters. The good Father keeps those in which I name names or locations. He tells me that they are beautiful letters and that one day they must be read by you but, for the moment, he will wrap them in paper and put them inside the chimney in his house.

Letters in the chimney; that accounted for the dirt.

'He was a *Maquisard.*' Is that not what Jon had said? The priest had also been with the Resistance. But these were two of the letters Jon had told her he had written and so who had sent them now and how had that person found out where she was? Her first thought was that it must have been Jon but Jon was on a battleship somewhere. Emmanuel was dead, murdered, but where was Jean-Jacques, his cousin, and where was the priest? Surely the priest was the only person who knew where the letters were, or had someone else taken them from their hiding place and ... it was obvious that they had been sent to her from England, not Corsica or France. Somehow the stained packet of letters had travelled from the priest's sooty chimney to England, but how?

Sally was sensible enough to realise that she would never find out the truth about the letters while she was in France – unless, of course, she received another letter, perhaps from Jon, or from whoever it was who had gone to the trouble of finding out where she was.

She wrote to Jon telling him that two letters, written while he was in Corsica, had turned up.

You painted such a beautiful picture of the island and of the lovely people who took such wonderful care of you and your colleague. I could see the maquis, *Jon, and even smell it and I would love to see the island when this war is over – and it must be over soon, please God. I want to thank Emmanuel's wife too, for taking care of you because although you say little about her, in my head I see a very busy, caring woman.*

'Jump, Sally, there's a line already for the shower thing the engineers rigged up. If you want to wash

388

your hair, come now.' Millie, who had peered into the tent from outside, abruptly closed the canvas again and disappeared.

Could the letter wait? Yes, and the hot water could not, would not. Sally put her pen down, pushed the papers into her bag and ran.

Sybil saw her later with her freshly washed hair hanging down her back dripping onto a towel. 'Not the best time to wash your hair, Sally; it will never dry for tonight.' She looked up at the sky, heavy with threatening clouds.

'There's a boiler in the laundry hut. I'll sit beside it and do my first read of *What Every Woman Knows*. Max thought a J. M. Barrie piece would go down well with the Scottish soldiers.' She looked at Sybil's face. '*Peter Pan*, Sybil.'

'I thought I knew the name, but I'm more familiar with choreographers. Well, better get over there and get that hair dry.'

Sally picked up her script and followed Sybil out. The rain had started and, as it had been doing for the past three days, it streamed down relentlessly, almost as if wherever Sally trod, someone with a huge bucket was standing above her, maliciously pouring. She pushed the script up inside her shirt and head down, ran.

Millie and several others were in the laundry hut where a huge boiler was sending out overwhelming amounts of heat. Millie was huddled in a corner and when Sally reached her, she saw that her friend had been weeping.

'Don't touch me, Sally; I don't want the others to know.'

Sally sat down, making a great show of pulling

the script out from its hiding place. 'What happened?'

'It's a laundry. They don't just wash shirts.'

Sally looked at the piles of washing still to be done and the sheets and cloths hanging on wooden pulleys that, once again, the engineers had managed to construct. She avoided thinking of the stains that were on some of the sheets. 'They're incredible, the army engineers, I mean, don't you agree, Millie? One day they're putting up bridges across swollen rivers, the next, they're fixing a place for us to hang our stockings.' She kept her eyes on Millie and decided to keep talking, anything to prevent Millie from jumping up and running out into the downpour. 'My mum had a local joiner put up a three-bar pulley in our kitchen; dried all our clothes a treat. Will you listen to me read this play, please? Sebastian says it's really enjoyable, has "sympathy, tenderness, and flashes of humour".'

Millie nodded and Sally read until the rain stopped. By then their hair had been dry for some time and, like so many of the others, they trudged back through churned-up mud, grateful to be wearing Wellington boots.

Millie seemed to have recovered from her sadness and talked easily about the Barrie play. 'It's a bit old-fashioned, don't you think, Sal?'

'They love Shakespeare and he's a few hundred years older.'

'Good point. I heard about a British marker today, Sal. The Scottish driver told me there's a British helmet among some markers he saw near Douai – only the French and the Lord know how to pronounce that, but it's not too far away; if I could just borrow a bicycle...'

'Max will never allow it.'

'If I'm careful he won't know a thing about it.'

Sally had no idea what to say or do. It was much too dangerous for Millie to go cycling; not only were there mines in some of the fields but there were occasional enemy patrols, hidden Resistance fighters and Allied and enemy planes flying over.

'I'm not stupid, Sally and I haven't arranged to borrow a bike, but I will not leave this area until I have seen this British marker.'

'But, Millie, it may not be Patrick.'

'And it could be. He was buried where he fell. No one knows where that is, just that it's near here somewhere.' She stood up and her face was fierce. 'Damn it, Sally, I mean to find it and I will.'

Wisely Sally said nothing. It would be extremely difficult for Millie to leave the base on her own. There were soldiers on guard at all exits, and surely she would not be foolhardy enough to try to squeeze under a barbed-wire fence. Sally would loathe herself for breaking Millie's confidence but if necessary she would have to tell someone what Millie intended.

She began with Sebastian.

'I haven't seen her as wound up as this for months, Sebastian, and I'm really, really worried.'

'One or other of us will be near her at all times, Sal, and I think we should rope in Sybil and Lal. I'm sorry I didn't tell you, mainly because I haven't seen you since, but I've been talking to our young driver, the Scots one, and he's got permission from the CO, if everything's quiet on the day, to drive that way when we're on our way to our next posting. There's an enormous Great War memorial and hundreds of graves at Arras and it might be better if Millie doesn't go near the place, but she's an adult.'

'She handled being in the laundry room today, drying bandages, etcetera, hanging about. She needs to say "Goodbye" to Patrick.'

'She'll never say goodbye to him.' Sebastian's voice was so low that Sally almost didn't hear him.

She smiled. 'She'll never forget him – we wouldn't want her to – but she will say "Goodbye, and sleep well".'

'I hope you're right, Sally. I think someone is more than interested in our little ballerina.'

Sally smiled. So he was more than friendly with Millie. 'I'm so pleased, Sebastian. I want everyone to be as happy as I am, and now I must finish the letter I started to write to Jon.'

When she sat down at the table to write she remembered that she hadn't told Sebastian about the two letters from Jon in Corsica but, vowing to discuss them with him later, she took out the unfinished letter and wrote what she had wanted to write for some time.

I treasure your letters, dearest Jon, and read them over although I don't need to as I'm quite sure I know every word by heart.

You talk about after the war. Yes, Jon, when this beastly inhuman war is over I would love to go to Dartford with you and to help you with your plans. To be a part of your life would make me the happiest woman in the world. Growing up I dreamed of stardom and perhaps some will come my way. My parents deserve to see that their sacrifices for me were worthwhile, but knowing them and loving them as I do I feel sure that what they want for me more than anything is personal happiness, and darling Jon, my own Just Jon, happiness for me is being where you are.

All my love, always,
Sally

She took the letter to the camp post bag and returned to her quarters to prepare for their next performance.

There was an almighty bang. A bomb? A mine? Dear God, where was Millie? Sally clambered out of the truck where she had been changing out of her uniform and into an evening dress.

Could anything be more incongruous than a lilac silk evening dress on a military base on the edge of a war zone? Those had been her thoughts as she had changed, but now she had no time to regret the sound of the delicate fabric tearing as it caught on a piece of metal on the side of the lorry. She picked up what was left of the skirt and began to run towards the plume of dust and smoke that still hung in the air. She could hear voices but there was no hysteria.

'Millie!' She screamed the name as loudly as she could and suddenly there beside her was Sebastian, in his white tie and tails.

'Sorry, darling, the bloody thing was tripped a little before it was meant to.'

'What bloody thing?' Sally who never swore

393

repeated his words. 'Where's Millie?'

'Over there, at the marker. I told you Rowan, our Scottish driver, found a British helmet. It was arranged for Millie to see it but first the bomb disposal lads went over the ground and they found a mine. There are several of the blasted things there and the experts are blowing them up before they let Millie near.'

'She's not hurt?' Sally was almost sobbing.

'No. We made sure she was in no danger but you see how sensitive the blasted things are.'

Sebastian had put his arm around her and pushed her forward. 'It was all supposed to be a lovely surprise. Just wait till you see what young Rowan has done. We'll be hearing from that young man after the war, believe me.'

'Sally, oh, your poor frock, what happened to it?' Millie had carefully walked back to them along the pathway the disposal experts had laid. 'There's a marker, Sally; it might be my Patrick, it might not, but he's British and so we'll say goodbye and honour him as we should. Follow me and please stay on the path.'

Sebastian led the way, followed by Millie and then Sally, trailing her ruined evening dress. Several of the company were there and some soldiers, including a padre and a Scottish bagpiper.

'Patrick believed in God, but not in religion,' Millie whispered, 'and he hated the bagpipes, especially close up but ... he won't mind, will he?'

'No, Millie, he won't.'

The padre said a prayer, the piper played and Millie, holding a small bunch of flowers a soldier had foraged for her, stood before the marker.

'Goodbye, my dearest love,' she said, so quietly that only those beside her heard. 'Sleep well.' She kissed the small bouquet and, bending down, put it on the ground before the pole.

She turned and walked back to the others. 'Thank you all so much, Max, I'll just thank the colonel and then I'll get dressed for the show.'

Sally had been remembering two of her dear friends as she watched Millie. The first was Daisy, who had lost the pilot she loved, Adair. How poignant Daisy's story of visiting his resting place had been. Then there was her twin sister, Rose, whose childhood friend, Stan, had been killed about a year after Adair's spitfire had plunged into the Channel. Occasional letters hinted at new loves for each of them. She watched Sebastian as he watched Millie and wondered if he cared for the young widow enough to wait for her until she was ready to begin a new life after Patrick.

There seemed to be a strange atmosphere in the canteen, which had been quickly rearranged so as to become, for the evening, a theatre. Usually there was an air of excitement and expectation; there was always noise, hearty laughter, the sound of relief exploding from often very tense men. But tonight it felt different somehow, and Sally could not put a finger on it.

'I suppose we'll have to wait and see,' said Sebastian, who denied emphatically that he knew something that he was hiding from his friends.

Neither believed him.

The small band of musicians started the programme and act followed act, a comedian after a scene – heavily edited – from a play, high kicks and somersaults from the girls, elegance and soft love songs from Sally, a Shakespearean soliloquy from Sebastian, a solo from the ballet *Giselle* by the exquisite Millie, accompanied on the piano by Sam Castleton. Every act was applauded rapturously, Millie more than any other, and then the makeshift curtain came down.

The colonel took to the stage and he called back a surprised Millie. He made a speech, thanking the company for their work in raising morale and then he gestured to the wings and Rowan, the driver, walked on stage. He was carrying a small frame, which he gave the colonel. Then the colonel presented it, with 'admiration and respect' from the entire regiment, to a puzzled Millie.

Millie took the frame as a ballerina takes flowers. Her hand flew to her face, 'Oh, how...?' she asked, and held the frame against her breast.

She turned to the audience, most of whom did not know what was in the frame and said, 'Thank you all from the bottom of my heart. I will never forget today.' She bowed and left the stage.

Later, in their tent, Millie and Sally made room for the others to crowd in and there were gasps of surprise and admiration. Inside the frame was a stark pencil drawing of a pole on which a British soldier's helmet hung. Kneeling before the pole was Millie in her ENSA uniform.

'How did it happen, Seb? How did he do it? He wasn't even there.'

'He did the programmes, Millie, and so I knew he was an artist. I offered to pay him to draw the area for you and he refused payment. He did a rough sketch of the field with the memorial and

I thought it was superb. But then he decided on his own to include you. He must have done you from memory. It's his gift to you.'

Millie's eyes sparkled with unshed tears. 'I shall treasure it, Seb,' she said very quietly.

'Good, when this damned war is over I've promised that we'll all go to his first exhibition – but we'll have to go to Glasgow and who knows, maybe the same piper will be there. But, that's life, the rough with the smooth. He's a really nice young chap and so talented. Unfortunately I don't know anyone in the Glasgow art scene – may have to saunter up there to have a look – but in the meantime he knows we'll find a corner for him if he wants to try London.'

'Best idea you've had yet,' said Millie, and bent her head so that no one could see the smile that had replaced her tears.

November 1944

News broadcasts told the company that the Allied armies had landed in North Africa. A few days later they heard that, whether by accident or design, Italy had invaded Corsica. Sally thought of the good people who had helped Jon and prayed that they would be safe.

But now, the ENSA company left France, travelled to Italy, where it was obvious that they were unwelcome, and from there, sailed to Egypt.

Just before they had left the area around Arras, mail arrived. Sally's heart skipped a beat when she saw that there was a letter from Jon. What if it had come the next day when they were gone? How long would it have taken to follow her around the Mediterranean? She scolded herself for needless worrying and read the letter in which he explained a little about the strange letters from his time hiding with the *Maquis*.

Those were two of the letters, Sally, that I wrote to you while I was in Corsica.

Perhaps Jean-Jacques escaped to England and took the letters with him but it's more likely that it was the priest. I would like that to be so, that he is safe and well in a civilised country. Perhaps the other letters will follow these first two, but there is little in them. I told you about working in the garden, and about fishing with Jean-Jacques. I could help there because I learned to sail as a child and, until Gibraltar, the sea had always been my friend. I suppose I must say it still is as it did not close itself over my head and I live with the joyful knowledge that one day, some day, you and I will be together.

She was almost more excited to find a letter from her old friend Grace, who was a land girl, now engaged to Sam, the oldest brother of the Petrie twins.

If only the war would end, Sally. Sam and I have decided not to marry until it's over, and Daisy and Tomas never seem to be in the same place so that they can make plans or arrangements. Did your mum tell you that Mrs Petrie hopes we'll have a double wedding? At least I have some money of my own now – a legacy from my grandmother – but Sam says he's not marrying me for my money. Isn't he funny? There is something special I would like to do with it and Sam will agree for he says it is mine to do with as I please.

I'm sorry I don't write much but I do think of you. I would love to see you on stage. One day, Sam says, and so we will.

Love,
Grace

In Egypt, the post rarely arrived, but one hot dusty after-noon there was mail on the desk in the tent Sally shared with Millie. 'Christmas is here,' she called to Millie, who was sitting on her bed desperately losing the battle – as she saw it – to prevent her skin from drying out. 'You too?' she asked happily, waving the envelopes.

Millie wiped the face cream off her fingers with the tail end of her blouse, reached behind her and held up an envelope. 'Long letter from my mum. Yours from Jon?'

'Christmas cards from almost everyone I ever met – except Jon. I won't complain. After all, Millicent, there's a war on.'

TWENTY ONE

Late February 1945, London

Sally woke, disturbed possibly by the change in altitude as the great bird gradually slipped down through the clouds on its descent into London. She shook her head as if to rid it of the crowds of thoughts that had filled it, and looked around. They had been away from home for such a long time and yet, besides the crew, she seemed to be the only one awake and staring out of a tiny window looking for a first glimpse of the city. There it was, its customary blanket of cloud, smoke and dust lying over it as if firm enough to walk on.

'Hello, home,' she whispered, and turned to look with affection on her travelling companions. Millie's head rested on Sebastian's right arm and still he slept.

Dear Millie, dear, dear Sebastian. Sally smiled fondly. She had, after all, awakened to find herself on his left arm. How many times had they slept like that, on lorries, on trains, on boats and now on a plane? How peaceful her two best friends looked, and somehow so right together. She sent up a silent prayer and turned again to look out of the window.

The company had, in a way, a debriefing not unlike that gone through by Jon. From the airport each one had been allowed to go home and Sally and Millie had spent the first night back in England in Sebastian's flat. Dmitri had looked after everything well and Sebastian retrieved champagne and some smoked salmon from the sparklingly clean refrigerator.

'Now I think I know where he found the bubbly, but where did our favourite Russian find salmon?'

'I don't particularly care,' said Millie. 'We're home safely; your lovely flat is untouched, and I have this beautiful drawing to show Patrick's mum and dad. In fact I may give it to them, if I think they would like to have it.'

'But what about you, Mill?'

Millie smiled at Sebastian as he struggled with the bottle. 'I saw it, Seb, I was there; I don't need it and I think they do.'

Next day they dispersed to their families, and Sally found herself at Dartford Station in the pouring rain. Unable to face the thought of a walk in a downpour, she looked round for a taxi.

'Sally,' a male voice called. 'Sally Brewer, is that you?'

A tall man in uniform was walking quickly towards her and for the first time in her life, Sally threw herself into Sam Petrie's outstretched arms.

A few minutes later they were driving out of the station and heading home. Sam, too, had just arrived with a few days' leave and was planning to spend one night with his parents before driving north to see Grace, his fiancée. 'Always the way, Sally; the girls are never here when I am, but

401

it's a joy to see you.'

They chatted about their work but not their private lives; that was not Sam Petrie's way.

'Good of your dad to leave the van for you, Sam.'

'Yes, annoyed he couldn't pick me up himself but I'm a big lad, I'll wait up for him.'

They turned into Sally's street and he drew up just beyond the cinema. 'Wish we had time to see that, Sally.' They looked up together and Sally read that Anna Neagle and Anton Walbrook were starring in *Victoria the Great*.

'I'm sure I saw it when I was still at school, Sam; educational, my mum thought.' She leaned across as she had never done before and kissed him lightly on the cheek. 'Good night and thanks, Sam, and give my love to everyone. I'm sorry I don't write much.'

'None of us has the time we want, Sally. Love to your mum and dad.'

Sally watched the little van pull away and wondered if the petrol would be put down as 'Delivery'.

Picking up decorated former POW, she said, a good reason.

Her parents, who had not expected her, were not at home, and Sally carried her overnight case back to the cinema where the girl with the sweets tray refused at first to let her in.

'I'm Sally Brewer.'

The girl emitted a small excited shriek but, pledged to silence, allowed Sally to go upstairs to the projection booth.

'Let me help you with that reel, Mr Brewer.'

402

Her father almost dropped the reel he was changing and so began a wonderful twenty-four-hour family visit.

It passed too quickly of course. There was so much to tell, so much to exclaim over and it was almost morning before they went to bed. Sally woke to familiar sounds and smells. Jumping out of bed, she threw on her ancient dressing gown and joined her parents in the kitchen.

'We expected to see you burned black by the sun.'

'I covered up all the time, Mum. Poor Millie says she dried up like a prune but it was all wonderful. I've seen things I never dreamed of, pyramids, Mum, and Egypt's not like a big beach, it's all mountains and rocks and every now and then a place with trees, an oasis.'

'Camels?'

'We saw some occasionally, and sometimes there were men in robes riding them. Looks terribly uncomfortable.'

She avoided talk of Jon deliberately because she had not really worked out what she wanted or needed to say. She had no idea what her mother had told her father and what his reaction had been. Finally, however, she could not avoid it and she told them everything. As they listened, their eyes never left her face.

'You're going to marry him then, our Sal?' her father asked her bluntly.

'If we still feel this way when the war is over.'

'And you will, Sally; you love him very much,' her mother said, but her voice was sad.

'He loves you too, Sally?' asked her father.

'Yes, Dad, he does.'

Ernie looked at his wife and smiled. 'Then, Elsie, love, that's really all that matters, isn't it?'

Next morning Sally took the first train back to London. She had hoped to see Maude but her mother could not bear to let her go and she did not visit the Petries for the same reason. She was glad that she had seen Sam, who had been so important to all four friends as they grew up, but he would tell the others that he had seen her and would send them her love.

'Oh, please, let this war end soon,' she prayed. Perhaps it would, for no matter how much of a secret it was supposed to be, everyone in England was aware that, almost monthly, American troops were arriving in Britain.

There had to be a reason. Was it the thing that was called the Second Front? If so, decided Sally, it could not come soon enough.

She had not told Sebastian when she'd be arriving and so she took her time making her way home. She had brought some tea leaves, a loaf of her mother's freshly baked bread and a bunch of curly kale grown at a local farm and which Elsie said she would not use.

'You remember Alf Humble, Sally – he's that generous – but the kale took over his "own use" plot and your dad says he can't face another bowl of cabbage soup. Flora Petrie could scarce wait for her Sam to get home on leave. "Always loved his kale, our Sam," she said.'

'Fresh vegetables are a real treat for us, Mum.'

Sally had been happy to take the kale.

Now she walked slowly along London streets, happier than she had ever imagined at being back in the capital city. Tomorrow they would discuss their experiences in France and Egypt – a few hours in Italy could scarcely be called part of their tour, and then they would be told what the future held for them. Even thinking the word 'future' made her go hot all over, for Jon, Just Jon was going to be a part of it. Her arms ached, not with the weight of her message bag and her overnight case but with longing for Jon.

At the Mansion she set her case down to open the door and the lovely welcoming smell of wood polish met her. Someone – Dmitri, she supposed, for he seemed to do everything – had polished the banisters and they gleamed in the light from the overhead window.

She climbed the stairs, stopped outside the door of the flat and listened, hoping to hear the sound of the piano or one of Sebastian's records but all was quiet. She went in and just as she closed the door behind her, she heard a giggle.

Millie's back, she decided, and she's giggling. How lovely.

She took off her coat and was just about to hang it on the heavily carved coat stand that must, she had always thought, have belonged to Sebastian's grandmamma's grandmamma when Sebastian's bedroom door flew open and out ran Millie without a stitch of clothing on, followed by an equally naked Dmitri.

The women shrieked and then all three laughed. Sally turned and looked at the door, and Millie and Dmitri, not at all discomfited, ran back into the bedroom. When she heard the door close, Sally picked up her bags and hurried along the corridor to the room she had shared with Millie.

'Sorry, Sally, that was quite a welcome.'

Sally, Millie and Sebastian were sitting in the kitchen drinking tea.

Sally smiled, looking across the table at Millie, whose eyes were downcast like those of a naughty child. 'Quite a surprise.'

'Actually,' she said slowly, enjoying her discomfort, 'after I got over the initial shock, I was delighted. I wouldn't announce your news to everyone in quite that way, though. I've made tea and Mum made us a loaf.'

'Damn, sorry, Sally,' said Sebastian. 'Should have said straight away. Jon rang.'

Sally's heart dropped into the pit of her stomach at the thought that she had missed him. 'When? Where is he?'

'Last night, and I've no idea. He was calling from...' He looked at Millie.

'Somewhere in the Mediterranean; it was a bugger of a line, Sal, lots of crackling, if you know what I mean, but he says ... where's the paper, Seb?'

Sebastian got up and hurried along the corridor to his bedroom, and Sally smiled and tried to be patient. In a few moments Sebastian returned waving a small piece of blue paper.

'Here you are. He said that Padre Vicenzo brought some letters to London and is now in hiding, probably until after the war and that he, Jon, will be here some day this week for two or three days; he's not exactly sure. I told him you were at home and he said something like feed a telephone.'

'Feed a ... honestly, Sebastian, he must have said my parents need a telephone.'

'That's what it must have been. Anyway, dear girl, it was a short call and he'll be on our doorstep any minute, I suppose.'

Sally thought she would burst with excitement. If only she knew exactly when Jon would arrive she'd be counting the minutes.

Jon turned up on the doorstep at the Theatre Royal and Sally was called from a meeting.

Max suggested they use his office and Sally, somewhat shyly, led the way, aware that the entire company was interested in the tall handsome naval officer.

'I hear he's a real lord,' she heard one of the chorus say, and blushed furiously but Jon merely smiled. As soon as the door of the office closed behind them Jon pulled her into his arms and for several minutes they stood and kissed and murmured nothings and then kissed again.

At last they gained control. Jon held her away from him, groaned and pulled her into his arms again. 'Oh, God above, how I've missed you, your voice, your smell, the feel of your skin. I don't know how long I have, Sally – today, tomorrow maybe. We're promised leave, a whole week, but when, I don't know. It all depends on–'

'The war,' she said. 'I understand, Jon, and I didn't hope even for this.'

'I'm free this evening. We could have dinner.'
There was longing and hope in his voice.

'I'm free, no shows for a week or two.'

'I'll find somewhere special.' He kissed her
again and then he moved away. 'I won't leave at
all if I don't leave now, and how embarrassing for
your friends to see me being led away by great
burly sailors. Seven OK? I'll come and meet your
chums, and then we'll go.'

They walked to the front door of the theatre
and there he turned to her. 'Goodbye until this
evening,' he said almost formally, and then he
bent swiftly and kissed her cheek.

Sally spent the rest of the day almost in a mist.
She attempted to pay attention but every moment
with Jon played itself over and over in her mind.
Max was patient although sometimes she was alert
enough to see him shaking his head as he looked
at her and she tried, unsuccessfully, to listen to
and understand every word he said.

Millie and Sebastian led her away at five thirty.
'What time?' asked Millie.

'Seven.'

'If we hurry, and the Gods of the underground
are on our side, we might make it. Thank God
the old lily doesn't need much gilding,' said Sebastian.

'Thanks, I think,' said Sally, but really she was
aware only of gathering excitement as hordes of
butterflies invaded her stomach.

She was not quite ready when Jon arrived; she
had tried on three different dresses, dismissed
them all and started again at the beginning.

'He hasn't seen you in any of them, Sal, so for

heaven's sake, get dressed or we'll throw you out in your skivvies,' Millie said as Sally again examined each dress critically.

At last she selected a pale pink evening dress with a cross-over bodice and almost medieval long filmy sleeves.

'Perfect.' Millie handed her the matching shoes before Sally could change her mind, took the full-length fur out of their shared wardrobe and almost pushed Sally from the room.

She stood in the doorway of the drawing room and looked at Jon. Her gaze had gone past him the first time she looked as she had expected a naval officer and he was wearing a dinner suit and, at that moment, she decided that he was much more handsome than any of the actors she had loved as she grew up. Clark Gable, Leslie Howard, even Jimmy Stewart, they disappeared out of her mind to be replaced by a tall, dark Englishman.

'Let me help you with your coat,' he said and, with a smile, took the fur from Millie.

'Have a lovely time,' said Sebastian.

'We won't wait up,' said Millie with a wicked wink.

Again Sally could feel a hot flush travelling up her neck and was glad that she could hide it with the fur. A taxi was waiting for them and she gasped at the realisation of the expense. Jon seemed to know what she was thinking and he squeezed her hand with encouragement.

'There are times, darling, even in war, when we say, "Hang the expense." Besides, it's not a terribly long drive. The club's on Piccadilly, not far from the Ritz but on the other side.'

He was right. They were there in a few minutes. It was a military club, of course, and portraits of famous flyers, sailors and soldiers, both living and dead, kept pace with them as they walked up the magnificently carved staircase. They went into an elegantly appointed drawing room where a uniformed steward took Jon's order and soon they were sitting in comfortable chairs, sipping champagne. Other officers passed, several stopping to greet Jon, shake his hand and introduce themselves to Sally, but for the most part, they were left alone. They chatted, discovering which letters had turned up, even out of sequence and which seemed lost for ever, and filling in the gaps.

Sally told Jon about Millie's search for her husband's grave.

'Poor girl. I saw her husband dance once before the war, in Birmingham. Very young and unbelievably talented.'

'I think between our reaching Arras and ... Sebastian's kindness, she may be able to move on.'

The steward came to tell them their table was ready and they moved to the dining room with its portraits, crystal chandeliers and soft music, and there, as they ate delicious food they were able to chat more intimately as no one was seated near them.

'I wish we had more time together, Sally. I had hoped to meet your parents, perhaps to take you and them, if they were free, to my home, but I have a letter to deliver tomorrow and it can't be late.'

'Next time, Jon. Will you be able to see Maudie?'

'No, and I know she's unhappy, but I did ring her and I might catch her at the shop before my flight tomorrow.'

'Your flight?'

'Sailors do use planes now and again, darling; they can go to places that ships can't reach.'

'Tell me about your childhood,' Sally said, because she could not ask where he was going.

He told her about his dogs and his favourite pony, and about his parents who had died ridiculously young, in a car crash in Biarritz.

'Oh, Jon, how awful.'

'They were together. Now that I'm an adult, I'm pleased about that because they loved each other very much.'

'The priest is safe, Jon?'

'I think so, darling; there is a worldwide network of people dedicated to helping. They couldn't save Emmanuel but the priest is safe and, I hope, Jean-Jacques. With you by my side I could help too. They need replacement livestock, farming equipment, and my farms can afford to provide that. In Emmanuel's memory, I have decided, I will educate both his children and Jean-Jacques' daughter.'

And then Jon asked Sally if she would return with him to his flat, instead of staying to dance. 'I want you to stay with me, Sally, but if you're not ready then I'll accept that, and we will stay here until they throw us out, when I'll take you back to Sebastian and Millie.'

Sally stood up. 'Dear Jon, I just couldn't bear to see you being thrown out.'

There was no taxi; hand in hand they walked, Jon, like Sebastian, seeming to have an unerring sense of direction. The moon was kind and a few stars twinkled as they made their way through the darkness to Charles Street where Jon had what he called a bachelor flat. It was not as big as Sebastian's but was beautifully appointed.

'Do look around while I make us a drink.'

'I don't want anything else to drink, Jon.'

'Then shall we dance? I have dreamed of dancing with you and that pretty frock was made for dancing.'

He wound up a gramophone; together they chose a record and then Sally slipped into his arms. 'Bliss,' said Jon as he held her close. They stood in the middle of the room, their arms around each other and they moved their feet in time to the music but it could hardly have been called dancing, and then Jon bent his head and kissed Sally. The music carried on for a few minutes and then there was only the sound of a record going round and round – and of soft sighs.

Sally woke first and looked at the sleeping Jon. Where their clothes were she had no idea, and neither did she care. There was no regret, no concern. Loving and being loved was absolute perfection. Jon stirred, opened a sleepy eye, smiled and closed it again but his body turned to Sally and they made love again, as fully and as beautifully as before.

Sally woke later to find Jon wearing a blue silk dressing gown and holding a cup of fragrant coffee.

'Coffee, darling.'

She took the cup and sipped. 'Beautiful.'

'Not nearly as beautiful as you. Sally, I love you so much; I want to stay here with you for ever, but they'd find us. Sally Brewer, will you marry me?'

Sally almost spilled the coffee. 'Oh, Jon, I love you too.'

'And *will* you marry me?'

'Yes, Jon, I'll marry you.'

He took the cup from her while he kissed her again. 'I'll keep my promise, Sally. We'll do our duty until this ugly war is ended, and then I'll buy you the most beautiful ring in the world. I'll tell the jeweller I want a special ring for a special lady, a ring no one else has ever seen, a ring just for Sally.'

Sally smiled. 'That's wonderful, Jon, I will treasure it always.'

Then she remembered what he thought of as his debt to the two families in Corsica and suddenly she knew exactly what to do with the money from the sale of the lovely ring that was spending the war in a safe in a Dartford Picture House.

The publishers hope that this book has given you enjoyable reading. Large Print Books are especially designed to be as easy to see and hold as possible. If you wish a complete list of our books please ask at your local library or write directly to:

Magna Large Print Books
Magna House, Long Preston,
Skipton, North Yorkshire.
BD23 4ND

This Large Print Book for the partially sighted, who cannot read normal print, is published under the auspices of

THE ULVERSCROFT FOUNDATION